In the hov...
an immense s... ... ...

At first, Zevaron thought it a trick of the rain, a sea-mirage. But no, something *was* there, insubstantial and wavering, mist condensing against the maelstrom of white and gray. He felt the thing in the sea, as if an unknown part of him, a sense that had lain sleeping all these years, now stirred.

The water around the shape churned and boiled, adding steam to the tattered, whirling whiteness of the storm. Voices echoed on the wind. The ship's timbers groaned.

The upper part of the figure rose above the plunging waves, human and dragon and sea-beast all in one. The massive head lifted, a mane like tangled kelp streaming over the shoulders. A crest of knobbed, interlaced coral sprang from the overhanging brow, arching over the domed skull and down the spine. The skin, what Zevaron could see of it through the foam, was green and mottled gray, patterned with pale incrustations and plated scales that shone like mother-of-pearl. Its eyes were huge and lidless, made for peering through lightless depths.

The monstrous fist descended, missing the *Wave Dancer* and passing instead through the maelstrom. A wall of water slammed into the ship. It surged over the deck. Timbers shrieked. The prow lifted, shuddering, reaching for the light. Zevaron staggered, thrown to his knees. Then the ship began to slip downward.

Zevaron scrambled to his feet on the tilting deck. He raised his own fist.

"NO!" he screamed. *"YOU SHALL NOT HAVE THEM!"*

For an instant, time itself seemed to pause. Although the wind and rain continued, the sea scarcely moved, as if the waves were mere painted images. The ship hung suspended in its descent.

The immense, distorted head swung around. . . .

*Coming soon from DAW Books

THE SEVEN-PETALED SHIELD

Book One

Deborah J. Ross

DAW BOOKS, INC.

DONALD A. WOLLHEIM, FOUNDER

375 Hudson Street, New York, NY 10014

ELIZABETH R. WOLLHEIM
SHEILA E. GILBERT
PUBLISHERS

http://www.dawbooks.com

First Printing, June 2013

1 2 3 4 5 6 7 8 9

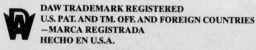

DAW TRADEMARK REGISTERED
U.S. PAT. AND TM. OFF. AND FOREIGN COUNTRIES
—MARCA REGISTRADA
HECHO EN U.S.A.

PRINTED IN THE U.S.A.

For Marion Zimmer Bradley, friend and inspiration.

By grace, all things are made,
By judgment, all things are unmade.
At the end of time, O Holy One,
Deliver us into the hands of peace.

PART ONE:

Tsorreh's Gift

Chapter One

SOARING above the besieging army, the ancient citadel of Meklavar stood stark against the volcanic cliffside. The sun dipped toward the jagged western peaks, and still the city held fast against the Gelonian invaders.

Tsorreh san-Khored paused along the top of the wall that surrounded the lower market city. Slender and honey-skinned, she looked more like her own servant than the young second wife of the lord of Meklavar. She'd thrown on her oldest clothes: a knee-length sleeveless vest over draw-string pants of faded cotton. Her hair, blue-black and long enough to reach her hips, was plaited into the usual seven braids, tied back, and covered with an old head cloth.

Once she had stood here for the sheer joy of feeling the winds through the Var mountain pass, of looking beyond the city gates to the fields and gardens, the livestock pens and villages, imagining the wide world beyond. Now the stench of blood hung in the air. The grassy paddocks and gardens had been trampled beneath the jumble of men and beasts, fire and dust.

Tsorreh lifted her gaze to the north, where the foothills tumbled down from rocky pastures to the *Mher Seshola*, the old name for the Sea of Desolation. On the day of her ini-tiation as a woman, from her vantage in the topmost spire of the temple high above the city, she'd glimpsed a line of shimmering brightness along the northern horizon. No sane army, she had been taught, would brave those waters.

No sane army? she repeated to herself. Then the Gelonian invaders must truly be madmen to have crossed it. They certainly fought with a singleness of purpose that swept through every defense Meklavar could rally. With every passing day, the fighting had become fiercer, more desperate. Although Meklavar overlooked the pass leading to the southern spice kingdoms, it had been built originally as a watchtower, not a fortress.

Below, shadows deepened. Men darted between piles of fallen bodies and smoldering fires that sent up streamers of greasy smoke. Dark pools stained the earth. Here and there a fallen animal, a horse or Gelonian onager, thrashed pitifully until one of the men reached it. Other beasts wandered free, shying when approached. Great-winged carrion birds wheeled and circled above the battlefield.

Horns rang out, echoing against the mountain. Tsorreh recognized them as Meklavaran, that throbbing tone.

Retreat.

The call sounded again. A Meklavaran banner caught the dying sun.

As Tsorreh turned, the light shifted, staining the sky the color of blood. A shiver passed through her. She was not superstitious; she could read and write, both the sacred languages and the modern. The heavens themselves now seemed to mirror her fears.

Tsorreh hurried down from the wall, a pair of maid-attendants at her heels. The outer gates opened to admit a stream of men and beasts. Soldiers supported their stumbling comrades. Riderless horses snorted, white-eyed, and many others carried limp bodies slung over their backs.

Maharrad, Tsorreh's royal husband, clattered by on his white horse, surrounded by his bodyguard. Along with the other women, she stood back to let them pass. The smells of blood and dust rolled over her like an invisible tide. So many hurt, so many she knew.

Zevaron, where is Zevaron? Where is my son?

Tsorreh's heart hammered in her ears, but she knew her duty. She pushed forward, directing the wounded to the areas she had prepared for them. The city's physicians and healer-women began sorting which soldiers needed immediate care and which could wait. Tsorreh sent her maid-attendants to help. Two of them looked panic-stricken, but the third hastened to her work. Tsorreh remembered that the girl's father had been outside, on the battlefield. Where he was now, she did not know.

The gates were barred again, for everyone who was able to get to safety had already done so. The way was cleared to transport the wounded to shelters and temporary hospitals.

Although fear threatened to swallow her up, Tsorreh forced herself to attend to her work. Before her lay a rider whose horse had been cut down beneath him. He was Zevaron's age, barely a man. The splinters of his thigh bone pierced his blood-soaked breeches. He was almost fainting from pain. His lower lip had been bitten through. Not daring to touch the wound, she called for a physician. When the healer arrived, she saw in his face that there was little hope for the young rider.

After the first wave of men, Tsorreh's ears went deaf with the piteous cries of the wounded. She reeled with the stench of slashed intestines and the coppery reek of blood. Once she thought she heard her husband's voice, shouting commands.

Zevaron, where is Zevaron?

He was a man now, for all his fourteen years. Like his fathers before him, he had stood in the seven-fold light of the temple and chanted the words of the *te-Ketav*, the most revered of all Meklavaran scriptures. Since the time he could lift a wooden practice sword, he had trained for this day, trained to be the strong and faithful second to his older brother. In ordinary times, he would have had years more to harden into his full strength. These were not ordinary times.

Zevaron must be alive. She could not bear it otherwise.

He would come to her when his duties permitted. The Most Holy would not let him die.

The next man in the row was an officer, an older man. He sat upright in the dust, insisting he was all right. His skin was gray in the failing light. When he tried to stand, his legs buckled beneath him. Tsorreh coaxed him to lie down on a pallet. She took one of his hands in hers, holding it as if she could hold him to life. Pain flickered like lightning across his face.

Her fortitude crumbled. "Zevaron," she said to him, hearing the urgency in her own voice. "Have you seen *ravot* Zevaron?"

He smiled and died. His palm between her fingers was still warm, but she felt the change, the sudden stillness. She pressed his eyelids, but they wouldn't stay shut.

Tsorreh stood up just as a commotion erupted at the gates. Through the mass of soldiers and townsfolk, she glimpsed a plumed Gelonian helmet. The soldier rode in a chariot pulled by a large, cream-colored onager. The beast's mane had been shorn and its lower legs and tail wrapped in striped cloth.

Muttering, people stepped away to let the chariot pass. By the pennons streaming from the standard—one of Gelonian blue and purple, the other green for truce—this must be an emissary from Thessar, the commander and son of the Gelonian king. He most likely carried a demand for the city's surrender.

A short time later, the emissary headed back to the gates. This time, Tsorreh got a better look at him, his cloak thrown back to reveal pale arms, his muscles flexing as he handled rein and whip. She saw nothing of his features, only the discipline of his upright posture.

"*Te-ravah*." A boy, one of Maharrad's aides, bowed to Tsorreh. He could not have been more than nine or ten, but his face, smeared with greasy smoke, looked haggard. His eyes were glassy. "The *te-ravot* has requested your presence in council."

"I thank you for bringing this message to me," she replied formally. Then, "Child, what is your name?" There were so many names she would never know. She wanted to be able to thank this one boy.

"Benerod."

Named for one of the brothers of Khored of Blessed Memory.

"Yours is an ancient and honorable name." When she smiled, her face felt stiff with dried tears. "You bear it well."

The boy's cheeks turned dusky. He ducked his head. "I almost forgot. I am to tell you that *ravot* Zevaron is unhurt."

Thank you, she prayed in relief. *Oh, thank you.*

"Come," she said to the boy, "walk with me now, and tell me of your part in the great battle, that it may be written down and remembered."

Together they made their way through the sloping streets of the market city. People filled the broad central avenue, hurrying to make use of the last light of the day. Scattered lanterns marked inns or shops, although many of the smaller streets lay dark.

They reached the King's Stairs, which led to the terraced upper city, called the *meklat* in the old parlance, and the citadel. At the bottom, the steps were wide enough for ten men to walk abreast, but they narrowed as they rose.

Set at the top of the stairs beneath a soaring arch, the wooden gates were weathered to the gray of the surrounding stone. The arch came to a tapered point, so that Tsorreh often felt as if she were passing beneath a pair of praying hands. In times of peace, the entrance always stood open and lit, even at night. Now only a scattering of torches illuminated the gates.

Tsorreh climbed into the shadows, the boy at her heels.

True night had fallen by the time Tsorreh hurried into the chamber that had once served as feasting hall and throne room, but now was used by the war council. It lay within the citadel, the tall, multi-storied edifice that dominated the upper city. During the day, air and light reached all the principal chambers through a series of mirrored vents. The art of making such things had been lost, yet their splendor endured, the seamless, fine-grained stone walls, the exquisitely carved furnishings, and above it all, the window of leaded glass depicting Khored's Shield. From noon to dusk, a shaft of brilliance transformed the colored glass into a luminous tapestry. Each petal glowed with its own symbolic color, six in all, around a heart of shimmering gold. Now night quenched the Shield and ordinary oil lamps provided a diffuse, flickering light for the meeting.

Maharrad bent to the map spread over the table that had been drawn up before his age-blackened cedar throne. His robe, snowy wool stitched with gold and black, the colors of his house, seemed to weigh heavily on him. There was more silver than ebony in his beard.

Shorrenon, elder son and heir, child of Maharrad's first wife, sat at his father's right hand. He was tall and well-built, with broad shoulders and dark, intelligent eyes. He still wore his armored breastplate.

Maharrad's general and his most trusted advisors ringed the table, as well as members of four of the six great houses founded by Khored's brothers. It was from the lands of these nobles that the Meklavaran army had been drawn. The most senior patriarchs occupied the few chairs, and the rest stood.

The lines of the remaining two brothers of Khored were broken, and other families had come to power in their place. Some said that the current struggle with Cinath, the Ar-King of Gelon, had begun with the disappearance of one of the heirs, which weakened Meklavar's magical defenses. Others insisted there was nothing supernatural, only Cinath's human ambition. Unlike his forefathers, Cinath did not content himself with harassing his neighbors and the occasional unsuccessful foray into the northern steppes. He seemed determined to conquer the entire known world.

Tsorreh knew some of her husband's advisors: the whitebearded scholar who had been her own tutor, the head of the city masons and representative of the craft houses, and the cleric who was her paternal grandfather's chosen successor as chief priest of the temple. She had less acquaintance with the officers. As she drew near, she saw the ash on their faces and smelled the dust and the sour miasma of despair.

Zevaron stood a pace behind the general, a somber man named Isarod. Her son's gaze flickered to Tsorreh. In her belly, a knot loosened.

He looked unhurt but weary. He'd tied back his hair like a soldier's and braided it with leather strips dyed in the colors of his house. Since the beginning of the siege, such tokens had become the custom, so that a man could be identified and returned to his family, even if his body was unrecognizable.

Maharrad looked up from the scroll. The vellum curled tightly, as if unwilling to yield to the weight of his hand. The casing lay beside it, tied with blue and purple cords.

At his gesture, Tsorreh took her usual place behind him. She sank down on her straight, narrow chair, wishing she could draw its unyielding strength into her own flesh.

"The Gelon have consolidated their position outside the walls," General Isarod said. He was a wiry man, as tough as the bones of the mountains. "Even now, they throw up new earthworks."

Zevaron stirred, bowing first to his father and then to Shorrenon. "If I may suggest a way to increase the defense of our walls?" he said with a trace of diffidence. "We have taken in many herdsmen who fled here as the Gelon drew near. They are not fighters but are skilled with the sling. It is their principal defense of their flocks against wolves and scavenger birds."

"The young *ravot* speaks wisely," the scholar Eavonen said, using the traditional word for *prince*. His reedy voice hesitated between each phrase as if he were turning it around on his tongue. "In the annals of Hosarion, we read, *And it came to pass, when the stone-drake drew nigh, that Hosarian went out to meet it. And fear smote the bones of Hosarion and he trembled. But Xianna his betrothed said to*

*him, Let not thy courage fail thee, for when a lion came nigh
to thy flock and seized a kid-goat, didst thou not smite the
lion, and deliver the kid-goat from the mouth of the lion?
Even so shall thou now prevail."*

Shorrenon suppressed a scowl, but Maharrad listened
with an expression of slightly distracted patience. Tsorreh
found herself smiling to hear scripture recited in the middle
of a war council. This was, after all, the traditional Meklavaran form of scholarly discussion, beginning with an ex-
haustive survey of historical references and commentary by
learned sages.

"And Hosarion gathered up seven stones," Eavenon went
on, *"and when he had come to the place the stone-drake had
laid waste, he took out the first stone and he slung it and the
stone-drake crushed the stone—"*

"Yes, yes, we know the verse!" interrupted one of the
nobles. "We know how the stone-drake turned aside six
stones, but the seventh could not be turned aside, and that
one slew it. But the old story cannot help us now! We have
no Hosarion in our midst."

Eavonen, looking affronted at the interruption, folded
his hands into his sleeves.

"Yet it is a good point," Maharrad said. "We have stones
in abundance and walls from which to throw them. Even a
pebble, aimed well and hurled from a height, can fell a
grown man."

"As I was saying earlier," the general continued after a
pause, "they have brought up engineers and miners. If we
push them back from the outer walls, they will move the
entrance to their tunnels beyond our reach."

"How long will it take them to dig from their present
position?" Maharrad asked.

The chief mason answered him. "Perhaps five or six days,
te-ravot. They are clever and skilled at such things. That is,"
he added, "if they are left undisturbed."

"Be assured," General Isarod said, "they will be well-
defended. The Gelonian prince, Thessar, is no fool. He has
studied his military strategy well."

"The more men they commit to the defenses of these tunnels, the fewer they will have to attack our walls." Shorrenon bent over the map. His voice, normally melodious, sounded as if he had screamed himself hoarse in battle. "We can harry them and whittle away at their numbers. If they breach the walls, we will be waiting for them."

"We cannot win such a battle," the general said, "not after today's losses. If they break through, they will take the lower city."

"Is there no way to keep them out?" Maharrad asked, his brow furrowed.

Murmurs rippled around the table. They were all reeling with the shock of the day, the flood of wounded men, and the implacable advance of their enemy. The general described their likely fate, once the outer walls were breached. The fighting, house to house, street to street, would be bitter.

So many had died already.

"There is an alternative." Anthelon, eldest of Maharrad's councillors, pointed to the scroll on the table. "Let us take what Prince Thessar has offered: an honorable surrender. Let us begin discussions now. The longer we resist, the more lives will be lost and the less favorable the terms we can negotiate."

"Treason!" Shorrenon leapt to his feet.

Maharrad restrained his son with a gesture. "It is never treason for a man who has served long and honorably to speak his mind. Shall we do the work of the Gelon for them and turn on one another?"

"Forgive me, *ravot* Shorrenon," Anthelon said. Tears glinted in his eyes, and grief and shame and things Tsorreh had no words for. She remembered he had served Maharrad's father as well.

"I sought only to ask," Anthelon continued, "whether it is not better to save our people, who would surely perish from starvation during a long siege, or to live on as a Gelonian province. Others have done so and prospered."

"Are you mad?" Shorrenon snatched the scroll from the

table and brandished it aloft. "No matter what soft words they offer, the Gelon will exile or slay every man of a noble house—"

The patriarchs reacted with cries of dismay. "May the Shield protect us!"

"They are not such savages." Anthelon raised his hands in a calming gesture, but Shorrenon would not be dissuaded.

"—and when there are none left to oppose them," Shorrenon continued relentlessly, "they will enslave the rest and carry away our holy things as booty! When they are done, we will no longer be Meklavar of the ancient heritage of Khored and Hosarion, but merely another vanquished outpost of Ar-Cinath-Gelon's empire!"

Tsorreh shivered, as if the blood-washed sunset once more cast its shadows across her soul. Was this the fate the heavens forewarned? She would not believe it. She dared not.

"What would you have us do?" Viridon of the ancient house of Cassarod asked in a quavering voice. "Sit here while the Gelon tunnel beneath our walls?"

"Go out to fight them!" Shorrenon cried. "Line the walls with archers, pelt them with rocks! Then create a diversion and attack their mining crews."

"We lost too many men in today's battle," General Isarod said grimly. "We do not have enough strength to defend the walls *and* create a diversion, *and* send a party to their diggings."

"Even if your plan succeeds," another of the elders began, "and the Gelon do not overrun the outer walls, I fear they can still hold us penned here."

Shorrenon's face tightened in the stubborn expression Tsorreh knew well. "The Gelon have no will for a long siege. They are far from their nearest port, alone in enemy territory. I say, let us hold fast. After a season of heat and empty bellies, they will give up and go home."

"I greatly fear they will not," Anthelon said, shaking his head. "We may have stores of food and water, but even those will be exhausted in time."

"We can bring in more, along the Shadow Road through the mountains. I say we sit tight behind our gates and let the Gelon starve outside."

"The way is narrow and perilous," the priest spoke up. The temple priests were said to know the hidden paths through the Var Mountains. "Only the most surefooted can travel the steepest parts, and we could not bring in enough supplies for the entire city."

"Aye, and the more frequently we use the road, the greater the risk of its discovery by the Gelon," the general pointed out. "Once they find out, they can use it themselves to advance a second attack upon us, one against which we have no fortification."

"All the more reason to begin negotiations now," Anthelon persisted, "while we can bargain for the best terms. Let us use their offer as a starting point to gain concessions—"

"Never!" Shorrenon moved as if he would strike the old man.

"Enough!" Maharrad rose to his feet and the entire room fell silent. "The *Gelon* are our enemy, not one another! I did not summon you here to see who can argue the loudest but to reason together, to find a way to save our city."

After a long moment, Shorrenon lowered himself back into his chair.

"In times past," Maharrad went on, "we have retreated behind our walls and let the invaders pass." He took the scroll from Shorrenon's clenched fist. "This Ar-King does not want merely more favorable terms, better stables for his caravan animals, or preferred access to the trade routes to the spice lands of Denariya. He means to rule here, to claim the Var Pass for Gelon. We must not permit that to happen. If we cannot defeat them or outlast a siege, then we must send for help. Shorrenon, for this we depend upon you."

"Father, do not send me away! My place is by your side, at the gates of our city. Let me stay and fight!"

Tsorreh glanced from father to son. Clearly, Maharrad and Shorrenon had discussed a plan earlier. Yet Shorrenon had not the temperament to let others battle in his stead. No wonder he argued for a strenuous defense of the walls.

"Your place is wherever you are most needed," Maharrad corrected him. "There is no one else I can send. No one else who can enlist the aid of the Sand Lands tribes or bring reinforcements from the Isarran outposts. This then is my command: You are to leave the city in secret, take the Shadow Road through the mountains, and gather as many fighting men as possible. We will hold the Gelon off as long as we must. Then you will attack them from the flank, and we from the front. Together we will drive the Ar-King's jackals from this land."

"*Te-ravot*, this is madness!" The city mason trembled with agitation. "Prince Shorrenon is our greatest warrior! Sending him away will cripple our defenses! It will destroy the people's hope. They will think he has abandoned us."

"Father," Zevaron said, his voice breaking, "can you not send me instead?"

Blood suffused Shorrenon's features. There was no better choice, and he knew it. Only once had Zevaron traveled the narrow road that led from the lower city, along treacherous mountain passages, and through the desert wastes. Shorrenon knew the trails and had dealt with many of the Sand Lands chiefs. He was known in Isarre, the country that was Gelon's bitter enemy. No man could do better in finding help for Meklavar.

Tsorreh realized why Maharrad had requested her presence. He might have chosen her as his second wife because she was of Khored's lineage through her Meklavaran father, but he also recognized the political value of her mother's royal Isarran connections.

"Isarre will not provoke retaliation from Gelon," the elder of a wealthy trading house grumbled. "Gelon threatens the port city of Gatacinne and pirates harry their seacoast. With few allies and with their resources stretched thin, Isarre will not divert its army. They will tend to their own and let Meklavar fall."

Tsorreh had never liked the man, and the courtesies between them had been of the chilliest and most punctilious politeness. In fact, she suspected him of opposing her marriage on the grounds that, unlike Maharrad's first wife, she was not of pure Meklavaran descent. Tsorreh herself might be only half-Meklavaran, but she had been born and educated in the city, and it was her only home. Her parents had died here, leaving no other issue. Whatever influence she might have with Isarre, she would freely give.

She drew herself up. "Isarre will answer the obligations of blood and honor."

"Enough!" Shorrenon said. "You are right, Father. Gelon is our enemy, not one another. I will depart this very night."

"Spoken like a true prince," Maharrad said.

Shorrenon went to his father and knelt. Maharrad placed his hands upon his son's head and blessed him. He used the old phrases, beseeching the Holy One to keep his son in safety, to bring him success in his mission. To Tsorreh's surprise, her stepson then approached her.

She unwound one of the ornaments from her braids, a coin bearing the image of a little silver horse. It had been her mother's, one of her few keepsakes from the land of her birth. The Isarran royal crest was stamped on the reverse. She pressed it into his hand.

"May this serve you well," she said, "and may you bring it back to me on the day Meklavar triumphs over its enemies."

Shorrenon then took his leave and the meeting dispersed. Tsorreh watched as Zevaron filed from the room in his proper place at Shorrenon's side. He would remain behind, here in the city, and if the walls fell before help arrived, he would fight and die with the rest.

A short time later, Tsorreh hurried to the royal stables in the lower city. Shorrenon would not linger, not while darkness was his ally, and she wanted to speak with him before he left. The stables were small, now crowded with animals; in normal times, horses were not kept within the city, except for a few reserved for use of the royal family. Meklavar had never had much cavalry, and most of their horses were crossbred from the hardy beasts of the Azkhantian steppe and the fiery steeds of the Sand Lands. Maharrad's white stallion had been an exceptionally fine gift from a Sand Lands chieftain. Shorrenon's rangy gray was big enough to support a grown man in battle, but such mounts were rare.

A single lantern hung outside of the main building, casting a soft yellow light. Just inside the opened doors, Tsorreh glimpsed saddle racks and ricks for hay. Three people and a horse stood in the saddling area. It was not Shorrenon's gray but a smaller horse such as Zevaron would ride, a brown mare with no white markings. Desert breeding showed in the fine bone of her head and legs, the wide-set eyes, and the strong, short-coupled back. She was already saddled, with breastplate and crupper-strap for mountain riding.

Shorrenon, wearing a dark leather jacket and leggings, rested one hand upon the pommel, ready to mount. His young wife, Ediva, clutched his other hand. Tsorreh could not make out her words, only the harmonics of sorrow in her voice. Zevaron held the reins of the horse, his face a glimmer in the shadows.

"There is no time," Shorrenon said in a tight voice. "I have already told you this. It is not my choice."

"The Gelon . . ." The rest of Ediva's sentence was muffled by a sob. Tsorreh felt a rush of sympathy for the young woman, newly a mother for the second time.

Shorrenon grasped Ediva's shoulders, holding her at arm's length as he gazed into her face.

"There is no other way," he said. "We cannot hold the outer walls if the Gelon are determined to bring them down. Should I risk your falling into their hands—our children taken as slaves—if I can prevent it?"

Tsorreh stepped into the lantern light. Noticing her, Shorrenon pulled away from his wife. The mare turned her head, ears pricked, nostrils flaring. Ediva gulped, her mouth working, and bowed deeply. Her eyes were red and swollen.

"*Te-ravah*." Shorrenon inclined his head. "Stepmother."

"I have given you a token of influence with Isarre," Tsorreh said, "but I would not have you depart without my own blessing. The fate of our city rides with you." The words flowed through her from a hidden wellspring. "Meklavar is honored by her eldest son."

Tsorreh lifted her hands and the sky itself, the firmament of stars, bent closer. A hush fell on the yard. She spoke not from the statecraft she had learned as Maharrad's second wife, daughter of an Isarran princess, but from her own Meklavaran heritage. She felt herself part of a lineage running unbroken through centuries past, to a time of miracles, of inexpressible evil, of enduring hope.

> "*May the light of Khored shine upon you;*
> *May his wisdom guide you;*
> *May his Shield protect you.*"

She had never heard those words spoken aloud, could not remember ever having read them, and yet their power rang through her like silvered steel.

The moment passed. Shorrenon kissed his wife and swung up on the dark mare. The horse pranced, pulling at the bit in eagerness.

Shorrenon paused, looking back at the two women. "Take care of them," he said to Zevaron. "And if—if you ride to battle while I'm gone, take the gray. He knows how to handle himself."

Tsorreh saw the leap of tension in Zevaron's muscles, the almost painful earnestness as he vowed to do so. Ediva shivered as Shorrenon clattered away into the night. Tsorreh folded the sobbing girl in her arms.

"Come now, sweetheart, you must not let your children see you like this. You must teach them hope."

"How can I do that, when there is none?" Ediva moaned. "He is gone, *te-ravah*! Oh, he is gone!"

Chapter Two

WITH a mixture of weariness and relief, Tsorreh returned to her bedchamber. Never before had she so desperately needed the solace of her own place. Unlike the suite belonging to her predecessor—a warren of interior rooms filled with ornate furnishings, age-darkened draperies, and the thick odors of incense and cosmetics—Tsorreh's chamber was a single spacious room with a balcony overlooking one of the terraced mountainside gardens. From her first days in the palace, she had loved its light, airy feeling, its walls unadorned except for a small tapestry that her own mother had woven as a bride. The finely-spun wool was patterned in shades of cream, brown, and black. Her cat, a spotted desert-breed, lay curled on the bed.

Otenneh was waiting. In the light cast by the bank of candles, wrinkles pleated the old servant's cheeks and redness rimmed her eyes. Wordlessly, Tsorreh held out her arms. The top of Otenneh's head barely reached her shoulders. Against the old woman's trembling body, the bones frail as eggshells, Tsorreh felt the straightness of her own spine and the strength of her own arms.

She held me in just this way on the night my mother died, Tsorreh thought. *Now it is I who must hold her.*

Otenneh had accompanied Tsorreh's mother, a princess

of the Isarran royal line, when she came to Meklavar to wed a noble descendent of Khored. Khored's heirs no longer ruled Meklavar, the throne having since passed to Maharrad's family, but it had been a politically advantageous match, carrying with it the possibility of an alliance with Isarre. Tsorreh's parents had been happy at first, but then her mother died in childbirth and her father had fallen fatally ill not long after. Now only Otenneh remained of Tsorreh's childhood household.

Tsorreh dozed off to Otenneh singing her favorite Isarran lullaby. She woke the next morning after only a few hours of broken sleep. Abruptly, with blood pounding in her ears, she jerked upright. The cat jumped off the bed with an aggrieved meow and stalked off in search of a mouse.

She was alone and it was almost dawn. A milky light swept the eastern sky.

Otenneh brought heated water, soap, and rose-scented oils, but Tsorreh took none of her usual pleasure in bathing. She allowed Otenneh to rebraid her hair in seven plaits tied together in back. From the carved chest, she took out clothing more befitting a *te-ravah* than the worn, blood-streaked tunic and pants of yesterday. She chose soft, warm colors like a harvest sunset; embroidery decorated the center panel of the tunic, worn over trousers of a darker shade.

Tsorreh ate a quick breakfast and, taking two of her maid-attendants, went downstairs. A crowd had gathered in the street outside the palace, nobles and merchants, even craftspeople from the lower city. A deputation of traders from Denariya was already meeting with Maharrad. A pointless exercise, Tsorreh thought, for no one had the power to grant safe passage through the Gelonian lines.

Below, in the lower market city, she found a whirlwind of activity. The area just inside the outer gates had been cleared of the dead and wounded. People rushed up and down the walls, archers and servants with baskets of stones and quivers of arrows. Drovers sorted and secured animals, and the most vulnerable shops and dwellings were already in the process of evacuation. In the marketplaces, women in cloaks of sand-pale cotton bargained with vendors for lentils and salt. The scene, Tsorreh reflected, resembled a festival in the fervor and pervasiveness of the preparations. Not an aspect of the city's life was undisturbed.

A man in the striped head garb of a Sand Lands caravaneer was pleading with a guard. He slipped one hand into the folds of his belt and brought out something Tsorreh could not see. "A family treasure," he said. "I would not part with it to any lesser man. It is one of the fabled *alvara*—the enchanted gems from Khored's own Shield. Yes, yes, hidden away all these centuries. It holds the key to undreamed power. But what are riches compared to the love of one's children? Seventeen little ones and their mothers! How will they survive without me? I must get to Gatacinne on the Isarran coast, and quickly!"

One of Tsorreh's maids exclaimed in dismay, quickly hushed by the other, "Is the situation so desperate? Must we all flee for our lives?"

Tsorreh had not the heart to scold her. Perhaps she ought to release the girl from service, to find whatever fragile comfort might lie with her own family.

As Tsorreh expected, the guard shook his head and gestured the trader back with the others. Every few years, some merchant claimed to have discovered one of the *alvara*, the magical petal-shaped gemstones of the Shield. Tsorreh was of the line of the great king himself, but had never heard of such an heirloom. The centuries had obscured the lineage of Khored's brothers. The descendants of the original Benerod were long gone, and those of Eriseth had disappeared a generation ago. The fate of the Shield was so shrouded in mystery, some now claimed the *alvara* had never existed except as mystical symbols. If they were real, Tsorreh thought, they would certainly not be bargained away so casually at the hands of a Sand Lands trader. Those offered for sale were usually ordinary gems, topaz or quartz or poor-quality emerald.

Tsorreh found Zevaron in the practice field outside the armory, surrounded by a group of children. Part of the area had been tented over for an infirmary. The soldiers there looked to be not so badly injured; a few of them were exercising.

She paused a short distance away and noticed that Zevaron's group included several girls. One was about her son's age, silent and lanky, with tiny bones tied to her single thick braid. Some of the boys were as young as seven or eight, for the teenagers had already been conscripted for heavier tasks. Most wore the clothing and rough sandals of goat herders, but a few were clearly city children, although barefoot. She supposed that even a beggar child could kill a rat with a sling.

Zevaron had not yet seen her. His expression was intent and animated as he spoke. Instead of armor, he wore a long fitted vest, belted at the waist over loose trousers and suede ankle boots. He raised his arms to gesture, his skin smooth and taut over muscles she had not noticed before. For a terrifying instant, Tsorreh saw that same golden skin slashed by Gelonian swords and washed in blood.

Her heart ached. She pressed one hand over her breast, willing herself to silence. No hint of her own fear must show.

Zevaron's gaze met hers. An expression she could not read flickered over his features, solemn and distant. As she approached, he bowed formally to her, as an officer to his *te-ravah*. The herder children watched with open mouths.

"You've done a fine job with them," she said.

"They need something they can do, not just wait helplessly while their fathers fight."

And die, he meant.

"They will become a generation of heroes," she said. "We must all turn ballad makers to sing their praises."

He smiled outright now, like sun breaking through clouds. In that moment, she realized why she had sought him out, how much she needed to imprint the sound of his voice and the light in his eyes upon her heart. Zevaron the babe and later the boy were already engraved there, as indelible as her own name. It was Zevaron the young man she needed to remember. In the hours and days to come, they might not meet. She might never see him again.

The moment stretched on, overlong. Zevaron looked away. He was still at an age to shrink from emotional scenes. Tsorreh held out her hands and, with a little movement of resignation, he reached out his own. Instead of taking him into her arms, she clasped his forearms, holding him at a distance.

Something in the physical contact shredded her detachment. Her eyes stung. There was so much she wanted to say: prayers, blessings, expressions of love and grief and a mother's worry. With an effort, she held them all back.

Zevaron nodded, looking even more a grown man than ever. To Tsorreh's relief, he offered no empty assurances. In this, they understood one another.

She drew herself up, releasing him. He bowed again to her, and at that moment, shouting came from the direction of the walls. The moment shattered. They were no longer mother and son, but a *te-ravah* with responsibilities of her own, and a *ravot* on the brink of battle.

That night and the next, after the Gelon had withdrawn to their earthworks, Maharrad, his general, and his senior captains walked the walls. Ignoring the scandalized whispers of the court ladies, Tsorreh went with them and without her whimpering, fearful attendants. Otenneh was the only one of her retinue with any fortitude, and she was too old to go climbing about the ramparts.

The Gelonian earthworks crept closer every time Tsorreh looked out at them. It seemed impossible the city could hold out five days, or even three, but she kept her fears to herself. Each morning and evening, she visited the wounded and stood at her husband's side as he addressed his fighting forces. Yet, as the hours stretched on, Meklavar held fast.

Another day.

Nightfall like the tolling of a knell.

Two.

Again, the slow creep of dusk.

Three.

A week.

Each day became a dance of advance and retreat. Shortly after dawn, the Gelonian infantry advanced upon the walls, only to be thrown back under the hail of arrows and stones. The Meklavaran cavalry rode out to attack the mining pits. On the second week, they set fire to the supply of timber the Gelon had gathered to brace their underground shafts. There was celebration in the city that night, but the next day, the Gelon brought up more supplies and began again. With each foray, fewer Meklavaran defenders returned.

Early in the third week, Tsorreh found Zevaron among the wounded. He lay on a pallet in the tented area of the lower city, among those not yet moved up to the *meklat*. In the uncertain torchlight, his face was dusky, streaked with something dark. Blood or smoke or mud, she could not tell. She threw herself to her knees and reached out to take him in her arms. Then she saw the rise of his chest. Her breath caught in her throat.

"Water!" she called to the nearest aide. "Bring me water!"

The boy brought a bucket with a little scummy water at the bottom. Tsorreh dipped the hem of her tunic into it and wiped her son's face. He murmured as she ran the cloth over his lips. The dark smears were not blood, at least not his own. He groaned. His eyelids fluttered open.

Tsorreh sat back, trailing the wet, filthy edge of her tunic between her hands. Breath swept through her; she had not realized that she was holding it.

"Of all the stupid—" His eyes widened when he saw her. He sat up.

"Are you hurt?"

"No, just stunned." Wincing, he got to his feet. "They singled me out because I was riding Shorrenon's horse."

"You must rest," she said, reaching out to restrain him.

He placed his hands on hers, gently drawing them away. She sensed his resolve, his certainty that if he did not fight to his utmost now, there might never be another time for any of them. She had the same feeling herself. She could not spare herself merely because she was weary. She let him go.

By the end of the third week, the Gelonian earthworks were even closer to the walls.

Tsorreh went to confer with Councillor Anthelon, to finish assigning temporary quarters for the families from the lower city. Maharrad had given her the task of housing refugees as well as residents. She and Anthelon sat together at a little table in the corner of the council chamber. One of the maid-attendants sat nearby, sewing. Tsorreh frowned as she compared her map with a list of the possible buildings, including the houses of the noble families, marking how many people she'd already assigned to each one.

"Twenty more can go here and here," she said, pointing to the map.

"Cassarod will object," Anthelon said. "They've already sheltered more than we originally asked. There aren't enough beds, or even blankets, to go around. These people will be sleeping on the floor in the sculleries, hallways—"

"Or the mountain tunnels, if need be!" Tsorreh snapped. Fatigue and anxiety had eroded her patience. "What else can we do? Leave them below?" That very morning, she'd overheard the officers talking about the treatment they might receive when the defenses failed. Even a disciplined army might go on a rampage once they'd overcome heated resistance.

Tsorreh sighed. "Somehow we will find room for them."

Anthelon gathered up his papers and record books and departed. A few minutes later, the clamor of running footsteps and shouting brought Tsorreh up sharply. She went to the door and flung it open. The household guard jumped to attention. The noise grew louder, a roar like a storm ravening from the peaks, but it came from the direction of the lower city.

Benerod, her husband's young aide, came running from the direction of the front doors.

"What is it?" she called to him. "What's going on?"

He slowed his steps, stammering in terror. "They've b-broken through! They're c-coming!"

The maid-attendant reeled in her chair. "Don't you dare faint!" Tsorreh snapped.

Tsorreh rushed to the balcony, where she could see a little of the lower city. Through the partly opened gates and spreading into the nearby streets, a mass of men churned up billows of dust. The bright midmorning sun shone on Gelonian spear points.

Enemy soldiers poured into the lower city. Tsorreh spotted Maharrad on his white horse and Zevaron on Shorrenon's gray, struggling to rally soldiers and townspeople.

"*Te-ravah*?"

Tsorreh turned around at the sound of the boy's voice. He stood on the threshold of the open door, chest heaving, eyes wide. He looked very young.

"Benerod, what happened? How did this come about?"

"They—they—" He straightened his small slender shoulders. "Our men rode out as they have before, to attack the place where the Gelon were digging. Suddenly their spearmen jumped out from the ditches. They were waiting for us! They charged us! We rushed to meet them. Then their chariots came! The onagers breathed out fire like dragons, and a demon strode in the fore, scourging them with whips of lightning!"

Fire-breathing onagers? Demonic chariot-drivers? The lad clearly had the makings of a storyteller, to have added such embellishments. Tsorreh had read of similar terrors in the holy texts. Had such creatures ever existed, beyond the imaginations of children and poets? Dragons and demons did not make war in the current age, certainly not in the service of the Gelon.

Seeing her look of disbelief, the boy paused. "Their archers fired but fell short. Before our men could turn their horses around, they shot another volley. We tried to stop them, but they drove on, to the city gates . . ." His young voice broke.

The maid-attendant had not fainted but was pale and

visibly trembling. She gripped the sides of her chair, her needlework in a tumble at her feet. Tsorreh told Benerod to see the girl back to her chamber. She must remember to speak to Maharrad about the boy. If there was ever again a time to discuss the future of bright young aides. If there was time to talk at all.

Tsorreh hurried through the palace to the front doors. One of the household guards, seeing her without attendants, followed her. Outside, a stream of refugees from the lower city milled about the courtyard with officials and *meklat* residents, palace servants and soldiers. It was so crowded, she could hardly move. The guard caught up with her and shouldered them aside, clearing a path. Tsorreh decided he was much more useful than a fainting, whimpering maid.

Aided by the guard, Tsorreh climbed to the wall beside the arched gates. Zevaron's sling-throwing youngsters had taken up their positions. White-faced, they readied their stones.

Fires had broken out in the wooden structures below. People rushed up the stairs to the upper city. Tsorreh shouted for them to hurry, to keep moving. A young woman struggled on, supporting a white-bearded elder with one arm and holding a baby in the other. Two old women in widow's robes clutched each other, weeping, as they climbed with painful slowness. A fat man with a crutch remained at the bottom of the stairs, urging the others on.

Tsorreh searched through the confusion for Maharrad's white horse. She spotted him at the center of a force opposing a mass of Gelonian spearmen. The closeness of the streets forced the Gelon to come at them a few at a time, but the Meklavaran horses had little room to maneuver.

He cannot hold them, she thought.

Moment by moment, the city's defenders fell back. The Gelon spread out, taking the smaller streets and alleys. The morning sun glinted on the points of their spears and the rims of their shields. They kept close ranks, each man protecting the weaker side of his fellow. When they encountered a cluster of Meklavaran defenders, they tightened their ranks like a wall. They moved forward, sometimes halting behind raised shields but never drawing back.

Ignorant as she was in the ways of battle, Tsorreh realized that Maharrad's own success worked against him. While he held back the main body of the enemy, they were encircling him. Any moment now, they would cut off his line of retreat.

There was nothing she could do to warn him, no way she could save those brave, desperate men: Meklavaran soldiers, few of them professional, and city folk—merchants, carpenters, smiths, herders. They had no hope against that shining wall of Gelonian shields.

And Zevaron. She could not see the gray horse anywhere in the smoke and dust.

A horn sounded. A Meklavaran horn? Yes. The pattern, the very timbre of the notes were etched into her memory. *Retreat.*

Street by street, Maharrad and his company fought to give the people of the lower city precious extra moments to reach the stairs. With a roar, the Gelonian soldiers rushed forward.

Through a rent in the smoke, Tsorreh glimpsed the gray horse, rearing, caught in perfect balance. She thought she saw a flash of brilliance reflected off a sword, but that might only have been the sudden blurring of her eyes.

The horns sounded again. The riders wheeled and raced for the stairs. The horses surged upward, slipping and clattering over the stone steps. A moment later, they rushed through the gates. Maharrad raised his sword in salute as his horse galloped past.

The last of the fighting men reached the *meklat* even as the Gelon set foot on the first stairs. The gates slammed shut.

Tsorreh closed her eyes, momentarily overcome by the thought of the people trapped below.

O Most Holy, be with them now!

The Gelon kept on, rushing up the stairs. They no longer moved in formation, but individually. A few outstripped their comrades.

Thwack! Thwack!

Stones hurtled from the slings of Zevaron's youngsters. The nearest Gelonian soldier fell backward, hands raised to his face. His body crashed into two soldiers on the step below him and all three went down, sliding and flailing. Before the Gelon could regroup, a volley of arrows and stones struck the foremost. They fell back in disarray.

Horses, wounded men, and families from the lower city jammed the outer courtyard. The palace steward came forward and began directing the refugees to shelter. Residents of the *meklat* emerged from their homes, enfolding the people from the lower city. Tsorreh recognized some of them. The woman in the brocade head scarf, bending to pick up a howling toddler and speak encouragingly to the mother, was the wife of the treasury warden. Many who had reached the *meklat* earlier in the siege came forward to help.

"Come this way."

"Quickly now! Make room for the others!"

"Are you hurt? Who among you needs help?"

Benerod darted up to Maharrad just as the King swayed in the saddle. For a heart-stopping moment, Tsorreh feared her husband would fall. Was he hurt, unconscious? She turned to climb down from the wall, and when she glanced his way again, he was sitting upright, drinking from a silver cup.

Tsorreh darted through an opening in the crowd and rushed to her husband's side. Around her, people murmured, "It's the *te-ravah*!" and let her pass. Maharrad saw her and smiled, but his face was drawn, his expression tightly set.

"Are you wounded, my husband?" she began, and then saw the trickle of blood from beneath the leather armor covering his thigh.

"Benerod!" she cried. "Get a physician, quickly!"

"No!" Maharrad said. "There are many in greater need. The wound is not deep. Ten years ago, I would have gone running after the Gelon, sword in hand, after such a trifling cut." He sighed, an old man's sigh.

Maharrad tilted in his saddle and this time, Tsorreh reached up to him. Too late, she realized that if he fell, she could not support his weight. The next instant, Zevaron was at her side, gently easing his father out of the saddle.

"That's a good lad," Maharrad murmured. "Now, if you'll just . . ." He slumped. Zevaron slipped his shoulder under Maharrad's arm, and Tsorreh took his other elbow.

"We must get him inside," Tsorreh said in a low voice. "I will care for him myself."

Chapter Three

TSORREH bathed and dressed Maharrad's wound herself. She rinsed it with boiled tincture of feverbane, wrapped it in clean, finely woven cotton, and prayed it would not go bad. He had been right, it was neither deep nor dangerous in itself, but at his age, a festering infection would finish him quickly. Benerod watched her every move, chewing on his lower lip, until Maharrad sent the boy down to the walls with a message for the officers that he would join them shortly.

As Maharrad struggled to his feet, Tsorreh confronted her husband. "Will you accomplish your own death, when the Gelon could not? Are you determined to finish what they began?"

"My place is below, with my soldiers. The people, they must see me—see me lead."

Nothing Tsorreh said could dissuade him. Short of carrying him to his bed and chaining him there, she could think of no way to restrain him. In the end, she accompanied him. If his aim was to give the people encouragement, then two could do it better than one.

Zevaron left his cadre of sling-throwers and joined his father on the parapet. General Isarod approached them, saying that he'd received reports of sporadic fighting in the streets, but Tsorreh could see none at this time. Most of the remaining city folk seemed to be hiding. The Gelon held the major marketplaces, open plazas where their disciplined tactics gave them an advantage.

"They have made no further effort to storm the stairs?" Maharrad asked the general.

"None, *te-ravot*. They cannot easily employ a battering ram from that angle, and we can keep them away from the gates. A shortage of stones is not yet upon us," Isarod added wryly.

"They seek to consolidate their hold on the lower city," Maharrad commented.

"Let them think so, and may it give them joy!" Zevaron said.

Tsorreh's belly clenched, thinking of the people left behind. Would the Gelon use them as hostages and threaten to kill a certain number every day if Maharrad did not surrender?

"Our granaries and cisterns are full," Zevaron continued. "Shorrenon will have returned long before we want for food or drink!"

"But—" Tsorreh burst out. The others turned to stare at her. "Shorrenon, if he does not realize the lower city has fallen—" Shorrenon would attack the Gelonian encampment, expecting a foray from the city to reinforce his thrust. Between them, the Gelon in the city and those outside would crush him.

"We must find a way to warn him," Zevaron said.

"We have time to plan," Maharrad said. "My elder son may not arrive for some days or more."

If he does at all. Tsorreh did not know whether to pray for her stepson's return or his failure to do so. As long as Shorrenon remained free, Meklavar might fall and yet be victorious in the end, rallying around its new *te-ravot*.

Maharrad swayed on his feet. He caught himself on the ledge, knuckles white with strain.

"Come, my husband," Tsorreh said, her voice low and urgent. "Nothing further requires your presence here. Come away and rest, that you may regain your strength."

Zevaron lifted his head. "The Gelon are at an impasse. Please, Father. When they move again, we will need you to lead us."

Maharrad drew himself up. He put one hand on Tsorreh's shoulder. She felt the weight bearing her down, but yielded nothing. Moving slowly, with heartrending dignity, he proceeded toward the palace. Tsorreh matched his pace so closely that his sleeves brushed the fine hairs on her arm. The people in the courtyard bowed. Hope shone in their eyes, hope and grief.

Only when they were within the walls of his own chambers did Maharrad give way, staggering to the chair just inside the door. His personal servant rushed forward, but Maharrad waved the man away. "I need nothing but my *teshurah*," he said, turning "Tsorreh" into the archaic word for *gift* or *treasure*.

Tsorreh gestured for the servant to remain. Gently but firmly, she guided her husband through the formal outer chamber to the more intimate bedroom.

The air smelled of beeswax scented with tiny grains of sandalwood, Maharrad's favorite. A tray bore pitchers of boiled water and wine, and a plate of honey-glazed almonds and dates. Tsorreh's eyes stung. He had offered her such a meal on their wedding night, and such she had also served him when she told him she was carrying their child. They would share a little comfort, then, in a moment of remembered joy.

Tsorreh and the servant laid Maharrad on the raised bed. His cat, a brown tabby, darted under the bed at their approach. Perhaps it scented the blood. Maharrad went limp, his body sinking into the soft surface. Tsorreh loosened the neck clasps of his robe and arranged the pillows beneath his head and knees. The servant removed his boots and brought water to bathe his hands and feet.

For a short time, Maharrad lay still, eyes closed, features frozen in an expression of gaunt endurance. Then he opened his eyes and bade the servant depart. Tsorreh mixed water and wine in a goblet and offered it to him. He raised his head, sipped a little, and lay back. Color seeped back into his flesh.

"You are as beautiful now as the moment I first saw you." Reaching up, he brushed her cheek with his free hand. "So young, like an unawakened flower, your petals still folded up."

Tsorreh lowered her eyes. At any other time, she would have accepted his words as a gesture of affection. She had not loved him at first, for she had been little more than a child herself, with no idea of what marriage meant, yet kindness had grown between them over the years. No matter how brusque and formal he might be in his role as *te-ravot*, he had always treated her tenderly in private. Now his words seemed as much farewell as remembrance.

Maharrad lifted one of her hands to his lips. For a moment, she thought he might heap additional praises upon her.

"I would speak to you of the fall of Meklavar." His eyes were dark and steady.

"What are you saying? Is there some new and dreadful turn of events that not even your council knows?"

He shook his head. "We are as determined as ever to defend ourselves. But we cannot deny the possibility that we may fail."

And it is the duty of a te-ravot *to plan for such a fate.*

"You will need all your courage in the days to come," he went on. "Our people will look to you. You must keep their hope alive, and protect and preserve them until the day they regain their freedom."

"I will serve as best I can," she answered, a little uncertainly. "Surely, there is still hope. Shorrenon will bring help and we will find a way to warn him. We can hold the *meklat* until he comes. We must not give in to fear. Even if—if we cannot keep them out, our plight may not be so dire. I have studied Gelonian histories and poetry. Anthelon is right. They are not barbarians."

"My dear, you are learned in many things, but military strategy is not one of them," he said, a smile hovering at the corners of his mouth. "I would not have you unprepared, should the worst come. Ar-Cinath-Gelon must have his victory and it will be brutal, a message to the world."

"If his purpose is to seize control of the southern passes, then he will need the city and its people," she said. "They will not destroy Meklavar—or its royal family."

"If Cinath had dispatched an emissary to negotiate a treaty with us, it would be no defeat if he came back empty-handed. In sending his own son at the head of an invading army, however, he has cast a wager he cannot afford to lose. The Gelon would have every other small kingdom know our fate, should they in turn resist."

Icy feathers brushed Tsorreh's spine. "Are we to expect no mercy from them?"

"*You* may, if you bend to their will." He paused, leaving unspoken the words, *But I will not.*

The people love him well, she thought in a burst of understanding, *and now he has become a beacon, a rallying point for every fighting man within the larger Meklavaran territory. Gelon cannot afford to let him live.*

"You must take sanctuary in the temple," Tsorreh said, the words tumbling from her mouth. "As chief priest, my grandfather will shelter you. Surely, not even the Gelon would dare to search among the venerable elders."

"No, no, my dear, the Gelon will not stop until they find me. Can you not see?" *They must have my body as a trophy.*

Tsorreh hardly dared to breathe. Somewhere in the far reaches of her heart, a voice began keening. There was nothing she could say to silence it. If their positions were reversed, she would not want empty reassurances.

Even as she trembled with foreboding, another part of her mind stirred. Meklavar was far older than Gelon; the temple had stood while the Gelon were half-naked hunters daubed with mud, stabbing one another with stone-tipped spears. Modern Gelon were not savages, true, but they were scavengers. Their cities, she had read, were museums of the cultures they had conquered and then looted.

Cities could be rebuilt, farms replanted, and another

generation born. But without knowledge of who they were and the heritage they safeguarded, they would no longer be Meklavaran, but just another nameless race fallen to a stronger empire.

Maharrad's hand had gone limp in hers. His breathing deepened, softer now. A hush suffused the chamber.

Tsorreh eased herself on to the bed, still holding his hand, and stretched out beside him. She lay with open eyes for a long time, thinking of Zevaron, the child they had created together. Perhaps she slept, for when she roused, no light came from the windows, and her body felt stiff, almost brittle. Maharrad slept on, his face peaceful. His cat had emerged from under the bed and sat at the foot, tail curled around its feet, tufted ears pricked.

Tsorreh slipped out of Maharrad's bed to her own chamber. The room was empty, for Otenneh was asleep in her own room and no attendants stirred at this hour. Tsorreh picked up her prayer book and sought the words written so many years ago, wondering if the scribe had set them down for this very moment, to be a voice when other voices failed, a thought when the mind had gone numb, an entreaty when hope was lost.

Written words had been her refuge since the time she'd come to the palace as a shivering, bewildered bride, not much more than a child, clutching her slim pile of books. Maharrad had gravely accepted them, a dowry whose value he recognized but for which he himself had little use, and then returned them to her keeping. When she'd felt their familiar weight once more in her hands, her fears had lifted. Now she had a place, something of her own amidst the confusion of the court. She was the Keeper of the Books. This she understood, and felt her own worth.

She had grown up surrounded by books. As a young child, she had spent many happy hours in the archives of the temple with her paternal grandfather, not yet risen to the office of chief priest but one among many. Her earliest memories were of lying in her bed, listening to the soft murmur of her mother reading verses aloud from a volume of

Isarran love poetry. Somehow her father had found it, bought perhaps from a trader, one of the hundreds who passed through the Meklavaran markets, and presented it to his homesick wife as a gift.

Tsorreh had learned the magic of words, the pulse and rhythm of speech preserved through the years. Even now, when she opened a volume or unrolled a scroll, she could almost hear the voice of the man or woman who penned it, sense the reverence of the scribe who copied it, and see the hands of everyone who had opened it and touched the written letters with their fingertips.

If ever you loved your people, she thought, following along with the formal phrases, *reach out your hand to them now, spread your sheltering wings over them. Even as you lifted Khored of Blessed Memory above his foes, protect my people.*

Save my son.

Tsorreh prayed as well for Maharrad, who for all the difference in their ages had been as kind and gentle as he could; for Shorrenon, that he lead wisely and justly; for the men and boys at mortal risk. And the women, too—the timid maid-attendants, the wives, the girls with their slings. She asked nothing for herself, as if by seeking even the smallest grace, she might diminish that granted to those she loved.

Deep within the citadel, Tsorreh made her way through the outer chambers of the treasury. She had dismissed her maid-attendants into the care of their families, which they interpreted as a gesture of generosity. Only Otenneh suspected Tsorreh's relief at her new freedom.

A single guard stood outside the treasury. The warden, keys jangling from his belt of office, preceded her and unlocked the first six locks, then handed her the key to the seventh. Entering, she passed coffers containing precious metals and jewels, pearls and jade from Denariya, age-darkened ivory from the Fever Lands where few men now ventured, amber and silver from Azkhantia. Crowns sat on their ornate stands, but a trick of light dimmed the gold. Here was a sword said to be Khored's own, and here, set in a swirl of wire, gold and silver and ruddy copper, the Stone of Hosarion. Whether it was the real stone or the real sword, Tsorreh could never be sure, but she felt, as an almost palpable weight, the centuries of veneration laid upon them.

Of all the holy things, nothing stirred her more deeply than the treasure waiting at the very end of the chamber.

Tsorreh stood before it, her heart rising in her throat. She felt presumptuous for daring to take such a hallowed object into her own hands. Yet, she argued with herself, how much more irreverent would it be for the Gelon to carry it off as a mere curiosity? They might present it to the Emperor as booty. They might also—and here her stomach knotted—they might also destroy the manuscript itself, keeping only its ornate outer cover.

This was not any *te-Ketav*, wrapped in layers of velvet of deepest purple, edged with cords of gold and crimson, and cradled in a holder of intricately carved ebony. It was the King's *Ketav*, said to be the first written version of the divine words.

The velvet-wrapped bundle was surprisingly heavy. She had never handled it before, had seen it only a few times. This was the *te-Ketav* by which she had been married, by which monarchs were crowned. When her grandfather died, the man who succeeded him as chief priest would pray for him from this volume.

The velvet folds opened beneath her fingers, and she touched the hard surface beneath. The richness of the cover took her breath away. The front and spine looked like silver, only without any hint of tarnish. Moonstones for night and clear yellow amber for day framed a central panel. An inlay of gold wires set with leaf-shaped emeralds, topazes, and jade represented the Great Tree. Set at its roots was a stylized emblem, six oval gems surrounding a single luminous heart. This was no blossom, she knew, but a representation of the *te-Khored-Magan*, the Shield of Khored. *The Seven-Petaled Shield.*

Like all Meklavaran children, Tsorreh had once asked why it was called seven-petaled, when clearly there were but six. Her grandfather had answered that only with the inner eye could one see the seventh petal, the heart of the Shield, so mysterious was its power.

For all its superb artistry and costly materials, the cover was only a shell. Turning it over in her hands, Tsorreh discovered a clasp on one side. When she pressed it, the lid slid open to reveal an inner compartment. Hardly daring to breathe, she lifted out the silk-wrapped contents. The sheaf of age-darkened parchment had originally been bound in leather and silk. Tiny holes along one side marked where it had once been sewn together, although the thread had long since fallen away. The ink had lightened as it aged until, in places, the words resembled shadows. There was no title page, no illumination or decoration, yet she never doubted what she held. In tiny yet flowing calligraphy, she read the opening phrases, the first prayer that every Meklavaran child learned.

> By grace, all things are made,
> By judgment, all things are unmade.

Tsorreh re-wrapped the empty cover in its velvet and put it back on its stand exactly as she found it, leaving no trace it had ever been disturbed. The Gelon would discover the jeweled housing, never guessing that the real treasure had been removed. She tucked the packet of silk-wrapped pages into the front of her tunic, its contours hidden behind the embroidery, and locked the treasury door behind her. Not even the warden would suspect she had taken anything. And if Shorrenon arrived in time to save the city, she could return the manuscript as secretly as she had removed it.

She emerged in the open courtyard between the palace and the citadel. Below, she heard a distant, muted clamor. A few servants ran past, slowing their steps only enough to bow to her.

At first, she had intended to take the *te-Ketav* up through the mountain tunnel to the temple. Now she realized she must first decide what else must be made safe, should the city fall. She might have time to remove only a tiny portion of the archives.

Passing halls where children's voices once rose and fell in unison, Tsorreh made her way to the library. There was no clerk at his station, and for a moment, the place seemed deserted except for the tortoiseshell cat who kept the mice at bay.

A movement startled her. Eavonen, the old scholar who had quoted from the story of Hosarion, rose stiffly from his desk. With exquisite delicacy, he closed the book he had been reading. As she drew near, Tsorreh saw tears shining on his withered cheeks. His eyes were so bright, so full of inner light, she wondered if he could see what she carried.

"You must go with the others to the temple," she said.

He bowed his head. A shudder passed through his thin shoulders. She saw how his scholar's robe hung even more loosely on him.

Tsorreh picked up the book he had been reading: *Shirah Kohav*, Poetry of the Stars. Some of the verses had been sung at her own wedding. She handed back it to him.

"Take this with you. It will be safer in your keeping." *And may it comfort you.*

Bony fingers closed around the slender volume. Even in these disordered times, he would never have taken it for himself.

"May the Shield of Khored ever protect you, *te-ravah*," he murmured, bowing as deeply as his aged joints would allow.

"May you return the book to its proper place in the fullness of time," she replied, managing a smile.

After Eavonen departed, a stillness settled in the air. The library lay before her, a realm of years and thought as well as landscape. Sometimes she felt as if each scroll and hand-sewn book contained the soul of a person. They were the only way those dead could speak. Each page sang of their wisdom, their pain, their joy.

How could she judge what to save and what to leave behind? However flawed her decisions, she must choose, and quickly.

The most ancient scrolls must go to the temple, the *te-Ketav* she carried next to her heart, as well as other holy texts, painstakingly copied by hand and illuminated with mystical symbols. She must also select from among more ordinary prayer books, genealogies, histories, commentaries on scripture, and the hidden names of things. All these defined her people, who they had been, what they had thought and dreamed.

An idea came to her, as she pictured not only what she would take but also what she would leave behind. Just as she had taken the most precious item of the treasury and left the rest undisturbed, visually intact, so she would disguise the changes in the library. No Meklavaran scholar would be fooled, but a Gelonian general might well be. He would look no further and would take back to Gelon those things that, while costly, had no deeper significance.

Let the invaders read how to plant crops and observe the stars. The books that spoke uniquely to the Meklavaran soul, the songs of praise phrased as only a Meklavaran could, the remembrance of saints and heroes, the deeds of Khored of Blessed Memory and his brothers, of the heroes Hosarion, Uzmarion and Faranoth— these must not be lost. The volumes of Gelonian history and language would remain, along with poetry and annals from Denariya and even the collection of Vasparon's travels to Azkhantia. Medical and astrological treatises, and books on mathematics and botany would remain in their proper places. These things were replaceable; other copies existed, and they did not speak to the soul of Meklavar. She must take only what was essential.

Tsorreh went to the nearest rack. Her fingertips brushed the spines of the volumes. They would have to be protected against the damp and the insidious dust of the mountain caverns. Wrappings of silk and oiled canvas would be best. Given the state of confusion in the *meklat*, she did not know what help she might find. Otenneh would do whatever was asked of her, but would it not be better to leave her in the relative safety of the temple?

No, she decided, the fewer people who knew about the hiding place of the books, the less chance of inadvertent betrayal.

Well past twilight, Tsorreh made her way along the tunnels leading into the mountainside. The passage, wide enough for three men to walk abreast, turned and then ramped upward. Vents carried a breeze to freshen the air. Fresh torches had been set in their brackets at regular intervals. She took one from its holder.

The tunnels had a strange way of distorting sound, and from time to time, she halted to listen. Even in times of peace, she had occasionally imagined footsteps behind her along these passages, or the slither of something long and scaly over the bare rock. Did she hear a faint vibration now, or was that only the thrum of breath through her own lungs? Was it the memory of distant horns, of sword against shield? Did the battle waken a resonance within the mountain, perhaps a longing?

If I do not take care, my imagined fears will me turn into a coward! She tightened her grasp on the torch. The enemy lay outside the city gates, she reminded herself, and not ahead.

As she went on, the air smelled less fresh. The darkness took on an almost palpable density. In the light of her torch, the walls glistened as if damp.

Twice a year, people ascended by this route to the temple set high above the city. The priests performed the ancient ceremonies, chanted praises, recited the story of the creation of the world, and sang of the times when the miraculous had been closer.

The temple had been created for many more people than now attended. Once, Tsorreh had been told, there were so many participants that everyone stood and the entire congregation bowed and swayed and sang as one. She wondered if Meklavar had lost faith, and that was why Gelon sat at the gates.

The temple was a marvel, a triumph of its ancient builders. Although most of it consisted of naturally formed caverns, a series of ducts and mirrors brought both light and fresh air. Even the chill of the mountain retreated. Somewhere deep in its heart lay a hot spring, and the builders had harnessed it for heat.

Tsorreh's sandals made no noise as she crossed the worn mosaic floor with its depiction of an endless circular river, teeming with fish and all manner of creatures: storks, stately egrets, fat ducks, birds with curved beaks and spindly legs, frogs and eels. Deer bent to drink, unafraid of the lions beside them, and snakes lay in graceful coils beside bees, badgers, dragonflies, and even an improbably long-necked camel. Tsorreh had loved playing on this very floor as a child, and now its familiar creatures brought unexpected comfort. One of the temple cats, pure black, glided over and rubbed against her leg.

She found Tenereth, her grandfather, directing activities in the outer sanctuary. He smiled when he saw her, but he looked as if he had not slept in days. The skin beneath his eyes hung in loose folds, and he moved stiffly, as if his bones pained him. As he bent to place a kiss of greeting on her forehead, his hands trembled. He grasped her elbow and leaned upon her as they proceeded to his private meditation chamber.

Two thick candles burned on either side of an opened prayer book, resting on its stand of ivory-inlaid cedar. The mingled scents of beeswax and citrus hung in the air. Tenereth lowered himself to the plain bench, resting one elbow on the reading stand. The carved screen cast patterned shadows across his face. He looked not just tired and old, but ill.

Tsorreh reached out one hand to him. He took it, his bony fingers wrapping around hers. Explaining what she meant to do, she drew out the *te-Ketav* and laid it in his hands. A shadow and then a radiance passed over his features. For an instant, it seemed as if his body were made of glass, lit from within. The faintest tracery of light passed over his skin. Then the moment shifted, and he was only a tired, elderly man holding a sheaf of pages as if they were the most precious thing in the world.

"This cannot stay here," he said.

She nodded. "When—*if* Meklavar should fall, the Gelon will not rest until they occupy the entire city, including the temple."

Their eyes met, and again she caught that curious, fleeting brilliance, like a living aura surrounding his body.

"Not *if*," he said. "Meklavar will fall."

The quiet certainty in his voice stunned her. "How can you know that? We have already held out far longer than anyone expected. We have even prevented the Gelon from undermining our walls. Any day now, Shorrenon will return. He will—"

"Gelon will take the *meklat*, the citadel, the fields, the Var Pass itself," Tenereth interrupted. "There is no time to explain. You must simply accept that I have been granted the power to see such things. When the city falls, do not linger, no matter what the reason. You must come here immediately, you and Zevaron. Do you understand? Promise me this!"

"I—I will come."

"And Zevaron as well?"

"Yes, of course."

"No matter what the price, some things *must not* fall into their hands."

Tsorreh's gaze flew to the *te-Ketav*.

"That and more," he said. "Come now with me, for your task lies before you and I have preparations of my own to make." He rose and gestured to her to follow. "I will tell you where what you carry may be safely stored."

"You aren't going to tell me any more than that?" Tsor-reh's nerves had been scoured raw by uncertainty and fear—and now these riddles!

Tenereth looked as if he were about to answer, but then a shadow, more felt than seen, came over him. "The time is not yet right. Just remember—do not delay. You and Zeva-ron *must escape.*"

Tsorreh bit her lip to keep silent. He was right, the line of Khored must survive, preserving the lineage that ran from Tenereth through her dead father to herself, and now her son. Her grandfather must have a plan in mind for their escape, one he dared not reveal prematurely. He led her to the back of the meditation chamber.

The little alcove was deep but not tall. A rack with pegs, for hanging cloaks, had been set into one side, along with a shelf for a basket of candles and a box with flint and tinder. In the alcove's center, on a raised slab of stone, was a wicker chest with a fresh supply of torches. At her grandfather's direction, she lit one of them.

"Reach behind the chest," he said.

Tsorreh slipped into the narrow space. After several attempts, her fingers found the deep groove in the back of the platform. She grasped the lever where he said it would be. With a creak, the platform slid forward, revealing an opening.

"Now go down." Tenereth gave her detailed directions to the storage place, urging her to commit them to memory.

The first steps were so steep, she had to turn around and face them as she descended, as if they were rungs of a ladder. She counted ten of them, feeling each one with her feet.

She descended a short distance further before the tunnel leveled out and began to climb again in a series of tortuous switchbacks. It was very narrow here and the walls were rough, yet she felt safe. The air was still, disturbed only by her own passing.

The tunnel branched and branched again. It occurred to her that it would be possible to hide for a long time in these tunnels. Food and water would have to be stored, as well as torches. But sooner or later, supplies would be exhausted and she would emerge to an occupied city. She was no outlaw, to attack and run, and she was of no use to anyone hidden away.

She eventually found herself in a large, dry cavern. In ages past, a hermit priest had lived here, for a sleeping ledge had been chiseled from the coarse dark rock. More recently, the central chamber and two smaller areas had been put to other uses: wooden platforms stood a hand's length above the floor and the wicker chests upon them looked new. The lids were tightly woven to keep out the dust. She opened one and found it was half-filled with silk-wrapped packets the size and shape of bound books. In addition, there were a number of lengths of the same fabric. Folding the *te-Ketav* in several thicknesses of silk, she laid it inside and carefully re-fitted the lid.

As Tsorreh turned to leave, a puff of air brushed her face. Her torch revealed an opening at the far end. The breeze gusted again, sending the flame flickering. There must be another opening, a way out of the tunnels, perhaps leading to the hidden mountain trails. If anything happened to her grandfather, she would be able to find her way this far, and the breeze would guide her the rest of the way. She prayed it would never come to that.

When Tsorreh returned to the royal quarters, the boy Benerod was waiting for her with news that a messenger had slipped through the Gelonian lines. Shorrenon was but a day's ride from Meklavar and would strike at dawn on the second day.

Amidst the rejoicing and excitement, Tsorreh's foremost thought was that she had only a little more than a day in which to move the library.

Chapter Four

AFTER a few hours of sleep, Tsorreh awoke, sweating and tangled in the light coverlet. Otenneh was absent, which was unlike her, but she had left a tray of flatbread and thin-shaved cheese, and a pitcher of watered wine.

She threw on her oldest clothes, the same she had worn on the fateful day the Gelon had breached the outer walls, and went to see how Maharrad fared. He was resting comfortably and seemed to be recovering. She told him her plans for the library and consulted him on who she might ask to help take it to the temple. His reaction was not what she'd hoped. He did not approve of her placing herself at risk, he said, although he respected her desire to be of use. Emphasizing that not a single able-bodied man could be spared from the defense of the city, he explicitly forbade her from enlisting others in her scheme. Tsorreh regretted confiding in him, although she understood his concern.

As soon as she could reasonably excuse herself, Tsorreh rushed off to the library. The enormity of her undertaking filled her mind with a feverish urgency, yet if she had not set herself such a task, she would surely have gone mad. What else could she do? Sit idly by while others fought and died for her? She could not, *would not* give up, even if she had to carry every book and manuscript herself. At least, Maharrad had not given her a direct command.

Even though dawn was still a few hours off, the *meklat* seethed with activity. Every man able to fight, every woman or child able to work the walls, was feverishly making ready. Arrows, stones for slings, even pots of water to boil, were being prepared. All of this took place in an atmosphere of hushed secrecy, so that the Gelon would have no sign of their defense preparations.

The library was not, as Tsorreh had expected, deserted. When she arrived, she found Eavonen and Otenneh bent over a table. Books and scrolls, a dozen or more of each, had been arrayed in neat piles. Otenneh clucked under her breath as she wrapped a book in a length of silk.

Tsorreh felt a jolt of irrational anger that the old scholar had not gone to the temple as she had bade him.

Eavonen looked up, his eyes bright. "I asked myself," he commented in the oratorical tone he used when reciting from the *te-Ketav*, "what purpose our *te-ravah* might have in examining the contents of the library. What did I know of her nature that might explain it? I know she is reverent, as the granddaughter of the chief priest should be, and that she is courageous, as the wife of the *te-ravot* should also be."

"From the state of your slippers last night, you'd been to the temple," Otenneh added.

"A logical place to safeguard our most precious records," Eavonen said, "provided they are properly protected against damp and dust. I would expect your grandfather to supply a suitably discreet hiding place. Which puts me in mind of a time when he and I were at school together—"

Otenneh shot Eavonen a sharp look. He cleared his throat. "Perhaps that story is better left to another time."

Tsorreh lowered herself to the nearest bench. "I don't know what to say. You know what I plan to do?"

"My dear child," Eavenon said, "do you think you are the only one who sees this place as the real treasure of Meklavar? For is it not written—"

"In short," Otenneh said briskly, "we came to help." She

gestured to a large basket of woven leather on the floor beside the table. "I found that in the kitchen. I think it came from the foundry. Will it serve?"

"I don't know how to thank you," Tsorreh said, acutely aware that amid all her plans, she had not worked out how she was going to carry the books.

"Don't," Otenneh said in the same tone she'd used when Tsorreh was a child and in a recalcitrant mood. "Try the basket on for size."

Tsorreh slipped her arms through the straps and hefted the basket on to her back. Tightly-woven and tough as iron, it was shaped to balance its weight securely against the back. The harness was sized for a broad-shouldered man, not a slender woman, but it fit better than she expected.

In a short time, the three of them had organized and packed the first assortment of records to be taken. Eavonen was too frail to carry even a single load of books to the temple and Tsorreh would not have permitted him to do so against Maharrad's direct order, but the old scholar's knowledge of the collection proved invaluable. Tsorreh had been afraid that she would not be able to transport all the books by herself, but between Eavonen's careful selection and Otenneh's help in preparation, the end result seemed within her ability, so long as she took her time.

Tsorreh picked up the laden basket. The leather straps creaked under the strain. She drew in a breath, summoning her strength, and hurried on her way. She feared she might encounter someone who would recognize her, even in old clothes and carrying a load like a servant, but everyone was so caught up in the frenzy of the impending battle, no one challenged her. If somebody did ask what she was doing, she was *te-ravah* and answerable only to her husband and her own conscience.

The trip to the temple was longer and more wearying than she'd expected. Perhaps her fears added to the weight of the basket. She passed the outer areas of the temple, weaving through the people who had already arrived. Tenereth was nowhere to be seen in the crowd.

Tsorreh passed through her grandfather's chamber and into the caves. She placed the contents of the basket in one of the chests on the wooden shelf, well above the rock floor. If anything happened, if she could not return when the city fell, this much of the library might lie hidden in its protective wrappings for a long time—years, decades, perhaps even centuries—before some hermit discovered it. But someone *would* come, she felt the certainty in her bones, and the library's wisdom would be waiting.

Meklavar will endure. We will wait, and we will remember.

The following morning, Tsorreh returned shortly before dawn from another trip to the caves. At Otenneh's insistence, she lay down for a short time and tried to sleep. She closed her eyes, caught up in an almost preternatural awareness, as if she had been touched with a prophet's dreaming vision. All around her, she felt the city, the men with their weapons ready and prayers upon their lips, the few remaining horses mouthing their bits in anticipation, the families sitting together, some women weeping, others clutching one another, and the herder children crouched behind the parapet along with those few archers who did not go out with the others. In the market city, she sensed skirls of fear, of festering wounds, of meals eaten quickly, and the thousand small activities of life now held in abeyance.

Benerod, who had become a private messenger between Tsorreh and Maharrad, knocked gently at the door. Tsorreh was instantly alert, her heart pounding. She slipped from the bed, her feet noiseless on the cool rock floor. Otenneh opened the door.

"*Te-ravah*, the signal has come. The *te-ravot* is waiting for you. They all are, to take their leave."

With solemn pace, Tsorreh, and Otenneh followed Benerod to the central hall and through the main doors into the courtyard. Light washed the eastern sky, for sunrise was almost upon them.

Maharrad waited at the head of his men, mounted on his white horse. Most of the other men were on foot, except for the captains and Zevaron on Shorrenon's rangy gray. Catching the tension of the men, the horses pranced restively.

Tsorreh took her place in front of the other noble women. A few wept, but most looked dry-eyed with exhaustion and shock. Otenneh waited, a silent shadow, behind her.

Maharrad took up his sword and held it aloft. The blade was desert-made, short and curved. Jewels had been set in the hilt and ancient words of protection inlaid in red gold along its length. The tip quivered, and it seemed to Tsorreh to fracture the light.

He called out, summoning his people to battle. She hardly recognized his voice.

"Arise, defenders of Meklavar! The hour of glory is nigh!" His words carried in the stillness, as if every man, woman, and child held his breath, each heart beat more softly, listening. "For ten generations, we have lived in freedom, following the ways of our fathers. We have watched; we have remembered."

Tsorreh heard the echo in the minds of the people, the same words in her own thoughts.

We watch. We remember.

The white horse danced beneath Maharrad. Its hooves clattered on the stone paving. "Let our children remember this day, and their children after them! Now we go forth! Now we fight for Meklavar!"

"Meklavar!" they answered. "Meklavar!" Their voices grew from a few isolated cheers to a rushing roar, drowning out Maharrad's final cry.

Tsorreh caught the sound of horns, some near, some far. The tones reverberated, overlapping. Building.

She waited with the others while Maharrad rode out leading the last of Meklavar's fighting forces. Every man able to wield a spear or sword or bow, gray-haired or stripling youth, hale or wounded, went with him. Those who were left behind, the women and children too young to fight, Zevaron's sling throwers and a sprinkling of lame archers, went to take their places along the *meklat* walls. If the day went badly, here they might make a last defense.

From the height of the *meklat*, Tsorreh noticed movement in the Gelonian encampment beyond the walls. She watched as Maharrad's mounted forces bore down on the enemy in the marketplaces. The plan was for him to keep them engaged while Shorrenon attacked the flank of the main army.

Tsorreh peered in the direction her stepson would come. Along the foot of the mountain, a swarm of orange lights, torches carried by mounted men, swept toward the city from one of the narrow passes. In the strengthening light, their horses appeared as an undulation of shadows.

As Tsorreh paced the walls, speaking briefly to each defender, she recognized the lanky desert girl who had practiced earlier with Zevaron, taut and silent, dark eyes watchful. She had noticed Zevaron sneaking glances at the girl.

"You are not Meklavaran, I think," Tsorreh said.

"No, I am desert-bred," the girl said, in a hesitant, accented voice. "My name is Shadow Fox. My family came here from Kadesh-Birna when I was a babe, and your king granted us pastures for our flocks if we would keep his laws. This we have done and so prospered."

"How did you come here, to the city?"

"When the men of the Rock Lands"—evidently the name the Sand Lands people used for Gelon—"invaded Meklavar, my family sent three of us here to defend the city."

"And you came? *You*?" Tsorreh asked, startled that a young woman should be sent to fight.

Shadow Fox smiled, her teeth white against the darkness of her skin. "It is the custom of my people. To the north, the women of Azkhantia ride to battle as well as the men."

And why not? Tsorreh thought. Swordcraft required strength and size, but not all combat was fought thus. Surely, this girl could aim a sling or use a bow as skillfully as any boy her age. She wondered if this was why the steppe riders had resisted Gelon so successfully. What allies those people would make!

Before Tsorreh could say anything more, one of the women stationed near the gates cried out, pointing. The Gelon were falling back from the lower city, keeping in tight formation as they moved toward the outer walls. On the western hillside, mounted men raced toward the city.

"Shorrenon is here—look what an army he brings!"

"He will save us!"

"Look, there they are!"

"He's come! The *ravot* has come!"

Tsorreh's breath caught in her throat. Around her, people cried aloud, some weeping, some dancing with joy. Others turned to their neighbors, embracing them.

Try as she might, Tsorreh could not make out anything beyond the mass of shapes and clouds of dust. The sun had not yet risen above the line of mountains, so the city and its surrounds were still bathed in diffuse gray light. It would be a clear, hot day.

The horns sounded again, closer. They echoed against the mountains, reverberating.

As Tsorreh watched, a small group of riders outran the rest. She frowned, wondering why they didn't stay together, but she knew little of battle tactics. Below, the main Gelonian encampment swirled with movement. They must have seen the oncoming attack as well.

Maharrad's forces continued to fight their way through the lower city. Watching them, Tsorreh felt a little shiver. She was witnessing a thing that would be written down and remembered: the day Meklavar threw back the Gelonian invasion. After this defeat, surely not even the power mad Ar-King would try again. Together, Maharrad and Shorrenon would put an end to the threat.

The sun crested the edge of the mountains, filling the city, the hillsides, and the Gelonian encampment. Maharrad reached the gates to the lower city. Tsorreh caught a glimpse of his stallion, white in the brilliance of the morning. Beyond, the Gelon struggled into their formations. They seemed to be very slow in coming to order, she thought, with the greater part still asleep in their tents or hiding in the earthworks. Once Maharrad broke free of the city, he would reach them. Unless ...

Heart fluttering, she bent over the wall, straining for a view of the oncoming riders. They were close enough now so she could make out the foremost. There was Shorrenon's hardy brown mare, then a few others, and behind them a large body of mounted fighters, whose slower mounts were *onagers*, not horses.

The Gelon had pulled back only to give the greater portion of their forces time to arrive.

As the two groups raced across the narrowing gap to the city, Tsorreh saw clearly the size of the pursuing army. No wonder the Gelonian encampment seemed to be almost empty. Her hands flew to her face as she stifled a scream. Around her, a few onlookers also noticed the pursuit. The sounds of jubilation fell away.

Somehow, the Gelon had discovered their plan. Perhaps they intercepted Shorrenon's messenger or merely followed him. In the night, the bulk of their army had stolen away and lain in ambush. A few riders, fleeing before them, were all that was left of Shorrenon's rescue party.

Maharrad's forces burst free of the city and swept across the earthworks, heading for the Gelonian camp. The white horse shone like polished marble, racing to the forefront. A length behind him, Zevaron spurred on the rangy gray. Shorrenon and the few riders with him reached the battle-ground between the city and the Gelonian encampment.

Horns blew again, clearer now. *Danger! Danger!*

In a heartbeat, a storm of men and beasts and dust rolled over the ground. The sound of the battle reached Tsorreh, a single inarticulate roar. For a wild moment, she thought of taking the sling throwers and few archers from the *meklat* and placing them along the outer walls. Folly, it would be rank folly, for there were still Gelon in the market city. Yet she had to do *something*.

Maharrad's words came back to her, *"You will need all your courage in the days to come. Our people will look to you. You must keep their hope alive, protect and preserve them, until the day they regain their freedom."*

Had he known, even then, how hopeless their position would be, how slim their chances?

The battle seemed to go on for an eternity of dust and screams and frenzied surges of movement. Cheeks wet with tears, Tsorreh turned away from the slaughter below. She sagged against the wall. There was nothing to do but wait for the end.

What was she thinking? If she, of the lineage of Khored, surrendered to despair, what was left for Meklavar?

Pulling herself tall, she turned to the Sand Lands girl. "Take as many of the others as you can and get them up to the temple! Quickly now, while we still have time!"

The girl gave her an uncomprehending look. Tsorreh grasped the girl's arm and spun her around. The girl caught her balance and hurried to obey.

"You, too, Otenneh," Tsorreh said. "You must go with them. I cannot protect you down here!"

"And you, *te-ravah*? What will *you* do?" the old woman replied in an equally determined voice. "You cannot present yourself as *te-ravah* without at least one attendant!"

Tsorreh knew when further argument was futile. She would need her strength for meeting the Gelon, all her wits for the negotiations to come. After today's battle, her people might have no one else to speak for them.

The end came sooner than Tsorreh expected. She had gone to the private chamber used by Shorrenon and his family, trying to calm Ediva and prevent her from some foolish action. One of the younger sling throwers, a herder boy with a twisted leg, hobbled up to the citadel. He moved with an odd combination of limping and scrambling, as if the urgency of his mission gave him an invisible crutch. Tsorreh gathered from his panting cries that the battle was almost over. A small number of Meklavaran soldiers had broken free, heading for the King's Stairs.

Ediva started for the door. "My husband! I must go down—"

Tsorreh managed to physically restrain her. "You will only impede their passage." *If they reach the gates, and if it is safe to open them. And if not . . .* "Come, we will watch together from my balcony."

Battle still raged at the *meklat* gates. The King's Stairs themselves were out of view from this angle, but Tsorreh could plainly see the sling throwers and archers along the wall, in a frenzy of spinning and hurling and shooting. Someone, perhaps an elderly guard who had stayed behind, had organized a group of men—or women perhaps, Tsorreh couldn't be sure.

Ediva made little gasping whimpers. Tsorreh put one arm around her, although she scarcely felt any braver. A wind had sprung up, blurring the sounds below. Her heart pounded in her ears. Her mouth went dry, and a dizzy sickness swept through her. *Save them . . . Save them . . .*

The wind blew away her prayers as well, but still they streamed from her mind like a fountain of tears.

Ediva cried out and pointed. Tsorreh, momentarily blinded by her own feelings, had missed the men slipping the bars of the gates free, the slender opening. Meklavaran fighters retreated through the gap—one, two, a handful, a few more. Below, in the market city, Gelonian soldiers followed them.

Together, Tsorreh and Ediva rushed down to the courtyard. Each of their footsteps pounded through Tsorreh's mind like another syllable of entreaty: *Please . . . Please . . .*

Within a few moments, the gates were once more barred. There wasn't much of a crowd this time. Most of the men had gone with Maharrad; the women and children were in hiding or watching from house or wall. Tsorreh spotted Shorrenon by his height, and one of the younger officers.

Zevaron.

Her knees went weak. She stumbled, so overcome with

relief and gratitude that she could barely stand. Ediva pushed past her and threw her arms around her husband. The impact, soft and slight as it must have been, almost knocked him off his feet. He twisted, struggling for balance, and Tsorreh saw the blood dripping from beneath his breastplate. His left arm dangled at an odd angle. Zevaron appeared at his side, calling for aid.

"Where is my father?" Shorrenon shouted, pulling free with the swift hot energy of battle. "Where is the *te-ravot*?"

Zevaron looked as if he had been pierced through the belly with a sword. "He—he fell—"

"I must find him—"

"You *will not!*" Tsorreh stepped forward. "The moment you step outside these walls, you will be taken or killed. We cannot risk both of you! You—" she pointed to the nearest men, "and you—escort the *ravot* into the citadel. Where are the physicians?"

For a moment, Shorrenon glared at her as if he would strike her down. Then the madness behind his eyes receded. He sagged against Zevaron. Ediva clung to him, her fine silk gown smeared with his blood.

A crash and a roar came from the gates. The defenders on the wall let loose a barrage of stones and arrows.

"Come away, my stepson," Tsorreh said, more gently. "For the moment, the *meklat* is safe. Let us tend your wounds and determine what is to be done next." To his rush of wild-eyed denial, she added, dropping her voice so that only he could hear, "If Maharrad still lives, they will bargain for his life. If not," her breath caught in her throat, "there is nothing we can do for him."

Shorrenon allowed himself to be taken within, to the quarters he shared with his wife and children. Zevaron supported him, silent and grim-faced, ashen beneath the dust and sweat. Ediva had lapsed from near hysteria into mute shock.

The physician arrived with needles and boiled silk thread. As she had done earlier with her husband, Tsorreh washed Shorrenon's wounds herself. Several were deep enough to require stitching. Ediva, looking pale and tense, excused herself to see to the children.

During the suturing, Shorrenon sat with a stony face, and only the catch in his breathing marked the passage of the needle through his flesh. When it was done and the physician had departed, Ediva returned. Her eyes were red and swollen, but she held herself calmly. She drew up a stool beside her husband's chair and took the hand of his injured arm in hers, stroking it gently. Tsorreh found herself unexpectedly moved by the younger woman's tenderness. Like her own marriage, Ediva's had been arranged for political purposes, but Tsorreh had no doubt of their mutual devotion.

Shorrenon gestured for Zevaron to draw near. Zevaron was shaking so badly, Tsorreh feared he could not stand.

"Now," Shorrenon said, "tell me of our father."

"We left the *meklat* at the appointed time and rode down the King's Stairs into the lower city," Zevaron began. "The Gelon had left only a small guard there, easily overcome. They fell away before us. We thought they were cowards at heart, without the will to fight. It seemed that victory would soon be ours. When we reached the outer gates, I was riding just behind Father. The earthworks looked abandoned, and we saw few enemy at their encampment. We expected to join up with your forces, my brother. But instead—what happened? Were you ambushed?"

Between the two of them, the rest of the story tumbled out, how the Gelon had lain in ambush for Shorrenon and his allies.

"They must have spotted the messenger and followed him in secret," Shorrenon said. Only by luck and skill of arms had Shorrenon survived, but with only a handful of supporters.

Attacked from forefront and flank, the city forces were quickly cut down. Maharrad himself was wounded, despite the desperate defense of his guard. Zevaron had been unhorsed and then faced the physical strength of larger, grown men, seasoned Gelonian warriors. He managed to bring together a small group of Meklavarans and, spying Shorrenon in the fray, made his way to his brother. Together they forced their way through the lower city. Most of the remnants of Maharrad's guard were killed either when he fell or in covering the retreat of the two princes.

"And here we sit," Shorrenon said after a painfully long silence, "waiting for their next move. Another demand for surrender, I would think, and under considerably worse terms than the first one."

"What will they do?" Ediva whimpered. "We have no choice now—do we?—but to accept their terms?"

Shorrenon paused, and Tsorreh sensed his thought, *There is always a choice.*

"There will be time for negotiations and decisions later, my dear," Shorrenon told his tearful, quivering wife, "once the fate of my father is known."

He turned to Tsorreh and took out the Isarran token from a fold in his belt. "I return this to you, stepmother. May its next bearer have greater success than I."

Tsorreh accepted the token. "You must rest and regain your strength. You are now our leader, *te-ravot* in deed if not in name. Your thoughts must be clear and your vision sure."

"For me, there can be no rest, not until—"

He broke off at a frenzied tapping at the door. One of the surviving soldiers stood there. "The Gelon—they came under a cover of shields. We could not hold them off, not by pebbles or arrows. They splashed the wood with black oil, some hellish mixture of theirs, and now they've set it ablaze. *Ravot,* the gates are burning!"

Chapter Five

CLOUDS of thick brown smoke billowed up from the gates. The ancient wood burned in a dozen different places. Some force, like an evil spell, fueled the blaze. A few of the city's defenders rushed to the top of the walls with buckets of water, but the smoke held them off. They fell back, coughing and clutching their throats. One of the boys from Zevaron's sling brigade toppled to the ground and lay there, unmoving.

The roar of the fire rushed over Tsorreh. She reeled under the heat and stench, greasy smoke and something more, some taint she had no name for. The next moment, a group of Zevaron's boys attempted once more to get close enough to throw water on the flames. Gelonian archers shot at any who showed themselves. One of the city men brought up his own bow and fired back at them. The next volley killed him, and Shorrenon commanded that no one else was to risk his life.

"As for the gates," he snapped, "let them burn."

The fire blazed through midday and into the afternoon, and still the Gelon did not move from their positions in the lower city. As the sun dipped toward the western peaks and the evening winds freshened, the air began to clear. The top and center of the gates were gone, but the sides continued to smolder.

Watching from her balcony, Tsorreh thought how the glowing embers resembled the eyes of mysterious beasts. The dusk felt curiously still, the struggles of the day utterly spent.

She sent a message to Shorrenon, asking for a private meeting. When he arrived a short time later, looking near the end of his strength, she insisted he sit down and eat a little from the plate of flatbread and dates Otenneh had left.

"Before the upper city falls," she said, "we must find a way of hiding Ediva and the children, a place the Gelon will not find them."

By his expression, he understood how difficult that would be. Even if he convinced Ediva, where would they go? Certainly nowhere in the palace or the citadel, and the temple would be thronged, all likely places for the Gelon to search. They could not reach the lower city and lose themselves in the poorer neighborhoods there.

Tsorreh's work in housing refugee families in the *meklat* had given her considerable knowledge of such households. She put forth her plan, which was for Ediva to disguise herself as a servant in one noble house while the children were fostered at another. A wet nurse could be found for the infant, and both would be treated kindly. When Shorrenon looked appalled, she pointed out that the Gelon would be looking for a noblewoman with two small children.

What if it were Zevaron? Would I find the strength to send him away if it meant saving his life?

"I know the separation will be painful," she said as gently as she could, "but surely it is better to survive separately than to be discovered?"

Shorrenon's resistance faded visibly as he considered this. At the same time, Tsorreh saw a hardening of his resolve, as if preserving his family had freed him to risk only his own life. He nodded when Tsorreh named the families she most trusted to keep the identities secret, and bade her leave the matter in his hands. From the tone of his voice, he would speedily overcome his wife's objections.

After Shorrenon left, Otenneh unbraided Tsorreh's hair and combed it, stroke after rhythmic stroke until Tsorreh sobbed, "Enough!" Then she saw the old woman's tear-streaked face and realized that the brushing had been as much for mutual comfort as for adornment.

"I'm sorry," Tsorreh said. "I had no cause to speak to you in such a manner."

Wordless, Otenneh held out her arms and the two women rocked each other.

The next morning, the Gelon approached the ruined gates. Tsorreh watched from her balcony, where she had waited since the first light, as a party of armed men made their way through the lower city. Behind her, Otenneh hummed tune-lessly as she tidied the room.

Morning light glinted off Gelonian spears and armor. Tsorreh guessed their strength at fifty, marching in formation with crisp precision. In their midst, onagers pulled a chariot and a wagon. At their head flew the green banner of truce. They halted at the bottom of the King's Stairs, and the soldier carrying the banner continued upward. From her angle of vision, Tsorreh could not see him pass through the gate, nor his reception when he got there. A short time later, however, she heard noises from the corridor outside, the slap of sandals and clatter of boots, then a knock. Otenneh hurried to the door.

Tsorreh had recognized the pattern of steps as belonging to the household steward, whose family had served the royal line for three generations, and to one of the few soldiers who had remained within, an older man with a severe limp who nonetheless held himself proudly. She went to them, extending both hands.

"My friends, what news?"

The steward's eyes glinted. He took her hands, shuddering as he gathered himself for speech. There was nothing she could do to make it easier for him. "The Gelon have sent back the body of the *te-ravot*."

"Yes, I saw." How steady her voice sounded, how removed from grief.

"Please, *te-ravah. Ravot* Shorrenon requests your presence when he receives the Gelon."

Tsorreh tried to take a deep breath but her lungs closed up. The muscles of her belly turned hard as rock around a core of trembling. Some emotion, hot and still, rose up behind her throat.

There was no time for a proper bath and she felt no need for purification before the Gelon, yet she dressed with care. Instead of a long robe, with skirts to tangle her legs, she chose a traditional vest and trousers of desert-pale cotton. Otenneh brought out a pair of thin brocade slippers, but Tsorreh set them aside, choosing her stoutest boots instead. She did not know what lay ahead, but she did not want to be crippled by elegant, useless shoes. The Gelon knew nothing of what a proper Meklavaran lady wore on her feet, so they would never realize they had been insulted. In recompense, she allowed Otenneh to touch her eyes with kohl and her cheeks with cinna.

When she was done, Otenneh sighed and said, "My lady, you are as radiant as the dawn."

"Do not say such things. What is the value of beauty on such a day?" Tsorreh shot back before she realized that comeliness could be both shield and sword.

Horns sounded below, the clear brassy call of the Gelon. The courtyard was already half-full, mostly with women, the elderly, and a few of the remaining household staff.

The Gelonian party ascended the stairs and passed the gates. They went armed, except for the drummers pounding out a doleful, insistent rhythm. In the center of the column came a litter, six men on either side supporting the long handles. They moved with solemn deliberation. The crowd drew aside as rank after rank of Gelonian soldiers filled the yard.

"Let's go," Tsorreh said beneath her breath. "Otenneh, you must go to the temple—"

"Don't ask me to leave you! Not now, when who knows what will happen and you may need me."

After a moment, Tsorreh relented. She could command

Otenneh but had not the heart to insist the old woman leave her side.

The steward and the old soldier, who had been waiting patiently outside the door, bowed deeply to Tsorreh. With Otenneh in attendance, they proceeded to the audience chamber.

Shorrenon sat on the throne that had been his father's, his sword bare across his knees. He greeted Tsorreh with a flicker of his eyes. Tsorreh had never seen him look so stern, the hardness of his jaw and taut brows masking his pain. Zevaron stood to the side, eyes glassy. Rethoren, the priest who was a healer as well as her grandfather's chosen successor, was also there, looking grim. He was a man of middle years and Tsorreh had always thought of him as a somewhat stern but kindly uncle. He inclined his head as she entered.

Tsorreh took her place on her usual, smaller chair. She'd sat in it so many times that it knew her weight and shape. The chamber before her was familiar, too, though the faces of the courtiers were strained. With an odd, atavistic shiver, she remembered the council of Maharrad, when they had determined the defense of the city. Viridon san-Cassarod and some of the other nobles were here now, but not Eavonen or the representative of the city masons. Only a few Meklavaran soldiers had returned with Shorrenon and Zevaron, and the most senior of these took the place of the slain general, Isarod. Otenneh stood along the wall near the front, beside some of the household staff.

A roll of drums boomed through the room, the doors burst open, and the Gelonian party entered. They filled the chamber, pressing the courtiers back. The litter-bearers set their burden down on the floor. A white cloth covered the body. Several of the courtiers gasped.

They mean to do him honor, Tsorreh thought. *They must not be aware that we do not shroud our dead in white.*

One of the Gelonian officers stepped forward. He was clearly a person of importance from the brilliance of his armor, his breastplate and shoulder guards inlaid with gold, and the crest of his helmet dyed brilliant purple and blue.

Six others, so alike they might have been cut from the same mold save for the plainness of their helmets, marched a pace behind. One carried the truce banner on a pole. They halted before the throne, and the nearest removed his helmet and swept the room with a glare.

At first, Tsorreh was taken aback by the Gelonian leader's shaven cheeks and close-cropped red hair. As best she could judge, he wasn't much older than Shorrenon. By his bearing, he was accustomed to command.

"I am Ar-Thessar-Gelon, come here in the name of my father, the most puissant and glorious Ar-Cinath-Gelon, may-his-reign-endure-forever, and charged with the subjugation of rebel lands," he barked out in his own language.

Every educated Meklavaran spoke at least one other modern language. Tsorreh spoke Isarran fluently, as well as simple Gelone and Sand Lands dialect, but only a little Denariyan. Scholars like Eavonen could read and write all these languages, as well as trade-dialect Azkhantian.

"The city now lies beneath my feet," Thessar said.

"*Te-ravot*, shall I translate?" Rethoren said in his mild, soft voice. He, like Tsorreh, knew perfectly well that Shorrenon understood Gelone, but there might be a small advantage if the Gelonian commander did not know that.

Without rising, Shorrenon said, and Rethoren translated, "I am Shorrenon, first son and heir to *te-ravot* Maharrad, King of Meklavar. I speak for my people."

"It is my father's will that Meklavar join the glorious empire of Gelon," Thessar continued, "and in token of this victory, I now return to you the body of your chief. After we have concluded your surrender, I will allow your people to bury or burn him, whatever is your custom. All that remains is for you to deliver your person into our custody."

Shorrenon tightened his grip on the hilt of his sword. The air crackled with tension. Something terrible was coming.

Now Thessar was speaking again, laying out the terms of surrender. He paused every few phrases for Rethoren to translate. Now and then, the priest made a simple mistake, a deliberate mistake, but the Gelon did not correct him.

So, Tsorreh thought, Prince Thessar does not understand Meklavaran.

Thessar's words rolled on, phrases that told her Shorrenon had not been far wrong in his fears. In Thessar's voice she heard that there would be no negotiation.

Thessar assured Shorrenon that the city would not be burned or torn down. Ar-Cinath-Gelon had given his personal guarantee of safety and order.

Did that mean no looting, no rampage? Could Thessar promise such a thing? Were the Gelonian soldiers so disciplined?

Thessar mentioned the royal family of Meklavar and heads of the noble clans . . .

Ah! They knew that much of Meklavaran history, then!

. . . who were to become hostages against the disobedience of their people, who could be sent to Gelon, either to Aidon, the capital, or to the port city Verenzza, as the Ar-King wished.

Was exile so bad a fate? Tsorreh's hand started toward her breast, where the *te-Ketav* had briefly rested. She remembered her grandfather's words, *"some things must not fall into their hands,"* and wondered again if he meant more than the ancient holy book. A shiver brushed her spine. No occupation could proceed entirely without brutality, especially when the city's inhabitants had fought back so hard.

As clearly as if he had spoken the words aloud, she knew Shorrenon's thought: *Resistance would give the Gelonian king the excuse he needs to end any possibility of an uprising or the return of an exiled ravot.*

The air took on a strange quality, thick and dangerous. Everything seemed to be moving slowly.

Two Gelonian soldiers drew back the white cloth that covered the litter. They had stripped off Maharrad's armor but not the undershirt and trousers, stiff and dark with blood. His hair lay wild and loose around his head. And his face—

Viridon cried out, as did the few women of the household. Tsorreh felt sick, yet drawn by an irresistible impulse to look. His body appeared to have been hacked and slashed, but his untouched face was the most terrible sight of all. His eyes, white as marbles, stared blindly from their sockets, his mouth drawn into a grimace so distorted that he looked barely human. With a smothered cry, Tsorreh looked away.

They left him thus—unwashed, unprepared—in order to shock us, to cripple our courage.

Shorrenon rose, his face a mask, and threw his sword down. It skittered across the stone floor, coming to rest halfway between the throne and Prince Thessar's feet. To reach it, Thessar would have to cross that distance and then bend down. Either that, or he must have it brought to him by one of his own men. He would never receive it from Shorrenon's own hand.

Thessar glared at Shorrenon. Arrogance burned in that glare like a flame, the tainted flame that had consumed the gates. Here was a man accustomed to power, to obedience, to mastery. He would make Shorrenon pay for even the smallest defiance.

To Tsorreh's surprise, the Gelonian prince chuckled aloud, as if appreciating a joke. "You there, boy." He pointed to Zevaron. "Bring me the sword."

Tsorreh searched for a way to prevent Zevaron from obeying, lest Thessar then turn the blade on Zevaron to demonstrate the consequences of insolence. They were all a breath away from whatever fate the Gelon decided to impose upon them.

Heart pounding, hardly daring to breathe, Tsorreh watched Zevaron leave his position behind the throne and kneel to pick up the sword. He offered it to Thessar without any hint of subservience, holding himself with such poise and pride, he seemed to be saying that doing so was a privilege, a way of offering service not to Thessar but to Shorrenon, his lord and brother, now his *te-ravot*. Every Meklavaran in the room knew it.

What a leader he would be, with such an instinct.

"Your men as well, order them to lay down their weap-

ons," Thessar said, through Rethoren's translation. It was
done in an instant, and the Gelonian soldiers began moving
about the room, gathering up swords and daggers.

Shorrenon rose, and Tsorreh felt him gather himself,
sparing nothing, every bit of will and strength that remained
to him.

He's going to do something.

And then: *This is the time Tenereth said would come. I
must get Zevaron to come to me, but without arousing suspicions.*

Tsorreh shot to her feet, then swayed dramatically, drawing the back of her hand across her forehead as if she were
on the verge of fainting. Zevaron moved swiftly to her side,
steadying her. She grasped his arm, pulling him close. With
the Gelonian prince and his officers watching, she dared not
say anything, but she saw their smiles: *the weak woman, the
boy who rushes to her aid—they will present no problem.*

Moving with stiff dignity, Shorrenon stepped down from
the dais. Tsorreh could not see his face, but there was no
mistaking the expression on Thessar's. He recognized
Shorrenon as a worthy adversary, noble in defeat.

The Gelonian prince made no move as Shorrenon approached. They came near enough to touch. Thessar was
slightly taller and more slender. His gray eyes flickered as
Shorrenon sank to one knee.

"You have taken my city," Shorrenon said in a voice that
rang through the chamber. "I have surrendered my sword.
There remains only one more thing to give you . . ."

Tsorreh's mouth went dry. She felt Zevaron flinch under
her grip and realized she had dug her fingernails into his
arm.

With a bellow, Shorrenon lunged forward. A dagger, long
and gleaming, slipped from his sleeve into his hand. He
struck upward, aiming for the gap under Thessar's breastplate.

With a yelp of surprise, the Gelonian prince twisted
away. His bodyguards hurled themselves at Shorrenon. The
center of the room erupted in a frenzy. A woman wailed,

high and shrill above the uproar. *Otenneh*, Tsorreh thought, *forgive me*. Still holding on to Zevaron, she sprinted for the door.

"Mother, what—" Zevaron stumbled after her. Desperate, she pulled on his arm. They had only an instant in which to escape.

The door stood open. Rethoren waited just outside, holding it ajar.

"Hurry, *te-ravah*! This way!"

Tsorreh darted through the opening, Zevaron now running hard at her heels. Rethoren pushed the door closed and slid a bolt across it.

The next moment, the three of them were racing toward the interior of the citadel. Walls sped by, corridors branching. Tsorreh ran faster than she had ever imagined possible. Her feet skimmed the rising stone floor as they started on the long tunnel leading to the temple. She blessed the impulse that had led her to choose clothing she could run in and boots instead of slippers.

The impact of her feet on stone rattled her joints. Her head throbbed with the thumping of her heart. She stumbled on an irregularity in the stone floor, hands outstretched as she fought for balance. Zevaron grabbed a hand and pulled her forward. They ran on, hand in hand. She leaned into his strength even as her muscles burned and she gasped for air.

Ahead lay the steepest part of the climb. She had passed this way many times with a basket of books on her back. Always before, she had been forced to slow her pace. Now she could hardly breathe, and her legs were rapidly turning into clay. A sudden cramp flared in her side. At any moment, she would reach the end of her endurance. Zevaron was pulling her along, almost carrying her, wasting his own strength.

It was no use. She could not force herself into that rising darkness.

Leave me here, she thought. *Go on*. But she had not the breath even for those few words.

Rethoren lifted one arm, signaling a halt. Without the impetus of flight, Tsorreh almost collapsed. Zevaron released his hold on her and braced himself against the rough-hewn stone wall. She bent over, pressing one hand to her side. Their hoarse panting filled the corridor.

Although her body shuddered with the force of her heartbeat, Tsorreh summoned the strength to gasp, "Leave me—I cannot run any farther!"

"I swore to Shorrenon I would protect you," Zevaron protested.

Don't ask me to break that promise, he seemed to be saying. *It's what my brother gave his life for, so that we would have a chance to escape. It's all I have left.*

"We've come far enough for the moment," Rethoren said between breaths. "Even after the Gelon get past the door," he paused, took a breath, "it will take them some time," he paused again, "to realize where—" and again, "where we've gone."

"Where exactly are we headed?" Zevaron asked, breathing more easily. "If we hide in the temple, the Gelon will eventually find us. They will not rest until they do."

Beads of sweat streamed down Tsorreh's skin. "Tenereth—my grandfather—he will get you out. Go on—"

Rethoren gave her a sharp look. "There is no need for anyone to be left behind. We can go more slowly now." He reached for a torch sitting unlit in its wall sconce. "We'll need some light."

It took the priest a few moments to get the torch properly lit with the flint from his belt pouch. His hands shook.

Zevaron took the lit torch, holding it steady. "It's better to keep moving, so your muscles don't stiffen."

With an effort, Tsorreh straightened up. The cramp in her side had eased, and although it seemed the drums of Gelon still throbbed in her ears, she found she could take one small step and then another. Her body radiated heat into the chill of the mountain passage.

They climbed, saving their breath and staying within the cone of torchlight.

Shorrenon is dead, and perhaps the Gelonian prince as well. What will happen next? Will their soldiers go mad and slaughter everyone within the citadel? At least Ediva and her children are hidden, as safe as anyone can be in the city. But Otenneh . . . surely they would not harm an old woman. She could not allow herself to think that. She must concentrate only on the next step, the next breath, the wavering light ahead.

Tenereth will get us out through the tunnel passages. Zevaron and I will go with him, and the te-Ketav, *the treasure of our people. Zevaron will survive, the heir of Khored and son of Maharrad.*

Somehow, no matter what the cost, she must find the strength to keep her son alive, to get him to freedom, to seek out allies—her Isarran kin, the Sand Lands tribes, the lords of Denariya, even the savage Azkhantian riders. She didn't care, just so he returned one day to free Meklavar.

Chapter Six

ZEVARON had been right about the need to keep moving. At first, Tsorreh's muscles felt as if they were on fire, step after agonizing step, but the pain eased as she went on. Her pulse no longer rampaged through her ears. Her breathing slowed to a deeper, regular rhythm. She could think and even talk a little.

She decided that her grandfather must have taken Rethoren into his confidence and sent the younger priest to the throne room to make sure she and Zevaron got away safely. They were in good hands and they had made their escape. Rethoren was right, it would be some time before the Gelon came looking for them, and it did not matter that Thessar's men would eventually search the temple. They had enough of a head start to be well away by then.

Zevaron, who had been in the lead, dropped back to Tsorreh's side. The orange light of the torch burnished his skin to bronze. His brows drew together, shadowing his eyes.

"Did you—" He stumbled over the words. "Mother, did you know what Shorrenon meant to do?"

"No, I didn't." She turned the thought over in her mind. "Even if I had, I would not have been able to stop him." It had been quite enough to convince him to separate Ediva and the children, but knowing they were hidden must have increased his resolve.

Had Shorrenon in turn known of her own plans? Had he created a diversion in order to allow them to escape, or had his attack on Thessar been the last, desperate act of a doomed man? She was certain he meant to kill the Gelonian prince, not just buy his own speedy death. What did he expect would happen then? By temperament, Shorrenon thought of glory and desperate causes, not of consequences.

She inhaled, shuddering inwardly. Even with Thessar dead, the Gelon still held the city. The Ar-King would send someone else to exact revenge.

Whether Thessar is alive or dead, it will go hard with Meklavar. And you, my Zevaron, will have to deal with the aftermath. She could not bring herself to say it aloud. There would be time enough, once they were safe, once he had grown to his role as the exiled *te-ravot.* She could not expect him to understand all at once.

Rethoren took the torch and led them single-file. The passageway narrowed and twisted, rising to a stair that Tsorreh had not noticed before. They must have taken a turn away from the usual route to the temple. During their first wild race, she had followed Rethoren blindly, not paying careful attention to their surroundings.

"This is one of the lesser routes," Rethoren said, as if sensing her thought, "one we priests use when we wish to come and go, unremarked. Many people now take refuge in the temple, and were you to enter through the front gates, you would surely be noticed."

"By people who do not have the strength to withstand interrogation by the Gelon," Zevaron added.

"If no one has seen us, there is nothing to tell," Tsorreh said.

"They will press them all the harder, hoping some elder or child will break." Emotion shivered through Zevaron's words.

"Save your anger for those who deserve it," Rethoren said.

Tsorreh lowered her gaze, holding her peace. There was no way to know what might happen. She felt a rush of understanding for Shorrenon and his choice.

As gently as she could, she said to Zevaron, "Do not take responsibility for whatever the Gelon choose to do. You cannot bargain for mercy from men who have none. Remember this always: As long as you are free, there is hope for Meklavar."

She felt him shudder under the weight of her words. It was too much to lay on him, too soon. *No*, she reminded herself, *he is a man. I must not—cannot—protect him from who and what he is.*

The stairs went sharply upward, spiraling to a hollow chimney. Light sifted from above, directed by mirrors from the temple. They climbed. Tsorreh's muscles started to burn again. She slowed her pace, taking deep breaths and holding on to the rough stone wall. They stepped onto a little platform, bounded by a heavy wooden railing that faced a door. Tunnels led away in two directions.

Rethoren lifted the latch and gestured for silence. The door led to a short passageway, stone on one side and wood on the other. At the end lay a second door and beyond it, the reverse side of a tapestry, reinforced with canvas. Rethoren pushed the edge of the tapestry aside and slipped past. Following, Tsorreh found herself in her grandfather's private meditation chamber.

How many secret entrances does he have?

The candles on either side of the prayer stand had burned down to nubs. The air was so still and the silence so thick that for an instant, Tsorreh thought the chamber was empty. As her eyes adjusted to the light, she realized that her grandfather was sitting on the bench, his hands composed on his lap, his eyes closed, his features reflecting an almost unearthly serenity. He might have been an exquisitely rendered carving. She wondered if her father, his son, would have looked like this one day, if he had lived.

For an instant, the faintest haze, a misty golden aura, glimmered around his body. Tsorreh blinked, and then it disappeared. The candle flames must have flared up with the disturbance of the air at their entrance, nothing more.

The old man moved, a shift of weight, a breath lifting his chest. He opened his eyes and raised his hands in greeting. "Children, you are welcome."

Rethoren set the torch in a holder just inside the door and left.

Tsorreh went to her grandfather and knelt, taking his hands. "Shorrenon . . ."

"Has made some grand gesture, rather than give himself into the hands of the Gelon." Tenereth's fingers tightened around hers. His skin felt chill. "Do not grieve for him, granddaughter. Think of him instead as fortunate. He has ended his life in the manner of his own choosing. How many of us can hope for as much?"

There would be time enough to honor Shorrenon's memory. "Are you ready?" she asked.

"As you see." Rising, Tenereth pointed to the corner alcove where packs and water skins lay beside the wicker basket.

Zevaron went to the packs and knelt to examine their contents. He straightened up, holding three long, hooded robes. Tsorreh recognized them as Sand Lands make, light on one side, dark on the other. By some trick of weaving, they protected the wearer against both heat and cold. The tribes did not readily part with them. How Tenereth was able to come by one, let alone three, she could not imagine.

"We will be off," Tenereth said, "as soon as Rethoren returns with our guide. It is a long . . . a long journey . . . to Isarre."

The next instant, the old priest's legs folded beneath him. He staggered, half-falling, and sent the bench crashing on its side. He clutched his shoulder. His breath came in labored rasps.

Tsorreh rushed to him and slipped his arm over her shoulders. "Zevaron, help me! He must lie down—let's get him to his bedchamber."

"There is no time!" Tenereth protested weakly. "I have rested too much already."

"You will be no good to anyone like this!"

With Zevaron's help, Tsorreh maneuvered her grandfather past the doorway and down a corridor a few steps long. The chamber beyond was sparsely furnished, a place for sleep and little else, simple rather than austere.

She lowered her grandfather to the bed. By the light of Zevaron's torch, Tenereth's skin shone like gray marble.

"Are you in pain?" Tsorreh asked, but there was no answer.

A few moments later, Rethoren came back. A young woman followed close behind. Tsorreh had seen her before, although she could not remember where.

Rethoren bent to examine the old priest. He touched the pulses at neck and wrist, and over the heart. Tsorreh, watching, caught a glimpse of dark brilliance, a scintillation more sensed than seen, passing over Tenereth's limp form. As quickly, it disappeared. Rethoren seemed not to have noticed anything unusual.

"What is wrong with him?" she asked Rethoren. "Can you tell?"

"He has had a seizure of the heart."

"What is to be done for it?"

"You can do no more for him," the physician replied. "I will bring medicines and tend him as best I can."

"Will he recover?"

"Only the Most Holy can say for certain. Tenereth has enjoyed surprising health for a man of his years."

Of his years. Tsorreh shivered. Her grandfather had been old when she was born. He had already outlived his children.

"You had best be gone," Rethoren said. "He will not be able to travel for some time now, if ever."

Tsorreh nodded, hearing the truth.

Then she was alone with her grandfather. Rethoren had vanished and the girl had taken Zevaron back to the meditation chamber. Tsorreh blinked back tears. They had given her a chance to say a private farewell.

"Come here, my child." Tenereth's voice brushed her like a shiver. "My heir."

He was going to give her some family treasure. She didn't want it. She only wanted to run away with him, with Zevaron, and for them all to be safe. She thought of staying with him in the temple, of nursing him back to health. Surely, a small delay would not prove fatal. But she knew, in the hard knot of her belly, that she dared not. For Zevaron's sake, she must leave while she still could.

Tsorreh searched for words of farewell, but none came. She knelt by the side of the bed and took his hand again. His fingers, the skin dry, the knuckles enlarged and bony, grasped hers.

"I wish . . . there had been time enough," he said. Then, as if a new strength surged up in him, he continued. "I should have instructed you, prepared you. I had hoped to pass it directly to Zevaron. But he is still too young."

"Hush," she said. "Do not trouble yourself. Whatever it is, I will keep it for him."

The power of his grip silenced her. Tears sprang to her eyes. Seeking to comfort him, she bent closer, her face close to his. She saw, through her own blurring vision, the look of pleading in his eyes. He released her abruptly, his hand falling away. His body tensed, his breathing turned sharp and quick, and he clawed at his chest with both hands.

"Grandfather, save your strength—"

Tenereth muttered under his breath as he pulled loose the neck fastening of his robe. Tsorreh could not make out the words, only the rhythm. It sounded like a chant, a prayer in the most ancient of the holy languages. She caught the name *Khored* and something about the Oath of Binding and the *te-alvar*. She dared not leave him in this state. He was raving. Rethoren would return at any moment, and he would know how to calm the old man.

Between Tenereth's hands, a mote of golden light flared. He cradled a sphere of brilliance. It was too bright to look at directly, like the sun at midday, yet Tsorreh felt no heat.

His voice gained strength, and the light seemed to pulse and grow in intensity with each spoken phrase.

Something slammed into her breastbone, smooth and hard, yet small enough to fit in the palm of her hand. She struggled against the sudden pain. The cartilage of her ribs flexed under the pressure. Her heart drummed wildly, like a bird flailing its wings against the bars of a cage.

Light exploded behind her eyes. It swept through her body. For a wild moment, she remembered stories of men who had almost drowned or been caught in winter avalanches. They had seen branching tunnels of light — was she dying, too? The words reverberated through her bones.

> By grace, all things are made,
> By judgment, all things are unmade.

White heat exploded outward from the point of agony in her chest. It shocked through her, blanketing out all other sensation. Then the pain slowly faded, giving way to unearthly stillness. She was a mote of brilliance, floating above a sea of light. Around her, radiant currents unfurled in elegant patterns. She sensed them, merged with them.

Now she was blue, a shimmering sky, an ocean steadfast and enduring.

Now green, eternal renewal, peace and healing, vibrant with compassion.

Now red, ebb and pulse, blood and courage.

She knew these colors and the attributes that went with them. She had walked this interwoven path before, traced the lineage with her fingertips, memorized the pattern.

Now yellow as the sun, as the pure clear light of dawn.

Now palest rose, the scent of blossoms, the faceted reflections of life.

Now purple, rich as the depths of a cavern, the shimmer on an eagle's feathers, the strength of mountains.

The Shield! She had, in some way far beyond human senses, journeyed through the essence of each of the sacred petal gems, the *alvara.*

And now, coming to rest at last in the clear center of creation, she felt a calmness, a certainty through every part of her spirit. She stood at the heart of the Shield, in the *te-alvar* itself.

No, she *was* the central gem, the *te-alvar.* She was Khored's gem, Khored's heir.

This cannot be happening, she thought. And then thought nothing at all.

"Mother?"

From afar, she heard a voice as familiar as the beating of her own heart. Male, on the edge between a boy's treble and a man's deeper tones. She should know his name—

"Mother, it is time. We must go, and quickly!"

Zevaron!

Tsorreh scrambled to her feet. Her grandfather's hand, released from her grasp, fell limply to his chest. She folded it over the other.

Grief shivered along her bones. She heard a wailing begin at the back of her throat, but she swallowed it. If she lingered now, she would jeopardize everything he had given her: a head start and a chance for freedom, her life and her son's, the mystical gem she now guarded within her own body.

"Sorrow and joy, each comes in its season." The words of the *te-Ketav* whispered through her mind. She would mourn him later, she swore to his motionless body.

Zevaron stood in the doorway. Tsorreh went to him. She held out her hands, trying to think what she could tell him. She had no words to describe what had just happened.

Rethoren waited beside the alcove, holding a lighted torch. Zevaron strode across the room, hefted one of the packs to his back, and helped the girl into another with a blush that surprised Tsorreh.

"Tenereth, he ..." Grief clenched her throat. The priest

met her eyes, and she saw the ripple of his sorrow, quickly masked.

Rethoren thrust the torch into her hands. "Hurry," he said in a voice only slightly roughened.

Tsorreh picked up the third pack. Now she remembered where she'd seen the girl before. It was on the wall of Meklavar with a sling in her hand—the Sand Lands girl. "Shadow Fox, isn't it?"

The girl lowered her eyes. "I didn't know if you'd remember me, *te-ravah*."

"Tenereth arranged for her to guide you," Rethoren said. "The trails through the Sand Lands can be treacherous."

Tsorreh pressed her free hand over her heart, over the sudden pulse of bright and lingering pain. Blindly she turned toward the hidden passage. Rethoren caught her, held her for an instant. His lips brushed her forehead, and he said in a low, urgent voice, "Go now with all the prayers and hopes of Meklavar, that you may speedily return."

"May it be ever so," she responded from long habit.

Then, as if her legs had a mission of their own, she hurried through the opening and down the steep steps. She counted, feeling each one with her feet. Zevaron followed, and then the girl, Shadow Fox, silent as her namesake.

They hurried through the tunnel and its labyrinthine twists. The rough walls sped by in the lambent torchlight. At each branching, her grandfather's directions sprang to mind.

"This way!" Tsorreh called, and they burst into a large, dry cavern. She paused, raising her torch. Light fell on the ancient chiseled alcoves and platforms, now bearing neat stacks of chests filled with wrapped books, just as she'd left them.

"What is this place?" Zevaron asked. Awe hushed his voice. "Who lived here?"

"I do not know," she said.

"Somebody's been here recently," Zevaron said, pointing to the chests.

"*I* have," she said. "That's the library, or as much of it as I could carry."

"Mother!"

A laugh surged up behind the knot of pain in her chest. "What did you think I was doing while you were keeping watch on the walls?"

"But—why *books*—?"

"And what else? Should we leave our heritage, our holy works, for the Gelon to plunder?" Tsorreh's voice rang through the cave. The Sand Lands girl, who had been looking about with curiosity, recoiled. With an effort, Tsorreh reined in her temper. "Whether by you, yourself, or by your sons, we will be free once more, and these things will be waiting. What greater treasure is there than our heritage?"

"Swords!" he shouted.

Swords shimmering in the dawnlight like blades of silvered grass . . . horses neighing and men's voices calling out, "Khored! Khored!"

From a high place, she looked out over the army while the sky condensed into darkness. Snow-crystal clouds flowed across the horizon. Wind whipped her cheeks, tasting of ashes and ice.

Tsorreh blinked. A shiver racked her body. The torch wavered in her hand. Beneath her breastbone, she sensed a flare of light, warm and golden. Above her arched the cavern with its rough stone walls. The Sand Lands girl stood at the far entrance, her face a pale oval. She gestured to hurry.

"Come on!" Zevaron shouted

Tsorreh started toward the opening. Her foot caught on an unevenness in the floor and she almost fell. Zevaron caught her arm and steadied her.

"You're unwell—"

"No, no, I'm fine," she insisted. The vision had faded, leaving a sick, heavy feeling in her stomach, but she knew she must go on. She tried to make her voice firm, stripped of all doubt. "From here, we must follow the air current."

"Give me the torch," he said. "Shadow Fox, help my mother."

"I don't need—" Tsorreh broke off her protest, as Zevaron had already plunged into the darkness. Saving her breath, she hurried after him. He might be showing off for the girl, but he was right. Within a few paces, the passage narrowed, and her pack brushed the stone sides. In moments, the torchlight revealed a high open space above them, the upper surface so far away she could not make it out.

They went on, the velvety silence of the mountain broken only by their breathing and the scuff of leather over stone. It took all Tsorreh's concentration to keep her balance. Zevaron rushed surefootedly along the passages, and Shadow Fox stayed close behind him.

Sometimes the tunnel widened or branched. Zevaron would halt, searching for the guiding air current, but never for long. When the torch burned out, he lit another from the bundle strapped to his pack. They rested and drank from their water skins and when appropriate turned politely aside to grant one another privacy.

How long they traveled like this, Tsorreh could not tell. Once she set her foot down on a loose stone and twisted her ankle. It throbbed for a time, as did the scrapes on her bare skin, but she ignored them. As long as she was able to travel, she must go on. She saved her breath for the next step and the next.

After a time, they began to climb. Sometimes Tsorreh had to use both hands and feet. Zevaron, above her, broke loose showers of dust and pebbles, sending Tsorreh and Shadow Fox into spasms of coughing.

Before long, Tsorreh's muscles burned. Sweat trickled over her abrasions, stinging. Once her foot slipped and she almost lost her hold. The skin on her hands felt raw, broken.

At last they reached the end of the climb and the entrance to a long, low-ceilinged cavern. It was rounded like a tunnel, and spherical depressions pocked the surfaces. Zevaron started across it. Too exhausted to protest, Tsorreh followed.

"We rest," came Shadow Fox's voice from behind her. She had hardly said two words together since the beginning of their flight, replying to Zevaron's solicitude only in monosyllables. "We will find no better place, and here we are hidden. Once free of these mountains, the spies of the Rock People can follow us. We must keep ourselves strong."

With a nod, Zevaron agreed. Tsorreh lowered herself into a large, rounded depression in the surface, which was so coarse it felt as if a thousand tiny teeth jabbed through the fabric of her trousers.

They ate a little from the stores of dried meat and fruit in their packs. Zevaron set out his flint carefully before extinguishing the torch to conserve it.

The darkness was so complete, Tsorreh could not tell if her eyes were open or closed. Her body craved sleep, and yet a formless dread held her back. She kept thinking of her vision of the hilltop, as real and vivid as if it were a personal memory, of Khored and his brothers preparing for battle with armies of monsters, creatures of the primeval incarnation of chaos, rendered from the ancient tongue as *Fire and Ice*.

Something whispered through the back of her mind, a sound like a hissing serpent, and then a long exhalation. Not Fire and Ice, the common appellation, but syllables of power, of conjuring.

A name. A secret name that only Khored knew.

She saw a hilltop and heard the glint and clash of swords. A man stood with his back to her. Wind tore at his braids, dark as the cavern. His skin glowed like honey. One bare arm lifted against the gathering storm, hand clenched. Then his fingers opened, cradling something infinitely precious and powerful—clear light, brilliant as the sun. She heard his voice, but whether he shouted or whispered, she could not tell. The syllables in their ancient rhythm called forth, gathered, summoned. Words became light, and light flowed through spirit, and spirit condensed itself back into words: BY GRACE, ALL THINGS ARE MADE.

How did she know this? How could she possibly remember this?

Retching and dizzy, Tsorreh curled herself into a ball. She held on to her knees, digging her fingers into her muscles, hard against her bones. She was here, she told herself, here in her body, here in this lightless cave with Zevaron, her Zevaron, and the girl from the walls of Meklavar, and it was now, at the fall of the city.

Now, and no other time.

Here, and no other place.

Gradually her heart slowed and she felt less sick. She sat up, spat out acid saliva, and wiped her mouth on her sleeve.

"Mother?" Zevaron sounded very young. He was frightened and doing his best to hide it. Darkness revealed as much as it covered.

"I'm here," she said softly. "It's all right."

Tsorreh heard the tap of flint. Slender tongues of orange caught the spark. Air ruffled the flame of the torch. She lifted her head and felt the breeze on her face, stronger than before. Her pulse quickened and strength rose in her. At the back of her mind, she could almost hear the stirring call of horns, the chomp and neigh of horses pulling at their bits, men's voices raised in song.

Memory of battles past or hope for the future? She did not care.

"Come on," she said. "We've rested enough. The road awaits us."

Chapter Seven

THE tunnel descended so sharply that they were forced to creep along, using finger-holds for balance. Tsorreh's hands and elbows stung. Her twisted ankle and the opposite knee ached with each slow step. Twice more they ate and rested, before a dim light appeared ahead.

At last, they came out to a narrow defile to see the sun a hand's-width above the western horizon. Mountains rose behind them, sloping down to rolling hills and the barren undulation of the Sand Lands. The colors were strange to Tsorreh, as if the sun had bleached and shriveled the grass. Even the stones beneath her feet looked as if they had been sucked dry. She licked her lips and tasted salt. A wind touched her face, quickly drying the film of sweat.

How could a person hope to cross that vast expanse of rock and dune?

Shadow Fox took the lead without comment, springing nimbly along the pebbled trail. Zevaron tied the extinguished torch to his pack and followed her.

A little way into the hills, they found a grove of wild olive trees around a spring. Tsorreh almost wept as she knelt on the muddy bank and dipped her hands into the water. It flooded her senses, cool and sweet. She drank it in, letting it run over her face, wetting her hair and the front of her vest.

Her belly clenched. She doubled over, gasping, and swallowed back the acid that suddenly filled her mouth. Through the sudden hoarseness of her breathing, she heard the splash of water, the movement in the grasses as Zevaron and Shadow Fox drank. She tried to call out for help, but could not force the words from her swollen throat.

Waves of nausea rose like tidal currents, sweeping through her. A rushing like the wind through the Var, like a mountain stream in flood, filled her skull. The edges of her vision went gray. The day, which had been so hot, turned icy.

The spring ... poisoned?

Her breath locked in her lungs. She felt herself falling, first through bitter cold, then fire, then through a sea of whiteness. Voices called to her, now human words, now the moaning of winter wind, now foam-whipped rapids, now the howl of a wolf, now the clash of swords ... *Swords.*

She gazed into a pool of colorless brilliance and in it beheld men's faces, stern, bearded. Four of them, five, six ... and then a great King, his head wreathed in the same light. He spoke words of power, *Eriseth, Benerod,* and *Cassarod—*

No, they were names, and as each was said aloud, one of the noble lords turned toward her, holding a gem in front of his heart. Dovereth, Teharod, Shebu'od, and the last, the King.

Khored.

She reached out to him. *Help us. Save your people, as you did once before.*

"What is wrong with her?" came a woman's voice, light and distant.

". . . don't know . . ." A second voice reverberated, fracturing into echoes. ". . . ever since . . ."

"Grief . . ."

The man's voice spoke again, rising in urgency. "We can't leave her . . ."

"What do you propose? We cannot carry her—"

A sigh, the mountains breathing . . .

Rock, black and glossy, jutted into the sky, and the sky

was torn with ice and fire and brightness beyond naming, beyond thought ... The vision fell away now, leaving her cold as death, as stars, as the high clear peaks of the Var before the snow. Cold.

"She's burning up ..."

"... do something ..."

Cold, and deep racking shivers shot through her. Sky and mountain broke into frozen splinters.

The world dimmed, shadow layered upon shadow. She made out the outlines of hills against a fading sky. They were strangely rounded, not the sharp mountains she knew. Creatures moved through the gathering darkness, tiny sparks that winked in and out.

Voices curled around her, like currents in a stream. "Keep going." "Just a little while longer." "We rest at dawn."

Motes of light spun into endless color. They wove in and out, making a pattern she knew and could not name. Closer now, they merged around a crystal center, a center that encompassed all color, all light, and a kernel of brilliance.

A man's voice shouted, "In the name of the One, the Infinite, I banish you!"

Silence.

Numbness.

Peace floated on the fading grayness. And warmth.

"I think she's a little better now. *Te-ravah*, can you hear me?"

Brightness fluttered, a dance of yellow streaks. She inhaled smells of wood and smoke, a green moistness. Faces, pallid ovals, bent toward her, and she recognized the touch and smell and voice that spoke to the depths of her heart.

"Zevaron? Zev? Are we still in the cavern?" Her own words came in stutters, like the beating of moth wings.

"Mother." Fingertips touched her arm. Her gaze met eyes dark with concern. "We're three days into the Sand Lands. You've been ill, don't you remember?"

Remember? The proud King shouting defiance? The creak and splinter of living stone? The dance of colored suns and the clear piercing light at the heart of things?

"Here." Gently he held a cup to her lips.

She swallowed, the water warm and slightly metallic on her tongue. Around her, sand exhaled heat into the night sky. Stars spun a milky swath across the heavens. Along the silvered dune, a shadow moved, and then another.

"Three days? I remember the little spring, when we came out from the tunnel."

"You were delirious for a time." He looked away, into the night. "You spoke of strange things. Ravings, fever dreams—"

Shapes moved closer, ribbons of light and dark, some able to fit into the palm of her hand. She could not make out their form, serpents or mice or tiny men. One carried a bit of brightness, like an ember, in mouth or claws, she could not tell. She watched as it neared.

"It's all right," Shadow Fox said. "They mean us no harm." She held out her hand, took the bit of brightness. It dimmed to a pale, almost pellucid blue. "It's a water-stone. With it, we can find the hidden springs between here and Karega Oasis."

"What—" Tsorreh started to ask, *What are they?* but she already knew. Part fable, part dream-vision, they lingered just beyond sight, drawn to her and what she carried. They were tiny elemental spirits, scattered during the first days of creation. Harmless, shy, and secretive.

She remembered little more of that night, past the rising of the moon. Walking, sand gave way beneath her feet, and a bitter chill descended from the arc of night.

The cold, the sickening jar along her bones as her sword met the hard, unyielding edge of ice. A creature with skin like mottled frost bore down on her, eyes like the glowing hearts of coals, mouth a jagged gap, breath an acrid gust of smoke: "Begone, foul creature, to the hell that spawned you! I banish you—"

Words poured through her. A man's deep voice echoed in her mind, speaking the ancient holy tongue that none now used. Before her, the ice-troll hesitated. Although it was twice, thrice her size, the power of the words held it back. She looked down at her hand, holding the sword. Notches marked where the blade had bitten into the ice-troll's hide.

No, it was not her hand she saw, but another's, as if she looked through other eyes, spoke through someone else's mouth. She felt herself draw back and lower the sword, then the sudden lightness as it left her grasp. Swords were of no avail against the spawn of Fire and Ice. Within her, the *te-alvar* pulsed with clear and piercing brilliance.

Someone held water to her lips. She swallowed. It was warm and brackish.

"Tell me," she gasped. "What did I say?"

"You spoke of Khored, of the enchanted *alvara*, of a mighty battle, of the birth of the Var," Zevaron said. "Then you said a name. I could not make it out."

Fire and Ice, in the ancient tongue, yet hidden from men's minds all these long years, until the very memory was lost. No, not lost. Waiting, preserved. Passed on with the te-alvar.

Tsorreh woke again, lying on her back on a soft surface, her head cushioned and her feet bare. She opened her eyes to a world of color, a sky of striped orange and white. The faint, tangy smell of animals and some kind of incense touched her nose. A tent, she lay in a tent, without any memory of how she'd gotten there.

She sat up. Intricately knotted rugs in dull red and ocher, the designs picked out in black silk, covered the floor of the tent. A waterskin and bowl lay within easy reach beside a plate of dried dates. The water tasted metallic, but she drank it all, pouring out bowl after bowlful. Her stomach shifted uneasily, then settled. Feeling steadier, she crawled to the partly open flap, found her boots, pulled them on, and slipped outside.

She emerged into a walled garden, bounded on one side by an arched walkway and a two-story house of sand-pale stone. Date palms waved gently overhead, creating swirls of dappled shade. She inhaled moist smells, a potpourri of unfamiliar spices. Sounds washed over her, people laughing, the whicker of a horse, the high delighted cries of children, a twitter of birds, others she could not identify. Turning, she saw that her tent was, in fact, a pavilion stretched over a lathe frame. It was one of several, each a different color. Enormous birds, the size of eagles, but with iridescent blue-green plumage and extravagantly long tails, moved among them, pecking at the white gravel.

"Look! She's awake!"

Shadow Fox and Zevaron emerged from the darkness of the walkway, both wearing knee-length, bell-sleeved tunics over leggings. With them came an older man in the flowing, striped robes and head dress of a Sand Lands chieftain. He carried himself with regal poise, yet with a quietness, an absence of bluster, that intensified the power of his presence. Here was a man, Tsorreh thought, who had no need to boast of his prowess or to compel obedience by force. He inspired respect by his wisdom and experience, seeing deeply and acting with forethought and deliberation. Such a man would make a formidable ally . . . or an even more formidable foe.

Shadow Fox performed introductions, referring to the chieftain as the Father of Karega. The Father inclined his head with a stylized gesture, delivered with the grace of a master swordsman, to indicate that Tsorreh should accompany him inside.

They passed through a foyer and into an inner chamber, with windows sheltered from the day by screens of intricately carved sandalwood inlaid with gold wire, mother-of-pearl, and ebony. They sat on cushions, and a small boy with the same dark, almond-shaped eyes as the Father, brought a tray of tiny pastries dusted with nuts and date-sugar, and served them cups of steaming tea. As Tsorreh sipped hers, the mint and honey sharpened her senses.

They ate and drank in silence. Zevaron, she noticed, kept his eyes carefully averted from Shadow Fox. The girl was a hopeless dream glimpsed in passing, but love—or, in this case, adolescent lust—knew no bounds.

When they were done, the boy brought damp cloths to wipe their hands and faces. The Father began to speak, pausing frequently for Shadow Fox to translate. Tsorreh understood him well enough, but to refuse the service would be ungracious.

Tsorreh replied to his inquiries that she was quite recovered from her sand-fever, as he called it, and expressed her gratitude for Shadow Fox's help and guidance, without which they would surely have perished a thousand times over.

"The Father says that our house is honored to be of service to the Lady of Holy Light, who brings water to the desert," Shadow Fox said.

"Please tell him, then," Tsorreh said, "of our gratitude for all he has done for us. If it is not too much to ask, we have a long way yet to reach Isarre."

"That has already been arranged," Shadow Fox replied. "Two of his sons will ride with you as far as the Hills of the Burned Trees, and from there, your own people can take you to Gatacinne."

Tsorreh considered. She had thought to go the longer, southern route through Barad's Gap, but she knew little of desert ways. She would surely have perished without Shadow Fox's expert knowledge. Whatever happened, Zevaron must survive.

No, pulsed a thought, like a fading echo in the place between her breasts—*she herself must survive.*

After the conference, she walked through the town, accompanying the Father as he selected horses and ordered supplies. Later that evening, she rested again in the Pavilion of Healing Smoke. Women in enveloping robes came and fitted her with full-cut trousers and a sort of veil that draped over her face and shoulders, leaving her hands and legs free. It looked uncomfortable, but these people knew the desert as she did not.

Before they set out the next morning, swirling sands descended upon the oasis. Tents were folded up, and animals brought within walls or underground. Heavy shutters kept out the worst of the wind. Tsorreh and Zevaron huddled in a corner of the house, listening to the wild shrieking overhead. After a while, she drifted through strange half-formed dreams, part personal memory, part visions from the past.

They set off two days later, mounted on swift, fine-boned Sand Lands horses. Tsorreh was not a skilled rider; she had only enough training to stay on the horse's back. The Father had chosen for her a sweet-natured mare with a soft gait. Zevaron could hardly contain his excitement as he swung up on his little gray stallion.

"What is his name?" Zevaron asked the groom, as he stroked the glossy, arched neck.

"He is called Rain-in-the-Night."

In a land where water was as precious as gold, Tsorreh reflected, only a steed of exceptional quality would bear such a name. In answer to her question, Shadow Fox said that the Sand Lands people did not geld their male animals, as did the Rock People, but as the mare was not in heat and the stallion was well-trained, there should be no cause for concern.

After the first few hours, Tsorreh was tired and saddlesore. Her horse followed the others without any effort on her part. She held on to the saddle and tried to keep her focus between the mare's ears. If she closed her eyes, if she allowed her mind to drift even for a moment, visions would rise up: *A plain of silvery grass rippled in the moonlight. Massive tusked beasts lumbered across a landscape of broken rock and sulfur-steaming vents. Lizards the size of horses belched fuming ice. She saw men falling, clutching one another in terror, blood running like dark rivers.*

Walk and trot . . . walk and trot . . . rest. Drink. Sleep. Walk and trot . . . So went the rhythm of the journey.

She thought of her grandfather, guarding the precious *te-alvar*, Khored's own stone, for all those years, waiting for a suitable heir. Not his son, for whatever reason. Perhaps her father had died too soon, before his training was complete. And not a daughter. In Meklavar, women did not ride to war, and the Shield of Khored was the weapon of a king.

In the ordinary course of events, Zevaron would have been carefully prepared for the transfer, schooled in history and lore. But he was too young when Gelon struck, too ready to die at his brother's side. If he perished while he bore Khored's stone, it would be buried with him and lost forever.

And so, the old priest had chosen a woman at the last, one learned in tradition, resourceful enough to preserve the holy *te-Ketav* and determined to save her son, a woman committed to the liberation of Meklavar, who would stay alive and flee beyond the invaders' reach.

Instinctively, she knew that with time, she would learn to use the power of the *te-alvar*. Already, the worst of the disorientation was fading. She could summon the visions of the past at will or dismiss them from her thoughts. The stone had other qualities, too. Sometimes she felt herself at the center of the Shield. If she concentrated, she could sense one or two motes of color and energy, other, lesser *alvara*, but too distant for any clear contact. The *alvara* were not ordinary gemstones; they were instruments of power, of magic.

They are scattered, and the Shield is broken. The thought filled her with dread.

Yet, why? Why should it matter? The ages when Fire and Ice walked the land and Khored of Blessed Memory created the *alvara* were long past. There were no more magical battles, no monstrous foes. The Gelon were human.

The te-alvar *is real, so what else might be real?*

It was a relic from the fabled past, an heirloom of her people, a precious part of their heritage, but nothing more.

The sand turned rocky, and scrub and thornbush gave way to greener growth. Trees, real trees instead of palms, clustered along a stream. Tsorreh's mare put her head down, snatching mouthfuls of grass. They rode beside pastures of sheep and long-haired goats, and now and again a few cattle. At one or another of the tiny villages, the brothers paid a few coins to refill their water skins and let their horses drink at the communal well.

"Are we in Isarre yet?" Zevaron asked at one of these pauses.

Another day would see them beyond the borderland and to a good road. From there, they would travel on their own; hoping for a swift passage to the port city of Gatacinne. If all went well, they could find a ship to take them west along the coast and then to Durinthe, the capital city and jewel of Isarre.

Chapter Eight

O N the last day's journey to Gatacinne, Tsorreh and Zevaron found a ride in the back of a farmer's cart amid
the sacks of millet and lentils. Strings of dried peppers and
braids of tiny purple onions swung from the crossbeams.
The farmer sang one boisterous, tuneless song after another, happy to have a few extra coins even before he
reached market. The gray ass plodded along at its own un-
hurried pace.

Tsorreh leaned back, pushed the coarse-woven sack into
a more comfortable shape, and closed her eyes. Sleep hov-
ered just beyond reach. Her feet were sore, but she'd found
it hard to rest since they passed into Isarre. Perhaps the visions that accompanied the *te-alvar* had left a lingering
sense of apprehension, of something terrible rousing now,
waking. It was not yet aware of her, but soon, soon . . .

They would reach Gatacinne by day's end. The Gelon
would be searching for her, but they could not yet know
where to look. Her mother's family would give her what
sanctuary might be found. She touched the token braided
once again in her hair, reassuring herself that it was still
safe.

She must have drowsed, for she startled awake at the
sound of unfamiliar voices. When last she noticed, they

were passing between low pastured hills. Now they emerged onto the flat land. Sitting up, she saw a scattering of buildings, pocket gardens, and a wide, well-traveled road. By the sea tang in the air, they weren't far from the port city. Zevaron lay curled against a sack, his head moving gently as the cart rocked.

"Whoa, easy there!" The farmer slowed his beast to a halt at the side of the road.

Tsorreh crept to the edge of the cart for a better look. A handful of travelers were trudging by in the opposite direction. A few pulled handcarts, and others led laden asses or carried the packs themselves. She blinked sleepiness from her eyes. Surely, traffic should be moving *into* the city at this hour?

The farmer called out to a tall man leading an ass. Tsorreh couldn't follow the idiomatic dialect, only a phrase here and there. She caught the word *Gelon* several times.

"What's going on?" she asked in Isarran.

"Gelon, they attack from sea," the farmer said over his shoulder. He clucked to his beast, and they started off again. "Happens sometimes. They fight, but they also must eat!" He laughed.

"Mother, what is it?" Zevaron had woken. "Where are we?" he asked in Meklavaran.

"Not far, I think. The Gelon have attacked Gatacinne. Those people were leaving."

Zevaron frowned. "Should we turn back and find another way? What if the Gelon take the city and we're recognized?"

"Even if word of our escape has reached the Gelonian fleet, we hardly resemble royalty. We're just a couple of Sand Lands strays, hardly worth noticing." She forced a laugh. "These attacks happen from time to time. There have been more in recent years as the rivalry between Isarre and Gelon worsened. The farmer doesn't seem alarmed, and this is his usual market. In fact, he sounded like the fighting would increase the price he could get for his crop. We'll be as safe here as anywhere, and it's still the quickest route to Durinthe."

In all likelihood, the fighting was confined to the sea and they would never see any of it. Once they had contacted the governor, he would take them under his protection until the way was clear and passage arranged.

Tsorreh's optimistic mood persisted as they wound their way through the outskirts. The farmer guided his cart into one of the market areas. He'd been right about the war not hurting business. Here people were still going about their affairs. Sellers of fruit and vegetables spread their wares on tables under canopies, along with jars of oil, strings of dried peppers and garlic, casks of wine, and tubs of olives.

An ache rose up in Tsorreh's heart, a longing for the bustle and richness of her own city. She wondered if the Gelon had permitted the markets to re-open, and how the trade fared. Her nostrils filled with aromas strange and familiar—bread brushed with sesame oil, lamb roasted on skewers with onions and peppers, Denariyan spices.

Selecting her words with care, Tsorreh asked the farmer where she might find the Hall of Judges. She tried to sound like the simple nomad she appeared. He pointed her north, where a white tower stood high above the roofline, and urged her to stay away from the wharves. She thanked him, nodded to Zevaron to follow, and headed in that direction, threading their way along the twisting maze of streets.

With a couple of wrong turns and a little help with directions, they arrived at the Governor's Palace. It faced the tower, the seat of the city government, across a wide, white-paved square. The open space churned with movement. Squadrons of armed Isarran soldiers marched toward the harbor, as did men in the robes of judges and officials, young boys in pages' tabards, and a trio of officers on horseback. Four guards with somber expressions and drawn swords bracketed the front door.

Tsorreh freed the Arandel token from her braid, clutched it in her hand, and placed her foot on the first step. The guards came instantly alert. She approached the one with the most elaborate helmet. Zevaron followed her like a shadow.

"We have no alms for you, Sand Lady. You'd best return to your own country." The guard meant no insult. In fact, he spoke like a man with some education. In his own terms, he was undoubtedly being courteous.

"My business cannot wait," Tsorreh said in slow, clear Meklavaran. It was a calculated risk, but one aimed at attracting his attention. She saw, by his immediate reaction, that she had succeeded.

"Please take me to the governor or, if you cannot, to your superior officer."

His brows drew together minutely. "What brings a woman of Meklavar to Gatacinne?"

Tsorreh held up the token so that he could see but not touch it. "That is for the governor alone."

She read his thoughts in the tiny movements of his eyes and corners of his mouth. *A Meklavaran woman, bearing the royal token of Isarre and dressed in Sand Lands robes!* He bowed and escorted her and Zevaron inside.

After the brightness of the late afternoon, the entrance hall of the palace seemed enveloped in gloom. When her eyes adapted, she recognized the Great Tree depicted in the frescoes that lined the walls.

They walked into a courtyard open to the sky, where Tsorreh and Zevaron were presented to a white-bearded man in a loose, flowing robe, who reminded her in a subtle way of the Father of Karega Oasis. After some discussion and a second look at the token, they were led deeper into the palace and up a flight of stairs, along an arcade of graceful columns, to a set of doors carved with images of a sea creature. The creature possessed the head and torso of a man, brows drawn in a stern expression, long locks studded with shells and pearls, affixed to the lower body of a fish.

The old man, a councillor of some sort, swung the door open without preamble and gestured Tsorreh to follow. She grabbed Zevaron's hand and went in.

The room was a sweeping arch of white stone. Frescoes inlaid with mother-of-pearl and jade echoed the maritime theme of the doors. Cunningly crafted folding doors had been drawn back along one side of the room, revealing an open balcony. At the room's center, a man sat at a table of pale, glossy wood. He bent over a pile of papers, much the way Maharrad sat in his war council chamber. His face and arms were tanned, and the hair that flowed from the high forehead to just below his ears was dark red. At their entrance, he looked up, a silhouette of shadow against the brightness of the vista.

"What is this? How dare you bring sand rats into my presence when I told you I was not to be disturbed!"

"Despite her unusually effective disguise, the lady is Meklavaran and she carries the royal crest," the elderly councillor said. "If I have erred in bringing her to your attention, I most humbly beg your indulgence."

The governor, frowning, walked around the table toward her. He was older than she'd first thought, a burly man with tiny seashells and golden bells braided into his beard. He took the token over to the balcony to study it more closely. "It's genuine, all right, and bears the insignia of Arandel."

"How did you come by it?" the old councillor asked Tsorreh.

She lifted her chin. "I didn't steal it, if that's what you mean. It was my mother's."

"Don't torment the poor woman, Chylan," the governor said. "Lady, what is your name, and how did you come here? By the dust on your feet, you have had a long hard journey."

"I am Tsorreh san-Khored, wife—*widow* of Maharrad, who was *te-ravot* in Meklavar," she blurted out. "My mother was Xianthe of the House of Arandel, and I have come here with my son and heir, Zevaron, to seek passage to Durinthe. There I can claim sanctuary with my mother's kin."

"Chylan, have wine brought for Lady Tsorreh. And food, too—she and her son must be hungry. Lady Tsorreh, please forgive my brusqueness. We have a military situation here."

"Yes, I understand. Thank you for receiving me."

Tsorreh sank into a carved, cushioned bench, and in a few minutes, servants arrived with a beaker of chilled wine, its sides dewy with condensation, a plate of flatbread and olives, and a pot of spicy bean paste. As she ate, she told the story of their flight, carefully omitting any reference to the *te-alvar*, the Shield of Khored, or the memories that had swept through her during the desert passage. The governor, whose name was Drassos, occasionally interposed questions that showed he understood a great deal of the political situation.

When she had finished, he nodded gravely. "We have never enjoyed an entirely friendly relationship with Gelon, but in the past the Ar-Kings understood the cost of conquest. They restricted their excursions to border skirmishes here and there, just often enough to keep us on guard. Ar-Cinath-Gelon, on the other hand, is power mad, or perhaps just plain mad." He shook his head, eyes somber. "He will ruin his own country, as well as those of his neighbors, in his quest for domination."

"I think he means to hold Meklavar and control the route to Denariya," Tsorreh said. "My people will resist, and I fear for them."

"I fear for us all. But take heart. We have weathered far worse storms than this. Even Cinath will not risk destroying the port. We will send his ships limping back to Verenzza to lick their wounds like the dogs they are. In the meantime, be as one of us. I will have chambers prepared for you, as befits a lady of your rank, and a place for your son with the other bachelors."

Tsorreh felt a jolt of apprehension at being separated from Zevaron. No matter how dismissive the governor might be about the seriousness of the Gelonian attack, conditions might change. "I am indebted to you for your hospitality. But I would prefer that my son remain with me."

"It is not our practice to house unmarried young men with women, even their mothers." Drassos scowled. "Perhaps the standards of propriety are different in Meklavar, but here such a thing would be intolerable for one of your standing, Lady Tsorreh."

"Pardon my ignorance of your customs. I meant no offense. Yet surely some allowance can be made for the hardships my son and I have endured and the natural desire of families to remain together."

"No offense is taken," Drassos said in a tone that implied the matter was settled.

Tsorreh realized that to press the matter further would risk offending the man on whose good will they depended. Drassos could easily declare the token a forgery and throw the two of them on the street. They needed his help to reach her mother's people in Durinthe.

She glanced at Zevaron, who had clearly been following the conversation. He looked pleased at being treated as an adult man, instead of a child too young to leave his mother. Swallowing her trepidation, she bade him go along, and they were invited to break their fast with the governor the following morning. Drassos inclined his head in dismissal and returned to his documents.

Chylan, the councillor, conducted Tsorreh to a sumptuous suite of rooms. The central chamber, like the governor's office, had a wide, open balcony. Mosaic panels studded with mother-of-pearl, lapis, and polished coral decorated the whitewashed walls. One entire room was devoted to bathing, with a tiled floor surrounding a deep round tub. Before Tsorreh could puzzle out how the tub was to be filled, flaxen-haired maidservants arrived to turn levers on the pipes, sending a stream of hot water into the tub. One added fragrant oils to the rapidly filling bath, another carried in a pile of thick towels, and two more coaxed Tsorreh to undress.

Tsorreh allowed herself to be washed with an enormous sponge, rinsed, dried and scented, and dressed in Isarran style. The robe was of pale yellow silk, gathered at the shoulders with golden clasps in the shape of sea stars. The hem was stiff with embroidery in the same pattern as the clasps.

By the time the maids had finished combing out and oiling her hair, rebraiding it with the Arandel token and smoothing her face and arms with scented ointments, the sky had gone dark. Tsorreh went to the balcony and looked out. Below her, the city stretched north to the harbor. Lights dotted the streets.

She inhaled, smelling a dozen unfamiliar flowers, a whiff of roasting chicken, the undertone of salty tang. Above her, clouds scudded across a full moon. A woman's laughter soared over the jingle of a harness, the distant call of gulls, men's muted voices, and a harp arpeggio alternating with the sweet low tones of a flute. At this moment, it was hard to believe that somewhere on the water, Gelonian ships waited for the morning to renew their attack. But they were, and she dared not forget it.

An under-steward presented himself while Tsorreh stood on the balcony. He was followed by servants bearing trays of food, and a young and rather nervous-looking guard. The steward explained that the guard would remain outside her door, in case the honored lady should require anything. She asked where the unmarried young men were housed, but since she did not know the landmarks he mentioned, the answer made little sense. The place was not far, however.

Tsorreh didn't feel hungry, but when the steward and his assistants left, she uncovered the dishes. She found a bowl of an unfamiliar grain, steamed with a sauce of apricots and topped with slivered almonds. There was more flatbread and bean paste, and a pot of stewed lamb and tomatoes. It all tasted wonderful, and she ate far more than she intended. With a full belly, lulled by the sound of music from the street outside, she stretched out on the silk-covered bed and fell asleep without even taking off her sandals.

She woke suddenly, to darkness and the sound of running feet in the corridor. The room around her lay dark, the oil lamps unlit. From the street below, she heard shouting, then a high-pitched scream. She went to the balcony and looked out. Men raced along the streets, some carrying torches. She strained to make out who they were, what they were doing.

She caught a glint of light off curved metal. A sword, perhaps.

To the north, close enough so she could almost feel the flames, the harbor was burning.

Zevaron, where was Zevaron? What a fool she'd been, to let down her guard even for an instant with the enemy so near! She had to find him, get him out of there. They must not be taken, should the palace fall.

Tsorreh threw the door open. The young guard was not at his post. From the direction of the stairs came more sounds of running and shouting. She started in that direction. Before she had taken more than a few steps, a woman appeared, holding an oil lamp and hurrying in the opposite direction. She saw Tsorreh and let out a shriek. Tsorreh grabbed her arm and forced her to a halt.

"What's going on?" she asked in Isarran. "Is the palace under attack?"

"Let me go!" The woman, barely more than a girl, began babbling. "We must flee! The devils will eat us all!"

"Nonsense! The Gelon do not eat their captives!"

The girl broke into hysterical sobs.

"Where is the—" Tsorreh could not remember the word for the unmarried men's quarters. "Where do the men sleep? My son! *Where is my son?* Take me there!"

The girl paused in her weeping. For an instant, the flame of the oil lamp illuminated her features, the wide uncomprehending eyes, the rounded cheeks, the flyaway, lint-pale hair. Her parted lips trembled. She was beyond speech.

With shrieks, a clatter of sandals, and a great deal of fluttering draperies, a small mob of ladies rushed down the corridor. Three or four of them carried little glassed lanterns.

"Come along!" barked a masculine voice. "Hurry! This way!" In the wavering light, Tsorreh saw several men among the ladies. They looked like soldiers to her, urging their charges along. Filling the corridor and leaving no room on either side, they bore down on Tsorreh.

She darted up to the nearest soldier. "Where is—" she began, but he grabbed her, none too gently, and shoved her toward the other women. The speechless maidservant hid herself in their midst like a frightened rock-rabbit. Between the shouted orders of the men and the women's cries of terror, Tsorreh could not make herself heard.

Like a stampeding herd, the women carried Tsorreh along. She tried to work her way to the outside, thinking to break away. The tallest of the ladies seized her arm and drew her close. Musky perfume mingled with the smell of adrenaline-laced sweat.

"You must stay with us!" the woman said in a surprisingly self-possessed voice. By her imperious manner and the richness of her dress, she might well be the wife of the governor. "It is not safe for a decent woman to be abroad, now with the city under attack. Come, we will take you to a well-protected place. Before long our brave soldiers will repulse the invaders. We have done so many times before. Truly, there is no reason for alarm. Menelaia! Stop your sniveling this instant! Your mother would be ashamed of you, carrying on this way!"

As the lady spoke, the party continued speeding through the palace. Tsorreh lost track of the turnings and stairs. Within moments, she had no idea where she was.

"My son!" she tried again, pulling at the other woman's arm. "I must find him—he is with the other men!"

"Then he is with them still, defending the city. Do not fret on his account, my dear. All young men seek glory in battle. It is their nature. I promise you, he will fight all the more bravely for your sake."

"But—"

They burst through a narrow doorway, jostling one another. For an instant, Tsorreh could hardly breathe in the press of bodies. Then they were out in the cooler darkness, stumbling down shallow steps. Lanterns and grease-smoking torches turned the plaza into a cauldron of shadows. From the direction of the harbor came a brighter orange light and the stench of burning.

People rushed by, men on foot bearing weapons, men on horses or mules, women with shrieking children, carts drawn by huge, ponderous, oxen-like beasts with but a single horn on their foreheads, lowing their distress. Dogs barked. The sounds mixed together into a roar like a mountain avalanche. Tsorreh flinched, thinking only that it would be impossible to find Zevaron in the roiling chaos. But somehow she must—

"Come on!" shouted the soldier in the fore, and they burst into a run. He managed to find an opening through the surging traffic. By now, Tsorreh was too disoriented to do anything but follow. Her sandals slapped flat stone, bare earth, sometimes gravel. She slipped and caught herself, but kept on. Her legs repeatedly tangled in the fabric of her robe. She longed for her Meklavaran vest and trousers and swore to herself that she would never be flattered into wearing such an impractical dress again.

The crowd thinned out, except for the sound of fighting in the next street over, and they raced the last distance to a squat, single-story building. Lanterns hung from either side of the narrow door, and two strong-looking men stood there, urging them on. As they filed through, Tsorreh noticed the metal straps reinforcing the wooden door, and the bars across the high-set windows. The place was either a fortress or a trap. Unless the builders of Gatacinne had dug an underground tunnel, there would be no escape.

The door slammed behind them, shutting out the noise of the street. They went through a short passage and into a large windowless chamber, furnished with couches, tables, and freestanding holders for the ubiquitous oil lamps. A number of these had already been lit, and even now, a pair of maidservants were placing more and bringing in trays of fruit and pastries, and beakers of wine. With a murmur of pleasure, the governor's wife draped herself across the largest divan.

"What an exhausting bother this all is!" she said. "I'm simply parched! Menelaia dear, bring me some wine, and then fetch a harp from the music room. We must have a song to soothe our nerves."

The other women arranged themselves about the room,

the ladies reclining, the servants attending to them. Tsorreh lowered herself to a bench. There was no cause for alarm, she told herself, repeating what the governor had said earlier that day. Gelon had sent many forays against Gatacinne in the past, without success. She looked around her. Clearly, these people were prepared.

Even if the Gelon took the palace, they would not find her here, in this fortress. But neither would Zevaron.

Zevaron.

She might be hidden, unable to leave this place, but *he* was at liberty. He would learn where she had been taken, along with the other palace ladies. The governor would be anxious to see his wife, once the fighting was done.

The sweet arpeggio of the harp rippled through the air, its notes evanescent as ghosts.

Zevaron was out there, in fire and darkness and confusion. *Fighting,* the governor's wife had said.

Tsorreh's heart stuttered. She waved away a goblet of wine and murmured an excuse to the concerned-looking older lady beside her.

Her son was no child, she reminded herself. He had been trained in combat, with weapons and his bare hands, since he could walk. She thought of him battling at the *meklat* walls, drilling the sling-throwers, fighting mounted at his father's side. Flirting with Shadow Fox. At that, she smiled.

He would survive. He would find her, and together they would flee Gatacinne. They would make for Durinthe, where she would raise an army to liberate Meklavar.

CR-R-RACK! CRASH!

The sound of snapping metal and splintering wood echoed through the room. Tsorreh, her nerves already taut, scrambled to her feet. Before any of the other ladies could react, a handful of soldiers poured into the room. There was no mistaking the Gelon—short leather kilts, helmets plumed with blue and purple, pale bare arms. Some had drawn their swords, those distinctive double-edged blades. The foremost wore a gilded helmet and carried a whip.

"Outside!" bellowed the officer.

The other soldiers shoved the women together roughly. The women whimpered in mingled terror and confusion. It was clear that not all of them understood Gelone. Tsorreh pretended to be as cowed as the others.

"Leave the servants," the officer said. "If need be, we can round them up later, once the city's secured. Right now, we don't need slaves, we need hostages. One of these is the governor's—you there!" He prodded the governor's wife with his coiled whip. "What's your name?"

The lady drew herself up, glared at him, and answered in accented but grammatically perfect Gelone, "I do not converse with rabble."

"That's her, all right!" The officer threw his head back and laughed. "From what I've heard, I don't know if His Excellency will pay more to get her back or have us keep her!"

The wife looked ready to scratch his eyes out, but one of the soldiers grabbed her, spun her around, and tied her wrists in front of her.

"How dare you!" She spat at him but missed.

"Let's get going!" The officer barked out a few more orders. Moving with ruthless efficiency, his men bound the rest of the ladies, Tsorreh among them, and tied them together. One of the women began sobbing.

As they were being led away, the governor's wife shrieked, "My husband will have you beheaded for this insult!" The officer laughed again as she went on. "Beheaded, and then flayed into little strips, and then—"

Tsorreh shuffled along with the others, her head down. As she drew near, the officer came alert.

"What's this?" He tapped her shoulder with his whip and signaled the soldier leading the string to halt. He lifted her chin for a better look. "You're no Isarran, not with that black hair."

Tsorreh jerked away, resolutely silent.

"You savage!" the governor's wife shrilled. "She is a noble guest and must not be harmed!"

"Noble? A princess of the sand rats?"

Tsorreh glared at him for an instant. Then, recovering her wits, she nodded.

"Do you have a tongue? A name?"

She considered refusing to give him even a single syllable, but decided that would only fuel his curiosity. "Shadow Fox."

She knew at once that she'd hesitated too long. The Gelon's mouth tightened. He issued more orders, and before she could resist, she found herself half-pulled, half-dragged out into the street, along with the others.

The eastern sky, cloudless, glimmered with pale clear light. The only people Tsorreh could see were Gelonian soldiers and their bound prisoners. Bodies, both Gelon and Isarran, lay in scattered heaps, and stains marked the paving stones where others had been taken away. From several directions, Tsorreh heard shouting. She hoped wildly that it meant fighting, armed resistance.

Somewhere out there, Zevaron was alive and free. He must be.

A squadron of Gelonian soldiers bore down on them, heading in the direction of the harbor. Their officer paused to confer with Tsorreh's captor. "Fall back! Orders are to consolidate our hold of the port area and palace," the newcomer said.

"I'll see this lot taken to the palace. I've got one for the priest. Might be nothing, but we were told to report anything strange."

They exchanged a few further comments, too quietly for Tsorreh to overhear, then parted ways. The other women seemed happy to be returning to the palace. They offered little resistance, even the governor's wife.

Tsorreh went along, saving her strength and trying to devise a strategy. It sounded as if she were to be interrogated, and she wanted to have a credible story ready. The best she could think of was to maintain her Sand Lands identity, hoping that the authentic name and the little she'd learned from her time at Karega Oasis would convince the Gelon.

And what then? With any luck, she'd be kept with the rest of the noble women. Governor Drassos would surely not endanger her, any more than he would his own wife. She tried to imagine how Shadow Fox would behave in such a situation.

When they arrived at the palace a short time later, the Gelonian officer untied the rope linking Tsorreh to the others. As he pulled her across the central hall, she saw none of the palace inhabitants, except for a few terrified servants. Morning light, stronger now, poured in through the open roof of the courtyard. Then they plunged back into shadow, heading this time not for the stairs to the upper stories but along an arched colonnade.

Two Gelonian soldiers, alert and grim, stood at attention to either side of an inner doorway. The officer rapped on the door and waited for a response before entering. He lifted the latch and the door swung open. Even before he tugged on Tsorreh's bonds, she had the sudden, overwhelming feeling she did not want to go in.

The chamber within was pleasantly proportioned, its white walls trimmed with ceramic tiles glazed with a simple geometric pattern. At a glance, her eyes took in racks of scrolls, a table, chairs, and a man bending over an unrolled parchment. Sun from the window on the far side touched his shaved scalp and pale skin. He wore a white robe and a cloth strip tied around his forehead.

The officer waited for the robed man to look up. When he did, a keen intelligence lit his eyes. Beneath his almost unnatural stillness, Tsorreh sensed an iron strength.

"We found this one among the noble ladies in their hideaway," the officer said in a deferential voice. "She claims to be a sand rat, and I thought so at first, for she's clearly not Isarran. I've brought her to you, as ordered."

"We are pleased." The voice, too, was strong and yet chill.

Tsorreh made out the emblem on his head cloth, some kind of animal, a stylized scorpion, she thought. She could not understand why it disturbed her. The Gelon worshipped many gods, so why not a scorpion? The Meklavaran varieties were small and gray, dangerous only to cats and other small creatures. She'd read that those of the Sand Lands were far more venomous. Something in that many-legged shape, pincers and stinger-tail upraised, now sent a shiver through her.

"You may leave us," the scorpion priest said. "Do not be concerned. She cannot harm us."

The departing officer seemed all too eager to remove himself. Tsorreh trembled as the priest glided toward her.

"Do not be afraid," he murmured. His voice was steel over snow. "All we wish is a little information, such a small thing to give, at no cost, no pain. So easy. Do you see? That's right, just open your thoughts to us."

As he spoke, the priest extended one hand toward Tsorreh's forehead. She tried to jerk away, but found she could not move, as if the mere proximity had paralyzed her with the scorpion's venom. She could blink and swallow, and turn her head a little, but her feet had been fastened to the floor, her muscles frozen. What had he done to her?

The voice rolled on, syllables rising and falling in waves. *Truly, there was nothing to fear.*

She felt herself softening like ice in an early thaw, melting, giving way. Her eyelids fluttered. Drowsiness lapped at her. She had only to let go a little, to sink into it. The voice kept on, so reasonable, so reassuring. Hands of misty gray reached out for her, fingers long and thin like ribbons or the strands of fisher's netting. They wrapped around her. Like the slender noses of serpents, the tips prodded, seeking a way through her, *into her.*

"Tell us . . . yes, that's right. Nothing to fear, just tell us."

Within Tsorreh, something pulsed gold and white, a second heartbeat. The half-fainting, half-dizzy sensation receded. Through the mist that covered her eyes, she made out the face of the priest, bending toward her. The scorpion emblem on his brow shimmered. Jointed limbs flexed. She sensed what it wanted: her name, her true name, the core and heart of who she was, everything she had ever wanted, and her darkest fears.

The voice no longer soothed and enticed, it commanded. The ribbon tendrils tightened, and the prodding turned sharp, insistent. "Why do you resist? You know you do not truly wish to. In the end, you will tell us. Yes, you will."

Pain shot through her. She staggered with it. Her vision turned white. Again came the demanding voice.

"Tell us!"

What was it she feared? No, whispered the voice, what did she *desire*? What did she cherish? Who would she give anything to see again?

Her mother, Maharrad, Shorrenon. Loss and anguish rose up in her. *Tenereth, grandfather.* She must not even think their names, lest the scorpion hear her thoughts, hear and learn—

Zevaron. The scorpion wanted *Zevaron.*

O Holy One, help me!

The pressure mounted. Her resistance was failing, brittle as eggshell. She could not breathe. Any moment now, she would give way, collapsing, shattering, and everything she knew—all she had experienced, her hopes and dreams and nightmares—would come spilling out.

The fall of Meklavar, saving the library, holding the te-Ketav *in her hands, the light streaming through the stained glass Shield of Khored. Zevaron. The* te-alvar *blossoming over her heart.*

In that instant, as if summoned by her thought, the gem flared into brilliance, not of sight but of spirit. Its living power surged through her. Recognition stirred, and she saw, with vision far deeper than her own, how the scorpion image wavered and grew thin. Behind it lay shadows of chilling cold, of infernal flame, a dim and distant *awareness*. It had slept long, but now it roused. Carefully it gathered strength, although it still remained hidden. In another instant, it would see her and recognize what she carried.

But she would die before she allowed the *te-alvar* to fall

into the hands of such an enemy. And with her death, the Shield would be broken forever. Meklavar would perish, and Zevaron with it.

NO!

Without thinking, Tsorreh reached into the core of pulsating radiance inside her and drew it forth. White-gold power filled her. Willingly she gave herself to it. She lost all awareness of herself, her surroundings, the man before her, and the invisible bands that encircled her.

She floated in the light. She *became* the light.

From afar, she sensed other motes of brilliance—blue and gold and palest rose—some faint and distant, yet resonant. The Shield, the harmonic union, was scattered, yet all its elements remained. As long as she lived to pass what she bore to another guardian, so would the hope of reunion survive.

Survive. The word echoed through her mind. Now she knew what she had to do. *Give them what they want to hear, and they will ask no further.*

Tsorreh came back to herself. The priest still stood before her, peering intently into her face. His voice still spoke in rhythmic phrases. Her body felt stiff, but she could breathe again.

She pitched her voice to sound as if she were overpowered and helpless. "I am Tsorreh, Queen of Meklavar. I fled here when the city fell to Gelon."

"Ah!" the priest exhaled.

Abruptly the sensation of pressure vanished. Nausea swept through her. She fell, retching, to her knees.

The priest bent over her, grasping the braid that held the Arandel token. Pain lanced through her scalp. She felt a sudden release as he slashed through the braid. She had not even seen the knife. He walked past her as if she were of no consequence, opened the door, and called in the guards.

"Put her on the next ship to Gelon," the priest's voice sounded as if he were far away. "A gift for the Ar-King from the Servants of Qr." He pronounced the name with a short, barely sounded *uh* between the two consonants.

Sickened and disoriented, Tsorreh struggled to her feet. She tried to walk, but her legs would not hold her. One of the Gelonian soldiers picked her up and slung her over his shoulder.

Zevaron, my son! O Holy One, keep him safe!

PART II:

Zevaron's Escape

Chapter Nine

PUZZLED, Zevaron glanced from the governor of Gatacinne to his mother. The flight across the Sand Lands had scoured his nerves raw, and although he spoke passable Gelone, his knowledge of Isarran was not good enough to completely follow their conversation. Even if he could not understand the words, he sensed the shifting undercurrents of power. Tsorreh wanted them to stay together, the governor had refused, and she'd backed away from an outright confrontation.

Zevaron sensed her unvoiced thought: *We cannot afford to insult his hospitality.*

"You are to have a place with the unmarried men," Tsorreh told him, "and I am to stay here tonight. Tomorrow morning, we will break our fast with the governor and arrange the next stage of our journey." She meant, *The sooner we are away from this place, the better.*

Although they were not out of danger, Zevaron was secretly pleased to be considered an adult and not a child too young to leave his mother. Maybe he'd have a chance to explore the city.

The quarters for the unmarried men turned out to be a dormitory situated just north of the governor's palace, between the city center and the harbor. Upon entering, he saw five or six men at the end of the ground-floor corridor, hunched around in a circle, playing a gambling game with knuckle bones by the light of an oil lamp. The dormitory itself was one of several long rooms divided by wooden frame beds, each with a space for a chest. Only one was occupied, at the far end, where someone lay snoring loudly. Zevaron set his pack down at the foot of the nearest empty bed.

His new companions, two ruddy-haired boys only a few years his senior, were good-natured and friendly in a boisterous, rough-housing way. If he'd understood them correctly, they were brothers from one of the coastal provinces. Neither knew any Meklavaran, but they were clearly curious about him. Between his simple Isarran, the few phrases of Gelone they understood, and a good deal of gesturing, he was able to sketch out the tale of his own adventures. They took him to an inn a short distance away. Dinner was a thick lentil stew, served with rice and onions, seasoned with unfamiliar spices and accompanied by watered wine, which he took care to drink sparingly. Gatacinne was, after all, a strange city and the Gelon fleet waited just outside the harbor.

It was late when they returned to the dormitory. The air rapidly surrendered the heat of the day, as if relieved of its burden. Once inside, Zevaron stretched out on the bed and waited for sleep.

It would not come. If he closed his eyes, he could feel the street outside, armed men, torches licking the shadows, the city like a restless beast. For a time, aided by the demands of thinking in three different languages, he had been able to set aside his fears. Now they returned, and he had no defense against them.

What exactly was he afraid of? Did he distrust the governor, suspect a plot or betrayal? No, the man was honest, of that he was as certain as he was of anything in this shifting world. What, then? The Gelonian attack?

Zevaron shifted from one side to the other, trying to find a comfortable position. His muscles were too tense for him to lie still, although there was nothing wrong with the bed. He had slept on harder surfaces during their journey. He tried breathing more deeply, drawing the air into his belly.

The Gatacinnes seemed to be going about the protection of their city as if such attacks happened regularly—unlike Meklavar, which had no standing army.

If the fighting were heavier than they expected—if the worst happened, surely there was no place more secure than the governor's own palace. If anyone was in danger, it was he, himself.

If the Gelon overran the harbor defenses, they would have to fight through him to reach his mother. He would find her, and the two of them would escape. With that thought, he was able to drift off to sleep.

Shouting jarred him awake. A man stood in the doorway, his body limned by torchlight. He yelled something in Isarran, too rapidly to understand more than *Gelon* and *fight*.

Zevaron rolled off the bed and scrambled to his feet. Around him, the room churned with movement. Men jumped up, pulled on boots, cursed, and shoved one another.

The man at the door shouted, "Hurry!"

"What's going on?" Zevaron asked one of his companions from the night before.

One of the other men grabbed his arm and pushed him toward the door along with the others. They scrambled up the corridor and down the single broad step, spilling out onto the street. The man who had shouted them awake urged them on.

Outside, the moon had set, leaving the city in darkness. To the north, orange light painted the horizon. The harbor was burning.

Stumbling, Zevaron half fell against the nearest man, who shoved him upright. His ears rang with the mingled clash of swords, and the cries of men, many men. Half a block away, he and the others reached a stone building. A single door stood gaping, and two men in battle gear were handing out weapons: swords, spears, long knives, shields. If they were arming the civilians, preparing for fighting in the streets, the situation must be desperate.

Mother!

Zevaron turned south, back toward the governor's palace. In the crowd, he could not go more than a few steps. A burly man in a soldier's tunic blocked his path, forcing him away.

"Let me go!" he cried. "I have to—"

But the soldier ignored him and dragged him along with the crowd.

The confusion let up at the entrance to the armory, where one of the soldiers shoved a battered, thick-bladed sword into his hands.

"You don't understand—" Zevaron broke off, realizing that in his desperation, he had reverted to his own language.

"Foreigner, fight-you for Isarre," the officer snarled, or so Zevaron understood his meaning. The second officer pointed him to a knot of similarly armed men. A couple were holding their swords, testing their heft and balance, as if they had training in their use.

"This way! For Gatacinne and the King!" The officer raised his own sword. The polished blade caught the light. "Gatacinne! Gatacinne!"

Zevaron hesitated, but only for a moment. He might be able to escape into the city, disappear in the confusion, and make his way back to the palace. And risk being cut down as a deserter or a traitor. The instant passed. His body moved as if it knew the way, racing up the street with the others, north toward the harbor.

I'll come back as soon as I can. As soon as the city is safe.

The streets were narrower here but less congested, and they were able to cover ground rapidly. Zevaron heard fighting ahead, not as one overwhelming uproar but as scattered islands of sound. They headed for the nearest one.

They burst out into a little square around a fountain. In the day, it might have been lined with outdoor food stalls, and children might have played in the water. Now fire raged across the south edge, devouring the wooden structures.

The square itself churned with smoke and falling cinders. Fighters were silhouetted against the brightness. The Gelon were obvious by their helmets and armor.

The Isarran officer screamed out an order, and the improvised company surged forward. After a moment's confusion, the two forces engaged and all semblance of order disappeared.

Zevaron leaped a fallen body—a woman's, he thought—and charged the nearest Gelon. The soldier swerved, bringing up his shield. Zevaron's sword, wielded with both hands, clanged against it. The impact jolted up his arms, for the man was larger, heavier, and much stronger. Then Zevaron veered out of the way of the countering blow. He couldn't think, not in the saturated chaos of fighting and night and smoke, but his muscles remembered their training. The drillmaster's orders sent him dancing beyond the reach of his opponent's weapon, then back in, using his speed and coordination. He struck again. His sword slid around the rim of the shield, piercing thin leather and slicing into flesh. The battered blade caught and dragged, sluggish. For a panic-stricken moment, Zevaron yanked hard, struggling to free the sword.

"Yahhh!"

A cry sounded behind him. Instinctively, he twisted away. The blade came free. A second Gelon bore down on him, so close and fast that if Zevaron had not already been moving, he would have been struck. He felt the sudden, whipping air as the tip of the Gelon's sword caught his tunic. The first soldier had recovered somewhat and lumbered toward him. Zevaron could not tell how badly injured the first Gelon was, only that he now faced two of them. He hurled himself toward the wounded one, bashing at the shield as he darted past. The wounded Gelon turned, a trace too slowly, and from the swirling firelit darkness, an Isarran in blood-streaked armor rammed a spear into his unguarded side.

The Gelon toppled, taking the spear with him. Before he hit the ground, the Isarran leaped forward and grabbed the invader's sword from his limp fingers. For a fleeting instant, the Isarran met Zevaron's gaze, then the soldier nodded and drove on to the second Gelon.

Zevaron turned back toward the center of the fighting, wondering for an instant how they were going to get beyond the burning buildings. The wooden structures looked like skeletons of flame. Shadowed figures moved through the conflagration, men struggling to contain it. Beyond them, through the smoke and falling ash, Zevaron glimpsed walls of stone and mud-brick.

One of those who'd come with him, one of the red-haired boys, staggered under a Gelon's assault, lost his footing, and went down with a shriek. Zevaron lunged toward him. Two Gelon came at him, blocking his path. They pressed him, putting their greater weight behind their shields. Twisting and parrying, he gave way. He could not stand before them.

Zevaron jumped over a fallen body—Gelon, yes—and for an instant, found a little clear space around him. On every side, however, Isarrans were falling back.

The next moment, he spied the Isarran officer who had led them. The man's armor had been hacked half to pieces and his left arm, covered in blood, hung uselessly at his side. He lifted his sword. Zevaron could not hear his words above the din, but his meaning was clear.

Retreat! Save yourselves to fight another day!

Zevaron hesitated, gazing once again at the line of burning buildings. The heat rolled over him, stealing his breath. Gaps appeared in the flames and disappeared as quickly. If he could find a way through or around—could he circle back to the palace?

The next moment, a wall of Gelonian shields bore down on him. With each step, the soldiers shouted in unison, but the words were swallowed in the uproar of the flames. The Gelon had fought like this before the gates of Meklavar, a coordinated attack, each defending his comrade's weaker side. The ragtag Isarran defenders gave way like paper.

Zevaron did his best to cover the retreating Isarrans. The unfamiliar sword felt leaden and awkward, his movements

slower with each blow. He had been wounded but felt it
only distantly. He could not remember how it had happened. There was no pain. Not yet.

A Gelon surged in from the side, slashing hard. Zevaron
jumped back and the tip of the Gelon's blade missed his
belly by a hair's breadth.

There was no room to fight and no way to stand fast.
More Gelon poured into the marketplace. They pushed
through the last shreds of resistance, driving the Isarrans
toward the burning buildings. To every side, Zevaron
watched the defenders scatter and vanish in the darkened
streets. Within moments, only a few remained.

The Isarran officer paused on the edge of the square,
gesturing encouragement to the stragglers. Zevaron raced
after them, dodging along the narrow, twisting streets. Once
or twice, he came upon a knot of fighting, Isarran soldiers in
retreat, or a corner where the Gelon were consolidating
their position.

The fading glow from the fire gave Zevaron a reference
point. They were heading toward the harbor. Each step
took him further from the governor's palace and his mother.
It was not difficult to slip away in the confusion and head
back the way they'd come.

For a short time, things seemed to be going well. Keeping
to the smaller streets, Zevaron managed to stay out of sight
as he worked his way south. He tried to skirt the worst of the
chaos, for he could not afford to be caught up in armed confrontation or risk being delayed or possibly disabled.

It was too bad this beautiful city had been invaded by
the Gelons, but it was not his battle. He had to find his
mother and get her out before things got any worse. The
battle adrenaline was fading, so that he was beginning to
feel half a dozen wounds. The sword felt heavier with each
step, but he could not stop now.

*I swore to my brother that I would look after her. I never
should have left her!*

The side street he was following debouched onto a
broader avenue, the center blocked by an overturned cart.

Wooden crates had crashed onto the paving stones, scattering their contents as well as straw packing. Fist-sized orange fruits rolled in every direction. Two men struggled with the draft animal, some kind of ox with hugely rounded, back-curved horns, while a handful of children snatched up the fallen fruit. Several Gelonian soldiers barked out orders that only seemed to increase the confusion.

Zevaron merged with the other passers-by, some jeering at the Gelon, others going about their business. Some carried bundles and hurried by as quickly as possible. A woman carrying a basketful of cloth, laundry most likely, was looking the other way when she bumped into Zevaron. The basket tumbled to the ground. As he bent to help her, she glanced at his bloody sword and soot-streaked clothing, smothered a cry, and scurried away, leaving him with a handful of dirty clothing. Quickly, he wrapped the clothes around the sword. It made a long, lumpy bundle, hardly a disguise against a watchful eye but better than nothing.

If his sense of direction held, the palace was off the plaza just beyond the overturned cart. A barricade might have been set up, but he couldn't be sure. He must not risk being noticed. With an effort, he slowed his pace, clutching the wrapped sword against his body. He lowered his eyes and slouched as if he were an insignificant nobody.

"You there!" one of the Gelon called.

Zevaron kept going. He pretended he had not understood, that he was of such little importance no one could address such a remark to him. He took another shuffling step and then another.

Although his heart thudded in his chest so loudly that the soldiers must surely have heard the racket, no hand reached out to restrain him. No cold steel pressed against his flesh.

He reached the fallen cart. Now he was passing the Gelon themselves.

"No, not you!" the same voice went on, still in Gelone. "The other one. Get back to your homes, where it's safe! Go on, all of you! Clear out!"

Zevaron hazarded a sidelong glance in the direction of the Gelon. One of them had sheathed his sword and was helping to right the cart, while the others stood guard and directed traffic as more onlookers gathered. A man in a ragged cloak drew back one arm and hurled a stone at the nearest Gelon. The stone hit the edge of the soldier's breast-plate with a clang. A rush, a gathering of anger, coalesced in the scattered crowd. Zevaron paused, thinking the stone-thrower had been a fool, and yet he understood what it was like to become caught up in the moment.

Faster than Zevaron would have believed possible, the Gelon reacted. He sprinted across the street. The people in front of him scrambled out of the way. The next instant, he had wrestled his assailant to the ground. Only then did he draw his sword, resting its tip against the throat of the hapless man.

Zevaron had seen the Gelon work together with their ruthless coordination, but he had not realized how deadly these men could be, fighting face to face.

If I am to free Meklavar, I must learn to fight even better.

Zevaron hurried away, using the cover of the scattering crowd. Trying to keep to the shadows, he reached the next intersection. The tower facing the governor's palace rose ahead of him. Torches dotted the plaza and the flat, broad steps.

Zevaron froze, watching in dismay as a line of prisoners, men and women, their hands bound in front of them, was led down those steps. Gelonian soldiers stood guard, and an officer in a plumed helmet shouted out orders.

He had come too late.

Chapter Ten

ZEVARON stared open-mouthed as the prisoners were led away. His breath racked his body in heaving gulps. All his efforts had been bent on reaching the governor's palace and taking his mother to a place of safety. It had never occurred to him that the Gelon might already have captured the palace.

He did not recognize any of the prisoners, but the women among them seemed to be serving maids. Their hands were tied and joined by a long rope. He had no way of knowing if Tsorreh had already been taken away or, if so, where that might be.

What should he do? Follow? Find out where the captives were taken? How? Who would know?

He felt slow and stupid as he tried to decide. What if Tsorreh were not among them? What if she were still in the palace and while he was following the other captives, the Gelon took her in another direction? On the other hand, to stay and watch might lose him precious time.

If he found her, then what? The convoy of prisoners was guarded, although not as heavily as the palace itself. Could he race up, cut her bonds, and snatch her away?

Get himself killed, more like.

"You there!" A Gelonian soldier called out and pointed in his direction. "Come here!"

Clutching the wrapped sword, Zevaron whirled and sprinted away. As he turned, fire shot up one thigh. He remembered taking a cut there earlier. For a terrifying instant, the leg threatened to give way beneath him. Limping, he headed for the darkest avenue of escape.

He turned a corner and plunged into shadow. Pursuit sounded behind him, the pounding of feet, the thump and clatter of shield and scabbard against stone walls. He had nowhere to hide, no familiar district in which to lose himself. But if he did not know his way around the city, he reasoned, neither did the Gelon. They would expect him to run in a straight line, so he turned here and then there, to make his path more difficult to follow.

Right, left, left, straight and then right again.

The pain in his leg slowed him to a hopping shuffle. Grimacing to keep from crying out, he held on to the sides of houses, to baked mud-brick and stone, to wooden railings, and once to a fence from behind which came the squawk of chickens. In his flight, the sword had lost its wrappings, but he dared not leave it behind.

He searched the horizon for light and caught a faint tinge in one direction but could not decide if it were the remnants of the marketplace fire, north toward the burning harbor, or east to the rising of the sun. How much time had passed? Where had his headlong flight taken him? From time to time, he heard the sounds of battle, but they were diminished and distant.

His heart labored, a hailstorm against the inside of his chest. Sweat crusted his face and sides. His wounds throbbed. The cut in his thigh bled, but sluggishly. His muscles were already stiffening in the coolness of the night.

The street, little more than an alley, seemed quiet enough. No one else was about. He came to a halt in the alcove of an entryway. The door itself seemed to be barred shut. When he lowered himself to the threshold, the stone felt satiny and cool. He would hide here, he thought, and wait for the worst of the fighting to die down.

Gradually, Zevaron's heartbeat slowed. His muscles felt like lead. He must rest, but for only a little while. The Gelon would secure the areas they had seized, the marketplace and surrounding streets, the governor's palace, and who knew what else.

The sound of running feet jerked him to full alertness. Sword in hand, he scrambled to his feet. Through the shadows that choked the alley, he caught a flicker of movement— two children, he thought—and a small animal. One child saw him and gave a startled yelp.

"It's right," he called out in his broken Isarran. "I am friend!"

The shorter of the children picked up the animal, wariness in every line of the thin body. Zevaron stepped from the alcove. If he could gain their trust, they might guide him to a place where he could hide. Almost anywhere would be better than stumbling around until he ran into a Gelonian patrol.

"I stranger," he said, "and friend to Isarre."

The two children had come to a halt. They bent their heads together, conferring in whispers. The animal yipped and wriggled free. As it ran toward Zevaron, he realized it was a dog. He drew back, for he had little experience with such animals. The Sand Lands people used them for hunting, thin long-legged hounds able to run down a gazelle. This one was small and loose-jointed, with a rounded belly and velvety hide. It bounded up to him, making excited noises, and licked his sweaty knees.

"Don't hurt her, she's only a puppy!" The child, a girl, darted forward and scooped up the animal in her arms.

"You're no Gelon," the boy said, stepping protectively in front of the girl.

"No, but I fight—fought—against them at the marketplace."

"Come with us," the boy said. "Hurry! They are sweeping this neighborhood. You'll be safe with my father."

Zevaron stumbled after the youngsters. Every joint and muscle in his body throbbed. He hoped he didn't have to run or fight any time soon.

Men's voices sounded behind them. Zevaron caught a phrase of Gelone. Gritting his teeth, he hurried after the children. They slipped down the street and through an alley that was barely wide enough for a grown man to pass, dodging here and there until he lost all sense of where they were going. Crossing a garden, they ducked between rows of herbs and bean plants climbing over a freestanding wooden latticework.

At last, they emerged into a courtyard bounded by two-story stone buildings. Lights burned in the windows. A woman appeared in a doorway, hands on her hips. When she saw the children, she rushed toward them. She caught the girl in her arms, peppering both children with questions and exclamations. Her speech was so rapid and her tone so agitated, Zevaron could follow only a little of it. It was clear, however, that she had been frantic with worry and was now furious as a result.

A man came out of the house, and then another. One carried an axe, the other a long staff. The one with the axe stepped forward, motioning the woman and children behind him.

Zevaron realized how he must appear to these people — a stranger, armed and covered in blood. He thought of running back into the night, but he doubted his legs would carry him. Now that he was no longer moving, he began to shake uncontrollably.

The boy spoke to the man with the axe, gesturing toward Zevaron. The man looked up, his features unreadable with the light behind him. "You fought for Gatacinne?"

"Yes."

"But you are not one of us."

"Gelon is my enemy." Zevaron thought he'd said it correctly, for the man nodded. The whole truth was too complicated, and he did not know these people. He reversed the sword and handed it, hilt first, to the man.

After a moment's muttered deliberation, the man gestured for Zevaron to come inside. The door led to an entrance hall of sorts, lined with benches, hooks for cloaks, and wooden racks for shoes. The children disappeared down a corridor, along with the puppy. Another man stood in the opposite doorway, and now Zevaron got a clearer look at them, the cut of their clothing, the length and color of their hair, their grim faces. They all bore marks of having been in the battle, wounds and grime, and streaks of soot.

"Bandages first, then talk," the woman said. She pushed Zevaron through an outdoor courtyard and into a smaller room, a kitchen by the wide hearth and work table. A small cauldron steamed over the remains of a fire. Strings of onions, garlic, and dried peppers hung in one corner, and the broad wooden shelves were filled with jars of oil and vinegar, lidded baskets, folded cloths, and other things he did not recognize.

As Zevaron sank down on one of the stools, the woman darted about the kitchen. Very shortly, she had assembled everything needed to bathe and dress his wounds. She clucked over the cut on his thigh, left him for a moment, and returned with silk thread and a metal needle, so thin and fine that it must be of Denariyan make. The man with the axe came in while she pierced Zevaron's skin and knotted the thread to close the cut. That done, she washed the wound again and wrapped it in strips of cloth. Cotton, he thought, but of a softness unknown in Meklavar. Then she insisted he drink a beaker of hot, thick, foul-tasting, greenish brew.

"It will keep your wound from *molynsi*," she urged. Zevaron did not understand the word, but it took it to mean the putrefaction that all too often followed deep cuts. "Drink, drink."

When she had finished, she conducted Zevaron to one of the inner rooms, where the rest of the men and a couple of women, dressed in the same tunics and leggings, were talking in low, urgent voices. One of the women had apparently been part of the crew that put out the marketplace fire. Zevaron understood from their discussion that most of the able-bodied adults of the city had helped to throw back previous Gelonian invasions.

"Never before have they fought so hard or come in such numbers," one of the men lamented.

"They may take Gatacinne, but they cannot hold it," said the woman who had fought the fire. She wore the same clothing as the men, which astonished Zevaron, and her manner was so commanding that he dared not stare. "We'll push them into the sea."

Everyone nodded, but beneath their brave words Zevaron sensed an undercurrent of fear. Or perhaps he imagined it, remembering the fall of Meklavar. No one had battled harder than Maharrad and Shorrenon and their men, and yet, in the end, it had not been enough.

"Now, stranger," said Aharros, the man who had carried the axe, "you have taken shelter in my home and my wife has bandaged your hurt. In return, we would hear your story."

The woman fighter, whose name was Sivran, smiled grimly. "If you have fought the Gelon as you say, you know their ways. Their weaknesses."

"I not Gelon, not Isarran," Zevaron began haltingly. "My name Zevaron. I come—came from Meklavar with my mother." How much more should he say?

He told them as best he could that his own city had fallen to Gelon. Aharros and his friends had not heard of the attack, but they readily accepted Zevaron's statement that he had come to Gatacinne seeking refuge with his mother's Isarran kin. Perhaps there were others of her countrymen here, people Zevaron could contact for help.

"Last night, she stay with the women of the governor," Zevaron said. "Gelon defeat palace, people taken away. Prisoners," he said, guessing at the word, though from the nods and grim expressions, he got it close enough.

"You fear your mother is among them?" Aharros asked, not unkindly.

"Where taken?" Zevaron asked.

"Sivran, do you know?" Aharros turned to the woman fighter.

She lifted her shoulders in a shrug. "No news, so far. The Gelon are said to hold those from wealthy families as hostage and send the others back to Gelon as slaves."

Zevaron's heart faltered. He had forgotten the Gelon took slaves as booty.

"There, lad," Aharros said, reaching out a hand to steady Zevaron. "We do not know. For now, regain your strength."

Already swaying with shock and fatigue, Zevaron went willingly as Aharros's wife led him to a narrow guest chamber. He fell asleep almost before he stretched out on the wood and leather-lattice bed.

Zevaron felt as if he had barely closed his eyes when the puppy, a velvet-skinned, loose-jointed creature with a perpetually wet nose, licked him awake. The boy stood grinning in the entrance, holding the door drape aside with one hand. He gestured with his other hand. "Come, come. Eat."

Zevaron tried to sit up and swing his legs over the side of the bed. Unlike the minor stiffness of the night before, near-rigidity had set in. Every muscle protested. At least, the wound in his thigh no longer throbbed.

In the kitchen, Renneh, the mistress of the house, had set out enough food to feed ten men: seed-topped loaves of bread, little round cheeses, bowls of beans stewed with tomatoes and peppers, and a grayish paste that reeked of olives and garlic. Sivran and another woman, dressed like her in tunic and short breeches, sat talking and eating. Renneh looked up from stirring a pot of something green and grinned at Zevaron.

"News?" Zevaron asked.

Frowning, Renneh took a wooden platter, filled it with the bean stew and bread slathered with the gray paste, and handed it to Zevaron. "Eat first."

Tentatively, he took a bite. The bean stew burned his mouth, bringing tears to his eyes, but the bread and gray paste tasted delicious. He accepted a beaker of watered wine, trying not to stare at Sivran and her friend, whose name was Hadela or Harela. The two did not speak or act like Meklavaran women.

"There has been fighting all over the city," Sivran said, speaking slowly and clearly. "The Gelon hold the harbor, the governor's palace and stronghold, and some of the northern district. Beyond the Boulevard of Flowers, however, they dare not venture. We will push them into the sea."

"And the prisoners?" Renneh asked, with a concerned glance at Zevaron.

Sivran's friend shook her head. "The governor's household is kept in the stronghold. My cousin's husband's sister brings them bread, and says there is no foreign woman among them. All are known to her."

Not there? Could she have been wounded in the fighting? Could she—Oh, Most Holy One grant that it not be so!—be dead?

Zevaron thrust the thought from his mind. In another instant, fear would turn his strength to water. "Other prisoners—where?"

"I have heard they will be sent back to Gelon as slaves, along with treasure looted from the city."

"Stop them! Must!"

She regarded him somberly. "Can you fight?"

"Give me sword, and I show."

Sivran's companion scowled at him. "You're barely more than a child, and you speak Isarran like a donkey."

"I not speak Isarran well," Zevaron said, biting off each word. Then he switched to Gelone. "But neither do the Gelon. Can you understand what they say in their own language?"

Sivran looked confused. Renneh laughed. "He makes a good point!"

The boy burst into the kitchen, flushed and panting. "*Theya* Sivran, *theya* Harela, papa says you must come to the Great Plaza. Please, come quick!"

"What? What happen?" Zevaron stammered.

"Soldiers! Gelon! They are going to kill the prisoners!"

Zevaron scrambled to his feet. "Where sword?"

"Mama, I want to go, too!" the boy pleaded. "I am old enough to fight, truly I am!"

"No, sweetling," said Renneh, "you must stay here and protect your sister. I cannot do without you."

The boy glared at Zevaron. Zevaron, unexpectedly moved, said, "Boy use sling?" He gestured as if to swing and release a stone.

Renneh scowled at Zevaron, the first time he had seen a harsh expression on her kind face. "There will be time enough for children fighting." She wrapped her arms around her son's thin shoulders. "Go now!"

A short time later, Zevaron followed Sivran and her friend through a mazework of streets, angling toward the plaza that fronted the governor's palace. His wounded leg still felt stiff, but it was sound enough. Renneh had returned his sword, wrapped in strips of leather and plaited straw. Sivran and her friend each carried a bundle of staves across their shoulders. With their faces smeared with dust, they looked very much like common laborers.

It was difficult to believe this was the same city through which he had fled in the darkness, these graceful buildings of white and gray with their bright red tile roofs. Pots of flowers stood in windowsills, and streamers of indigo cloth trailed from woven lattices strung between buildings, shading outdoor food shops. People went about buying and selling on the streets, workers carrying tools, donkeys pulling carts laden with barrels or piles of mud-gray bricks, women with baskets tucked under their arms or bundles balanced on their heads, and a page in livery leading a brace of nervous, long-legged dogs on bejeweled leashes.

"Boulevard of the Flowers," Sivran said in a low voice. "We must go carefully here."

They passed through the merchant district without challenge. The streets here were broader and yet less populated, and many of the buildings—shops, Zevaron supposed, or apartments—had been shut up.

As they neared the plaza, the foot traffic thickened. Zevaron noticed the tense expressions of the people. Ahead, he heard raised voices, bursts of shouting against a rolling mutter.

A crowd had gathered in the plaza. From the periphery, it was difficult to see what was going on. Zevaron glanced up at the governor's palace. Several men stood on the open balcony, most likely the commanding Gelonian general and his aides. And there was someone else, cloaked in shadow. Zevaron shivered, as if ice had brushed his skin, and quickly turned away.

A man in Isarran dress stood on the topmost step, addressing the people. When the speaker finished, there was a flurry of activity. Muttering swept the assembly.

Zevaron touched Sivran's arm. "What is happening?"

"It's an execution," Sivran muttered. "Someone dared to stand against them."

"We must find Aharros—look, there he is!" Sivran's friend, Harela, shoved her way through the crowd with Sivran hard on her heels.

Zevaron followed them for a short way, then a path opened up and for an instant, he could see the space right before the palace steps. The scene looked like a theatrical presentation, with the players frozen in dramatic postures. The blue and purple plumes of the Gelonian helmets glowed in the sun. Their armor and bared swords caught the light. Zevaron halted, horrified and fascinated, as he recognized the man who had thrown the stone at the soldiers. He was one of a handful, ten at least, all of them bound, some bloodied, one or two struggling weakly.

That could be me.

Around them, people shifted uneasily, cutting off his view. Cries of protest arose here and there, as quickly choked off. The crowd wavered between action and horrified paralysis. A spark would set them off. All they needed, Zevaron thought, was a leader to bring them together.

"Stop them!" a woman whimpered. "Oh, someone must stop them!"

"Not now," said a familiar voice. It was Aharros, working his way through the assembly. "Hold fast, do nothing."

"He knew the risks," someone else said.

"We can't stand by—"

"Hold fast!" Aharros repeated. "Let them think they've won."

"We will not forget this day!" Sivran muttered, her voice harsh and very close. Zevaron turned to see her bent in conference with a cluster of onlookers. He made out a few phrases: "Harbor tonight," and "Pass the word."

"Aye," said the man who had spoken of risk. "They'll take no slaves from Gatacinne."

Slaves. Harbor.

A silence fell on the crowd. The sky pressed down on them and in an instant, broke open. An invisible storm cracked the air and a great cry arose from the people, mingled terror and grief.

Zevaron shuddered as if he himself had been struck, as if something bright and hot chilled his very soul.

Source of Blessings, look upon this thy child, he began the prayer of departure. The words came sluggishly to mind.

Zevaron could not remember the last time he had prayed, not since leaving Meklavar, not since the Gelon had come pounding up to the gates. His mother prayed, he knew. He had heard her murmured words while the fever had her. She had kept faith with the ways of their ancestors, for all the good it had done her. Yet, he admitted reluctantly, *something* had sustained them and brought them free from Meklavar and across the barrens. They might have died ten times over, and yet they had reached Gatacinne.

She had kept faith, and so would he. Tonight, he would go with the others to the harbor, would free Tsorreh and the other captives. Tonight, they would continue their journey together.

Chapter Eleven

"**I**T'S time."

A hand on Zevaron's shoulder shook him awake. Around him, the house lay dark but not silent. He heard voices, muted and urgent, then footsteps. Renneh bent over him, a slipper-shaped oil lamp in one hand. Her eyes glittered in the light.

He sat up. His body felt as brittle as if he had slept for a week. She offered him a beaker of watered wine and bread with olive paste. He ate what he could, took his sword, and went to join the others. They gathered outside, ten or twelve of them, mostly men. Sivran was among them, talking in hushed tones with a man wearing an Isarran breastplate, but her friend Harela was absent. Although Zevaron's was not the only sword among them, many were armed only with staves or axes.

A second Isarran officer, the one from the marketplace battle, outlined the plan, the routes they were to take, and the signal to begin the attack.

"Tonight, we will take our city back!" Although he spoke softly, his voice rumbled like muted thunder.

A shiver of excitement passed through the company. Zevaron felt it, too, the sense of standing on the brink of something momentous. Then he remembered feeling the same way before riding out to battle Thessar's army.

Tonight, Zevaron thought grimly, he and Tsorreh would turn their backs on Gatacinne and leave these people to their own destiny.

The party set off, moving quietly and swiftly along the back streets. Here and there, a light shone from a window or a torch over an arched entrance. After a short distance, the company broke into smaller groups to avoid notice. Sivran led Zevaron's party. His heart raced as his body prepared for the fight ahead. Around him, the others muttered prayers, urging each other on. The sword felt light in his grasp, eager.

Streets sped by. They passed the marketplace without incident, then swerved wide around the palace district. Once or twice, Sivran signaled for them to wait at an intersection, then sent them across singly or in pairs. Once, a barricade set up by Gelonian soldiers blocked their path; the mass of splintered wood was mostly likely the remains of a food stall. They had to go round it for several blocks and even then they went carefully to make no sound.

The detour cost them time. Zevaron could not stop thinking of all the things that could go wrong. The attack could start without them. It could go badly, even end in disaster with the Gelon slaughtering the prisoners or he did not know what else. Now that the plan was in action, now that he was on his way, things were both better and worse than while he'd waited. All he could do was to plunge ahead.

Still some distance from the harbor, they came out from an alley, barely more than a trench running along the back of two buildings, and onto a road that was broad enough for two carts to pass. It was lined with storage sheds and an inn or two. Lights clustered ahead.

Sivran called out, "There they are!"

In an instant, Zevaron saw torchlight flashing on metal and men struggling, surging ahead.

Screaming, "Gatacinne! Gatacinne!" Sivran brandished her staff and burst into a run. The others pounded after her,

Zevaron amongst them. As part of a rushing, hurling mass, he came up against a wall of Gelonian shields.

In an instant, Zevaron saw the pattern of the battle. The Gelonian line wasn't deep, but it didn't need to be. Nothing could get through. They fought in formation, even as they had at Meklavar, with a precise linking of shield and sword. Each man covered the weaker side of his comrade, giving no opening. The Isarrans broke on the shield wall like water against granite.

Zevaron slowed his pace and the others rushed past him. Sivran disappeared into the crush of bodies. With an effort, he held back, thinking only that if he could not get past that line of shields, what else might he do? Where could he use his strengths—his coordination and agility, his smaller size—to any purpose?

Get away! The thought came upon him suddenly, ambushed him.

The Gelon were advancing, pressing them back, and now Zevaron saw that the line had curved. The Gelon were using the blocked-off streets as a funnel.

More Isarrans went down. The air stank of fresh blood and battle fever. Zevaron drew it into his lungs, the reek of sweat and adrenaline. For a horrible instant, he was back in Meklavar, fighting at his father's side, watching the gates burn, watching as the Gelon kept coming and *coming*, and he could not stop them.

I will stop them now!

Fury came howling up from Zevaron's belly and burst from his throat, with screams that seared his lungs. Charging, he passed through the ranks of Isarrans. To his heightened sight, the Gelonian shields no longer formed an unbroken wall. In an instant, he saw the cracks, the way one sagged here, the gap as another soldier pivoted, the pulse and rhythm of their swords.

"Yahh!" Beside him, an Isarran thrust a spear at the nearest Gelon.

Zevaron sensed how the shield would raise and tilt even before it moved. He sidled, low to the ground, and swept outward with his sword. Though it was not balanced for circular strokes, he was able to compensate. The edge of his blade slipped below the shield and dug into flesh. It raked bone below one kneecap, then sliced through tendon.

The Gelon staggered, folding forward. Screaming, the Isarran thrust his spear even deeper. He pushed the Gelon backward and to the ground.

The Gelon's shield-side partner turned, momentarily unguarded. Zevaron, still low and balanced, reversed the arc of his sword, angling it upward. The Gelon turned away from the thrust, and the blade edge ripped across the back of one knee. With a shriek, he crumpled, shield flailing. To either side of the two fallen soldiers, Gelon struggled to reform their line.

With an inarticulate roar, the Isarran fighters surged into the gap, striking the newly opened flank. They pushed through the Gelonian line. Attacking from the side and rear, they forced the Gelon to fight singly. More Gelon fell or stumbled back in disarray. The breach opened still further.

Zevaron drove hard against the next Gelon. He no longer planned, he thrust and hacked his way through the enemy line. Above the clamor of the fighting, he heard shouted commands in Gelone. He could not make out their meaning above the yammering of his blood.

The Gelon fell back, but no longer in disorder. They were reforming, their officers gathering them together, using their strength and training. Renewed, they advanced on the Isarrans. Zevaron retreated a step before their shields, then another. Around him, the city's defenders fought on, but less effectively now. Zevaron twisted aside and barely escaped being caught between the advancing Gelon and the Isarrans who still pressed from behind, unaware that, in a few moments, they would all be trapped.

"Retreat!" Zevaron shouted, realizing a moment later that he'd used Meklavaran. What was the word in Isarran? He couldn't think. Things were happening too fast, and he was still half-crazed with fighting fever and the stench of blood.

"Back! We'll do no good here!" Sivran's voice rose high and shrill above the tumult.

An Isarran charged the Gelonian line with his axe. The soldiers met his attack smoothly, precisely, two men blocking and countering as if they were one. The Isarran collapsed, and Zevaron saw it was Aharros.

"Out of here!" Sivran shouted. "Back! Back! Save yourselves!"

Zevaron hesitated, for a stunned moment looking down at Aharros's face. In the uncertain torchlight, blood shone dark across the front of the Isarran's tunic. His eyes were open, the whites like silvered crescents.

Another debt to lay at Ar-Cinath's feet.

Zevaron turned and raced back the way they had come. Already, the Gelon were closing in. In a few minutes, there would be no escape. He stumbled — over what, he could not see, a fallen body by the feel of it. He got up and kept going.

Sivran was somewhere behind him, lingering to guard the rear, screaming out encouragement to her people. Zevaron swerved down the first side street he came to. The way felt familiar, shade upon shadow, the pavement falling away to dirt beneath his feet. He had run down a hundred alleys like this, or so it seemed.

He turned down one narrow lane and then another, and only when the sounds of the battle died down and he was left with the pounding of his heart in the cooling night, did he realize he was alone. He bent over, gulped air, braced himself with one arm, and cradled the sword with the other.

He was unhurt, except for yesterday's cut on his thigh, which burned from the salt of his sweat. That was of little consequence. He could still run and fight.

Fight? What utter folly!

Zevaron had no way of knowing if the Gelon had been warned of an attack on the harbor or if their readiness was part of the general occupation of the city. He did not care. Only one thing was clear: the only way Tsorreh would be rescued was if he did it himself. He would have to go alone, using stealth instead of a frontal assault. The Gelon were too strong to be overcome by force. If he ever went up against them directly, he would need all the hordes of Az-khantia at his back. For a moment, he envisioned himself riding down the streets of Aidon as the city burned, even as the King's Gates had burned, as the port of Gatacinne had burned—and in that vision he looked down, his heart filled with dark exhilaration, at the battered, lifeless body of Ar-Cinath-Gelon. Yearning shook him, fracturing the vision. He was momentarily stunned by the ferocity of his hatred and how readily it engulfed him. And why not? He had lost a father, a brother—and now a mother—to that monster!

He could make no specific plans until he knew where Tsorreh was kept, how guarded, whether against escape or rescue or both, and by what force. That knowledge must wait for daylight.

Zevaron found an alley, narrow and smelling of rotting cabbage and soured wash water, but well off the traveled streets. He searched out a relatively uncluttered spot and slumped down.

He debated what to do with the sword. He couldn't think of it as *his* sword, only a thing with which to hack and stab. Much as he disliked the idea of going unarmed where he would almost certainly encounter Gelon, he would attract their immediate attention if he entered the harbor area with such an obvious weapon. He buried it in a pile of re-fuse, marking the area in his memory. It might not be there when he returned, and if that was so, he hoped its new owner would be Isarran and put it to good use.

Zevaron sensed the change in the air as he neared the har-bor the following morning. Sea birds swooped overhead, and the breeze carried a salt tang. Underneath it, he caught the bitter taste of ashes. He passed the warehouse district, where he had seen wooden structures ablaze two nights be-fore. As he came into view of the water, he saw that the damage here had not been as extensive as he'd feared, given the size of the fire. A single row of buildings had taken the brunt. Their northern sides were gone, leaving blackened beams. He could not determine the condition of the piers and ships.

The smells of pitch and smoke combined with those of rotting fish and seaweed. The docks seethed with activity, far better organized than Zevaron expected so soon after the invasion and the fires. Isarran laborers passed through with carts of coiled ropes and bales of canvas, huge timbers, barrels, and oiled baskets. Gelonian guards questioned anyone entering the area.

Zevaron found a corner to slouch in, listening and watching. Workmen passed, as well as sailors. They spoke in a polyglot of tongues, phrases here and there in Gelone, in Isarran, even a version of the trade-dialect used in the steppes of Azkhantia. Hope rose in him, for his outland accent and poor command of Isarran might well pass without notice. Heartened, he moved closer to the piers.

The sea smell changed, no longer unpleasant but invigorating. The sound of the water as it surged against the pilings resonated through his bones.

The ships drew his gaze, some barely more than dugouts lashed together, others sleek and brightly painted, their furled sails of plain gray canvas or striped red and black. The thought came to him that he could be happy out there, lost in wave and sky, but he set it aside. He was Meklavaran-bred, a creature of rock, of mountains and ancient lore, trained since childhood to be the loyal shield of his brother. All that had changed when Ar-Cinath-Gelon sent his armies across the Sea of Desolation. Meklavar would never be the same, any more than Gatacinne would be the same. Zevaron shivered in the sudden realization that he might never see home again.

He spotted a warehouse guarded by two armed Gelon. One stood beside the door while the other watched over the approach. Although damaged by the fire, it looked sturdy enough but windowless. As the day heated up, the place would turn into an oven. There was only one door visible.

Zevaron watched while several Isarrans, fairly well-dressed, attempted to approach and were turned away. It seemed he was not the only one trying to discover the fate of a relative.

He nodded to one of the sailors, Isarran by his clothing, who was hurrying toward the ships. The man maneuvered a handcart that creaked under the weight of an enormous cask.

"A fair day to you, friend," Zevaron said in trade-dialect, trying to sound casual.

"Fair skies, but no fair day," the other responded, resting for a moment. Zevaron had never seen a man with skin so leathery, his eyes bright chips among the scars and pleats.

"I seek news—" Zevaron began.

"You and half the city. The bunch inside is bound for the *Wave Dancer*, that's to sail tomorrow. Come back in the morning and say your farewells then."

"Is there a woman, dark like me, foreign accent?"

"Nay, lad. But the *Silver Gull*, she set off yesterday. Marsus there, he helped load supplies, for the Gelon what commanded her were in a terrible hurry, as well he should be, bringing news of what they done here." The sailor turned his head and spat. "May every coin they took bring them a hundred year of curses."

Zevaron muttered agreement.

"Don't let them hear you say it, lad," the sailor said. "Keep your head down and your thoughts to the seas, that's the way." His narrowed eyes turned to the horizon of blue-gray water stretching north from the jumbled, half-burned pier. "There's things out there that even Gelon cannot stand against, and not all of them are men."

Zevaron supposed he meant the force of the sea, the storms and waves that might drown friend and enemy, good men and bad, without discrimination.

The man wheeled his cart past the Gelon at the base of the pier, who stopped him and inspected the cask. Zevaron turned away, lest he appear overly interested in the *Wave Dancer*. If Tsorreh were not among the palace captives and not here, then where was she? The sailor could be mistaken, after all. He might be going on rumor and hearsay. There was another possibility: she might have already sailed on the *Silver Gull*.

Marsus, who had helped load supplies on that ship, which one was he? A couple of discreet questions resulted in a sympathetic onlooker pointing out the laborer. Marsus had neither the aspect nor the coloring of an Isarran, although his skin was so weathered and seamed, and his sparse hair so streaked with white, that it was hard to tell he might have come from. Thin and stooped, he sagged under the load of two huge coiled ropes. Zevaron greeted him politely in trade-dialect, and was surprised when the man answered in pure Meklavaran.

"Is it true that Meklavar has fallen to the Ar-King?" Marsus asked.

"Though it breaks my heart to say so, it is indeed true." Zevaron kept his voice low. "I was there myself. I watched the King's Gates burn."

"Aye! That I should live to hear such a thing!" The old man rolled his eyes. "Come, we cannot stand here, or the jackals will get suspicious. Take this rope and walk with me."

Zevaron hoisted one of the rope coils over one shoulder. It was far heavier than it appeared. He did not have to pretend to trudge along under its weight. "What is a man of Meklavar doing here in Gatacinne?" he asked between breaths.

"I should as soon ask you, for you have not the look of a wanderer."

"My mother and I fled here after the Gelon took Meklavar."

Marsus whistled under his breath and glanced at Zevaron out of the corner of his eye. "So that was her."

"You have seen her? Here in port? On the *Silver Gull*?" Zevaron dropped the rope. The way was narrow, and he jostled a pair of sailors struggling to carry a tangle of netting in the opposite direction.

Zevaron resumed his burden, and soon they came out onto the pier, alongside a large ship and well past the Gelonian guards. "Please," he said, his voice suddenly choking. "Please, tell me."

"What's that gabble?" came a raucous shout from the deck of the ship. The words were a choppy mixture of Isarran and badly accented Gelone. "Marsus, you lazy oaf! Can't even carry your own load but must trick some half-grown boy? You there, gutter-rat!"

Zevaron looked up to see a hugely muscled giant of a man, dressed in outlandish colors, standing at the ship's railing. "We were just—"

"Off with you! Work to be done! No time for talk!"

Marsus reached out for Zevaron's rope. As it was passed it to him, he said, "Yesterday, the *Silver Gull*. Remember my name. Marsaneth."

Zevaron stared at the old man's retreating back. With the big sailor staring down at him, he dared not follow. The deck crawled with men. Some were obviously seamen, but others appeared to be shore laborers. He stepped closer, into the sailor's glare.

"I want a job."

"Get away!"

Zevaron took a breath. "I'll work for my passage—carrying, hauling, scrubbing. Anything you say!"

"Row like slave?" The sailor's mouth curved in a cruel line.

"If that's the work to be done," Zevaron insisted. "I must get to Gelon."

"Ha! We have crew enough, too many! Bring money, I take you as passenger."

Zevaron was about to continue bargaining when he glimpsed a Gelonian soldier heading their way, perhaps alerted by their conversation. He ducked his head in what he hoped was a properly naval gesture and hurried away.

Money? Where can I get money? He had no coins or anything to sell ... or did he?

Scarcely daring to pause long enough to think, lest the

audacity of what he was doing overwhelm him, Zevaron searched out the alley where he'd spent the night. The sword was still where he had left it. Now, in daylight, it did not look at all valuable, with its dried blood and nicked edge. He should have cleaned the blade better to prevent the blood from etching pits into the metal. Still, it must be worth something. These sailors might want weapons to use against pirates.

Trying to stay out of sight, he made his way to the poorest, most disreputable tavern he could find. He hoped it was the sort of place where a sword with obvious recent use and in none too good condition could be sold without questions. The room inside was dim and rank-smelling, with a row of ill-patched tables, one of which bore a line of pottery jugs and trays of coarse bread, dried figs, and olives. Flies buzzed around the food and the unwashed wooden bowls.

Zevaron slid onto one of the benches, rested the sword against his good leg, and tried to look calm as he surveyed the handful of men. All he had to do was display his wares and let them come to him. He wouldn't take the first offer. He'd just sit here until he got a sense of how much they would pay.

One of the drinkers, a thick-bodied, grizzled man who had been sitting at the far end of the bench, glanced pointedly at the sword and then at Zevaron's face. He heaved his bulk to his feet and began to walk toward the back.

Before Zevaron could follow, the door burst open and a handful of Gelonian soldiers rushed in. Swords drawn, they fanned out, pushing the tavern customers against the rough walls.

Zevaron grabbed the sword and leapt to his feet. A Gelon lunged for him, attacking with his own blade. Zevaron took a step backward, lost his balance, and came up flat against the wall. In a split instant, the Gelon parried, sending Zevaron's sword spinning free, and jabbed the tip of his sword against Zevaron's throat.

"What have we here?" A Gelon in the plumed helmet of an officer stepped into the middle of the room. A sword hung from his belt. He carried a short whip of the sort used on cattle.

"What do you want with us?" The bartender's voice quavered so badly, his Gelone was almost incomprehensible. "We've done nothing!"

"This," the Gelon picked up Zevaron's sword, "is not *nothing!* I see a nest of criminals."

"No! No! We are innocent men, quietly drinking!" the tavern host protested. "I know nothing of this, I tell you! Nothing!" The Gelon who held a sword to his belly shoved harder. The man squeaked, gulped hard, and swallowed any further protest.

"As I was saying," the Gelonian officer went on, "in the interests of peace and order in this city, we cannot allow such dangerous men to roam the streets. That one—" He pointed. "That one and, oh yes," he said, voice turning silky, "the boy with the sword. We can't very well have *him* roaming around, threatening innocent civilians. Bring them!"

The next moment, Zevaron was spun around, his wrists bound in front of him in rings of rough iron, and shoved out through the door. The brightness of the day stung his eyes. A central chain linked him to a dozen or so men. Some had freshly bleeding wounds or swollen lips. When he stumbled, one of the Gelon cuffed him on the back of the head, almost sending him to the ground. The shackles on his wrists pulled him up.

The officer emerged from the tavern. "Get them on board. And you prisoners! A word of advice, which is the last anyone will give you. Pray if it comforts you, but abandon all thought of ever seeing your families again. You are no longer free men. You are the property of Ar-Cinath-Gelon, the Scourge of Isarre and Protector of the One True Land, may-his-power-ever-increase, to do with as he wills. And what he wills is that you spend the rest of your miserable lives rowing his ships back to Gelon. Your lives can be short and painful, or shorter and filled with agony beyond your wildest nightmares. The choice is up to you. Or rather, up to me!"

The sound of the officer's laughter rang in Zevaron's ears. Let the fool boast, he told himself, if it would mean passage to Gelon. He could keep his head down, do as he was told, and work as hard as anyone. Once he was in Gelon, he would find a way to escape. His Gelone was good and—

"Stop!" the officer shouted, and the train of prisoners came to a shambling halt. "That one—the boy with the sword and the smirk on his face. As an introduction to your new lives, I will now provide you with a lesson."

One of the guards jerked on Zevaron's manacles, dragging him forward. The officer took up a position in front of him, tapping his shoulder with the coiled lash. Zevaron forced himself to stand still. He kept his eyes downcast and his expression bland. After all, the Gelon could not read his thoughts.

Thwack!

The Gelonian officer brought the lash across Zevaron's face. Shock took his breath away. Parallel lines of fire seared his cheeks. He hunched over and tried to cover his head.

Slash-thwack!

Backhanded, the lash struck again, this time striking Zevaron's arms and shoulders. How could this be happening? He'd offered no resistance—maybe they thought he was someone else.

Thwack! Thwack!

He felt the individual strips of knotted leather as they rained down on his back. His shirt afforded him little protection.

"S-stop!" he gasped. "This isn't f-f-fair! I've done nothing!"

"Silence!"

Zevaron tried to twist away, but the officer kicked his legs out from under him and kept hitting him, over and over again. Within a few moments, his back and shoulders had turned into a tangle of criss-crossed welts.

"The first law—"

Thwack! The blows fell and fell, too fast and heavy to

count. More cuts lacerated his buttocks and the backs of his thighs, but the main force was directed at his back. The Gelon struck with such a vicious frenzy, it was as if he were hitting every slave who'd ever been insolent, every person who'd ever offended him.

"—of the slave—"

Thwack!

"—is that I will do whatever I wish—"

Thwack!

"—whenever I wish—"

The hiss and slap of the lash filled Zevaron's ears. Tears spilled down his cheeks. He tried to scream, but he couldn't draw a breath.

"—simply because I can!"

Where the flails overlapped a previous blow, the pain was unbearable. Blow after relentless blow landed, sheets of white agony, cold and burning at the same time. His skin seemed to melt under the onslaught, so that each cut went deeper and deeper. Something hot and wet trickled down his sides. His back turned into a single pulsating mantle of fire.

He tried to crawl away, wriggling this way and that to protect his back from the worst, but he could get no traction on the wooden deck. Someone kicked his head. His vision whirled with the impact and the sickening, distant sound of laughter.

Then his throat opened and he screamed.

Chapter Twelve

ZEVARON drifted in and out of nightmares, of half-waking dreams of fire racing across his back, of the world dissolving beneath him as legend said would happen at the end of time, of voices weaving in and out in the distance, often in languages he could not understand. Of something cavernous opening up beneath him and a low deep thrumming, a sound below sound.

Gradually, the periods of consciousness lengthened. He became aware that he was lying on his belly on a rough wood surface, jammed between boxes or crates, he couldn't tell. From time to time, a someone knelt beside him, sponged his back and face, and spoke to him.

Zevaron wanted Tsorreh more than ever. But she was gone, sent off to Gelon and slavery or death. All because he had failed her. Whatever happened to her was his fault, his misjudgment, his weakness. The pain in his back and the pain in his heart ran together and wet his face, a storm of tears.

"There now, boy," came the man's voice, rasping and curiously familiar. "Wilt live. Wilt mend. Though it might have been a blessing otherwise."

Wilt live? Was he not dead already?

Uneasy sleep swallowed him up again.

He woke to the sound of a man's voice speaking Gelone, a voice he ought to know. Instinct kept him motionless, pretending sleep.

"So the cub has survived, after all. Who would have thought he had it in him? Perhaps there's more to this one than meets the eye. All right, I'll allow him a share of rations. Put him on the oars as soon as he's able. He'll work his way, all right. When we reach Verenzza, we'll see what else he's good for. Too bad about the scars. He's pretty enough to be a rich man's ducky."

Footsteps, this time leather over wood, receded into the constant rushing sound. Zevaron slitted his eyes open to glimpse a man in Gelonian clothing, wearing a bandolier of braided leather and a sword in its belted scabbard. He watched the man clamber up a ladder and disappear into a wash of brilliance. The world shifted rhythmically. Salt tang and the smell of fish hung heavy in the air.

"'M'on a boat?" Zevaron's throat ached as he formed the broken words.

"Ship, not boat. Drink this." A man, stout, with thinning white hair, helped Zevaron to sit up while carefully avoiding touching his back. "We're three days out of Gatacinne. That's three days closer to Gelon."

Zevaron took the dented metal cup in both hands. The movement was awkward because his wrists were encased in iron manacles, joined by links of chain. Thirst swept through him, and he gulped down the tepid brew. It was some kind of ale, bitter and well-watered. His throat felt as if he'd swallowed sand or screamed himself voiceless, but he had no memory of it. There was food as well, dry flatbread, salt-cured meat, and boiled millet. Zevaron ate it all, even though his stomach rebelled at the smell. The old sailor brought rags and a thick, stinking ointment for Zevaron's wounds. They were on the *Wave Dancer*, headed for Gelon with a load of slaves and booty, mostly from the governor's palace and the Gatacinne treasury.

"That Haran, he meant to make an example of you, d'you see?" the old sailor told Zevaron. "He'd be just as happy if you died. Then he could feed your body to the fishes. You belong to the Ar-King now that we're at sea, so he dare not. But he'll make you wish he had."

"Why—why are you helping me?" *Am I to be your ducky?*

In the half-light, Zevaron caught the glint of the old man's eyes. He saw a secret recognition, an affirmation that *the enemy of my enemy is my friend.* A chance to defy Gelon, to wrest one small victory from their hands.

With food in his belly, Zevaron felt strong enough to move about, as the old sailor urged. The cuts on his face were shallow and had already scabbed over. The hold was cramped and dank, and the constant rhythmic movement left him nauseous and disoriented, but he persisted as if his life depended on it.

Although every movement sent fresh spasms of pain through his back, Zevaron gritted his teeth and clambered onto the rowing deck. Here he joined the rows of oarsmen, one above and offset from the other. The *Wave Dancer* had previously been crewed by free men, so there were no bolts on the floor to attach the leg shackles. Instead, the Gelon knotted a loop around one ankle of each prisoner and anchored the ends to the bench brackets.

The old sailor left to attend to his own work. "Do your best, lad, keep your nose out of trouble, and the others will look after you."

When the ship moved easily under sail, the oarsmen rested. After a short time, however, the wind fell off, and Zevaron took his place with the others on the bench, who were mostly Isarran, newly made slaves. Some had sea experience.

Zevaron grasped the oar as he was shown and did his best. After a short time, the barely healed cuts on his back broke open and began bleeding. He felt wrung out, exhausted. He kept going, telling himself that the only way he was going to get strong enough was to push himself.

He was shaking all over when a halt was called. His hands were scoured and blistered, and the salt from his sweat set his back on fire. They rested, drank a measure of water, and returned to work. He wanted nothing more than to crawl back to the belly of the ship. He sat, staring at the oar and wondering where he was going to find the strength to pick it up.

Haran, the whip-bearing Gelon in charge, spotted him. Glaring, the Gelon made his way on the planking between the banks of rowers. Terror overcame exhaustion as Zevaron hastily grabbed his oar. He thought of that whip laid over his torn, oozing back. He ducked his head, throwing his weight into the next stroke. Out of the corner of his vision, he saw the Gelon come closer, the gleam in the man's eyes. The whip uncoiled.

Slash!

Zevaron flinched at the sound. His muscles tightened reflexively. His throat clenched, and bile rose to his mouth. No lash of fire bit into his flesh this time. He hauled on the oar, his heart pounding. The whip snapped again and a voice cried out, but not his. The Gelon cursed aloud in his own language, something about *lazy scum.*

Shivering in the close, hot air, Zevaron rowed.

Stroke ... stroke ...

He tried to settle into the rhythm, but the oars required coordination and the skill was slow in coming. As minutes built one on the other, his muscles ached and the palms of his hands burned and swelled. Each torment added to the next, until he felt he could bear no more, do no more. Then he would catch a glimpse of Haran and his whip, the gleam of those eyes, remember the sound of the lash laying open his skin, and he would row. And row.

As the eastern sky grew dark, the wind came up again. The oarsmen rested. Zevaron slumped over, hands hanging limp between his knees. As soon as he stopped rowing, the agony of salt on his open wounds sprang up again, assailing his back and his torn palms. The man with the water bucket came around, but Zevaron did not have the strength even to reach for the cup. The man who rowed in front of him held it to Zevaron's mouth and coaxed him to drink. No one protested the delay, although the other rowers must have been thirsty, too.

The water had been dosed with wine and something else, some restorative herb. It brought a small measure of renewed strength. Zevaron felt the ship gliding under him, and looked up with the others as someone on the top deck called out the approach of land.

The old Isarran sailor brought a pot of ointment and rags, and set about tending to the abraded hands of the new rowers. As he worked, he told them what was happening. They had made land, one of the islands in a chain called the Sea King's Necklace, where they would pass the night at anchor, rather than risk straying from their course. It was along the route to Verenzza, and the *Wave Dancer* had stopped here many times before. The island provided a sheltered cove, as well as inland springs and wild goats.

A shimmering twilight hung in the western sky as the ship dropped anchor. Zevaron heard the change in the waves and the shrill cries of the sea birds. Haran had taken ashore a party of seamen, the old Isarran among them, to hunt and to refill water casks.

The Gelon on watch untied the slaves, several at a time, so that they might move about and relieve themselves over the side of the ship. Zevaron could not imagine any of them having the strength to rebel. He certainly didn't. He patiently waited his turn for the ration of water and boiled grain that was his evening meal. When he started shivering, one of the sailors gave him an old shirt, stiff with sea salt.

Full dark had fallen by the time Zevaron was allowed to move about. He had been dozing fitfully in his place when the rower behind him touched his shoulder gently. Lantern in hand, a Gelon stood guard while another untied the ankle loop. The muscles of Zevaron's arms and back were so stiff, it hurt to breathe, but he forced himself to follow the others to the main deck.

"Something's going on," someone said. "There—on shore."

Zevaron was too tired to care.

Still, it was good to be on deck. The night was unusually clear, and the moon, barely past full, was so bright it cast faint shadows. Sounds carried above the gentle plash of the waves: shouting, the rustling noise of bodies moving through brush, then a scream. Zevaron saw the darker shadow of a small boat heading toward them.

"Ambush!" Haran's voice sliced through the night. "Pirates! Flee! Flee!"

"Sir? What about the others?" one of the Gelon onboard asked, glancing wild-eyed toward the shore. "Shouldn't we—"

"Never mind them!" The slave-master hauled himself up the knotted rope and onto the deck. He was alone. "All men to the oars! Row! Row for your lives!"

The other slaves began shuffling down, but Zevaron lingered. His knees threatened to give way beneath him, yet something came boiling up in him. His one friend on this ship, the old sailor, was still on the island. He could not endure being tied up once again, serving the man who had beaten him almost to death, abandoning yet another person who needed him. What he would do when the Gelon noticed his defiance, he could not imagine. He glanced at the railing, wondering if he could scramble over it, his hands still fettered, and somehow make it to shore.

The next moment, the pirates hurled themselves over the railing and onto the deck. Their approach had been silent, no more than the sound of the waves, but when they burst over the sides of the ship, they let out a unified, blood-curdling scream.

Haran and the handful of Gelon readied their swords and rushed to engage them. A heartbeat later, the deck swarmed with struggling bodies. The air rang with clashing steel.

Zevaron scuttled out of the way as men slashed and charged at one another. The other slaves had disappeared below, but he remained on deck, heedless of the risk. He knew nothing of these pirates, whether they might be his enemies as well, or *the friend who is the enemy of my enemy.*

The battle was quick and bloody. Within moments, all but one of the Gelon had jumped overboard or were lying inert on the deck. Only Haran remained. He'd lost his sword, but he struck out with his whip, again and again, keeping his opponents at a distance. The pirates backed off, as one of their number, a short lean man, his features unreadable in the uncertain light, stepped forward to engage Haran. The pirate had no sword, only a long knife, and as he and the Gelon circled each other, Zevaron noticed the slight drag of an injured leg.

Haran must have seen it, too, for he moved in, striking hard to close the gap between them. He kicked at the pirate's good leg. The pirate fell, rolling. Before he could scramble back up, Haran lunged for him. The sound of the lash cracked the air, followed by the sickening slap of knotted leather across flesh.

Zevaron's throat filled with bile. His muscles locked for an awful instant. Then his vision went preternaturally sharp. The moonlit deck, shadowed by railings, tackle, and beams, seemed as clear as a street in full day. The Gelon's back was to him, so that he looked full upon the face of the fallen pirate. He saw each one of the parallel cuts across cheek and brow, the eyes shock-wide, the angle of Haran's arm as he brought the whip around for another stroke.

Suddenly Zevaron could move. He took a deep step forward, pivoted slightly, and brought the edge of his heel down on the back of the Gelon's knee. The Gelon folded, twisted away. The blow aimed at the pirate went wild, but one of the flails of the lash caught Zevaron's upraised hand, cutting open a strip of skin.

Zevaron hardly felt the cut. With that same clarity of vision, he watched Haran surge to his feet.

"You!" Haran snarled, "I'll get you—"

Again the whip came up, flails spread wide as they began their terrible arc. They hissed, as if they were alive and hungering. Zevaron saw the familiar gleam in the Gelon's eyes,

the shape of his breastplate like that of the soldiers who had
cut down his father and then his brother, who had rampaged through the streets of Gatacinne.

No! howled through his mind, along the marrow of his
bones. *No more!*

Faster than thought, Zevaron darted forward. He
matched his movement to the arc of the blow. Although he
was still too far to reach the stock of the whip, the heavy
braided leather at the base smacked against his manacled
hands. This time, the flails did not bite. They slid into his
grasp. His fingers closed around them. Still moving along
his own circular path, he stepped back and, using his momentum, yanked hard.

Haran, holding tight to the stock of the whip, was caught
unawares. He lurched forward, his balance broken. Zevaron
shifted his weight and struck out with the ball of one foot.
He missed his target, catching the Gelon high on the thigh.
By chance or unexpected luck, he hit a nerve and Haran's
leg went out from under him.

Fire exploded behind Zevaron's eyes.

Screaming curses in Meklavaran, he jumped on the
fallen Gelon, kicking and pummeling. His blows landed
with satisfying impact, one after another, some aimed at
groin or knee or upward under the curving breastplate
toward the heart, but most were just anywhere he could
reach.

Haran tried at first to defend himself. There was no room
to swing the whip, and after the first few resounding kicks
from Zevaron, he curled into a ball, knees drawn up to protect his belly, arms covering his head.

With each kick, the rage inside Zevaron surged higher.
His breath sizzled through his lungs. Every nerve and fiber
shrieked. Roaring filled his skull, incinerating thought.

The Gelon's cries turned to frenzied yelps, no longer human to Zevaron's ears, but those of a beast. Zevaron saw his
prey twist and scrabble in a frantic attempt at escape. He
followed, closing tighter with each round.

Someone shouted at him, syllables that held no meaning.

He bent and grabbed the beast's sweat-damp hair in both hands and hauled the body upright.

"Sur—surrender!" the beast mewled.

Surrender?

There could be no surrender, only revenge. Only justice. Only death.

A sword was in his hands, the Gelon's sword, although Zevaron had no memory of picking it up. The beast twisted away, crawling on its belly. Shuddering with adrenaline and emotion, Zevaron placed the tip of the sword against the beast's neck.

"Enough." It was a different voice this time, not that of the beast, but human, both gentle and harsh. A hand closed around Zevaron's, fingers covering his on the hilt of the sword.

"Enough, now. He has yielded, this one." Something in the voice, an undertone of quiet authority, pierced the wall of flames in Zevaron's mind.

Zevaron staggered backward and other man slipped the sword from his failing grasp. He felt as if he had been encased in fire, in ice, a brittle shell now falling away into shards.

Two men rushed on to the deck, one carrying a lantern. The other strained under the weight of a small, ornately decorative chest. They halted, eyes widened. The one with the lantern drew a wickedly curved knife from his belt.

"There's no need for Shark's Tooth here. We have another guest," Zevaron's pirate nodded toward Haran with a suggestion of drollness, "—one whose family will be grateful to ensure his safe return."

"And this one?" the pirate pointed his knife at Zevaron.

"I am no friend to Gelon," Zevaron said in the same trade-dialect.

"No," the pirate chief replied, eyes thoughtful. "But the question remains, are you *my* friend?"

If you will take me to Gelon—

Zevaron bit off the thought. Gelon would be the last place these lawless men would go. Even if Haran and the other officers were ransomed, an exiled Meklavaran never would be. The only fate he would meet at the hands of the Gelon was a speedy execution.

Weariness washed over him. He leaned against the railing. The chain joining his wrists made a hollow clanking sound.

One of the pirates had set about removing the armor from the half-conscious Haran, tying him up, and hauling him into the captain's cabin. Zevaron waited at the door, as the lantern filled the low-ceilinged space with honeyed light. The other pirate placed the chest at the feet of his leader.

". . . no ordinary ship," Zevaron overheard. "Treasure from Gatacinne . . ."

"On an Isarran ship, under Gelonian command?" The chief rubbed his stubbled chin. From his seat on the built-in bed, he leaned forward to touch the chest.

"Gatacinne has fallen to the Ar-King," Zevaron mumbled.

"Ah, yes, that explains much. Let's take a look." He lifted the lid. "By the leviathan's pearly bones!"

Stung by the frank astonishment in that otherwise sardonic voice, Zevaron crept closer. The chest itself was silver, cunningly set with precious gems. It was about as long as his forearm, lined with crimson Denariyan silk, and filled almost to overflowing with coins, gold and silver, pearls, rings and torques, and arm-bands set with emeralds and rubies, most of exquisite Isarran artistry.

"What is a slaver ship doing with this?" one of the pirates exclaimed.

"Loot, both the chest and the slaves," the chief said.

"They took the governor's palace," Zevaron said. "May their souls never find rest." Was it three days ago? Four? Six? He couldn't remember.

"You, lad," the chief fixed Zevaron with that dark, uncompromising gaze. "What is your name?"

"Zevaron."

"A Meklavaran name, if I'm not mistaken. I am Chalil, that is *little horse of the sea*."

Zevaron nodded, recognizing the name and accent as Denariyan.

"And yon fellows are Omri and Tamir. Whatever lies the Gelon may have told you, we men of the sea pay our debts. I owe you twice if you count leaving that piece of slime alive for us to ransom. What would you have of me?" Chalil sat back, inviting Zevaron to select a piece of the treasure.

Zevaron lifted his manacled hands. "What good is silver to a slave?"

"Ah, yes. That goes without saying. Omri, find the keys."

"And the others?" Zevaron said. "They would do Gelon far more harm if they take back Gatacinne than their price would do you good. You will have the treasure and more, once Gelon pays for the return of its donkey."

For a long moment, Chalil stared at him, and Zevaron wondered if he had made a terrible blunder, if he had asked for something so outrageous, so offensive, as to sacrifice all the pirate's good will.

"I see you have no need for silver, for you carry it in your tongue!" Chalil replied. "The sea holds the only true freedom, for possessions that can turn on you are the worst kind of enslavement. Now we have two ships but loyal crew for only one, an excess of riches. Ransom messages must be sent and men exchanged for gold. We will discuss the fate of your friends in the light of morning."

Omri returned with a set of keys and a wide, gap-toothed grin. When Zevaron's hands were freed, Chalil said, "Now come, choose something. Debt weighs heavy on a sea horse."

A coin or two would satisfy the pirate leader's honor and might buy passage to Gelon, Zevaron thought. That was, if he could find a ship to take him there. He bent over the chest and reached out for the nearest large silver coin. Something dark, like a piece of ragged silk, lay beneath an ornate armband. He grasped it in trembling fingers and knew the instant he touched it that it was a braid of human hair.

Black, like strands of midnight. Black, like Tsorreh's hair.

He held it up. A token shaped like a little silver horse gleamed in the lantern's golden light.

Arandel.

A voice he scarcely recognized as his own said, "Where did this come from? How did it get here?"

Zevaron hurled himself across the room. He grabbed the front of Haran's tunic and pulled him up to sitting. The Gelon moaned, his eyes crescents of white. Zevaron slapped him once, twice, stopping only when he saw the return of awareness.

He shoved the token, its cord still wound in the severed braid, in the face of the Gelon. "Where did you get this?"

"Leave him be," Chalil said. "He knows nothing."

Zevaron could not tear his eyes from the curve of Haran's lip, hovering between a sneer and something darker. "He knows! He will tell me or I will rip it from him, bit by bit. An ear, then an eye—"

The Gelon burst into a fit of coughing. "I'll tell you, for all the joy it will bring you. Belonged to a lady, did it? Someone you cared about? Your ducky?" He turned his head and spat, a wad of bloody froth. "Took it from her dead body, I did."

Crimson jagged across Zevaron's vision. He locked his hands around the Gelon's neck. His fingers dug into flesh. He felt the springy tension of cartilage flex and give way.

The Gelon went limp in his grip, but Zevaron kept pressing, as if he could force death itself to give back his mother's life. Behind him, someone shouted orders. He could not understand the words through the rushing, pounding clamor in his skull.

Hands closed around his shoulders and pried his fingers open. He fought, but they pulled him back, two or three of them, he couldn't tell. The Gelon wheezed and gasped.

Through waves of shuddering nausea, Zevaron heard Chalil say, "Get him out of here," and it took him a long moment to realize the pirate leader meant Haran, not himself.

"Boy." Chalil came up from behind and put his hand on Zevaron's back.

The explosion of agony sent Zevaron reeling to his knees as rough, salt-encrusted cloth rubbed against weeping sores. His vision went white. He could not breathe. Gentle hands lifted the shirt over his head, pulling away new-formed scabs.

Chalil swore in gutter Denariyan, words so foul-sounding Zevaron could only guess their meaning. "He did this to you?"

Zevaron could only nod mutely. His back was nothing. It would heal, he would live with it. But Tsorreh—

O Holy One, she is gone . . . dead . . .

"I'll kill him," Zevaron sobbed. "I'll *kill him!*"

The pirates dragged the Gelon away. Chalil left Zevaron in the little cabin with Omri as guard and nurse.

Zevaron curled on his side on the built-in bed, too numb to weep and too wrought up to do anything else. He wavered in and out of darkness, shivering one moment and sweating the next. Eventually, light crept across the sky and in through the open porthole.

After a time, the old sailor took Omri's place, sponging the crusted sores on his back and murmuring to him. Zevaron slept then, or thought he must have, but could not remember anything beyond waking dreams, dreams of fire and blizzards, of mountains crashing down upon him, of men burning like torches in the night. Of Tsorreh.

Always of Tsorreh, her strong arms about him, her voice singing him a lullaby or reading to him from the *Shirah Kohav*. Tsorreh lending Shorrenon her courage and calm during that last terrible fight, her lightning reflexes in getting them out of the palace, her determination to keep going, through the caverns, across the sands.

I would never have made it this far without her.

And now what did it matter? An exile in Isarre, a slave in Gelon, a captive of the pirates, his life was over, useless.

I should be dead instead of her.

Tears spilled down his cheeks. His body rocked with sobs, and yet no sound came from his mouth.

"Boy." Chalil again, his voice rough with concern. "Zevaron. You are free now. Your back will heal."

Zevaron heard the question behind the kindness. It was not for the beating and the lingering pain that he wept. "She is dead. She is dead . . ."

"The woman of the braid? Someone you knew?" Chalil sat on the edge of the narrow bed. The mattress, coarse cloth over straw, shifted under his weight.

Zevaron nodded. "My mother."

"Ah."

"He killed her, he must have. You heard him. Why did you stop me?"

"Aside from his value at ransom, you mean? Zevaron— I can't keep saying that name, it's too long, my tongue will take sea sickness. Zev, then. Zev, it is the nature of such a man to be cruel, even when there is no profit in it for him. He saw that you knew the woman and therefore he aimed his words like a spear at your heart. To wound you in any way he could."

"Why would he lie to me?"

"Why would he tell the truth? Is he an honorable man?"

A pirate speaks of honor?

"As you would have it, then," Chalil said with a sigh. "Meanwhile, what are we to do with you? The Gelon is safely ashore with the other hostages, and I cannot let you go wandering about the ship. Not unless you have sworn in as my crew, subject to my command. What do you say to that?"

Zevaron's thoughts went spinning. "You are asking me to become a pirate?"

"What other choice have you? You cannot go back to Gatacinne, which is still in Gelonian hands, or on to Gelon itself. One look at your back and they will take you for an escaped slave and kill you, or worse. Listen to me, young Zev. The world is wide and the sea is filled with gifts. What have you to lose?"

Indeed, Zevaron thought, what had he to lose? At least, this might give him the chance to take vengeance upon a few more Gelon.

Someday, someday, he would return, and then he would make Gelon pay.

PART III:

Tsorreh's Test

Chapter Thirteen

DIZZY and disoriented, Tsorreh came to herself. The world around her shifted, rising and then plummeting. Her stomach lurched, sending acid up the back of her throat. She tried to sit upright and found herself netted down in a bed that occupied most of one wall in a small chamber. An unlit lantern swung from the low beamed ceiling, and the only other furnishings were several chests strapped to the walls. A slit of a window revealed a gray, overcast sky. The air was filled with the smells of brine, fish, and pitch.

I'm onboard a ship, headed for Gelon.

Tsorreh fumbled with the netting. Her hands were stiff, and her vision slid in and out of focus. She had to stop when the rocking motion grew worse. Praying she would not vomit, she forced herself to breathe slowly. Her muscles felt as weak and watery as if she'd lain abed for a month with a fever, yet she had no memory of illness. She wondered if she had been drugged.

Before she could free herself, a door on the opposite side opened and a man entered. He walked easily and confidently across the tilting floor. Even in the subdued light of the cabin, his clothing blazed in shades of crimson, green, and yellow, an open-necked shirt, breeches, and a wide sash into which were tucked at least two knives that she could see.

"Now you're awake, my lady, let me help you with that." He spoke Gelone with an accent, but his fingers were gentle as he slipped the netting free from the hooks along the side of the bed.

"Thank you." She sat up. Another spasm knotted her stomach, and she looked around wildly. Just as she lost control, the seaman retrieved a bucket from an unseen niche. He steadied her with one hand as she retched. There wasn't much to bring up, just a little foul-tasting liquid. Her throat burned, her eyes watered, and the muscles of her belly cramped.

The seaman slipped away and returned a moment later with a towel and a cup of tepid water. She rinsed her mouth. The water tasted delicious.

"Captain!" A crashing knock sounded, the door swung open, and a hugely muscular man, bald and naked to the waist, his skin a labyrinth of blue tattoos, stuck his head inside. Carefully not looking at Tsorreh, he rattled off a string of phrases, nautical terms, she supposed. The first seaman, presumably the captain of the vessel, hurried away.

Tsorreh used a little of the water to wash her face and hands. Feeling refreshed, she tried standing up. She discovered several cabinets built into the cabin walls, filled with an assortment of clothing, maps, and small boxed instruments, nautical and medical, rolled maps, even a collection of books. She recognized a history of the Gelon Empire, the *Odes* of the Empress Cilician, and a volume in the spiky calligraphy of Denariya.

An interesting collection for a seafaring man, she thought, smiling to herself.

This cabin must belong to the captain. Probably, she was the only woman aboard, and this was the best accommodation that could be devised for her, especially on short notice. The captain clearly wasn't Gelon, nor were his possessions those of a military man. She'd been put on a merchant vessel, most likely as part of a cargo of treasure looted from Gatacinne.

With each passing moment, Tsorreh's nausea and weakness lessened. Although she had never been on an ocean-going vessel before, she had heard of the sickness that afflicted many. It was supposed to take days for the worst symptoms to pass. Strange, how she had recovered so quickly. One hand moved unconsciously to her chest, fingertips brushing her gown above her breastbone. A pulse of warmth answered her.

The te-alvar *protects its own.*

She lowered herself to the bed and tried to focus her awareness on the gem, to reconcile what she had been taught with what she had seen and felt in these last tempestuous days.

The petal gem held impressions of people and battles long ago, that much was clear. But it was more than a repository of history. That priest—the one with the scorpion image on his headband—had been searching for something hidden, something secret. She shuddered, remembering the pressure of his mind against hers. A power had flowed through him, but the *te-alvar* had shielded itself, had shielded *her.* If the stone had not spoken for her, giving the priest the very answer he would accept without questioning further, then he would have pushed harder and deeper. She very much did not want to think what would have happened then.

Not that I'm safe now.

Yet her situation was not so bad. She was in no imminent danger, and much could happen between now and her destination. There might be a chance, many chances, to act.

There was a hesitant knocking at the cabin door.

"What now?" Tsorreh muttered. When the tapping repeated, she called, "Come in!"

The door opened, revealing a sliver of bright day. One of the young women who'd attended the wife of the Gatacinne governor slipped inside. It was Menelaia, the one who'd played the harp, and she was sobbing. Tsorreh guided her to the bed and made her sit down. There was no more water in the cup, but the towel was still damp. She wiped the girl's face and slowly drew out her story.

Menelaia had been taken onboard in the night with a handful of palace women and some men, too. She had been roughly handled but not otherwise molested, and had been told she was now a slave. If she failed to please her new masters, she would be thrown overboard. She had no answers when Tsorreh asked about their specific destination or the whereabouts of the priest, but she had noticed a number of armed Gelonian soldiers. None of the male captives bore any resemblance to Zevaron.

"I'm to attend you, lady." She gave Tsorreh a look of desperate, tear-drenched appeal.

"And so you shall, once you are feeling better," Tsorreh said. "Do you think you could eat a little or drink something?"

Menelaia shook her head. The ship gave another lurch. To Tsorreh, it felt like a gentle shift, like the rocking of a cradle. The girl moaned and clutched her stomach.

"I'll get you some water." Tsorreh found the door unlocked and went outside. The ship moved beneath her, and although she found the sensation pleasant, she had to grab for the nearest rail for balance. Beyond stretched an immensity of blue-gray water rising to a hazy boundary with the sky.

The only vessels she'd ever seen were much smaller, river-going craft. From her position, she made out a long row of oars extending from openings along the side and moving with a strong, even rhythm. The cabin behind her was the only structure above two half-decks, fore and aft. The hold between them was open, with benches for the oarsmen along either side. Wind ruffled the large square sail.

Everywhere, Tsorreh saw structures and items she had no names for. Men, sailors by their garb, hurried about their work, doing things with the ropes of the sail. One group she

did recognize, however—a Gelonian officer and a handful
of guards, some of them looking just as sick as she had first
felt. The officer turned toward her and she saw his face. He
was the one who had led the raid on the hiding place in
Gatacinne, the one who had taken her prisoner. Seeing her,
he scowled.

"Who let *her* loose? Why isn't she shackled?" He nodded to the nearest of his men. "Do it immediately."

The captain appeared from behind an open hatch and
climbed nimbly on deck. "See here, sergeant. This is my ship
and no one gives orders but me."

"You forget yourself, Bynthos. You sail at the pleasure
and command of the Ar-King."

An easy smile widened the captain's face, although his
eyes did not soften. "So I do, and so do you. If you wish to
sail this ship yourself, I'll not hinder you." He turned to the
crew on deck. "Up oars! Cease all work! Lord Mortan, the
Silver Gull is yours. Her men await your orders."

The officer's face turned a paler shade of green. "I am a
soldier, not a sea-rat, and I am responsible for escorting the
Meklavaran Queen to the Celestial Court at Aidon. I cannot permit her to go scampering about the deck."

"Gods, man, where do you think she can go in the middle
of the ocean?"

Mortan glared at the captain. "Have it your way, then,
and on your head be it if she comes to any harm."

"As you wish," Bynthos replied. A stride or two took him
to Tsorreh's side. "This way, my lady. You will be more comfortable if you stay inside."

Tsorreh allowed herself to be guided back to the cabin.
"I was looking for water for the girl."

"Not got her sea-legs yet, the poor thing?" Bynthos
opened the door and stepped back for Tsorreh to enter.

"'Sea'—oh, I see. No, she doesn't."

Menelaia lay as Tsorreh had left her, curled into a ball,
moaning with each rocking motion of the ship.

"I'll bring more water and have Cook make up a brew
that might help." The Captain moved to close the door.

"You are very kind," Tsorreh began, and then panic rose in her at the prospect of being caged in this narrow space, isolated except for a helpless, miserable girl, unable to see what was going on around her. Most of all, unable to do anything, cut off from even the solace of her books.

"If you please, sir," she stammered, "I think it would ease her mind if I could read to her. May I borrow one of your books?"

Bynthos paused, his face a silhouette of shadows against the sky. She read the surprise in his posture. Then he recovered himself and said, "Help yourself."

Having a task gave Tsorreh something to focus on. At first, her hands shook too badly to manage the flint and tinder to light the lantern, but in the end she managed. Its small cone of light added to what came through the slit window.

She paused over the Gelonian history, thinking that even if Menelaia could not pay proper attention, she herself might learn something of value. It could not hurt to learn more about her captors. But her heart hungered for something more than the chronicles of kings and generals.

Her eyes went to Cilician's *Odes*. They were a series of poems, a cycle that began in anguish and homesickness, flowered into extraordinary eroticism, and concluded in grief, written over the course of a decade by a young woman who had been given in marriage to an Ar-King a century or more ago. Eavonen had said they were some of the most beautiful love poems in all of literature.

She had not gone more than a line or two down the first page when Bynthos returned. She sensed him standing there, just outside the door, his shoulder against the salt-weathered wood, heard the sudden catch and softening of his breath as she read on:

> *I hear the song of the flute.*
> *The flower blooms, although it is not spring.*
> *The sky roars and lightning flashes.*
> *Rain falls.*
> *Waves arise in my heart.*

The shadows filled with light. Across the chasm of a century, the dead woman poured out her longing, a perfume just beyond the senses.

Tsorreh paused at the end of the verse. While she read, Bynthos had slipped into the room. On the bed, the girl Menelaia lay quiet.

"I—" the captain's voice sounded rusty. "I had no idea that was here."

Tsorreh looked up, startled. Surely, such a volume was to be treasured and savored. Could it be that he had never opened its covers? Or perhaps, she thought in a flash of understanding, a man such as himself had little time for poetry.

"Now you know," she said gently, folding the book and holding it out to him. "And you can read those words for yourself whenever you desire."

He crossed the narrow space and took the book from her hands, running his fingers over the worn leather covers. "No," he said, "I can't."

Would he lose the respect of his crew if it were known that he indulged in poetry? Tsorreh had heard of such attitudes, but never believed them possible.

"None of your men need ever know," she said.

"No, it's not that."

For a long moment, she stared at him, the strong features softened by the lantern light, the rough skin, the bright eyes. Then, setting down the metal pitcher of water, he was gone.

It came to her that he had just entrusted her with a secret, like the long-hidden chamber of his heart—not only that he could not read, but also how much he longed to.

After a time, Menelaia woke, and the two women sat together while the ship pitched and rolled. One of the Gelonian soldiers brought bread and olives and a small stoppered bottle of resinated wine. Tsorreh ate with an appetite and then went back to tending the frightened girl.

Her thoughts went to the battle at Gatacinne and all that

had come before. She prayed for Zevaron's safety, but the old fervor, the terror of any harm coming to him, had lifted somewhat from her heart. The sensation of warmth and steadiness from the *te-alvar* faded with the passing hours but never entirely departed.

Zevaron might be young, but he was strong, well-trained, and resourceful. He had kept both of them going during the flight across the desert wastes. Tsorreh wondered what he would do next, whether he would return home or stay in Isarre to fight the Gelon there. She had no influence over his decision. There was nothing she could do to help him, nor he, her.

He was alive—she would surely have sensed his death. Now their lives followed different paths. He would take what she had already given him and do with it what he willed.

As for her own future, she felt surprisingly tranquil. For the moment, she was safe and well. As royal hostage or spoil of war, she clearly had value to her captors. That might change once they arrived in Gelon, but she could not summon any amount of worry. The most frightening thing to happen to her since leaving Meklavar was the interview with the priest, and the *te-alvar* had protected her. She was its guardian, its safe-keeper, and it was hers.

By the shifting of light through the slit window, it was toward late afternoon when Tsorreh detected a change in the motion of the ship. They anchored at a little island, forested hills sloping down to a crescent of white sand. Most of the crew went ashore, where their fires glowed against the falling night. Tsorreh caught snatches of their songs through the surge of the waves, for she and Menelaia had remained onboard, guarded by a pair of grim-faced Gelon. Except for a brief foray on deck, enough to see the encampment on the beach and smell the salt air, they were confined to the cabin.

After a time, Bynthos entered, bringing a meal of the same flatbread, olives, and resin-wine, along with dried fish. When Tsorreh asked, he explained that the captain always remained with his ship. Even here, she wondered, with the sea so calm, the night so peaceful?

After lighting the lantern, he unfolded a table, a slab of oiled wood hinged into one of the walls, and brought up a pair of stools. At Tsorreh's command, Menelaia sat on the bed. Bynthos listened gravely as Tsorreh recited the customary blessing for meals.

They ate in silence. The air grew thick with unasked questions. Menelaia, having finished her meal, curled up and soon fell asleep.

"I find it comforting to read aloud," Tsorreh said. "Would it disturb you?"

Deftly she moved so that the pages fell open to both of them. She began to read, slowly and clearly, tracing each word with her fingertip,

> *O that I might see my country once again.*
> *There wisdom fills her pitcher from the well,*
> *Yet needs no rope to draw the water.*
> *There no clouds cover the sky,*
> *Yet rain falls in gentle waves.*
> *Let us not sit on the doorstep,*
> *Let us bathe in the holy rain!*

At first Bynthos followed her finger surreptitiously, but within a few phrases, he leaned forward. His gaze locked upon the page, his whole body intent.

"Can you see this letter here?" Tsorreh said softly. "It begins both 'rain' and 'rope.' When I was a child, I always thought it looked like a spiked head of grain. In Meklavar, we call it *ran*, but the Gelonian word is *reth*."

"*Reth*."

"Yes, like the ancient word for barley. They each have names, these letters, and once you know the sounds, they tell you the words."

"*Reth*," he repeated. Then, bending once more over the book, he pointed. "It is here, and here . . . and here. Show me another."

Smiling to herself, Tsorreh went on. "Here is *lam*, like the neck of a camel. And here, this little mark that is almost no mark at all, it is *aph*, the indrawn breath before you speak."

In Tsorreh's memory, her mother held her close as they traced the letters together. Even so had she herself read to Zevaron. Candles had burned in a many-branched holder, their light sweet and warm. Beyond the walls of the house, night had lain like a velvet cloak over the city. A cat mewed plaintively, bells jingling from its collar. Someone played a lullaby on a wooden flute.

"Here is the first breath, and the last, and all between," Tsorreh's mother had said. *"Here is love and hatred, folly and understanding. Here is the story of Khored, and how his magic saved the world, that we might remember and honor him."*

They went on in this manner for some hours, letter by letter, until the lantern burned low. Menelaia roused, the reading lesson came to an end, and Bynthos took his leave. Menelaia made a pallet for herself on the floor from a folded blanket they discovered in the compartment beneath the bed. Tsorreh extinguished the lantern and went to sleep.

The next day passed very much as before, a day of confinement in the tiny cabin, of monotony broken only by the arrival of food and water, the unending rise and fall of the ship, the smells of salt air and fish. Again the ship came into harbor as the sun fell. When Bynthos brought dinner, Tsorreh asked him why they spent each night near land and not at sea.

"It is the custom, whenever possible, and Lord Mortan has ordered it. Perhaps he believes that the monsters who roam these waters attack at night. More likely, it is to keep us out of the way of pirates. And then, it is more difficult to navigate out of sight of land when the stars cannot be seen."

Tsorreh mulled over the implications of his words. Lawless seamen, many of them Denariyan, were said to ply these waters. She had not considered the difficulty of staying on course when surrounded by waves in every direction.

The strange sense of disorientation returned, along with the image of floating on a vast sea. She felt adrift, even here, even at anchor.

Monsters. Something beyond the motion of the ship that made her ill. She imagined lightless depths and strange beasts rising from them, moving slowly, inexorably. The room slipped sideways.

She stood on a cliff above an ocean. Waves rose at her call . . . no, not her call but that of the great king. From deep in the shadows beneath the waters, power stirred and took form: a great head, eyes huge and pale as pearls, mane like tangled seaweed, horns of polished coral.

"My lady?" Menelaia stepped to her side, touched her arm. "Is anything amiss?"

Tsorreh blinked. The cabin, now familiar in the light of the lantern, filled her vision, blotting out the image of the sea beast.

"I'm quite well," she said quickly. "I was just thinking." She turned to Bynthos. "Captain, you sound as if you do not share these fears."

"I'm not Gelon-born, for all that I now sail under her command," Bynthos said. "I'd just brought a cargo into Gatacinne when the invasion began. With Gelon barricading the harbor, the only way any of us leaves is at their bidding. One cargo's as good as another, it's said."

"What cargo?" Tsorreh asked.

"Loot from the city, whatever they could pile together as prizes for the Ar-King." He did not add that she herself was booty.

"Where are we bound?"

"First to Verenzza and then across to the mainland. That's as far as the *Silver Gull* can sail. You'll go upriver by barge to Aidon."

"Have you been there? What is it like? What sort of man is the Ar-King?" *Besides an arrogant, power-hungry tyrant?*

"Aye, I've visited Aidon once or twice," Bynthos said. "A marvel it is, that city, with wide streets and gardens everywhere, and palaces of white marble shining in the sun. I've heard it called the Crossroads of the World, the Pearl of Gelon."

Tsorreh found herself smiling. This sea captain was a poet! After that, they walked on deck together and he showed her the various parts of the ship. They watched the waves, slightly luminescent along the curve of beach and the black line of the headland. Points of light glimmered through a rent in the clouds. On the following nights, Tsorreh continued the reading lessons, this time from the Gelonian histories.

As Bynthos had said, they came eventually to Verenzza, formed from massive jagged peaks that thrust upward from the ocean. The harbor was deep, its wharves built out from the narrow rocky beaches. Tsorreh had learned from her reading that the island was an important center for Gelonian naval power. The attack on Gatacinne had been launched from here. Even as she had sensed a deep, brooding intelligence below the waves, so now something reached out to her from the dark volcanic peaks, a wordless elemental power, long slumbering, beyond human comprehension. She felt it even in the confines of the cabin.

At Verenzza, they rested for a few days while the ship was reprovisioned. Tsorreh glimpsed wharves of weather-bleached wood, ships with square or triangular sails, white sails, red sails, black sails, prows carved with dragons and sea beasts, all crowded in between smaller vessels, boats laden with fish and sponges, and coracles paddled by half-naked boys who shouted and held out strings of shells for sale. The smells of fish and salt water, of refuse and seaweed, filled the air. Seabirds wheeled overhead, emitting shrill cries. Once or twice, Tsorreh caught sight of a sleek-headed creature keeping pace with their boat. It was not a dolphin, but she could not think what else it might be.

She and Menelaia were not allowed to go ashore, but sufficient fresh water was brought onboard for them to wash themselves and their clothes. By this time, Menelaia had recovered from her seasickness. She took charge, hanging the clean garments from ropes strung across the deck.

To Tsorreh, even the abbreviated bath in a small tub of cold water with a knob of strong smelling soap was a relief. The soap stung her skin as she scrubbed away the grime. She lathered her hair three times and used the last of the water to rinse it. At home, she remembered with a pang, the last rinse would have been scented with chamomile or citron to leave her hair silky and sweet-smelling. Since there was no oil, either, her hair dried rough and knotted. She made no sound as Menelaia yanked the bone comb through her tangles.

They set to sea again. At night, Tsorreh emerged from the cabin to walk the *Silver Gull's* deck. The moon, almost full, swept the sky with glimmering light. Brightness reflected off the waves. She could see her own wavering shadow on the deck. The ship stood at sea-anchor, moving rhythmically with the gentle surge and pull of the water. The *te-alvar* in her breast had gone quiescent, as if the peace of the evening had laid all past sorrow and present fears to rest.

In two or three days, they would reach the mainland and she must bid farewell to the *Silver Gull.* For the journey to Aidon by barge, Mortan would undoubtedly order her chained. Bynthos came to stand beside her. He held something in his hands. He waited until she had noticed him, and then held out a book. She held it up to the moonlight to read the title.

It was the *Odes.* A lump rose in her throat for all the things that meant, for the beauty of the words, the solace of their sharing, the heartache that the author had penned into those words.

She shook her head. "I cannot accept this. It is too rich a gift."

"I will find another copy." *And someday I will be able to read it.*

For an instant, her fingers closed over the worn leather. Even in Meklavar, such a book would be a treasure. But she was not in Meklavar, nor was she *te-ravah* or even the daughter of an Isarran princess. She was a captive of war and, in all likelihood, a slave. Nothing she owned from now on would be hers.

"The offer is gift enough," she said, and this time she pressed it back into his hands. "If you would have it be more, then remember me whenever you read it."

"Aye, that I'll do." He glanced away, and she read in his movement that if either of them said more, the perfect grace of the moment would shatter, gone beyond recall.

In silence, they watched the first pale light seep into the east.

Chapter Fourteen

HALFWAY to the mainland, a storm came up. Tsorreh heard a clatter and running feet outside the cabin. The ship heaved under her, timbers groaning. She felt the rigging vibrate through the wooden planks. The ship tilted alarmingly. Menelaia, losing her balance, let out a shriek that pierced the sound of the wind.

Tsorreh went out on deck. She could hardly see through the downpour. Day had turned almost as dark as night. Waves surged over the decks. Wind whipped the water to a froth. Flying spray drenched her.

In snatches, she heard men's voices, shouted orders, and cries of alarm. Water, bone-chillingly cold, engulfed the deck. She clung to the railing. Behind her, in the cabin, Menelaia shrieked again.

Tsorreh was no sailor, and only a fragile craft stood between everyone aboard and the long cold plummet into darkness. If the ship split apart or crashed on the jagged rocky shore, she would drown and what she carried would be lost.

Between her breasts, she felt the steady pulse of the *te-alvar*. With it, Khored of Blessed Memory had conjured Fire and Ice, had raised mountains from meadows, and caused the very bowels of the earth to open. She pressed both hands over the living gem and tried to imagine its power flowing into her, into the sea, the waves calming to green and slate-blue instead of wind-whipped gray, the wind softening, a warm breeze stirring the clouds, blue sky above glassy swells.

Almost, *almost* she felt an answer.

The ship lurched under her like a great beast rising to its feet, then seemed to catch its balance. The clamor of the gale hushed, and the voices of the sailors rose like a fractured chorus.

Deep beneath the waters, something moved. She sensed a shifting of dark upon dark, of cold within cold. Strands of pearls, sea-jade, and coral glinted in the abyss.

"Rocks to port!" a man's voice rang out, his next words swallowed by the rising wind.

Through a gap in the seething gray, Tsorreh looked where the seaman had pointed. A promontory jutted from the sea, its black stones drenched and gleaming.

Bynthos shouted out orders. Men leaped to their ropes.

Slowly, the *Silver Gull* turned. The rocks disappeared in a swirl of flying spray as the ship pulled away. Then the storm closed in on them once again, and Tsorreh sagged against the railing. She felt utterly drained, caught between astonishment and terror.

Hands closed around her arms. She turned to see the hard, set features of the Gelonian officer, Lord Mortan. Yet there was nothing of cruelty in the way he guided her back to the cabin, only the disciplined focus of his purpose. In all probability, he'd been afraid she would seize the moment to throw herself overboard, and he would lose his prize.

Two steps further, and she fell into Menelaia's waiting arms. Sobbing, the maid took her to the bed, sat her down, and stripped off her sodden clothing. In her brief exposure, Tsorreh's skin had gone numb with cold. Menelaia found a length of cloth to rub her dry, then wrapped her in blankets.

As Tsorreh sank back on the bed, bone-deep shivers rippled through her. There was nothing hot to drink, and no fire with which to prepare it. She would have to trust the resilience of her body, even as she relied on the skill of the sailors.

She felt Menelaia's weight beside her, the arms enfolding her, heard the little wordless cries. Reaching up with one hand, she felt the girl's fingers, knotted in the blanket. Gradually, warmth seeped into her muscles. Her shivering faded, replaced by a heavy lassitude. She felt drained in spirit as well as body.

Lying cradled by the young Isarran woman, Tsorreh tried to sleep. Images continued to flare and dance behind her closed lids. She saw again—was it *seeing?*—the beast in the shadowed deep, trailing strands of benthic gems.

Almost, *almost* it had answered her call.

Two oxen, their horns sawed off near their shaggy, white-and-gray spotted heads, drew the barge. The barge itself was large and flat-bottomed, topped by an open-sided shed. Flaps of canvas, heavy and stiff, could be rolled up during the day for fresh air or dropped for privacy. As Tsorreh had expected, Mortan attached her chains to a ring set in the deck.

Once away from the port, the air turned dense and sticky. The heat drained Tsorreh's strength, so that she felt no desire to move about the barge, even if she were free to do so. The occasional breeze was delicious beyond words.

Enervated as she was by the unaccustomed climate, Tsorreh watched the passing countryside. The histories she had studied had given her little idea of what the land and ordinary people of Gelon were like. The pastures and farms, the rivers teeming with fish and waterfowl, presented a panorama of fertility. Green plants grew everywhere, trees, vines, bushes, hedges, waterweeds, and reeds. The Gelonian guards, as well as the people she saw working in the fields, astonished her with their discipline and energy. On first glance, she had thought the land so naturally bountiful that its inhabitants must be fat and lazy. Quickly, she modified her opinion. The lush green and gold, the plentiful water and crops, covered an iron core, a ruthless determination. Gelon was not a weak and idle land.

On the last day of travel, they passed through the outskirts of Aidon. Tsorreh had no idea the capital city extended so far nor how many villages lined the river itself. Most of what she could see were piers and landings, buildings of sun-bleached wood and beyond them, warehouses, barns, roads, and taverns. Strings of fish hung drying in the sun. The mud, red like rust or old blood, smelled like dead weeds.

In her heat-drenched sleep, motes of colored light roused from water and sky and riverbank. They drew near her, their motions hesitant and indirect, as if they were shy to approach. She felt their curiosity, and then realized what they were: tiny elemental spirits of land and air and water. The countryside was rich in magic, even as Meklavar was, but these were domestic spirits, each content with its own small domain. In their swirling bits of color, she sensed their pleasure in the humble shrines, the curl of aromatic incense, and the offerings of flowers or fruit or new-spun wool.

The closer she drew to Aidon itself, the fewer and weaker the spirits became. At first, Tsorreh thought the buildings along the bank damped the voices of the river, the fish and frogs and reeds. Then, in the long hours of daylight, when she had nothing to do but stare at the passing shores, she realized that the nature spirits were still there but hiding, as if cowed. Frightened?

A shadow crept over river and earth, at first very faint, like a colorless mist. The closer they got to Aidon, the darker it became, clotting into darkness below the pillars of the wharves and in the hidden places between the buildings, in the rotting felled trees.

Aidon itself swept all thought of nature spirits from Tsorreh's mind. Its hugeness struck her like a wall of brass and granite, like the clangor of a thousand gongs. It rose into hills, revealing layer upon layer of white and gray and sand-colored stone, rows of lacy branched trees, towers of gleaming marble or painted wood, spires and shaded colonnades, and high-rising arches. Flags and pennons trailed from balconies, ribbons intertwined with dangling ivy or massed blossoms of purple, yellow, and orange.

Meklavar had been Tsorreh's world and the birthplace of her world, deep with the wearing of ages, of rock dust and books. This place, the heart of Gelon, was deep in a different way, with the weight of looted riches and the passionate energies of engineering and commerce.

They disembarked and joined several other parties heading into the center of the city. The officers rode standing in a chariot drawn by three dun onagers. The harness was studded with medallions of brass. Fringe covered the beasts' faces, and their long, tapered ears had been painted blue.

Tsorreh walked behind them, along with the other captives, more than a dozen but no more than two or three from any single land. An Isarran man, gray-bearded and limping, was tied at his wrist to the knotted rope that joined them all, but he was too far along for her to speak with him. She recognized a Xian, naked to the waist, eyes impassive, tattoos covering face and scalp. A slash of crusted blood ran across his cheek, and one eye was swollen shut.

No one tried to speak. Several of the captives had made an attempt while being tied to the rope, and the guards had used their whips freely. Tsorreh did not think they had any language in common, save Gelone. A conqueror's tongue now became a slave's tongue as well.

Morning light splashed hard and brittle off the whiteness of the city and yet, as if her bones had grown eyes, Tsorreh saw shadows shifting beneath the brightness. Their weight pressed against her heart. She thought of how the priest in Gatacinne had probed her and how the *te-alvar* had hidden itself, throwing up a lesser truth as a shield.

They have me now, but they do not know what they have. They must never find out.

Her mouth went dry. She tried to think of Zevaron, to see him in her mind free and unhurt, on a Sand Lands horse, the one he had been so pleased with, racing through the desert or into the fastness of the Var, or fighting among the free Isarrans. No images came to her, no fleeting comfort. She shuddered under the invisible density of the shadows. Something in them elongated, like articulated limbs.

"You there!" A voice lashed out in coarse Gelone. "Move along!"

The rope jerked. The loops binding her wrists dug into her already raw flesh. She lurched forward. The *te-alvar* lay quiescent, silent, yet something within her turned adamantine.

Tsorreh lifted her chin. The pain in her wrists and the cramping in her belly receded. She drew the ancient grandeur of Meklavar around her, a mantle woven of holy languages, of texts and light and prayers, of song and stone and blood. The shadows would not touch her.

They proceeded up from the harbor, past warehouses and shanties, to a broad avenue. Here they followed a mass of soldiers, accompanied by the sounds of flutes and drums. People watched from outside the buildings or on balconies. Their clothing gave them the aspect of gaudy birds in mating plumage, robes from shoulder to ankle, draperies and high-collared vests, garments that flowed or hugged the body in a riot of concatenated styles.

The crowd cheered and pointed at the captives, and tossed flower petals, bits of red paper, and apples. One went wild and hit Tsorreh on the shoulder. She tried to catch it, for she had been given no food that day, but it rolled free and she could not reach it with her bound hands.

A handful of half-grown boys in mud-colored tunics ran alongside the procession. Some hurled pebbles and hooted in glee as the black-skinned woman beside Tsorreh stumbled. One of the guards raised his whip, but he did not use it and only laughed. Tsorreh was close enough to reach out her hands to the other woman and steady her. Their eyes met in understanding.

The road led up, curving between the two nearest, lowest hills. Beyond them rose a third hill, flat-topped, that commanded a view of the harbor in one direction and the city in another. Wide, terraced gardens striped its slopes, interrupting the sweep of buildings. Tsorreh, gathering herself for the climb, tried to establish landmarks, but the city was too dense, too strange. The entire *meklat* could have fit on one hill.

As they went on, Tsorreh saw that they were headed to a palace of columned silver-white stone. Each corner supported a huge bronze statue, and she wondered who or what they represented. Figurative sculpture was rare in Meklavar, but she had seen many examples in Isarre. She had no chance to examine them as the chariot pulled up at the wide step. The soldiers shifted their formation, and the rope was untied and the captives separated, their hands still bound. They went up the steps, each pair between two guards with drawn swords.

By the time Tsorreh arrived at what was clearly a chamber of audience, she was thoroughly disoriented. The size of the entrance hall, the riotous color and strange shapes of the furnishings—statuary, tapestries, pillars—battered her already saturated senses. Her ears caught snatches of a dozen different languages; some she recognized from a word or two, but in others, she heard only strangeness.

The lesser halls and corridors were filled with people, some standing in groups talking, and some on raised platforms, perhaps performing rites or orations, she could not tell. Others stood in attendance or hurried about their business. As before, some wore the familiar armor of Gelonian soldiers, others loosely flowing robes, yet many more were in outland garb.

Tsorreh's vision blurred as she tried to take it all in. Moment by moment, she felt herself retreating into the inner sanctuary of her own prayer.

> *In the desert, my soul cries out in thirst,*
> *On the heights, my heart is filled with longing,*
> *In the temple, I find no rest.*
> *All is dust between my hands.*
> *My fire gives no warmth, my bread no savor.*

> *Come to me, O Holy One of Old;*
> *Speak to me as you spoke to my fathers!*
> *Let me not perish alone.*
> *Reach out your hand, lift up my soul,*
> *Be with me now, be with me now . . .*

Silently, Tsorreh chanted the ancient words until their rhythm matched the beating of her own heart. The thought came to her, as if in answer to her prayer, that these same words had been spoken by her ancestors, loudly or in whispers, over more years than a man could count. Her father had prayed in this way, as had her grandfather and the grandmother she had never known, perhaps even Khored of Blessed Memory. Her trembling eased, and her vision cleared. Calmly, she looked about her at the courtiers and the king seated at the far end of the hall.

The procession came to a halt, followed by a good deal of ceremony, most of which made no sense to Tsorreh. She and the other captives were left standing toward the back of the room. At the front, men and women in ornate dress, some holding what looked like instruments of office, sat in a half-circle.

At the center, raised above the others, a man in robes of pristine white, edged with blue and purple, glared down at the assembly. Like the other Gelon, he was pale-skinned and clean-shaven. His red-and-gray hair had been cropped short. The sleeves of the robe had fallen back, to reveal large, thick-fingered hands and muscular forearms. He was a tall, well-made man, broad in the shoulders and now run a little to fat, but he radiated a power beyond the strength of his physical body. Although he wore no crown, he could be none other than Ar-Cinath-Gelon.

Of the others, she was not so sure. Several of the men seemed to bear a resemblance in their features, although she could not be certain.

One man in particular attracted her notice, but not for the richness of his apparel or the arrogance of his features. Subtly unlike the others, this man wore the long courtly robe of white edged with only the thinnest bands of blue and purple, and no jeweled chain or other ornament. Only a single ring circled one of his swollen fingers, and that bore a small, dark-red stone. His face was as puffy as his fingers, and his distended belly stretched the fine fabric of his robe. Lines, as if from unremitting pain, were etched into his misshapen face. Tsorreh observed the awkwardness of his posture and the crutch resting against the back of his chair. He frowned and shifted in his seat, looking very much as if he wished he were elsewhere.

One by one, the captives were brought forward, and one of the officers presented each to the court, describing their origin. They were trying to impress the Ar-King with their value, Tsorreh thought.

Cinath listened with an expression of grave attention but no other visible emotion. He waved away the first few, and they were taken away by their guards, back the way they had come. Tsorreh had no idea what would become of them, except for the Xian, who was to be trained for some sort of combat spectacle.

The black-skinned woman was next, and her guard told a long, elaborate story of her capture. She was from one of the tribes along the Fever Lands border, known for their savagery in combat, and had been taken on board a pirate ship off the coast of Verenzza. Apparently, this one woman had killed three Gelonian soldiers. The rest of the pirates had been summarily executed.

As the tale unfolded, the entire assembly, the court on the dais and the audience below, came alert. Eyes shone, and the murmur and rustle died down. Several of the men leaned forward from their seats. Cinath did not shift his posture, but his eyes narrowed. One of his hands clenched into a fist.

The officer finished the story by shoving the woman forward and then tripping her so that she fell on her face in front of the throne. She caught herself with her bound hands and scrambled to her feet, to the sound of raucous laughter.

Cinath straightened on his throne as the noise died

down. Something in the intensity of his gaze alerted Tsorreh. Here was a man who would never question his own opinions or the rightness of his actions. His mouth twisted into a sneer. "So this *person* has dared to threaten the peace of my provinces? To lift her hand against my own sworn men?"

The woman stood, posture erect, face impassive, giving no sign that she understood him.

"What shall answer such insolence? How shall we set an example to any who dare follow?" Cinath paused dramatically.

"Give her to the Xian for entertainment at dinner tonight," one of the younger men called out. He had the same pale skin and ruddy hair as Cinath and wore a robe of blue edged with gold.

Tsorreh recoiled, but the reaction of the audience was the opposite. One of the ladies clapped her hands. There were scattered hoots and cheers from the audience. Only the man seated to the left of the throne, the one who so strongly resembled the Ar-King, made no response.

"Cut off her feet," another of the court suggested. "What a fine jest, to see her crawl about like one of those monkeys!"

"Aye! Being from the Fever Lands herself, she's little better than one of *them*!"

One of the courtiers from the audience stepped forward. "Your Majesty, worthy nobles, they say the women of the Fever Lands fight as well as the men. Why not test this one against the brother-regiment of the men she has killed?"

Cinath lifted one finger to his temple. The room fell silent. "Send her to the barracks."

"An excellent plan, Your Majesty!"

The guards to either side of the woman exchanged a glance, fierce and lascivious. Tsorreh had no doubt how they would pass the evening. An outright execution would be far more merciful.

The woman herself stood unmoving, but a new tension came into her muscles. The air around her seemed to quiver.

One of the guards nudged her in the back with the tip of his sword.

"Let's go. We look forward to offering you our hospitality."

In a movement as quick and heartless as a striking serpent, the black-skinned woman darted forward, only a step or two, but close enough to spit at the Ar-King. The gobbet of slime struck him full in the face. A gasp shook the assembly.

Shouting a curse in Gelone, the guard lunged at her, slashing with his sword. One of the ladies shrieked.

The Fever Lands woman pivoted and reached out with her bound hands. The sword edge sliced through the rope at her wrists. She curled and rolled, agile as a gymnast. Coming up to her feet, she faced her guards.

The circular attack had carried the guard's sword past his body. He had put his power into the blow, and now he stumbled, struggling with the weight and momentum of the blade. His partner, caught unawares, brought his own sword to ready. The woman stood with one foot before the other, hands raised, knees bent. White gleamed around the darkness of her eyes. She bared her teeth in a feral smile.

The nearest soldier moved to join the attack. In only a moment, the woman would be encircled. Even with her hands free, what could she do, unarmed, against a dozen or more?

The guard who had first struck out at her regained his balance. The initial attack might have been one of surprise and impulse, but he was no green recruit. With deadly economy, he brought his sword around in a backhand slice. The arched path of the blade would catch the woman obliquely across her belly.

At the same moment, she hurled herself toward the blow. The edge of the blade slashed through her skin, but she was already moving, twisting around it. She seemed to draw the length of steel into herself, to embrace it like a lover. For an instant, the sword lifted her up. The tip slipped along the angle of her ribs, toward her heart.

A look of fierce, almost transcendent joy lit her face. Then the light went out of her eyes. Her body folded in on itself. Her weight pulled the sword from the hand of the guard.. The guard wrenched his sword free. The coppery reek of blood filled the air.

Tsorreh could not breathe in the silence.

Several courtiers rushed forward with cloths to wipe the spittle from Cinath's face. One of the soldiers, an officer by the colors across his armor, went down on one knee before the king.

"I offer my life in payment for my failure," the officer said.

Again, the crowd held its breath. Tsorreh's mind whirled with the sudden turn of events. She was too numb, her thoughts too slow, to make any sense of what she'd witnessed. The alien nature of the Gelon made her shudder. How could the officer be responsible for the captive's death—or did he mean the woman's insult to the king? What kind of honor would exact such a penalty?

Cinath rose and stepped down from the dais. With his hands, he lifted the officer to his feet. His voice was low, so that Tsorreh could catch only a few phrases, something about *loyalty* and *a strong sword arm*. Now she sensed something familiar in the crowd, for she had seen it in the faces of her own people. Such a leader they would follow gladly, joyfully, even into the jaws of darkness.

The moment passed, and Cinath took his seat on the throne once more. "Get rid of that." He indicated the body of the black-skinned woman with a jerk of his chin. "Feed it to my dogs, if they will eat it."

After the corpse was removed, the officer returned to the presentation of the captives. One of the courtiers suggested that the two remaining prisoners, Tsorreh and another woman, might be sent to the barracks, since the soldiers had been deprived of their sport.

"Perhaps," Cinath said carelessly.

One of Tsorreh's guards stepped forward and bowed

deeply. After the proper salutations, he gestured at Tsorreh. "This woman was taken at Isarre, a refugee from Meklavar."

"Mortan sent her all the way here?" Cinath sounded bored and irritated. "One more filthy, scrawny female slave? Gods, as if I haven't enough of them already!"

The courtiers tittered.

Gathering all the grace of movement she could summon, Tsorreh sank to the floor in a deep obeisance.

"Your Majesty! Ar-King of all Gelon!" She lifted her head to free her throat, sending her voice into the room as her grandfather often had, addressing the congregation of Meklavar. "I am Tsorreh, second wife and now widow of Maharrad, King of Meklavar. My kingdom lies in the hands of your army. After the city fell, I fled through the mountains to seek refuge with my kinfolk in Isarre, in Gatacinne, and was taken prisoner there."

By Cinath's expression, and those of his courtiers, he did not believe her. The man to the king's right, the one with the crutch, came alert, clearly interested. He leaned over and said in a mild voice, "The timing would be right, according to our own reports. Consider also, my brother, how well she speaks Gelone, yet with an accent one could well describe as scholarly. Clearly, she has studied it properly and not just picked up a few phrases from the gutter. As to her appearance, what woman would look better after so many days at sea?"

Tsorreh got a closer look at the man. He was not as old as she had first assumed, although his hair was so thin that he appeared almost bald. An expression of keen intelligence lit the eyes that looked out between swollen folds of flesh.

"Majesty, she was interrogated b-by the Q-Q-Qr priest," the guard said. "He v-v-verifies that she is indeed the Queen of M-M-Meklavar."

Through her rising panic, Tsorreh caught the whispers at the back of the chamber. They were laced with fear, she thought, rather than respect.

"Qr does not rule here," Cinath said darkly. "Yet its servants have powers beyond those of ordinary men, and an uncommon ability to detect the truth beneath layers of falsehood. Bring her forth."

Praying she would not stumble, Tsorreh got to her feet, waited for the guards to take their places as if they were an escort of honor, and walked forward between them. She kept her features composed, her head lifted, and her step stately. All the while, her thoughts churned, searching for a way to convince this king that she was worthy of his protection. Cinath glanced at the man at his right, the one who had called him "brother."

"What seeketh thou, O my sister," the bloated man recited in surprisingly musical Meklavaran, *"so far from the mountains of your birth?"*

Tsorreh startled, for he had not only spoken in the ancient holy language, but had quoted from an early version of the *Shirah Kohav*. She had not thought to hear the poet's words, not so far from home nor spoken with such reverence.

She drew in a deep breath, raising her voice in the lilting chant:

> *"When I left the tent of my fathers, O my brother,*
> *I thought only of fame and treasure,*
> *I found only parched sand and empty skies."*

> *"Then seek no more,"*

the crippled Gelon answered,

> *"but abide with me,*
> *And I will pour cool water for your thirst,*
> *And fill the heavens with songs of rejoicing."*

The king's brother regarded her gravely. At first, she had thought him old, but now she saw the lines around his eyes and mouth were those of suffering and ill health, not age.

He shifted again on his hard wooden chair, and she saw that one of his sandaled feet, like a sickle, crooked inward. That would explain the crutch.

"She is Meklavaran, of that there is no doubt," the king's brother said. "And she's an educated woman. If she is not the runaway queen, she must surely be of a noble family. It would be a waste to turn her into barracks fodder or a scullery maid."

"Since the priest of Qr took an interest in her, I suppose we must keep her under guard. You have evidently taken a fancy to her, brother. I give her to you."

The man blinked, clearly surprised. "I meant for you to place her as a lady-maid here in the palace—"

"No, no, I want her close but not that close. Come now, Jaxar. What's the problem? Is Lycian jealous? Who rules in your house, you or your wife? Besides, if this woman is as well-educated as you claim, she'll make you an adequate assistant. Call her a guest or a hostage if you don't like the word *slave*. From this moment, she is your responsibility. I'll hear no more objections."

"And I will offer none," Jaxar replied after the faintest hesitation. "In this, as in all things, I serve the Ar of Gelon."

Chapter Fifteen

TWO days later, Tsorreh found herself in the entrance hall of Jaxar's city estate. She had not been sent directly there, but had passed the intervening time in the custody of Cinath's lady-steward. No one spoke to her in Cinath's palace, except to give her brief instructions—*go here, wait there, lift your arms*—spoken as slowly as if she were a child or a simpleton. In the women's slave quarters, she had been bathed and scrubbed, her hair combed and tied in a single thick plait down her back, her nails trimmed, and her ragged clothing taken away and replaced with a short gown, clean but worn. The garment was no more than a length of lightweight undyed cotton, folded and stitched along the sides, with a hole cut for the head. A few fraying tears bespoke previous hard usage. The hemline fell ungracefully to the middle of her calves. She felt half-naked with so much of her legs exposed, until she realized that many of the other women—slaves or servants, she could not be sure— wore even shorter ones.

On the brief trip to Jaxar's compound, she saw a little more of the city's broad paved streets, plazas with fountains shaped like leaping dolphins or men with the tails of fishes, avenues of blossoming trees, and walls of weathered gray stone.

Through a gate set in one of these, her guards conducted

her to an inner garden. Beyond the jewel-bright beds of flowers, the dwarf orange trees and hedges, stood the house itself. It was at least two stories tall. The walls might once have been as white and shining as those of Cinath's palace but were now worn to a grayish sheen, veined with delicate darker streaks. The house looked old and dignified rather than shabby, as if the hopes and dreams of those who had lived here still hummed softly in its bones.

A steward greeted them, a pear-shaped man with sallow, sagging skin, a nose that looked as if it had been broken several times, and slanted almond-brown eyes. He moved soundlessly, gliding over the tiled floor. Tsorreh could not imagine much happening within these walls that he did not know about. Such a man could be an invaluable ally or a formidable enemy. She must proceed carefully, avoiding even the appearance of a challenge to his authority until she had a better sense of his temper.

Tsorreh followed the steward inside the house and through a spacious entrance hall. Exquisitely wrought mosaics covered the floor and one long wall. Their path skirted an inner courtyard, open to the sky and bounded on two sides with graceful colonnades. Tsorreh faltered at the sight of the garden. Someone had put a great deal of care into its design and nurture, here placing a thicket of roses, there a tiny meadow of blue and yellow starflowers. Through the meadow wound a trail lined by benches that invited her to rest beneath the trellised vines. Beyond, she glimpsed a fountain and flagstone-paved patio with table and chairs.

She drew a breath, inhaling the fragrance of flowers, the scents of rich, moist earth and growing things. Longing filled her. She wanted to weep among the lilies, like the poet of the *Shirah Kohav*.

She came back to herself, standing at the edge of the garden. The steward had paused as well and was looking at her curiously. She sensed sympathy in that oblique gaze. He could have hurried her away and castigated her, and yet he waited, the creases at the corners of his mouth deepening, as he allowed her this moment of comfort. Eventually, they passed along a colonnade into the shaded darkness of the house and then up a flight of stairs.

The steward tapped on a door of honey-toned wood whose carved panels depicted the four Gelonian primals: fire, water, earth, and air. Inside was a library unlike any Tsorreh had seen, with not only bookshelves, but also work tables bearing instruments of glass and metal and reed tubes. A wooden ladder at the far end rose the entire height of the room and into a wide opening in the ceiling. Light streamed down, bathing the chamber in gentle brilliance.

"My lord?" the steward called, for the room appeared to be empty.

A muffled sound came from beneath one of the work tables. Jaxar's head emerged. Cobwebs laced his sparse hair and dust smeared one puffy, flushed cheek. He clutched a scrap of yellowed paper in one hand. Panting, he pulled himself up, using the table for support. When he saw Tsorreh, a smile lit up his homely face.

"Oh, there you are. We didn't expect you until this afternoon."

"My lord," the servant said in an aggrieved tone, "they sent her over from the palace just now."

"Then, Lady Tsorreh, I bid you welcome to my laboratory." Jaxar fumbled with his crutch, got it into position, and limped toward her.

"Thank you for your graciousness, Lord Jaxar," Tsorreh said in her best Gelone. "As you see, I am your prisoner. Or rather, your brother's. You need not flatter me with honors."

An unreadable emotion touched Jaxar's face, a tightening of the expressive lips, a shadow evanescent behind the eyes. "There are neither slaves nor hostages in my house. As for being a prisoner, where are your chains? Do you see any bars upon these windows? I told Cinath, may-his-reign—well, we're not in court, so never mind what I wish for him. I told him I would keep you safe, and so I shall, as best I can within these walls."

Jaxar's mood shifted. The corners of his mouth twitched upward and smile crinkles appeared around his eyes.

"Whether I can protect you equally well against boredom is another matter. Where to start?"

Waving for the steward to depart, Jaxar motioned Tsorreh to approach the apparatus laden table. "Do you know what any of these are? Go ahead, take a look. Just don't drop them."

Uncertain but curious, Tsorreh approached the table. She picked up a length of polished reed, banded at either end with rings of brass. It looked like a flute without mouthpiece or holes, and was far heavier than she expected. Peering inside, she saw discs of glass, but had no idea what a such a device might be. She set it down carefully and looked over the other items. The flasks and tubes were as fine in quality as any she had ever seen, and the glassblowers of Meklavar were highly skilled. White crystals coated a flat glass plate beside a row of jars containing small dead animals—frogs, fish, a snake with tiny legs—floating in yellowish liquid. There were also stacks of papers, ragged and yellow around the edges, covered with diagrams and strange symbols, a very dusty stuffed owl, several implements consisting of engraved, hinged metal plates, and what looked very much like a piece of moldy bread.

"I'm sorry," she said, for naming the owl and the bread would be impertinent at best, "I don't recognize any of this." She touched a fingertip to the center of the table and held it up, smeared with grime. "Except the dust."

Jaxar shrugged. "Ah, it was too much to hope for. At least, you can help me keep the place a bit cleaner. I have always wondered where the dust comes from. . . . Do you know?" He paused, as if hoping for an answer, then shrugged again. "It is said the Meklavarans teach their women to read. Is that true?"

"Yes, of course." Tsorreh frowned, a little taken aback that there should even be a question. Certainly, there were uneducated people in every land, including her own.

"Excellent!" Jaxar brightened. "Then you can help me with note-keeping and those infernal letters. How about translation?" He settled himself on a bench. "There's a stack of books on the shelf behind you. Read a little of each one aloud to me. In the original and then translate into Gel-one, if you can."

Tsorreh picked up the topmost volume and turned it over, feeling the weight of it, noticing the water-stained leather covers. Opening it to a random page, she recognized the angular Denariyan script, and sighed, for although she could understand it well enough, her pronunciation was terrible. Still, she took a breath and, as Eavonen had repeatedly urged her, tried to think of her voice coming out the top of her head. It was a treatise on the magical properties of crystals. Jaxar stopped her after half a page.

The second volume, to her relief, was in Gelone, and described the proper methods for training onagers for various uses. The language was simple enough for even a soldier, and she found herself interested in the description of the beasts best suited to riding, pulling a cart, or even warfare. Jaxar let her read on for a few pages.

She could make nothing of the next book, save for a few phrases in Gelone. It was so old, the ink had faded to illegibility in places. She made out numbers and strange symbols, like those on the papers on the table. "I'm sorry," she said, "I don't know what these mean."

Jaxar sighed. "Alas, neither do I. That is a copy of an even older text, Isarran from the shape of the numerals."

"I can read Isarran and write it as well."

"Let us hope another version shows up, one you can make sense of."

She reached for the next book, the last but one, a slender volume bound in what had once been beautiful cream-colored leather. It bore the same traces of water damage as the others, but, unlike them, had seen harsh handling. The covers opened easily, the pages separating as if they had been recently read.

> *Exiled from Thy sight,*
> *My soul is a realm forsaken,*
> *Filled with lamentations,*
> *Strange portents —*

Tsorreh's breath froze in her throat. She could not speak. She would have known the phrases of the *Shirah Kohav* anywhere.

"Where—where did you get this?" she whispered, hardly able to hear her own words above the sound of her heart. Of course, she thought haltingly, Jaxar had recited one of these very same verses at the audience before Cinath, and she had completed it. He must have learned it from this very same volume, for how many more could there be so far from home?

Through tear-blurred eyes, she saw him bend over her, his movement unexpectedly graceful, the bulk of his ungainly body comforting. Gentle hands lifted the book from her. "Of course you can read this. It's your own language."

She felt rather than saw him straighten up. He read,

> *By day, I long for Thee,*
> *I thirst for Thee at night.*
> *The shadowed avenues of my soul*
> *Wait in stillness for Thy light.*

Something gave way within her. The tears spilled over her cheeks. Her breath stuttered and great shuddering sobs came boiling up from the very core of her. She covered her face with both hands, as if her fingers could contain all the nameless emotions within her. It had been so long since she'd wept. All she was, all she felt, was pain too great to be contained within. It split her open in a thousand jagged cuts, grief pouring out.

"Come this way."

She took a few shambling steps and allowed herself to be lowered onto a bench and pulled close. Jaxar wrapped her in his arms. Her body felt all bones and eggshells. She rocked with weeping.

"You've had a hard time of it, child. I can't imagine how difficult it's been, losing your family and your home, fleeing all the way to Gatacinne. And then to be captured and brought here, and that dreadful scene with my brother. Any man would be broken, who had to bear half so much."

Isolated words echoed through her, sparking memory: *Your family, your home. Zevaron . . .*

"You are safe with me," Jaxar murmured. "No harm will come to you if I can prevent it."

Safe. Where was there safety in all this blood-drenched world?

As if in response, she felt a kernel of warmth deep within her chest, a beacon through the swirling loss and pain. With it came a shimmer of astonishing tranquility, like clear, cool water in the desert.

Her heart beat steadily, like the slow inexorable movement of a tide. The ordinary sounds of the day swirled around her, distant voices, birds singing in the garden, the clank and clatter of housekeeping tasks. She raised her head. The moment of clarity fell away, leaving an awkward, almost embarrassing awareness that she had been embraced, as a child is embraced, by a man she barely knew—her jailor, her guardian, perhaps someday her friend?

"Father, please come," came a voice from across the room, a boy's clear voice. "Mother's all in a dither over some slave and demands to see her immediately, if not sooner."

Tsorreh lifted her head, sweeping away tears with the back of one hand, and saw the speaker. Not a child, but a boy on the brink of manhood, he could not have been more than a year from Zevaron's age. The light from the corridor behind him cast his features into shadow, so that all she saw was a slender, well-formed body, knee-length belted tunic, and a shock of curls.

"Oh!" the boy said. "Please excuse me."

"It's all right," Jaxar said. "Come in and meet my new assistant."

The boy stepped into the room, and the light shifted, revealing a pleasant, open face framed by red-gold hair.

"This is my son, Danar."

Tsorreh did not know what form of greeting might be appropriate. She inclined her head, as if she were being introduced to a noble youth of her own class. Danar bowed deeply in return.

"And this is Tsorreh," Jaxar continued. "She's from Meklavar, where she was once a queen. She's better educated than ten of you put together, so you'd best show proper respect for her. And she is most definitely not a slave."

"Please forgive me, I meant no offense," Danar said to Tsorreh. He looked at her with disarming curiosity.

"Then I will take none," Tsorreh said.

Reaching for his crutch, Jaxar heaved himself to his feet. "You can rehearse better manners while I'm gone. I'll see what I can do to settle Lycian. Once Tsorreh has regained her composure, bring her along to the garden."

Tsorreh stood silently while Jaxar hobbled from the room. She could not think what to say to this young man, who reminded her so poignantly of her own son.

Danar bent toward her and said in a conspiratorial whisper, "Mother's not allowed in here, which is why she sent me. When she and Father were first married, she insisted on helping him, or so Issios—he's our household steward—tells me, and, well . . . there was a big explosion. *Really* big. It took the servants *weeks* to clean it up. Now Father won't even let her through the door."

A bubble of something like laughter rose up behind Tsorreh's throat.

"Is it true you can read five different languages? That's what the servants are saying." Danar picked up an empty flask and ran his fingers over the smoothly rounded glass. "You don't look old enough to be a scholar. Is it a secret of the mountain folk, some magic in the water?"

Tsorreh managed to keep a straight face. "In my country, every well-born child learns to read and write both modern Meklavaran and the holy languages. We are such a small land and we depend on trade, so everyone must study at least some Gelone and Denariyan, and trade-dialect Azkhantian, if they can." Seeing the boy's astonishment, she subsided. "Besides, I am not all that young. I have a son," her tongue stumbled on the word, "of your years."

"That cannot be possible!" Danar said, wide-eyed.

"Oh, indeed. You are what, fourteen? I had already borne Zevaron when I was your age." The syllables of his name echoed through her, and her heart resonated with aching.

"Was he—" Danar said, his young features suddenly solemn, "was he slain when Meklavar fell?"

Tsorreh shook her head. "No, we fled the city together, and he was well when I last saw him. We were separated during the battle at Gatacinne. I hold in my heart the hope that he escaped, although I do not know where he might have gone. I miss him, I . . . pray for his safety."

"You pray? To which god?"

"Why, to the only one: the Most Holy, the Source of Blessings."

Danar set down the round-bellied flask and shrugged. "I think there are as many gods in Gelon as there are donkeys. Forgive me if I'm blasphemous, but Father says it's all nonsense. He believes in only what he can see and measure."

He strode over to Tsorreh's bench and sat beside her, even as Zevaron might have. "He's always scandalizing Mother with such talk, and *she's* always looking for a new shrine. I think if a talking water-pig would give her a son, she'd worship it."

"Danar, is it wise to speak so frankly of your parents, and to someone you barely know?"

"Oh, none of this is secret, and I think it's best to be prepared. Before you meet Mother, that is. She's my stepmother, you know, not my real mother. I only call her that so she doesn't get mad."

Tsorreh looked away. It was not easy to be a second wife, to stand in the shadow of another woman. What if she, like Lycian, had been childless? How much of Maharrad's love arose from the son she had given him? But no, he had cared for her, she was sure of that.

Even though Jaxar seemed a kind and decent man, Lycian's plight might be very different. Or she might be well-treated but tormented by her failure. Either way, the woman deserved compassion, not scorn. She said, "I hope you try to be a loving son to her."

Danar shrugged, an adolescent's careless dismissal. "I like you already, and I know Father does. I can tell you now that Mother won't approve of you."

"Why not?"

Danar blushed and stammered something about her being much too young and pretty. "Even if all you do is dust this place and help me with my history lessons, you'll be more fun than my stepmother."

"Then it is best to get the ordeal over with. I cannot believe any woman who would marry your father could be dull, but I am forewarned."

From Danar's description, Tsorreh expected Lycian to be an older woman with hard, assessing eyes and a pinched mouth, one whose fear of losing her attractiveness colored her every interaction. She had seen the wives of the noble houses behave in that manner, even if she did not understand it. To her, beauty was a thing to be put on like a garment, and sometimes better discarded.

Lycian, standing in the inner garden in the dappled shade, was no fading blossom, but a confection of crystal and silver. Glistening wires, formed into shapes like fantastical flowers, twined through her ash-gold hair, and jewels winked from the folds of her gown. Huge gray eyes outlined in kohl regarded Tsorreh from a face as faultless as alabaster.

A fluffy white creature, no bigger than Tsorreh's cat, sat at Lycian's feet. Button eyes lit upon Tsorreh, and the dog scrambled to its feet, yapping wildly.

"Hush, Precious Snow!" Lycian lifted her chin and turned back to her husband. "So *this* is your new assistant." Her tone was impeccably polite, and yet she managed to convey the impression that no better use could be found for such a disgusting wretch.

None of the ladies of Maharrad's court had ever dared

treat Tsorreh with such rudeness, but she had seen these games played out before. She bowed. "I am happy that I can be of some small use in this great house."

"Since," Jaxar said heavily, "it is the command of the Ar-King himself, may-his-wisdom-never-fail, that we extend our protection to her."

"Yes, my dear," Lycian said, her tone poisonously sweet. Her gaze flickered from Jaxar to Tsorreh, and beneath the glittering beauty, Tsorreh sensed a jealous mind, fueled by thwarted ambition. Such a woman would make a dangerous enemy, against whom Tsorreh had little power.

Tsorreh did not think Lycian would make any overt move against her, not with Cinath's command so fresh in memory, but there were always accidents, a bit of meat gone bad in the heat, a slip on a stone stair, a hundred ways she might come to harm and no one would know.

Danar would suspect, came to her mind. Tsorreh quickly suppressed a shiver as she realized that if Lycian should bear Jaxar a son and the son survived his infancy, Danar's own days would be short in number.

"We must find her a place to sleep where she will not be in the way," Lycian said.

"Yes, yes," Jaxar said soothingly. "You need not trouble yourself, my wife."

Lycian sniffed elegantly and was about to say something more, when Danar touched Tsorreh's arm and drew her away. Once out of the courtyard, she heard him exhale, as if he'd been holding his breath through the interview.

"Would it," she asked hesitantly, "would it be possible to make up a pallet for me in the laboratory? So that I could watch over—whatever needs watching over?"

And where I will not find Lycian bending over my bed with a dagger?

"It's up to Father," Danar said. "Just tell him you're fascinated by his astronomy studies, and he'll keep you up all night, taking notes while he peers through his telescope."

"His what?"

"Come on, I'll show you." As Danar led the way back to

the laboratory, he explained. "It's another of Father's devices, and ever since he met this Denariyan trader—they're marvelous at polishing lenses of quartz and glass—he's been using them—the telescopes, not the traders—to look at almost everything."

Danar closed the door behind them and gestured to the end of the work table, where an assortment of clear glass disks and reed tubes were neatly displayed on racks. Tsorreh listened with growing interest as he explained that, depending on the shape of the lens, objects would appear to the viewer as larger or smaller.

"Father started on this project when his eyes got too bad to read. You can imagine how frantic that made him, and at that time, I couldn't read anything but Gelone, so I wasn't much help. With a lens like this, he could see even very small writing. Like men, the lenses strengthen each other when put together." Danar held up a piece of smooth glass the size of Tsorreh's palm, set like a mirror in a ring of silver, and one of the tubes.

Looking through the various lenses, Tsorreh was swept up in a exhilarating blur of light and color. Shapes rushed toward her, suddenly huge.

"This is wonderful!" she cried, delighted in spite of her earlier fears. She tried to imagine looking through the far-seeing tube from the heights of the temple, toward the line of brightness on the horizon that marked the Sea of Desolation. What more could she have seen, what strange wonders made clear to her sight?

"Is it some kind of magic?" she wondered aloud. "Like the tiny spirits of fire and water, only of air, that bring these visions?"

"Hardly magic," Jaxar answered her from the doorway. Limping on his crutch, he crossed to take the tube from her hands. "This is based upon the principles of the natural world, which any reasonable person can understand. What you call 'magic' is superstitious nonsense. There are no tiny spirits of air, any more than there are of any other element."

No matter what Jaxar said, she had seen the spirits of fire

and water, and she had seen Khored of Blessed Memory stand against the powers of Fire and Ice. For a dizzying instant, she felt herself astride two worlds, one in which only what she could see or touch was real, and the other, a place of unimaginably vast powers, a place that legend and scripture struggled to evoke. Khored would have had no doubt which world was real. But Khored had long since passed from the face of the earth, his people diminished and scattered. *Khored was glorious in his day, but his time ended. It is now the age of men like Jaxar. And Ar-Cinath-Gelon.*

She said nothing of her visions, only commented that the priests who had built the temple in Meklavar used mirrors to bring light deep within the mountain.

"Yes, yes!" Jaxar said, plainly excited. "The same principles hold true everywhere! Can you draw it for me, this system of mirrors?"

They cleared off one end of the table, sat down with paper and sticks of charcoal, and spent the rest of the day discussing the properties of light. Servants brought in a mid-day meal, a cold soup made from cherries, bowls of spiced lentils and cucumbers, and unleavened bread.

The three of them talked long into the night.

Chapter Sixteen

W HEN Tsorreh woke, she was in the laboratory, curled
on the pallet that had been made up for her. Softness cushioned her body, and the stuffed pad gave off the
faint scent of dried lavender. The coverlet was finely woven
wool, dyed in a pattern of bright stripes. The degree of comfort had surprised her, for she had expected something thin
and hard, a servant's meager bed.

A hush filled the spacious chamber. Radiance sifted
from the open door of the rooftop observatory and through
the windows. By the angle and tint of the light, Tsorreh
judged that it was morning. The enclosed space, filled with
strange but curiously reassuring objects and the familiar
smell of books and ink, created the sense of a place set
apart. It was a place not utterly alien to the things and val-
ues she had always known, a place enclosed by walls visible
and invisible.

From the rooms and corridors beyond the grounds of the
estate came the sounds of everyday life. Footsteps, voices
calling to one another—servants about their morning
chores, she supposed. Once or twice, she caught a trill of
birdsong from the garden courtyard. Within these walls,
stillness held sway. Stillness and a blessed, fleeting solitude.

Since her arrival yesterday, Tsorreh had left the laboratory only a few times. It occupied one corner of the second floor, down the hall from a small toilet chamber. A bucket of water, kept filled, served to rinse the porcelain facility. Where the soiled water went then, Tsorreh did not know. Gelonian sanitation was efficient, judging by the absence of smell.

She could not hide here, she knew. She must learn the layout of the compound, the house with its courtyards and garden, the grounds. She must get to know the servants and determine which ones might help her and which she must avoid. If possible, she must build the alliances that would gain her access to the city beyond.

And then what? If she escaped Jaxar's custody, where would she go? Nowhere in Gelon would be safe. Could she evade being caught, as well as the many hazards of a woman traveling alone in unknown lands, long enough to make her way back to Isarre? To Meklavar? The prospect of such a journey, undertaken in secrecy and attended at every turn by fear of discovery and in the absence of allies and resources, was daunting.

Tsorreh got to her feet and stretched. Her spine popped and her muscles ached in relief. She'd been too long abed, she thought, and needed something active to sharpen her wits. She went to the nearest bookshelf, noting with dismay the thickness of the dust. The scrolls had been placed neatly in slots, but without a system of identification. She suspected they were in as great disorder as the bound volumes. She drew in her breath for a sigh of exasperation, then quickly swallowed it, rather than risk sending billows of dust everywhere. She could easily tell which books Jaxar consulted frequently, for the bindings were relatively clean and little avenues of bare wood amid the grayish dust marked where the books had slid in and out. Dust coated her fingertips from brushing against only a few.

She glanced around the room. There must be a rag somewhere, perhaps buried in one of the piles of odd objects, bits of wood and metal wire, and unspun wool.

The door opened with a faint click of the latch. Tsorreh

flinched at the sound. A girl, not much older than Danar, slid through the opening. Her nose was short and snubbed, and her black brows almost met in the center of her forehead in a single straight line. She would have been homely, except for the sweetness of her expression and the beauty of her hazel eyes. Her hair, a darker shade of chestnut than the usual Gelon red, had been tied in a single, severe braid, and she wore a knee-length white tunic, belted with a braid of brightly colored ribbons and pinned at the shoulders with little copper ornaments. Embroidered flowers brightened the neckline and sleeve hems. She carried a tray with a bowl of boiled millet, a pitcher, and a napkin.

A napkin! Perfect! Tsorreh stopped herself before she could snatch up the scrap of cloth and begin cleaning.

The girl came to a halt and inclined her head shyly.

"Is that for me? Thank you. It smells good." Mixed with the faintly nutty aroma of the millet, Tsorreh inhaled the subtle scents of apricots and honey.

The girl looked startled, as if she had not expected to be addressed in understandable Gelone. She handed over the tray and began to scurry back through the doorway.

"Wait!" Tsorreh cried. "I don't know your name."

"Astreya, lady."

The name certainly did not sound Gelon. Remembering Jaxar's emphatic statement about not keeping slaves, Tsorreh asked, "Are you a servant?"

"Yes, indeed! My mother is the cook here."

Cooks often knew more about the doings of their households than did their masters. "I wonder," Tsorreh ventured, "could you take me to your mother? And to a place where I might wash, as well?"

Astreya inclined her head again. "Eat the food while it's hot. I'll be back for the tray." With a sideways smile, she slipped through the door.

Tsorreh set the tray down beside her pallet. A spoon of carved horn had been tucked beneath the edge of the bowl. She dipped it into the porridge and found the millet was still warm. The sweetness of the fruit and honey filled her mouth. Her stomach rumbled, and she felt suddenly ravenous.

The girl came back just as Tsorreh was finishing the last tiny grains. She picked up the tray. "Come on, then."

Astreya walked along at a business-like pace, indicating the direction of the family apartments in the wing that stretched to the south. The main building had been constructed as an open rectangle, with the central courtyard garden open to the sky. Apparently, Lycian had her own separate suite, with a balcony view overlooking the city. Lycian's rooms, Tsorreh noticed, occupied the opposite end of the house from the laboratory. Tsorreh glimpsed the garden below, then followed Astreya down gloomy stairs and along a brief stretch of the shaded colonnade that ran around the courtyard.

The kitchen and bakery stood apart from the house itself, down a path of fine-grained gravel. A well and a large freestanding oven, rounded like a beehive, flanked the kitchen building. As they traversed the outdoor compound, Astreya pointed out servants' quarters, gardening sheds, a little stable for Lady Lycian's onager and Lord Danar's horse, vegetable and herb gardens, and an orchard, the apple and pear trees pruned and espaliered for easy picking. The smell of sun-warmed herbs filled the air. Beyond the orchard, Tsorreh glimpsed the high stone walls she remembered from her arrival.

Astreya led the way through the wide open doorway and into the kitchen itself. The kitchen comprised a series of adjoining rooms, with areas for storage, preparation, and cooking. Piles of dishes, mostly metal pounded thin, were stacked in the washing area. Shelves held an array of pottery canisters, wooden boxes, and other containers. Braids of onions and garlic hung from the beams in one corner, as well as strings of sausages and what looked like wax-dipped cheeses.

A ruddy-faced woman bent over the iron pot that hung over a wide cooking hearth, stirring the contents with a long-handled wooden spoon. One girl chopped leeks and carrots on the table, while another scrubbed pots at the massive stone sink. A half-grown boy maneuvered a yoke with two buckets of water through the back door.

The woman at the hearth looked up from tasting the pot's contents. Beneath the flush, presumably from her nearness to the banked fire, her complexion resembled Astreya's, and the line of her dark brows and curve of her lips left no doubt in Tsorreh's mind that this was indeed the girl's mother. Like her daughter, the woman wore a simple, loose fitting dress, but hers fell to her ankles, and the shoulder clasps were fashioned from black wood, polished to a high sheen, and carved like entwined snakes. A bibbed apron strained across her ample breasts. Clearly, she enjoyed her own cooking.

"Ah, you must be our new guest, the foreign lady," she said, without setting down her spoon. "I'm Breneya, cook here, and I see my girl's got you fed."

"Yes, thank you," Tsorreh replied. She found herself liking both mother and daughter. "The food was very good."

"A sight better than you'd find in uncivilized parts." Breneya looked pleased. "We'll put some meat on your bones."

Tsorreh glanced down at her body. She had always been slender, and the long, desperate flight through the Sand Lands and Isarre had pared her even further. The unbelted dress hung on her like a shapeless sack.

"Mamma," Astreya said, "might I show this lady to the bathhouse?"

A bathhouse? Despite the awkwardness of the moment, Tsorreh's muscles went weak with longing. Hot water, soap that did not leave her skin scoured raw, a soft towel, and the leisure to enjoy them — the prospect was marvelous beyond words.

"So you shall." Breneya put down the spoon, wiped her hands on her apron, and bustled Astreya and Tsorreh toward the door. As they left, Tsorreh heard the older woman muttering, "That dress! Not fit for a decent woman to wear!"

Heat rose to Tsorreh's face. Clearly, Cinath had sent her forth in nothing more than a slave's robe. These women, *free* women, showed their status by adding personal adornments. Jaxar had said nothing. Perhaps he had not even noticed. But Lycian had.

Paying no heed to her mother's comments, Astreya led Tsorreh back toward the main house, then down a branching, rock-lined path. The bathhouse itself was a compact stone structure with high-set, unglassed windows and a roof of glazed blue tiles that curved up at the edges, giving the appearance of frozen dancing waves. Willowy trees lined the path. White, intensely fragrant blossoms covered their branches, but could not entirely disguise the faint sulphuric tinge to the air. Tsorreh sniffed, recognizing the reek characteristic of natural hot springs. No wonder the baths were situated some distance from the main house.

They went around to the entrance, a series of broad steps leading downward to a landing. Passages opened to either side, presumably separating bathers either by sex or class.

A statue of a woman occupied a niche in the wall; she held a jug on one shoulder, one leg bent as if paused in midstep and the other hip forming a graceful curve. Fresh flowers, both the white ones from the trees and a scattering of brighter petals, had been mounded around the statue's feet.

Tsorreh paused before the statue. A gentle, benign presence radiated from the sculpted face, and something in the softly lowered gaze of the marble eyes suggested compassion, or so Tsorreh thought. How she sensed this, she did not know. Perhaps some force, kindly and welcoming, inhabited the statue.

With a rustle of silk, a pattering of sandaled feet, and a flurry of attending servants, Lycian burst from one of the bathhouse entrances into the lowered courtyard. Rosy color suffused her face, and her bright hair fell in damp curls over the nape of her neck. Her gown followed the same basic pattern of women's dress in Gelon, but the iridescent rose-and-yellow silk was gathered at each shoulder into tiny jewel-studded pleats and held by golden clasps in the shape of flowering vines. Matching bands coiled around her upper arms and wrists. More gems winked along the hem of the scarf that fluttered about her shoulders. One of her attendants carried the little white lap-terrier, which began to yip as soon as it spied Tsorreh.

Lycian's gaze lit upon Tsorreh, and she paused in mid-sentence, her lips parted. Frowning, she swept up the stairs.

Astreya backed up against the wall while attempting a deep obeisance. Tsorreh, unsure of the proper salutation in such circumstances, inclined her head. "Lady, your pardon."

Lycian's perfectly arched brows drew together. "Explain your presence here!"

"I was just going to—" Tsorreh began. Were servants not permitted access to the bathhouse? If that were true, why had Astreya brought her here? Why had Breneya, who had seemed so friendly, suggested it?

Have I stumbled into a nest of household plots and subterfuge?

She glanced at Astreya. Keeping her eyes lowered, the girl stammered, "Gracious lady, Lord Jaxar gave orders that this guest be made comfortable. I beg forgiveness if—"

"We'll see about that!" Lycian cut her off. "It seems to me a scandalous indulgence to bathe in the middle of the day, when there is work to be done. If *she* has nothing better to do than idle around, splashing about in hot water, she can just as well be of use. She will go with you to the washery. See to it, girl, or you will soon find that slaves are not the only ones who can be whipped!"

Round-eyed, Astreya bowed again. "Lady—"

"Now!" Lycian drew back one hand. "Or have you forgotten where the dirty linens are kept?"

Acting more by instinct than rational thought, Tsorreh stepped between Lycian and the cowering girl. Lycian's open palm, aimed with surprising force, caught Tsorreh flat on the cheek.

Tsorreh's head snapped back with the force of the blow. Her face stung where Lycian's long fingernails raked her skin. She staggered and caught herself against Astreya.

Tsorreh's temper flared, fueled by pent-up anxiety and frustration, the days of fear and confusion, grief and horror. To have survived the siege and fall of a great city, the deaths of so many loved ones, flight and capture and the hideous mind-touch of the Qr priest in Gatacinne, only to be slapped about by this silly, pampered woman!

She took a step toward Lycian, only dimly aware of the fierce expression on her face and the menace in her posture. One of Lycian's attendants yelped.

A hand touched Tsorreh's shoulder. She spun around, a heartbeat away from striking out. Astreya stared at her, eyes white-rimmed and desperate. She took one of Tsorreh's hands between her own and pulled her back up the steps. The girl's grasp was surprisingly soft, entreating rather than compelling.

"Gracious lady," Astreya bowed to Lycian, "she's confused, she didn't mean anything. She doesn't know our laws or customs! Please, if you must punish anyone, it was my fault—"

"Get out of my sight! Immediately!"

"Yes, of course, gracious lady. Thank you, gracious lady." Astreya whirled Tsorreh around and shoved her bodily up the path. Tsorreh started to speak, but Astreya hurried her away even faster.

By the time they were beyond Lycian's hearing, Tsorreh had regained a measure of calm. If she had hoped Jaxar's patronage would protect her within the compound, she now knew that to be an illusion. She did not know what power Lycian might have over non-slaves, but Astreya's reaction suggested it was considerable. She did not know the customs here, whether Breneya and her daughter had any rights, if they were free to leave if they were mistreated, or what hold Lycian might have over them. Grimly, she thought that she would soon find out.

"I'm sorry to have brought trouble upon you," she said to Astreya.

"You took the blow meant for me," Astreya breathed.

"She had no right to strike you."

"You don't know what she's like, what she can do! How

she never forgets." Astreya glanced back toward the bath-house entrance. She bit her lower lip, clearly thinking she had already said too much.

"But you are not slaves! Surely you have the freedom to leave, to refuse her orders."

"Once that was true. My mother has told me how it was when she was a child." Astreya shook her head. "Now the laws are different. It is said that obedience is ordained by the gods for the greater glory of the Ar-King, may-his-splendor-never-grow-dim, and the Golden Land. If you or I dared, dared to—and Lady Lycian made a complaint against us for disruption of social order, it would become a matter for the public court. She could have us whipped. Or worse," she added in a whisper.

"I don't suppose the washery is that bad." Tsorreh shrugged, resigned. "It's useful work, after all. Someone has to clean the clothes."

Astreya gave her another astonished look. "Oh, we don't do that here! We take them to the best establishment in the cloth-groomers' district. It's on the other side of the city."

Excitement tingled along the edges of Tsorreh's mind. An image tantalized her—eluding the fragile custody of this young girl, bolting down a crowded street, hiding herself in a warren of alleys . . .

"Why so far?" she asked to cover her reaction. "Don't you have a laundry for a household this size?"

"What do you think we are? Only poor people wash their own garments. Besides, the smell is terrible! You wouldn't want to live anywhere near, if you could help it." Astreya frowned. "It's not the usual day for laundry, so Is-sios won't be pleased."

"Issios?"

"Steward here. He likes everything in its place, you know."

"Oh yes, I've met him."

"Don't mistake me. He's strict, but he's fair. It's just that he never smiles. Never. Not even at the Festival of The Bounteous Giver of Wine!"

"I'm sorry, I don't know what that is."

Astreya rolled her eyes, looking very much like an adolescent, but said nothing. They'd reached the house. A side entrance, one of many, led to a separate wing where the steward and other household managers had their quarters and offices.

The steward frowned when Astreya explained to him what she and Tsorreh were to do. He shook his head. "I cannot authorize *her*," meaning Tsorreh, "to leave this compound, not when she has been given into the custody of my Lord Jaxar."

And certainly not on the word of a mere servant girl, his tone indicated as well.

Astreya's voice shook as she answered Issios, but she stood her ground. "Shall I send for Lady Lycian, then, so that she can repeat her words to you? Whose orders must I obey—yours or *hers*?"

For a moment, Issios looked as if he might strike Astreya. Then his angry expression vanished into a mask of tight control. "It is not your fault that you have been placed in such a position. I see that you are a dutiful child and have no wish to make mischief. A household runs best when there is one set of clear orders and a hierarchy that everyone understands."

He suppressed a sigh, pressing his thin lips together. "If Lady Lycian has commanded you both to perform such an unusual duty, it is not for any of us to question her right to do so. I warn you that any deviation from the most proper behavior will place you beyond my protection. You will not be able to say in truth that I authorized this errand, only that I did not forbid it."

He regarded Tsorreh, his eyes dark and hooded with warning. *Lycian will not vouch for you if you get into trouble. You will be on your own.*

Tsorreh thought Lycian would take great delight in disavowing all responsibility, should anything befall.

Under the direction of Issios, a bevy of servants soon assembled piles of sheets, towels, ordinary robes of cotton and fine-spun wool, and linen underclothing for both men and women. Regarding the sheer quantity, Tsorreh decided that either the household was much larger or more amply supplied than she had first guessed.

Tsorreh wondered how two women could manage such a bulky load, but with the aid of shoulder yokes and capacious wicker baskets, they were able to carry it all. The baskets were heavy, although not unbearably so. As she settled the curved wooden yoke across her shoulders, Tsorreh remembered carrying load after load of library books into safety in the temple cavern. At least, if she dropped this burden, she would not damage it.

She saw very little of the outside streets once they had left the compound itself. All her concentration went to keeping the panniers steady. She kept her eyes on Astreya's legs, moving in slow, patient steps before her.

The edge of the yoke, which had felt smooth at first, pressed into her flesh. The muscles of her shoulders went from aching discomfort to agony. After a short distance, the rope sandals rubbed blisters on her feet.

I can do this, Tsorreh repeated silently to herself.

They went around and down, following the natural contours of the hill. The streets curved so that after a short period of time, Tsorreh lost sense of direction. Eventually, they reached the bottom of the hill and wound through one district after another. They passed along rows of shops and progressively poorer-looking dwellings. Astreya explained that, as well as washing finished clothing, the cloth-groomers treated newly woven cloth, rendering it soft and pleasing to the skin. The smells of the substances used to treat the cloth, however, were apparently so vile that the groomers were, by law, relegated to areas far away from any respectable residences.

Tsorreh could not tell how long they had been walking. She tried counting steps. She counted backward and forward. She counted in Gelone, in Denariyan, and in tradedialect Azkhantian. The distraction helped take her mind off her physical discomfort.

Once down from the hill, they passed all sorts of people, many on foot, others riding donkeys or onagers. Occasionally, a chariot rattled past. Now and again, a runner would dart by, well-shod and swift. The first time this happened, Tsorreh jumped in alarm before she realized that no one took any particular notice of the runner. His even pace suggested that he was a courier rather than a fugitive.

Armed men moved through the streets in twos and fours. Pairs of them stood at the major intersections. Tsorreh's heart raced the first time they came near. The sun gleamed on their helmets and blurred her vision. They were vivid reminders of the soldiers who had marched through the gates of Meklavar and Gatacinne. One of them called out a slang phrase that she did not understand.

"Watch your tongue," Astreya snapped back, "for it's more use to any woman than what wags at your other end." Laughing, the men turned away.

Tsorreh wavered on her feet. Her panniers swung dangerously. For a long moment, it was all she could do to regain control and keep the yoke steady across her shoulders. She was sweating and breathing hard, not entirely from the physical effort.

Astreya, who had gone ahead, paused. "What's wrong?"

"I'm sorry," Tsorreh stammered. "I'm not used to—I was surprised by the way those men spoke, that's all."

"They thought you were a slave. That's why they talked to you in such a disrespectful fashion."

Tsorreh bit her lip. Better that than an escaped prisoner, one Cinath would be as glad to have done with.

"It's not your fault," Astreya went on as they walked side by side. "It's the dress."

"It doesn't matter what Gelonian soldiers think of me."

"Soldiers? Oh no, those were just ordinary city patrol! Riff-raff with no decent manners! No properly trained soldier would speak to a woman in that way, even if she were a slave." Astreya sounded very much like her mother.

"I don't understand. They were armed and in uniform."

"I suppose that all men with swords must look alike to

anyone who hasn't lived in Gelon. See those men at the corner? They're military; you can tell by the cut of their tunics and see, their breastplates and the medallions on their scabbards. Some of the noble houses have their own armed escorts, and you can identify them by the sashes with their lord's colors. City patrol don't wear armor, just helmets."

Astreya lowered her voice "The ones you really need to watch out for are the Elite Guards, the Ar-King's private enforcers. Just pray to whatever gods you have in Meklavar that you never see one of that sort."

Chapter Seventeen

AFTER detouring to avoid the center of the city, Tsorreh and Astreya reached one of Aidon's many plazas. Although pleasing in shape and clearly designed as a public space, the plaza had seen better days. The paving stones were worn and cracked with the passage of years. Despite her weariness, Tsorreh lifted her head. Booths ran halfway across the plaza in widely spaced rows, while buildings of weathered wood and stone formed a perimeter. Many of these were shops, their entrances sheltered from sun and rain by overhanging eaves. At each corner, a cluster of shrines stood amidst offerings of wilting flowers, ribbons, and fruit.

In front of the shops and at the ends of rows of booths, old men sat gossiping or dozing in the shade, their heads lowered. A woman in baggy, faded pants and tunic, clearly too poor to afford a booth of her own, crouched behind baskets of peaches, nut candies, and fist-sized green melons. Another man, his face a toothless grin, offered crude beeswax idols and pots of honey for sale. A pair of teenagers laughed and flirted as they sold skewers of some kind of meat from a cart.

Women flocked around a fountain of eroded pink stone that had been carved with sea creatures and human figures, now faded and indistinct. One by one, they dipped their jugs and carried them away on top of their heads or braced against their hips. Boys watered onagers and donkeys. Between the fountain and the wall of shops, half-grown children played with pebbles, and street performers plucked stringed instruments, rhythm drums, and finger cymbals. The place had the slightly dangerous atmosphere of a festival. Tsorreh would have liked to stop and stare at the rich variety of costume, listen to the unfamiliar dialects, perhaps sample the strange food. Astreya hurried her on, saying they still had far to go.

As they passed through the crowd at the far end, Tsorreh caught a phrase in Meklavaran, or thought she did. By the time she turned to look, however, the voice had stopped. She searched the milling crowd, but none of the faces or clothing looked familiar. From the plaza, they made their way past crumbling apartment rows.

When Tsorreh stumbled with fatigue, they set their panniers down beside a street shrine that Astreya explained was to honor The Source of Fertility. Tsorreh arched her back, feeling the joints of her spine crackle. The buildings here stood two or three stories tall and might have been comfortable enough once, judging by the ample windows. Overcrowding, disuse, and, most likely, the passage of years, had taken their toll. Greasy stains ran from the cracked roofs and window ledges. Emaciated dogs picked through the piles of refuse that were heaped along the sides of the buildings. Several figures squatted in the shadowed doorways, tipping their heads back to drink from a common wineskin.

The air reeked of stale urine, old wine, and moldering garbage. "What is this place?" Tsorreh asked.

"Haven't you seen slave quarters before?" Astreya said.

Tsorreh shook her head. "We have nothing like this in Meklavar. If these people are slaves, where are their masters? Why don't they run away, leave the city? Go someplace clean, where they can live like human beings?"

Astreya explained that being able to live in a place like

this was a privilege, and that the penalties for any slave who failed to appear for work at the designated time were extreme. Slave-owners liked the arrangement because they no longer needed to supply food or shelter. Slaves were usually given a little time off to work on their own for enough money to buy the cheapest sort of food and share the meager rent, crowding into the old apartments.

Tsorreh's temper rose. She did not know what made her more angry, the plight of these poor wretches or the sudden suspicion that Lycian had intended her to see this place as a warning. Her face hot, she turned to the younger woman.

"Were you told to bring me by this route?"

Astreya looked puzzled. "There is no other way. All the outer areas are like this."

The streets dwindled into lanes of hard-packed dirt lined by fenced yards and sprawling, ramshackle buildings. As Astreya had indicated, the street of the cloth-groomers was well isolated from the richer neighborhoods, in a district that included tanners. When they left Jaxar's compound, the day had been mild, the breezes cool and laden with pleasant scents of herbs and flowers. The air here reeked of noxious substances. In the stench, Tsorreh smelled sulfur. Within a few moments, her eyes were burning and her lungs felt raw.

Astreya led the way to a yard of modest size. Under an airy lattice canopy, half a dozen youths barely out of their teens marched in place in broad wooden tubs. They had tucked their tunics above their knees to avoid being splashed. The tubs, easily wide enough for a grown man to bathe in, were filled with dark water and sodden cloth. The rest of the open space was taken up by drying racks, frames of wicker on which clean cloth was stretched.

The boys chanted in unison, sweating in the mild morning, but grinned and waved as Astreya and Tsorreh maneuvered their panniers through the gates.

"They're grooming new cloth," Astreya said, and headed for the squat stone building. "The laundering is done inside."

Stepping into the washery was like entering a furnace.

Despite the high-set openings, the large single chamber was dark and close. Tsorreh's breath caught in her lungs. The air was laden with moisture, although the stench was not so bad.

In the center of the room, an enormous vat perched over a roaring fire. The flames cast a red glow over the walls, racks, piles of clothing and linen, and the sweating faces of the washers. An aperture in the ceiling let the worst of the steam and smoke escape.

The washer-chief grunted in greeting and straightened up from where she and two others, a boy and a middle-aged woman, stirred clothes around in the bubbling water. Tsorreh had never seen such a large, muscular woman before, easily a head taller than Shorrenon, and he had been a tall man. Tsorreh did not know the Xian folk well, but guessed that this powerful-looking woman must be one of them.

The washer grinned, revealing a missing front top tooth. "A fair day to you, young one." She spoke with a slight twang.

Astreya set down her panniers with a sigh of relief. "We've brought the laundry from Lord Jaxar."

"Xathan's hairy balls! You're days early! All my apprentices are at work on a rush order from the Palace." The woman peered at Tsorreh. "What's this? Has Issios sent me some extra help to make up for the inconvenience?"

"Tsorreh, don't take anything Czi-sotal says seriously or she'll have you doing all the work by yourself," Astreya said tartly. "Everyone knows how lazy Xians are."

Czi-sotal gave a low, rumbling laugh. She shuffled closer, her bulk shutting out half the room. Although sweat rolled off the folds of her skin, she smelled surprisingly clean.

"Sor-ra, is it?" she drawled as she took Tsorreh's panniers, lifting them as if they weighed nothing. "You ever wash clothes?"

Tsorreh shook her head. Of all the things she had done in her life, laundry was not one of them. In Meklavar, as here, skilled workers prepared the finished cloth and cleaned it for others.

"Come, then, and I'll show you how it's done."

Astreya went outside to gossip with the boys in the tubs; one was apparently a distant cousin. Czi-sotal showed Tsorreh how she stirred and beat and boiled the tangled lengths of cotton. When they were sufficiently clean, Czi-sotal explained, she took them outside and draped them over drying frames to expose them to the sun, or on curved frames over pots of fuming sulfur for further bleaching. Then more heaps of rumpled, soiled linens and robes would go into the vat.

The enormous woman was clearly deriving a great deal of enjoyment from her captive audience. Years of assuming a polite expression during court ceremonies had given Tsorreh the ability to look interested while her thoughts wandered. She nodded now and again as her thoughts drifted.

The light in the room changed. Something moved in the shadows, something cold and sweltering at the same time. Tsorreh no longer felt the waves of heat from the fire. The red-tinged light went gray.

A massive hand on her shoulder jerked her awake. The grip was hard, the calluses like armor. The large woman shook her, peering into her face.

"Nothing but a wet rag, you are. Outside with you, then. Can't have you fainting into the wash pot." She pushed Tsorreh toward the door.

Tsorreh stumbled to the entrance. Daylight blinded her for a moment. She reeled, caught by the sudden brilliance and the cool, sweet air. Her lungs ached when she drew a deep breath.

I must be delirious with the heat, Tsorreh mused. Her cheek throbbed where Lycian had struck her.

Whistling cheerily, Astreya sauntered up. "Come on, if you've had enough lessons in laundry. Czi-sotal's happy to have something to complain about, but our order will be ready in time. She won't risk losing Lord Jaxar's custom."

A smile lit the corners of Astreya's mouth, and her eyes took on an expression both eager and dreamy. Reaching into a pocket, she clinked two coins together. "We don't have to go straight back. It will be some time yet before we're missed, so let's enjoy ourselves. I saw you looking at the market performers."

Tsorreh followed Astreya along the dusty avenue toward the center of the city. Perhaps she might find the man who had spoken her own language. It made sense that there were other Meklavarans in this cosmopolitan city, with its diversity of cultures.

If she found a countryman, what then? Her spirits leapt as the thought came to her that she might, with the right help, be able to make her way past the borders of Gelon and eventually return home.

They stopped at a food stall, and Astreya bought pastries: dough twisted around a fruit filling, then fried crisp and dusted with cinnamon and powdered almonds. Then she made for another line of booths that had been set up along one side, and Tsorreh followed. Wares were arranged on tables beneath sun-shades of open-weave fabric, draped over slanted frames. They passed baskets of apples and other fruit, as well as tubers of a dozen kinds, smaller baskets of seeds and dried beans, then on to a row where clothing in bright colors was spread out on tables or hung from ropes strung between the poles of the booths.

They approached several sellers of footwear, leather shoes that looked soft and supple, thick-soled boots, sandals, knitted wool socks, and brocade slippers. Some clearly were samples, to be custom made, but there also appeared to be a stock for direct sale. Tsorreh's feet burned where the rope sandals had rubbed blisters.

Astreya, seeing Tsorreh's interest, halted. "Wait here and promise not to wander off. You can look all you want. Just don't steal anything, or we'll both be in trouble."

Tsorreh was about to protest that she was not a thief, when she reminded herself that nothing from her former life was the same. She was no longer *te-ravah* of Meklavar, wife of Maharrad. She did not know what she was.

"Well, don't look so covetous, then," Astreya said. "I

know these merchants. If they see a slave eyeing their goods a little too eagerly, they'll call the city patrol."

Tsorreh's mouth dropped open in surprise. The girl was proposing to leave her here, in the market plaza, without supervision? What would prevent her from disappearing into the crowd?

Or was that what Lycian had intended, sending Tsorreh and Astreya on this errand? Escape would be easy. Too easy.

Lycian must be very sure that I would be captured again.

Whether Tsorreh were arrested or if by chance she managed to escape, the result would be the same. She would be gone from Lycian's house.

Tsorreh composed her features into a suitable expression of indifference. "I'll wait for you here, then."

Astreya nodded and headed toward the far end of the shops. Her pace increased, her feet flying over the ground. Tsorreh followed for a step or two, in time to see Astreya reach a doorway. The shop looked ordinary enough. A sign painted with a two-handled jar hung above the open door. A young man in a canvas apron had just carried out a similar vessel, easily as tall as his own torso, its neck sealed with red wax, and placed it in a donkey-drawn cart. Spying Astreya, he rushed over and caught her in his arms.

Tsorreh smiled despite herself, but the pulse of warmth faded quickly into sadness. She had never been in love like that, certainly not with Maharrad, not even with the occasional noble who had sought her favor before her marriage. She had become pregnant with Zevaron almost immediately, and then her life seemed to revolve around him and the city and the care of her aged spouse. She'd had a husband, a son, rank, and ease. What more could a woman dream of?

Love was a thing for fools and poets, those without duty.

Then what was this empty ache in her heart, as if it had broken without her knowing why?

The ache shifted to the now-familiar pulse of warning from the *te-alvar*. Tsorreh glanced around, but the market seemed perfectly normal. People stood bargaining with the vendors at their booths. The tinkle of a dance melody wafted through the air. The sun shone as brightly as before, and yet a shadow seemed to have fallen over the plaza, or perhaps behind her eyes.

Nothing.

Still nothing, as the ache faded. She wondered if the *te-alvar* had warned her against longing for what she could never have. Had it been trying to remind her that her life was not hers and had never been, but belonged to a greater purpose?

If so, she thought with a tinge of acerbity, it was going to have to speak more plainly to her.

Tsorreh turned back to the cobbler's booth. At least, the *te-alvar* had no objection to her hungering for decent foot-wear. If she could not dream of a lover, at least she could imagine the comfort of a well-made pair of shoes instead of rope sandals.

The young man who was minding the booth, an apprentice, she thought, looked up as she approached. He had the loose, gangly frame of an adolescent in the midst of his growth spurt, and acne blotched his face. By the plain pewter ornaments on each shoulder of his coarse-woven tunic, he was poor but free. His gaze flickered over her plain dress, her *slave's* dress, and his mouth tightened. Clearly, he intended to keep a close eye on her, and hurry her off as soon as a paying customer arrived.

Drawing her shoulders back and her head up, she strode up to the booth and faced him across the table where the shoes were displayed. "I'm to examine the quality of your wares," she said, meeting his gaze directly. "It's for my mistress. If I give her a good report, she will send me back with a substantial order."

"Whom have I the honor of serving?"

Tsorreh tossed her head. "My mistress does not reveal her identity to common craftsmen. You may take it that she is newly arrived in Aidon."

She almost giggled at the sight of the poor cobbler's apprentice quickly laying out a row of the most expensive-looking merchandise. Tsorreh picked up a slipper, finding the sole as thin and supple as satin. Bright embroidery and tiny pearls embellished the top. As she pretended to examine the stitches, she reflected that once she would have worn such shoes. She would have given little thought to how durable they were or how her feet would feel after hours of scrambling through volcanic tunnels or trudging across the sand. Or even walking from one end of Aidon to the other, she thought, shifting to ease the cramp in one arch.

She must have been frowning, for the apprentice quickly handed her another. "See the quality of the leather, fine enough to grace the tender foot of a lady."

"I suppose." Tsorreh sniffed. She was having fun at the poor boy's expense, which was unkind but would produce no lasting harm. In fact, she decided, demanding to see a pair of dancing sandals, a little intimidation might improve his manners. As she inspected the merchandise, she hazarded an occasional glance at the sturdier shoes and boots in one direction, and the oil merchant's shop into which Astreya had disappeared, in the other. She could not linger here indefinitely. The apprentice's patience undoubtedly had its limits. Then she'd have to move on.

What was taking Astreya so long? At this rate, they would be so long in returning that Lycian would not have to invent a reason for punishing them.

I'm seeing schemes and plots everywhere!

Just as she made up her mind that, in order to play the part she had created, she must stalk off in an aura of disapproval, she felt a presence behind her shoulder. A voice, low and masculine, murmured in her ear.

"Forgive my rudeness in speaking. I know every one of our people in this city, free or slave, trader or money-lender or craftsman, but I do not know you."

The words were spoken in Meklavaran, yet too low to be easily overheard. Startled, Tsorreh turned her head to see a man, slight of build but tall, dressed in the robes and intricately folded cloth cap of a Meklavaran physician. At once, she took in the trimmed, gray-streaked beard, weathered skin the color of honey, the creases around the eyes, the arch of cheekbone and nose.

The man's words and the kindness in his voice brought Tsorreh an absurd rush of joy. Until that moment, she had not known how deeply she missed seeing a face like her own—with her bones and skin and wavy dark hair—and hearing the music of her own language.

The man's eyes softened as he took in her response. "You are new in Aidon? Taken as a slave?"

The day seemed suddenly too bright.

The Meklavaran said, under his breath, "This place is not safe." His eyes narrowed as he looked out over the market. His body tensed, jaw clenching. Tsorreh tried to make out what had alarmed him, but she was too short to see easily through the crowd. In comparison, he was a head taller.

"What—" she began, still in Meklavaran, and then a space opened between the strolling pedestrians.

A pair of helmeted men, city patrol, strode through the crowd. A brief glimpse revealed their intent, set expressions and the arrogant set of their shoulders. From the way they walked and held themselves, they were on an urgent mission. The more poorly dressed people scurried out of the patrolmen's path and the street urchins disappeared. Even the more wealthy made way.

Tsorreh masked her shiver of fear. She reminded herself that, to such men, she would look like any other slave woman. In a public place like this, they might direct a few crude remarks in her direction, but nothing worse. She wished that Astreya had returned. Perhaps the best strategy was to take no notice of the patrolmen and do nothing to bring herself to their attention.

The Meklavaran had vanished, melted into the market crowd as if he had never existed. How would she ever find him again? She didn't even know his name. There were so many answers she needed from him.

The gaze of the foremost patrolman lit on her face. His eyes widened and his expression shifted. He pointed at her.

"You there! Halt!"

All Tsorreh's resolve to remain calm vanished. Her heart hammered so fast and loud, she could not think. Wildly, she searched for an avenue of escape. She knew, before she could take a single step, how futile that would be. The moment of flight had already passed. Any street urchin could have evaded the patrol more readily than she. If she tried, she would be captured, if she were not killed in the attempt. Neither anonymity nor flight could avail her now. Her only hope was to offer no resistance, to pretend innocence.

The next instant, the two patrolmen were upon her. One grabbed her and spun her around, expertly jerking her arms behind her back. "Got her!"

"The Lady Lycian reported you'd escaped custody," said the other, who appeared to be in command.

Lycian!

"There has b-been a m-mistake." Tsorreh tried not to stammer, and failed. "I w-was not running away."

The patrolman gave her arms a vicious twist. "That's what they all say. You will soon learn not to lie to those in authority over you."

"What—?"

"No questions!" The patrolman shoved Tsorreh forward so hard that she stumbled. Fire shot through her shoulder joints.

"Everyone out of the way!" the older patrolman ordered. The crowd, which had drawn nearer out of curiosity, pulled back again.

"What's this? What's going on here?" Danar's voice rose above the sounds of the market crowd. Through eyes watering with pain, Tsorreh saw him pushing through the milling pedestrians toward her. Two tall, muscular men followed him closely. They wore sashes in Jaxar's house colors.

Danar glared at the nearest patrolman. "What do you think you're doing? Is this how you were trained to greet dignitaries? Do you not recognize this noble lady or know she is in Lord Jaxar's care?"

The man holding Tsorreh's arms snorted insolently, but

his fellow paused. His expression wavered from annoyance to hesitation.

"Who is asking?" The patrolman's gaze shifted from Danar's youthful features to his tunic of silk, the gold clasps at his shoulders, the chain of ruby-studded links around his neck, and the cloak of purple wool. Danar's escort had taken up positions to either side of him. From their postures and grim expressions, their eyes narrowed and their hands ready on the hilts of their swords, they stood ready to defend him against the city patrol or anyone else.

With an aggrieved sigh, as if anyone who needed to ask was beneath his attention, Danar gave his name, followed by a long stream of titles, few of which Tsorreh recognized. Her panic melted into near-exhilaration at being rescued by a boy the age of her son.

"I see you are woefully ill-informed on current events at court." With a sneer, Danar addressed the senior patrolmen. "I shall report this lapse and your superiors will be duly disciplined. This lady is in my father's charge and *I* am escorting her about the city. I suggest that if you value your jobs, not to mention your skins, you unhand her immediately. Well, what are you waiting for? Is something amiss? Anything I ought to report to my uncle?"

"Nothing at all, young lord! Everything is in perfect order!" The older of the two patrolmen sputtered as his comrade released Tsorreh.

Tsorreh lifted her chin, assuming as regal a posture as she could. The muscles of her shoulders burned and she longed to rub them, but she was determined not to display weakness in front of such men.

"It is unpleasant to be the object of so much common attention," Danar said to the patrolmen. "Disperse this rabble and then take yourselves off to your next duties, so that we may proceed without hindrance about our own business."

The patrolmen shouted for the crowd to break up, then hurried off as quickly as they could with any degree of dignity. With their departure, the shoppers and vendors lost interest. Danar's guards maintained their watchful stance.

"Thank all the gods you're safe!" Danar said. "Astreya told Father what Lycian did! Or rather, she told Breneya. Father was furious at Lycian. I haven't heard them fight like that—well, *she* screams, but he just listens and then does what he wants. He sent me to find you. When you weren't at the washery, I didn't know where to look!"

"We were on our way back," Tsorreh explained.

"Where's Astreya? Isn't she with you? She didn't leave you here to find your own way home?"

"No, no. She just stepped away for a moment. To see a . . ." Tsorreh hesitated, unsure how much to reveal. How easy it was to slip into a conspiracy of the powerless, to lie by omission. "A friend, I think."

Somewhat to her surprise, Danar nodded. "Yes, the oil merchant's son. We'll lose her as soon as the boy's father settles him with a share in the business. Father says it won't be long now."

For an invalid and a crippled recluse, Jaxar appeared to know a great deal about the goings-on in the city. Certainly, he was no fool about what went on in his own household.

"Father said not to hurry home, to keep you away from the house for awhile. I wonder if you'd like to see a bit of Aidon." From Danar's tone, the outing was clearly not a burden, but an adventure. He had shed the arrogant self-importance with which he had confronted the patrolmen. "What would you like to explore first?"

Chapter Eighteen

"I HARDLY know," Tsorreh replied, still dazed at the rapid reversal of events. First she had been sent on a menial errand, which turned out to be a scheme by Lycian to have her arrested. Now she found herself in the company of a young man eager to indulge her wishes.

"I've been in your city only a short time," she pointed out, "and most of that I've been confined indoors, either at the Palace or in your father's laboratory. Won't Astreya worry if she returns, and I am not here? I did promise not to wander off."

Danar appeared not to have heard her last comment. He was already turning away from her, gesturing to one of the ragged children who had followed in his wake.

Glancing nervously at the two guards, the child approached. Dust obliterated the original color of his rough-cropped hair. He looked to be about eight, slender and wiry, but the bright, calculating look in his eyes made Tsorreh suspect he was older.

Danar held out a coin that glinted copper in the sun. "Here, boy. Do you see that shop, with the two-handled jar above the door? I will give you this coin to tell the oil seller there that there is no hurry on his order. I will have another such coin when you return with his answer."

Beaming, the boy snatched the coin in one dirt-encrusted hand. He darted back into the crowd, weaving in and out of the shoppers like a liquid shadow. The boy was so clearly a creature of the city, of alleys and stolen apples, of cleverness and desperation, Tsorreh wanted to laugh and weep.

A few minutes later, the boy returned.

"He says he is most, um, most overjoyed." With an exultant glance at Danar's bodyguards, the boy thrust out his hand for the rest of his payment.

"I doubt he really said that, but you have earned your fee." Watching the boy disappear once more, Danar said, "I believe he may have a future as a speedy but not necessarily accurate messenger."

The incident lightened Tsorreh's mood. "You choose our destination. Take me to one of your favorite places."

"Let's go up to Victory Hill," Danar said, motioning for his escort to follow. "It's got the best view of the city. That will give you a general idea of where things are."

The slopes of Victory Hill were almost as steep as cliffs. A road wound along the sides, switching back frequently. Its natural defenses made it an ideal location for both lookout and fortress. A handful of archers could easily hold the heights. At the highest point, to the southwest of the relatively flat top, a windswept field surrounded the crumbling remains of a watchtower. Leaving the two guards at the base of the tower, Danar and Tsorreh clambered up to the top of the heaped stones.

Aidon was more vast than Tsorreh had imagined, a patchwork of regularly laid-out avenues lined with greenery, marked by open spaces and markets. It flowed like a carpet of white and green and red-brick roofs between the encircling hills. Jaxar's compound, as she had seen from her first day, was situated near the top of one of three eastern hills.

The hills, Danar explained, were the oldest part of the city. Each had originally possessed its own fortifications, villages that at times warred against each other. The first Ar-King had united them as a single city. He had also, Tsorreh recalled from her study of Gelonian history, codified the various legal systems. For this, he was now known as Ir-Pilant, a divine avatar of The Giver of Justice.

As Danar talked, Tsorreh studied the wide Serpan River that formed the western border of the city. The water shifted from green to a blue so deep it was almost black, but along the shore, churned silt turned it brown. Here and there, fortified bridges, marvels of Gelonian engineering, spanned the river. As Tsorreh watched, a pair of long-necked white birds swept across the surface, dipping now and again to brush the waves. She had read about such birds. The sight of them, with their wings outstretched as they drifted on the air currents, moved her unexpectedly.

In the early years of the city, a second river, flat and shallow, had flowed into the Serpan. The old river had long since dried up or been diverted. Now the royal palace, municipal buildings, temples, and courts occupied the dried watercourse. The most fashionable noble families had relocated their compounds there from the inconvenience of the hilltops. Danar explained that Jaxar remained in the ancestral family dwelling. Unlike other nobles, he did not leave the city during the summer, although his estates on the slopes of the northwest mountains were rich and pleasant.

Beyond the Serpan, Tsorreh could just make out a ribbon of road and fields, the dust-blurred shapes of men and beasts, tents and wagons. In response to her questions, Danar confirmed that the fields were for army encampment. Once the site had been temporary, but now, with one campaign following another, no crops had been grown there for years. He hesitated, as if in realization that the soldiers who had conquered her homeland might have mustered and trained on those very fields.

In the awkward moment, Tsorreh found her voice thick with unexpected emotion, "Who does Cinath make war upon now?"

"He's always sending expeditions to Azkhantia, for one

thing, for all the good it does. Those riders have powerful gods, and they're marvelously fierce archers. If they ever decided to invade Gelon, we'd be hard-pressed. It's just as well that they keep to the steppe. And there's Isarre. Isarre, the Eternal Enemy. I don't know where my uncle will turn next. Through the Var Pass to Denariya? The Sand Lands? Or west to the Mearas? Only the gods know. He wants it all."

Tsorreh looked at the young man with curiosity. Danar did not sound enthusiastic about his uncle's military ambitions. "You don't approve?"

Danar leaned on a bit of stone wall and looked away, but not before she caught the shift in his expression. He seemed suddenly much older than his years. The wind tugged at his red-gold hair. "It's not seemly for me to have any opinion at all," he said tightly. "My uncle is the Ar-King, the Voice of the Gods, the Glory of the Golden Land. How can anything he commands be otherwise than right?"

Some impulse drove Tsorreh to say, "If you did have doubts, would it be prudent to speak of them to an enemy, even one as defeated and powerless as I am? And yet, even if I did repeat what you say, who would believe me?"

He flashed a grin, and she decided she liked him very much. She wondered if he and Zevaron might have become friends if they had met in times of peace.

"My father says trust must be earned." Danar's voice was softer now, more thoughtful. By chance, the wind died down so that she heard him clearly, not just his words, but all the harmonics below them.

A smile touched the corners of her mouth. "Your father is a wise man."

"My father is a man who, only a generation ago, would have been drowned as an infant!" he said, his voice laced with sudden fervor. "He's seven years older than my uncle, but because of an accident at his birth, he cannot rule. Yet he never lives a day without being suspected of coveting the Golden Throne!"

"*Does he?*" she shot back, masking her horrified reaction

to Danar's casual reference to infanticide. "Does he covet it?"

"How can you ask? How can anyone who's spent a hour in his presence believe such a vicious lie? You've seen his laboratory! All he wants is to be left alone, to study the marvels of the natural world. He is the best, most honest man I know. I would say that even if he were not my father."

Tsorreh could not think of a response. Children did not always judge their parents wisely, thinking too much or too little of them.

"Steel wears thin," Danar said, sounding so much like Jaxar, Tsorreh suspected he was quoting his father directly. "And gold grows dim, and men discover they have spent their lives in pursuit of shadows instead of stars. How can we fight and die and kill one another, when there is so much wonder in the world?"

The phrases lingered in Tsorreh's mind. Eavonen would have been delighted beyond words with such a student. She thought of the library she had struggled to save, how much knowledge and how many fine minds had already been lost. Anger, or something very like it, curled through her belly.

After a pause, she said, "My son is your age, you know. And he had no choice. He *had* to train in fighting. He *had* to defend his city, his family, his life. *You* have the luxury of living far away from the battle, while it was carried—by *your uncle*—to my son's doorstep."

The wind had whipped color into Danar's cheeks, but not enough to disguise the sudden rush of blood. "I am truly sorry. My father says that someday we will no longer strive to conquer each other, but will see the world as filled with friends yet unmet and be eager to learn their wisdom."

Tsorreh shrugged. Danar's words were pretty, but she could not imagine such a world. Since the beginning of time, one enemy or another had threatened her people.

Does the struggle ever end? Or is it the same story, over and over again?

The wind shifted suddenly, buffeting her face. A swirl of dust blew into her eyes. Her eyelids burned and watered.

The weathered stones of the old watchtower blurred. She blinked, sending tears down her cheeks. The sky turned preternaturally bright. She lifted a hand to shield her eyes.

The next moment, when she lowered her hand, she still stood on a windswept hill. Now, however, she was alone, and no city stretched below her. No river gleamed like a vast, silver-green ribbon, nor could she make out red tile roofs, temples, and marketplaces. Instead, she looked out over an army, a mass of glittering armor and upraised swords. The whiteness of the sky congealed. Snow-crystal clouds glowed between billowing thunderheads. Across the horizon, something moved, pale as ice and black as ashes, something indistinct and terrible, a ripple of light and darkness, of white-hot flame and bitter cold.

The air tasted of unspent lightning.

A man stood beside her, tall and strongly built, regal in bearing. The wind tore at his hair, tossing braids as dark as night. His skin was the color of honey and his eyes gleamed with inner fire. Unaware of her presence, he lifted one bare, muscular arm, holding something just beyond her vision.

Something infinitely precious, infinitely powerful.

Once before, she had stood at Khored's side, looking out on this same battlefield. She had seen what came next. Like a dreamer, she could not move, could not speak, could only witness the unfolding events.

Her heart leapt as she lifted her eyes to what Khored held. She recognized the distinctive pattern of the Shield, each petal glowing, the clear center as brilliant as the sun.

Words came from the mouth of the great king, words shouted, whispered, prayed. Ancient syllables called forth, gathered, summoned. Words became light, and light flowed through spirit, and spirit shaped itself into words.

BY GRACE, ALL THINGS ARE MADE . . .

In Tsorreh's vision, Khored once more held the Shield aloft. Its light streamed out in all directions, the Seven-Petaled Shield that would conquer the forces of Fire and Ice. The Shield that stood between the armies of chaos and the living world.

What does it mean? she wondered. *Why does this vision come to me here in Gelon?*

As Tsorreh watched, the lowering stormclouds shifted. For a moment, things once hidden came into focus. Shapes moved through the mists, reaching down from the north with tendrils of shimmering gray. She could not tell if the wavering forms were streamers or weirdly articulated legs. Whatever they were, their power increased as they gained in solidity. In another moment, they would become solid forms, potent and malevolent presences in the world.

She knew what would come then, what had come before: monsters of frost and flame, stone-drakes belching ice and molten cinders, ice trolls. Fertile lands would be turned into shattered rock and sulfur-steaming vents, awash in tides of blood.

Tsorreh had no doubt that the tendrils were an incursion by the ancient powers of Fire and Ice, long held at bay by the Seven-Petaled Shield. It was written in the *te-Ketav*, in the Book of Khored, that as long as the Shield endured, the ancient enemy would remain imprisoned, and righteousness would reign.

Then why did her spirit falter? Why did her heart tremble?

Khored shouted again, words that blew away in the wind. In response, light blazed forth from the Shield. The heavens shimmered in multi-hued glory. The shadowy forms halted, writhing and twisting in on themselves. Slowly, they withdrew.

All is well, Tsorreh tried to reassure herself. *The Shield protects us still.*

Between her breasts, the *te-alvar* surged to life, filling her, searing her from within. Her first thought was that it had responded to its counterpart in her vision. Perhaps it remembered the past and was eager to perform its duty again.

Like a sword that thirsts for the blood of its enemies.

Without warning, one of the *alvara* in Khored's Shield broke away from the magical device. It hung in the battering storm for a moment, glittering as if with tears.

Tears of fury? Grief? Despair? Tsorreh could not tell. Her breath burned her throat. Her mouth stretched wide, and yet no sound came forth.

The wind fractured the detached gemstone into nothingness. Still the great king held the Shield high, his stance as determined as ever. But the colors in his skin and eyes faded, as if a cloud had passed across the sun.

Another gem tumbled loose, shattering on the hard ground. One of the shards flashed blue, a fragment of reflected sky.

When Tsorreh was a child, Eavonen had drilled her in the names, colors and attributes of each of the crystals. She had memorized them all, Dovereth's true yellow, the pale rose of Teharod's wisdom, Shebu'od's purple strength, and more, all united by a single clear uniting purpose, the *tealvar* of Khored.

Blue was for Eriseth, for endurance, for steadfast loyalty. *Eriseth!* she realized with a jolt of white fear. The heir to that lineage had been lost a generation ago in Denariya—and the *alvar* with him! And without Eriseth's unwavering steadfastness . . .

Sweat covered Khored's brow and trickled down his cheeks. He trembled with effort to keep the remainder of the Shield intact. Tsorreh reached out to cover his hands with her own, to bind together what was left of the Shield.

As long as the center holds, there is hope.

The wind increased in force, buffeting her. She held tight to Khored's hand, to the Shield. The brightness of the day dimmed; the storm was almost upon them. Her muscles stretched and strained. Silently, she prayed for the endurance of Eriseth, the wisdom of Teharod, the courage of Cassarod, the might of Shebu'od. Until that moment, Tsorreh had regarded her noble ancestor as a colorful legend. Now she felt within herself his strength as well as his sense of duty. Khored would never relent in his purpose, and neither would she, his heir. Resolve flowed through her like a river of gold. Whatever was required of her, whatever the cost, she would hold fast.

Moment by moment, the storm gained in power. Dust, fine and white as ice crystals, billowed up to blind her. Through watering eyes, she could see only swirls of gray and darker gray. Her hands turned cold, then numb. She could no longer feel Khored's fingers beneath her own, only the adamantine facets of the Shield gems.

Thunder boomed, at first distant, then closer. The rumbling shook Tsorreh's bones. For an instant, she felt as if she would fly apart, along with what remained of the Shield.

Desperate, she clenched the precious central crystal and drew it close. She curled her body protectively around it, pulling her arms close, hunching her shoulders. In the shelter of her body, the gem flared up again. Light, fierce and golden, filled her, spilling through her flesh.

"Tsorreh." From afar, a voice spoke her name.

The storm dissipated as quickly as it had sprung up. A breeze, sweet and cool, caressed Tsorreh's skin. She stood blinking in the brightness of normal day. Looking down at her hands, she was surprised to find them empty. The joints of her fingers throbbed as if they had been dislocated.

"Tsorreh? Are you ill? What is wrong?" Danar was leaning toward her, his young face furrowed in concern.

She forced her lips into a smile. "I'm sorry, I don't know what came over me." And prayed to be forgiven for that small lie. There was no possible way in which she could explain to this Gelonian youth what she had just seen.

"Can we go down?" she said. "I fear this wind has given me a headache."

"Yes, you do look weary. For a moment, I thought you might faint. My father would never forgive me if you became ill while in my care."

"It is of no matter. See, I am quite well again."

They started down the path, once again trailed by Danar's escort. Tsorreh wondered if he went anywhere outside the compound without them. She could not imagine Zevaron willingly enduring such constant surveillance. A thought came to her, teasing a smile from the corners of her mouth: Danar, sneaking out after dark for an hour's freedom, perhaps in one of the less savory districts, intoxicated by the taste of danger. Perhaps Zevaron had, unknown to her, done the same.

"Just as you turned white, you called out a name," Danar said. "*Khored.*"

"Khored was my ancestor, the founder of my father's house," Tsorreh explained as they walked along. "His deeds form the basis of our most sacred texts."

"I haven't read them," Danar admitted. "Is he one of your gods?"

"No, of course not. He was as mortal as you or I. But he was a great king and war-leader."

"Here in Gelon, we believe that our kings are descended from gods—*god-begotten*, we say. Perhaps that's why we have so many."

"There is only one god, the Source of All Blessings."

"In Meklavar, perhaps. It is such a small country, perhaps there isn't room enough for more than one. Here in Gelon, we have many gods. But not all of them bestow blessings."

A quick retort rose to Tsorreh's lips, but she managed to hold her tongue. Danar was trying hard to be her friend, and he was so clearly in need of one, living under the same roof as his stepmother. She wondered if he now spoke of his own troubles.

Once they had left the flat top of the hill, the wind died down. They passed through a wealthy residential area of walled compounds, tree-lined avenues, and public gardens with elaborate fountains.

"Which god do you worship?" Tsorreh asked in a carefully neutral voice.

"My family follows the usual household gods suitable for those of royal descent. The servants have their own. Until I come of age, I belong to The One Who Lends Fame, a very fickle god, I confess, for what is lent can be as easily taken away. My favorite comes to us from Denariya, The Remover of Difficulties."

At this, Tsorreh laughed, and Danar grinned back, continuing, "I'm told that my mother was a devotee of The Lady of Mercy."

The Lady of Mercy sounded benign, if heretical. "What about Lord Jaxar?"

"Not the King's-god, of course, that one's for Cinath himself. Father was consecrated as a baby to The Giver of Justice, or so they tell me. Privately, I don't think he bothers with any of the rituals. He believes more in what he finds in his books and laboratory than any idol. Lycian finally gave up trying to convert him to whichever god has her favor at the moment." The muscles in Danar's jaw tensed as he said this

The chance to learn more about the household in which she must survive was too tempting to pass up. "What god does Lycian pray to now?"

"Oh, she's taken up with the Scorpion god. Just trying to impress the other court ladies, I think. She thinks that next season, the Scorpion priests will have the Ar-King's favor, and she will be their foremost devotee."

A shivery touch pass over Tsorreh's skin. She remembered the form on the headband of the priest who had questioned her after the fall of Gatacinne. "Scorpion? Do you mean Qr?"

"You've heard of it? Qr? It's unlucky for a god to have a public name, for how then can it speak to our innermost hearts?" Danar scratched his chin. "The Scorpion never appealed to me, but that's the good thing about having so many gods."

"Yes, I see that. If one god displeases you by demanding righteous behavior, you turn fickle and choose another."

Danar seemed unaware of her sarcasm. "It's funny, you know, Lycian devoting herself to the Scorpion, because she hates things that crawl. One time, a real scorpion got into her bedroom, one of the big black ones. She screamed so loud, she woke the whole household and raised such a fuss that Father finally agreed to let her move to an entirely new suite of rooms. You should have heard the commotion!" Danar rolled his eyes. "Otherwise, though, Qr suits her."

"Maybe she doesn't look too closely at the headbands the priests wear," Tsorreh suggested.

"Maybe she thinks they can give her a son."

"I'm sure they can." The words popped out before Tsorreh thought what she was saying.

Danar flushed and looked away. "They say that when Qr returns to the world, it will repay their loyalty. Its followers will have unimaginable power. They will become gods themselves."

"And Cinath permits the worship of a god who makes such claims? Wouldn't these followers overthrow him, if they became so mighty?"

"Oh, the priests are careful in what they say directly to him. Father says they promise whatever that particular person wants to hear. Of course, if those promises don't come true, they can always claim that the worshiper wasn't devout enough. Or didn't give them enough money."

To Tsorreh's mind, that proved only the greed of the priests. The Most Holy One bestowed blessings freely, opened the hearts of the people, and filled them with compassion.

"Father won't have anything to do with Qr," Danar said. "He says it's a criminally ambitious cult and not true godworship. Of course, he'll let Lycian have her way, as long as she doesn't ask him for money for her tribute. She's got her own fortune from her family. But she can't force anyone else—and that includes you—to go with her."

He sounded so earnest in his reassurance that Tsorreh laughed. Being compelled to worship the idolatrous gods of Gelon had not been among her worries. *Staying alive, however, is,* she thought, sobering.

Tsorreh fell silent. When Danar pointed out the various sights, she nodded without comment. After a time, the glitter of marble and limestone, of gold-foil decorations and rainbow garlands began to dull. She found herself longing for the clean, dust-scoured lines of Meklavar instead of this brilliant opulence.

As they passed through the valley between Victory Hill

and Cynar Hill, Tsorreh remembered Danar saying that Lycian had been banned from the laboratory. She decided that, for the time being, she would restrict herself to that suite, the better to avoid the schemes of the mistress of the house.

When Tsorreh returned to the laboratory, aching in spirit and body, she found that someone—Astreya, most likely—had left a basin and ewer of lavender-scented water beside her pallet, along with a towel and a lump of soap. Tsorreh almost wept at the sight.

Curled up on the surprisingly soft pallet, Tsorreh felt the day's tension slowly drain away. Her body felt thick and heavy, like that of an exhausted child. She murmured thanks to the Most Holy One, Source of Blessings, and tumbled into sleep.

Chapter Nineteen

WHEN Tsorreh awoke the next morning, she found a breakfast tray waiting on the floor beside her pallet. The food was much the same as the day before, except that the millet porridge had gone cold. Folded on her blanket was a dress of white cotton, as fine and soft as silk. White embroidery ran along arm openings and ankle-length hem, and the fabric had been gathered at each shoulder to drape gracefully. Underneath, she discovered a pair of low boots of supple suede and a belt of braided white silk, fringed with little gold beads. The accompanying shoulder clasps were ivory set with pearls, worn to a softly shimmering luster. Holding them, tracing the craftsmanship of the carving and the smoothness of the pearls, she realized that such a costly treasure could not have come from Breneya. She wondered what woman had first worn them. Surely, such a gift came from the heart, in love and hope, and not out of obligation.

After she dressed, Tsorreh untied her hair and, using her fingers, began to comb and braid it. The patch that had been cut off in Gatacinne, along with the Arandel token, was beginning to grow out and was already long enough to catch the ends in a braid. One plait, two . . . until seven glossy braids swung freely down her back. She gathered them together with the leather thong.

Jaxar's smile upon seeing her confirmed that he was the giver. Tsorreh began to thank him, but he changed the subject, clearly uncomfortable with expressions of gratitude. Later, she learned from Danar that the pearl clasps had belonged to his "real mother," Jaxar's first wife. Lycian had never worn them and in all likelihood knew nothing of their existence.

Tsorreh could not entirely let down her guard, not here in the capital city of her enemies, but Jaxar appeared to be a rational, civilized man. So far, he had given her no indication that he meant her ill, but she did not yet trust him. At any moment, he might turn her back over to the Ar-King. Moreover, beyond the gates of his estate, armed Gelon patrolled the streets. Soldiers and police and Cinath's Elite Guard and what more, she did not know. Strange, half-formed shadows lurked just beyond her senses.

Very gradually, Tsorreh's life assumed a new rhythm. At first, she kept indoors as much as possible, except to visit the bathhouse, and then only when Lycian had gone out. The laboratory became her world. She cleaned the dusty shelves and organized the library. Jaxar was an easy task master. Often, he was so absorbed in his own work, most of which was incomprehensible to her, that he took no notice when she curled up with a book for hours at a time.

Danar came to Tsorreh for lessons in Meklavaran, trade-dialect Azkhantian, and even a little Denariyan, although Tsorreh insisted her own accent was dreadful. After a time, Tsorreh noticed that Astreya, who still brought her meals, lingered to listen. It was not difficult, after Tsorreh's experience teaching the captain of the *Silver Gull* to read Gelone, to arrange circumstances to include the girl.

Days melted into weeks. Tsorreh became more restless and less fearful of venturing out of the house itself. She began taking her meals in the kitchen with Astreya and her mother. Breneya's easy warmth was as nourishing as her meals. Tsorreh thought of Otenneh, of the loving care the old woman had lavished on her. What had happened to Otenneh—was she still alive? Did she pray for Tsorreh, as Tsorreh prayed for her?

Silently, in the still corners of the night when no one else was awake, Tsorreh recited the prayers for the dead for Maharrad and Shorrenon, for her grandfather, who would never know what befell the *te-alvar*, for the captains and defenders of Meklavar, for all those whose names she did not know.

From time to time, Tsorreh heard bits of news from Meklavar. Prince Thessar had survived Shorrenon's suicide assault and remained in the city. Cinath declared Meklavar to be a Gelonian protectorate and appointed old Anthelon as governor under the watchful presence of Thessar's loyal generals.

Anthelon, Tsorreh remembered, had been the only councillor to urge acceptance of the initial terms of surrender. He had argued that other lands prospered under Gelonian governance, and it would be better to save the many lives that would be lost in battle, or due to thirst or starvation during a long siege. Anthelon had always struck Tsorreh as a man of compassion, fiercely devoted to his *te-ravot* and his people. She did not doubt he would do everything in her power to soften the occupation, including suppressing any activity that might lead to official reprisals. Tsorreh did not know how to respond to the news of his appointment. It seemed to be happening far away, involving people she no longer knew. She supposed she should be glad that Thessar had not been killed, so Cinath could not use his son's death as an excuse for even more brutal reprisals. Or was that only a matter of degrees of evil?

As for Anthelon, she had nothing against the old man personally. But could he reason or bargain with the conquerors? Did he have any means of persuasion? Could he advance any compelling argument for justice or mercy?

Could anyone moderate Cinath's implacable ambition?

As the last light seeped from the western sky, Tsorreh and Jaxar climbed to the top of the ladder. For a crippled man, he moved with great determination, if slowly. They emerged onto the flat roof, with its benches and stands for equipment. The city spread out before them, its hills arching like the backs of grazing camels. Pinpoints of light, yellow and orange, shone from the more densely inhabited areas. Tsorreh exclaimed that they looked like jewel dust scattered on a velvet cloth.

"Very pretty, I'll admit," said Jaxar, "but deep night is better for observing the stars."

Mounted on a wooden frame was a telescope larger than the one Tsorreh had examined below. When Jaxar explained its use, Tsorreh drew back. She was not sure it was entirely reverent to peer into the heavens. Then she decided they were part of the natural world, and if the Most Holy One had truly intended to keep them secret, then the far-seeing-tube would not work.

More stars, not just dozens but what looked like thousands, became visible. These same points of light shone upon Zevaron. She imagined him free and safe. He must be, or surely the heavens would weep, not shine with such glory.

"Here, my child, look at this," Jaxar said, interrupting her reverie.

With her own eyes, Tsorreh saw nothing more than a smudge of gray in the direction Jaxar pointed. When she bent to look through the telescope, however, she made out a ball of shimmering white. Behind it trailed smoke, as if it were a torch in a storm. A torch to set the world ablaze? Or carried by an enemy who cloaked himself in darkness?

"What is it? A falling star?" She frowned, for the object did not seem to be moving, and yet the luminous streamer suggested great speed. She searched inside for a hint of alarm from the *te-alvar*, but it had gone quiescent. If the celestial torch posed a threat, it was not imminent.

"A comet. Of those I have observed over the years, none have plunged to earth, but I suppose it is possible. They appear even as you see, grow brighter for a time during their journey across the sky, and then fade away."

"It looks to be on fire, but a frozen sort of fire." Tsorreh had no idea what prompted her to say such a thing. What did she know of this smear of gray against the black of night?

Jaxar's voice drew her back to herself, as he spoke quietly about his system of notation and his thoughts on the aetheric nature of comets and whether they ceased to exist when they disappeared or merely traveled beyond the range of his telescope. Tsorreh fetched paper and charcoal from the laboratory and attempted to sketch the comet according to Jaxar's direction. She did not think the results were very good, but Jaxar seemed pleased.

A deep weariness crept along her bones. Jaxar noticed her stifled yawns and, at his urging, both clambered down the ladder.

Her last conscious thought as she drifted into sleep was that she would not find true rest until the comet was gone, no longer hanging like a miasmatic sword above the living world.

Jaxar did not come into the laboratory all the next day, and Danar rode out to the country estate, leaving Tsorreh alone. She went about her usual work, copying out a badly damaged Gelonian scroll, a history of finance under Ar-Dethen-Gelon. She did not worry about Jaxar's absence until late in the day, when twilight stained the sky. She climbed the scaffolding up to the roof and waited for him to join her.

The day had been warm and still, and now heat rose in shimmers, as if the land itself were exhaling in relief. Dusk, which often seemed to go on forever, came to an end. Stars bathed the heavens in milky light. Such a sight never failed to delight Jaxar, to draw him to his precious telescope.

Jaxar had previously been absent for a single day, sometimes two. Most of the time, he had advised her the day before. He had duties at court and at the Temple of Justice, called Ir-Pilant after the Ar-King who first codified the Gelonian laws. He was often gone on business regarding legal matters or the running of the country estate that furnished his income.

Surely, she thought, he would have returned to take his dinner, and then to watch the stars. The comet was already fading from the night sky, but there were plenty of other celestial objects to excite Jaxar's interest. Where was he? Had something happened to him? Clearly, Tsorreh could not find out while hiding in the laboratory.

I've become a prisoner of my own fears.

Resolved, she got to her feet and descended the ladder. She had forgotten to leave a lamp burning, and shadows shrouded the laboratory. Dim light filtered through the opening in the ceiling.

In the hallway outside, a torch burned in its wall sconce. Tsorreh made her way through the house, not altogether certain where she was going. Pausing at the second-story balcony overlooking the central courtyard, she heard the ripple of a harp and the trill of a flute, and caught glimpses of servants about their work.

At the bottom of the main staircase, Tsorreh passed a servant, a boy of eight years or so, with a round-eyed expression and bony knees. He was carrying an armful of folded cloths, blue-and-white striped cotton, bed linens most likely. When she spoke to him, something in his astonishment reminded her of Benerod, the page she had befriended during the siege of Meklavar. She wondered how Benerod, with his earnestness and talent for imaginative stories, had managed since the fall of the city.

When she asked the boy how Lord Jaxar fared, he only stared harder at her. She went on, "Would you show me to the steward's office?"

The boy darted away the way he had come, clutching his armful of linens.

Tsorreh did not know whether to be amused or offended. Was she so terrifying? She had heard that many Gelon regarded her people as sorcerers, powerful and malevolent. No, surely the boy could not think of her as a demon. He must be shy of strangers, nothing more.

And yet, stories of evil Meklavaran witches would be exactly the sort of thing Lycian would use against an unwanted guest. Tsorreh knew only a few people within the compound walls. Except for Lycian, she believed that none of them intended her harm. On the other hand, if something had happened to Jaxar, she would lose her best protection.

I am neither slave nor servant, and Jaxar himself has said I am not a prisoner. I will not cripple myself with fear!

Tsorreh strode back up the main stairs, determined to wrest an answer from the first person she encountered, even if it were Lycian herself.

The house was a sprawling, open rectangle. The inner rooms looked out over the central courtyard where even now, the lilting strains of music and the perfume of night-blooming flowers filled the open space and wafted upward. Lycian's suite lay somewhere in the newer annex, situated to overlook the center of the city. Jaxar had maintained his rooms in the older part of the house, close to his laboratory.

As Tsorreh reached the top of the stairs, Astreya came down the hallway opposite the laboratory. She carried a tray with a pitcher and bowl. Her gaze lit on Tsorreh's face. "What is the matter, lady?"

"I was just looking for someone who might answer that question!" Tsorreh calmed herself. "I have not seen Lord Jaxar all day. I am concerned about him. Perhaps it is foolish of me and there is nothing unusual in his absence, but I will not be easy until I know."

"Oh! He has been taken with one of his spells. Issios has been tending him all day." Astreya lowered her voice. "Lady Lycian wanted to send for a Qr priest to perform sacrifices for Lord Jaxar's recovery, but he wouldn't have it. We were all terrified he'd do himself a harm, he was so fierce. She's been at the temple ever since."

Tsorreh smothered the revulsion that rose in her at the mention of the Scorpion god. "Spells? He is ill, or more so than usual? May I—I wish to see him."

"Come on, then." Astreya turned, gesturing with a tilt of her head for Tsorreh to accompany her.

Jaxar's suite of rooms had been designed on a grand

scale. An entry hall was furnished with marble benches and niches containing idols of carved wood and ivory. They looked very old.

Tsorreh caught her breath as she stepped into the next room. A pair of torches set in freestanding iron holders, wrought like the intertwined branches of willow trees, cast a warm light. Mosaics of brilliant bits of tile, shards of colored glass, intricate gilt filigree work, and glimmering mother-of-pearl covered the ceiling and walls. In them, she saw surging oceans, mountains belching fire, men on foot and in chariots drawn by fierce-eyed onagers, men and woman—she supposed them to be representations of Gelonian gods by their halos of gold and seed pearls. A number of divans and chairs, carved from glossy dark wood and buried under velvet cushions, had been arranged around the room. To Tsorreh's mind, however, the room was to be traversed instead of lived in. Perhaps Jaxar used it for formal entertainment when he wanted to impress his guests. She could not imagine him at home with those elaborate murals or sitting comfortably in those ornate chairs.

Astreya passed through the mosaic chamber without a glance. At the far end, she opened one of three small doors and slipped through. Following her, Tsorreh immediately felt the difference in atmosphere. The proportions of this room were perfect, the walls unadorned except for a single faded banner. A door on the far side opened onto a balcony, admitting the night air.

A bed dominated the center of the room. It looked very old and could easily have accommodated three or four people, not just the single occupant who lay with his head propped on a thick bolster. A table bore a tray with bowl and pitcher and several shallow bronze dishes of the sort used to burn incense.

The steward, Issios, slumped beside the door on one of two modest benches, his head to one side and his mouth slightly open. He jerked awake as Astreya and Tsorreh entered. "You have no reason to be here, girl. The master is resting."

Astreya flinched at the steward's tone, but she held her ground. "Lady Tsorreh required me to bring her here."

"Out, both of you! He must not be disturbed."

"Please, may I not see how he fares?" Tsorreh pleaded. "If he is ill—" No, that would not work. She had no claim on a place here, no right to care for him. But she had noticed the chest standing beside the open balcony door and the pile of books there. "Let me read to him. Perhaps that might comfort him."

The steward's scowl deepened. Before he could refuse, Jaxar stirred, lifting one hand. "Is that you, Tsorreh? Issios, let her come near."

Tsorreh approached the bed. Seen in the faint light, the change in Jaxar's condition shocked her. His face was no longer puffy but bloated. He inhaled, wheezing as if each breath were a struggle. His skin had taken on an unhealthy flush. Yet the eyes that regarded her from that swollen face were as kind as ever.

She took his hand in hers, feeling the sodden texture of his flesh, and could not speak. Her expression must have revealed her emotions, for Jaxar said, "It is not so bad as all that, my dear. I have lived with this malady for many years now. Sometimes it is better, sometimes worse. It will be the end of me one day—"

"You must not speak so, my lord!" Issios objected. "You will recover! You must! I myself have offered prayers of intercession to The Dispenser of Justice, to my own patron, The One Who Blesses Commerce, and even to The God of Forgotten Hopes and Unspeakable Desires—"

"Enough!" Jaxar broke off in a fit of coughing. Tsorreh detected an alarming wheeze and rattle in his chest. "You may pray any way you wish for yourself, my old friend, but do not inflict your gods on me. I have enough difficulty in my life as it is, without their help." Gasping, he sagged back on the bolsters.

Tsorreh turned to the steward. "Can nothing be done to ease his breathing and the swelling of his flesh? What has his physician advised?"

Issios glared at her. "We are not superstitious folk, to consult such a person!"

Tsorreh paused on the brink of outrage. Then she realized that in Gelone, the words for *physician* and *soothsayer* were identical. Surely, Gelon must have healing professionals.

"Who do you send for if you have a broken bone or an aching tooth?" she asked.

Issios snorted. "A tonsorial, you mean? They're all very well for cauterizing a boil or amputating a gangrenous toe. On the battlefield, they have ample chance to practice their arts, so they are very skillful. This malady," he gestured at Jaxar, "is clearly a spiritual matter."

"I'm sorry, I don't understand."

"I will explain the way of such things in Gelon." Moderating his tone, Issios took Tsorreh aside. "Lay practitioners— tonsorials or country herbalists or even the priestesses of She Who Blesses Childbirth—use ordinary means of observation to determine what injury or ailment has beset their patient. You or I could do the same, yes? We see the same wound, we feel the same tumor."

"Yes, of course," Tsorreh agreed.

"Therefore, we will in most cases agree on the appropriate remedy. We can objectively evaluate the course of recovery. But for conditions that are invisible to ordinary senses, that manifest in strange and subtle ways, what can we do? We cannot see or touch or smell out the cause. This is because the disease is not physical, but *supernatural* in nature. Only the god to whom that person has sworn himself can diagnose and cure it."

Tsorreh was so appalled, she could not think of a reply.

"In most cases, the priests of the patient's patron god perform auguries to reveal the unique, specific cause of each patient's malady. Treatment may involve making sacrifices, or ingesting certain foods or herbs. If that does not avail," Issios hesitated minutely, "then a more powerful god must be invoked."

Tsorreh suddenly understood Astreya's comment about Lycian wanting to bring in a priest of Qr.

Issios glanced back at Jaxar. Although his face was impassive enough in frontal view, when he turned, a trick of the light revealed his deep worry. He returned to the bed and began wiping down Jaxar's face.

Astreya touched Tsorreh's arm to signal that it was time for them to leave. Jaxar was clearly slipping into restless sleep. Tsorreh hoped that the ministrations of the steward were soothing, that the patient might improve with rest. At least, the water was clean and had been scented with a refreshing herb.

Thoughtful, Tsorreh bade good night to Astreya and made her way back to the laboratory. Jaxar's illness had been evident from the first time she'd seen him in Cinath's court. Until now, she had not realized the seriousness of his condition or how quickly it could deteriorate.

Jaxar was not young, and he had been ill for a long time. Eventually, even the strongest constitution must give way under constant assault. The same principle applied to men as well as cities. Without proper care, with only rest and whatever remained of his innate vitality, Jaxar might die. Pausing with her hand on the latch of the laboratory door, Tsorreh bit down on her lower lip.

If Jaxar did not survive, she would lose her protector, her best defense against not only Lycian but against Cinath himself. The acquaintances she had made so far were new and the bonds fragile. She did not want to consider what her fate might be without Jaxar to take her part. But more than that, she realized as she closed the door behind her and stood gazing at the darkened chamber, she did not want to lose her friend.

Surely, something could be done to help him. If they were back in Meklavar, she would send for a physician, one trained not only in the best of her own people's medical knowledge, but that of Denariya and Isarre as well. Meklavaran physicians often traveled to study and learn.

A Meklavaran physician ...

At least one such man lived here in Aidon, unless his professional robes had been merely a disguise. But how could she find him again?

Perhaps Jaxar would come through this episode. If he had not improved by the following morning, she decided, she would find a way, even if it meant leaving the compound without leave, thereby risking Lycian's wrath and the city patrols. She would hazard even worse, for she had no doubt that if she were caught by Cinath's Elite Guards, she would have no possible defense.

Chapter Twenty

THE next morning, Tsorreh woke early, rising sluggishly through the borderlands between dream and day. Her limbs felt heavy, as if she had not rested. Astreya had not brought breakfast, which might not be a good sign. Tension twisted her belly, and even after she had scrubbed her teeth with a stick and rinsed her mouth, a cottony tang remained, like the dregs of fear. Although she wanted to rush to Jaxar's chamber to see how he fared, she forced herself to sit still, to breathe deeply as she had been taught. There were prayers of supplication, prayers of thanks, and simply prayers of listening, of gradually quieting the mind.

"Reach out your hand, lift up my soul," went the verse from the *te-Ketav*. *"Be with me now, be with me now."*

As she repeated the holy words, Tsorreh's fears gradually lessened, until she felt ready to deal with whatever she might find beyond the laboratory.

When Tsorreh knocked gently at Jaxar's door and there was no answer, she lifted the latch and went inside. A bitter, chalky smell hung in the air, and an enameled bronze dish held a pile of brown-tinted ashes and lumps of melted resin.

Astreya was asleep on one of the benches beside the door, her mouth open, her cheeks gray with fatigue. Her legs splayed out in the awkward grace of all young sleeping things. There was no sign of Issios.

Jaxar, too, slept. Not wanting to waken him, Tsorreh tiptoed closer. It was good that he rested, but she saw little improvement in the puffiness of his skin or the sound of his breathing. She had not studied medicine in any formal sense, but she had read enough books on the subject to know that incense and prayers and a pitcher of parsley tea would not cure what ailed Jaxar.

She had made a plan, a bargain with herself, and now she must fulfill it. Clearly, Jaxar fared no better than the day before. For all she knew, he was worse. She touched the back of his hand, felt the too-soft flesh. Eyelids opening, he stirred. She saw in an instant that he still retained his wits, for the eyes that looked out at her glittered with intelligence.

"Jaxar," she began, "this treatment is not working. You know that my people have knowledge in such matters. Will you allow me to consult a physician?"

"Tsorreh, my child, do not bring trouble upon yourself on my account." His voice sounded weaker and reedier than ever. "My illness and I are old friends. In the end, it will win. I have known this for a long time."

"But not yet," Tsorreh shot back. "Not now. Danar needs you, Gelon—" the name stuck in her throat but she forced it out, "Gelon needs you." Then, softer. "As do I."

For a long moment, he made no answer. Perhaps he was struggling to take in what she said. Perhaps he lacked the strength to speak.

"Please." She fought to keep her voice confident. "Let me go for help. If it is not the will of—of whatever god who watches over you, then at least we will have tried."

Another pause, then a slow nod. The light in those bright, intelligent eyes shifted.

"I won't try to escape," she went on. "I promise."

"Then go with my leave . . . and my blessing."

Tsorreh squeezed his hand and felt the answering grip of his fingers around hers. She turned toward the door. Astreya was awake, watching. Issios stood in the half-opened door. For a moment, Tsorreh feared that the steward would prevent her from leaving. As she passed him, she saw in his face the love he bore for Jaxar. Issios would not stop her, not if there were the most remote chance that she might be able to help.

As Tsorreh descended the stairs, Astreya pattered after her, flushed and breathless. "I'm to come with you."

"I don't know how much risk this involves," Tsorreh replied, hurrying across the courtyard toward the front doors.

"Less than if you were alone," Astreya said with dry practicality. "Wherever you're going, I've been there more times than you have."

Tsorreh paused with her hand on the massive bronze handle of the front door. "True enough. But do you have any idea what I'm looking for?"

"Should I care?" Astreya closed the door soundlessly behind them.

"All right, then. We'll start at the marketplace."

The sun was well overhead as Tsorreh and Astreya reached the bottom of Cynar Hill. Every time they passed a pair of city patrolmen, Tsorreh tensed. Lycian had not seen them leave, and according to Astreya, the lady had left before dawn to pray at the Qr temple. She might well return before Tsorreh did and take action, if Jaxar were sleeping, or too ill to make his wishes known, or unable to testify that Tsorreh had gone on her errand with his permission.

The market had been busy before, but now it teemed with buyers and sellers, beggars and sightseers. The number of stalls had doubled. Between the rows of booths, more food-sellers had set up their wares. Fruits and vegetables, some of them looking so fresh they must have been brought into the city that very morning, covered tables and overfilled baskets and crates. Sights and smells filled Tsorreh's head: a dozen kinds of greenery, turnips and radishes glowing like jewels, vats of olives swimming in their own oil, heaps of dried plums and apricots, fresh grapes like tiny purple globes, garlands of tarragon and oregano, braided strings of garlic and little red onions, and jars of vinegar.

"What are we looking for?" Astreya asked.

"Not what. Who," Tsorreh replied. "A Meklavaran physician. I met him while you were visiting your friend at the oil shop." She paused, turning slowly to survey the plaza. Between the booths with their slanted awnings and the press of the customers, she couldn't see far.

"I was hoping . . ." Tsorreh stumbled to a halt. She felt like a fool. It had been such a slim, unlikely possibility of finding him here again. "Perhaps someone knows him, where he lives."

"We can ask." Astreya did not seem taken aback by the magnitude of the search. "I know these merchants. But we're more likely to find your physician in the Reaches, down by South Gate. That's where most foreigners live."

Was there—even here, in the capital city of the conqueror—a quarter where Meklavarans gathered, preserving their traditions and learning?

Astreya pushed her way to first one and then another of the stalls to ask if anyone knew the foreign scholar. Yes, that was how these people would see him. With his somber robes and hat of folded cloth, he would bear little resemblance to their own priest-physicians.

The market was noisy, and people called out greetings, shouted out what they wished to buy or sell, bargaining and commenting on the quality of the produce. Tsorreh heard the high-pitched laughter of gossiping old men and the shrieks of children playing between the booths. Astreya managed to make herself heard above the din.

The first vendor was too busy to answer. He waved them away, impatient to greet a paying customer. The next had seen such a person but not this morning. The one after, scowled at Tsorreh and shook his head. Astreya pulled Tsorreh to the fountain, out of the press of traffic, and then to the shop of the oil merchant.

The young man in the canvas apron was energetically wielding a broom over the already spotless threshold when

Astreya called to him. He looked up, grinned, and waved to her.

"Varan, this is Tsorreh, Lord Jaxar's guest by order of the Ar-King himself."

His gaze flickered from the ivory clasps at Tsorreh's shoulders to her black hair. Tsorreh could not help noticing the shift in his expression, the tightening of his mouth.

"We can't talk out here," he stated.

They went into the shop, cool and dim after the brightness of the market. The shop smelled of olives, sesame, and aromatic herbs. Jars of varying sizes lined the walls, the larger ones stacked in neat rows on the floor, several rows deep, with smaller vessels on the shelves. A cabinet sat beside the door at the far end, the only other furniture in the room. The floor and shelves were scrupulously clean.

"We've no time to visit today," Astreya's voice was businesslike, even as a smile dimpled her cheeks. "We're looking for a Meklavaran scholar who was at the market the other day."

At Varan's questioning glance, Tsorreh added, "He is of my race, tall and thin, wearing long brown robes and a cloth hat. Do you know him?"

"Such a person has come into the shop once or twice." Varan shifted uneasily from one foot to another. "I remember him because he purchased only a small amount of oil but insisted that it be of the finest quality."

He went to the cabinet and drew out a bound sheaf of papers, flipped through them, and found the entry he wanted. "Yes, here it is. First pressing, fit for the Ar-King's own kitchen, may-his-glory-never-diminish. It wasn't a sufficient amount to cook with, which puzzled me at the time."

But pure enough for medicinal purposes, Tsorreh decided.

"Did he give a name?"

Varan peered at the sales record. "Mar—Marvenion, I think."

Astreya glanced at Tsorreh. "That's certainly a Meklavaran name," Tsorreh said. "And his address?"

"Try the South Bathar Hill district, I suppose. He looked rich enough to have moved out of the Reaches."

Tsorreh supposed that was good, a sign of the physician's status and success. She was anxious to be on their way once more. Who knew how long it would take to walk to this South Bathar Hill, let alone find the physician there? How might Jaxar fare in the meantime?

"Thank you!" Astreya planted a kiss on Vanar's cheek.

Varan glared at Tsorreh, took Astreya's arm and pulled her toward the back of the shop. In a hushed voice, he said, "Whatever is going on, I don't want you involved in it."

"What's happened?" The girl's tone turned worried. "What have you heard?"

"Only that it is not good to associate with *her kind*. They bewitch people and force them to do terrible things. Unholy things ..."

Tsorreh looked away, her cheeks burning. She fled through the open doorway.

"That's ridiculous!" Astreya's voice rose, clearly audible from the interior of the shop. "Who told you such hateful lies?"

Standing outside the shop, blinking away tears that arose more from anger than pain, Tsorreh heard only fragments of Varan's reply, which included the words, "omens" and "priests of Qr."

So it was not she herself who had been the target of the priest's inquisition back in Gatacinne but her entire race. No, somehow that did not seem right. She was too distraught to remember the interview in its entirety, but had the priest become interested in her only when he sensed the presence of the *te-alvar*?

"Lord Jaxar does not believe in such superstitious nonsense and neither do I!" Astreya stormed out of the shop with such vehemence, she almost knocked Tsorreh over. Fury turned her face red and taut.

"I'm sorry—" Tsorreh trotted to keep up with Astreya. But sorry for what? For causing trouble between Astreya and Varan? For being what she was?

They angled through the periphery of the crowd and onto a medium-sized street, heading east. Between the buildings, Bathar Hill rose low and flat, a short distance away.

"No, it is Varan who should be sorry," Astreya said. "His family have always been devoted to The Protector of Travelers, who extends kindness to all, especially the poor and homeless. He should be ashamed to speak so of any stranger! And within your hearing, too! How could he be so—so *rude?*"

Tsorreh could not think of a reply. Would it have been any better to say such things in secret?

They walked on for a time without speaking. The street began to rise as they passed from a working-class district to one of more prosperous shops and dwellings. Once Astreya burst out, "Oh, my mother will be furious!" and Tsorreh thought it better not to make any comment.

After several inquiries of passers-by, they were directed to a modest street where tastefully discreet signs indicated a scattering of tonsorials and herbalists. A temple, sparse and gray, dominated the corner; the only visible offerings were tiny stones, moon-pale shells, and white ribbons. When Tsorreh asked what they meant, Astreya explained that it was dedicated to The Remover of Sorrows, and it took Tsorreh some time to understand that this god represented death itself.

The houses here were well-made, joined in rows, with bright blossoms in pots or on wooden balconies whose railings were carved like graceful, intertwining vines and painted soft green and purple. A row of dwarfed apricot and plum trees, some of them in fruit, ran down the center of the street. The shade and the smell of the fruit blended with an occasional waft of incense from one of the opened windows. It was, Tsorreh thought, a pleasant street, a street of hope.

"I can't tell which house it might be," Astreya said, pausing. "We'll have to ask again."

"This is it." Tsorreh pointed to the small painted sign

beside a door. Meklavaran script formed the initials, MRVN PHY.

Marvenion, Physician.

Tsorreh went up the single broad step and knocked. A moment later, a young girl of maybe ten or twelve opened the door. Instead of the usual Gelonian tunic of simple white cloth, she wore a long sleeveless vest of blue-black cotton, split along the sides for easy movement, over full pants gathered at the ankle. Her hair had been braided with little bells and tied back, and her smooth round cheeks were the same honey-gold as Tsorreh's own. If Tsorreh had not been so anxious, so single-minded in her errand, she would have embraced the girl with delight at seeing a face so like her own, and familiar clothing, even the sound of the bells and the faint smells of cedar and sandalwood used to keep the clothing fresh.

The girl stared, wide-eyed.

"It's all right." Tsorreh spoke in Meklavaran and noted the girl's instant comprehension. "We're here to see the physician about a patient."

Shortly, she and Astreya were ushered into a ground-floor room fitted as an office with chairs, divan, and table. Shelves held rows of jars and canisters, wooden boxes, and stoppered glass vials. It looked like a tidier version of Jaxar's laboratory.

The girl returned in a few minutes with the very same man who had spoken to Tsorreh in the market. He wore his physician's robes but no hat. When he recognized her, he hesitated. His gaze rested for an instant on her ivory shoulder clasps, the sure token that she was not a slave as he had first supposed.

"I never expected—" he murmured in Meklavaran, glancing at Astreya, with her pale skin and red-tinted hair. "Is this wise?"

"I have not come on my own behalf," Tsorreh said, switching to Gelone, "but for the sake of my protector, who is in need of your tending."

At Marvenion's invitation, Tsorreh and Astreya sat

down, the physician in one of the chairs, the two women on the divan. Tsorreh described Jaxar's condition in as much detail as she could remember. He nodded from time to time. Occasionally she paused to consult with Astreya regarding what treatments had already been tried.

Some instinct prompted Tsorreh to avoid naming the patient. She did not know how a Meklavaran exile would react to the prospect of attending a member of the Ar-King's own family. The physicians she had known in Meklavar were bound by solemn oaths to devote themselves to the welfare of their patients, regardless of rank, fortune, or political connections. She felt confident that once the physician had accepted the commission, he would treat Jaxar with the same scrupulous care as if Jaxar were his own father.

"You were correct to come to me," Marvenion said, when Tsorreh had finished her description. "Symptoms such as these, the difficulty in breathing and the sogginess of the flesh, often indicate a grave condition. It is difficult to say whether the problem lies in the kidneys or the heart or another indisposition, not until I have examined the patient, but yes, I can treat him."

A sigh escaped Tsorreh's lips. Until that moment, she had not realized how shallow and tight her breathing had become. Her shoulders ached with tension.

"Then you will come at once?" she said, getting to her feet. "I fear the risk of every passing hour."

"Then we will not delay to offer you the hospitality of my house," he replied. "I will bring those medicines most likely to be indicated. It will take me only a few minutes to assemble them."

From the cabinet, he took a box of patterned wood inlay, strips of pale cream alternating with russet and gold. The inside was divided into sections and padded with quilted cloth. A clasp secured the lid, reinforced by a braided carrying strap.

"Where is the patient?" he asked, as he selected several stoppered vials and placed them in the box's compartments.

"Cynar Hill." As she answered, Tsorreh's heart gave a curious thump.

Marvenion frowned. "He must be a person of importance, your protector. He's not—?" He turned to face her. "He *is* a Gelonian noble, then."

She lifted her chin.

He paled visibly, his lips soundlessly repeating the name of the hill. With trembling hands, he set the medicine box on the table. "No, no. What you ask is quite impossible."

"You accepted him as a patient! Will you now renege on your word?"

"I did not know what he was. If you had told me, I would never have agreed."

"Why, because he is a Gelon?" she demanded. "Do you base your decision to treat a man on his rank?"

"He is of the race of our oppressors!" Marvenion shouted with such vehemence that Astreya cringed. "Besides, he must have a host of his own priests to tend him. There is no need for me to become involved."

"Those priests are worse than useless, and you know it!" Tsorreh said. "I am no physician, but even I know you cannot properly evaluate a patient by reading burnt entrails! I know that diseases follow certain principles, regardless of whom they afflict. If the priests could have cured him, they would have done so by now. His only hope lies in Meklavaran medicine." With an effort, Tsorreh reined in her impatience. "Think of the good—to all of us—that will arise from this man's gratitude when you have made him well again."

"You cannot know what you are asking. Please, sit down. I will try to explain."

Reluctantly, Tsorreh lowered herself back into the divan.

"The situation is a difficult one," Marvenion said, his voice thick. "If what you have told me about this lord's condition is true—"

"It is!"

"Then he is seriously ill. But he is no ordinary patient. I

cannot simply walk up to his compound and expect to be admitted."

"He has given me leave to search out a physician of my own people," Tsorreh pointed out, struggling to keep her voice calm.

Marvenion met her gaze, his irises a rich dark brown, deep and expressive, so different from the washed-blue of Gelonian eyes. In them she read fear, and not merely for himself.

"Surely, when a sick person asks for our help, we must answer," she said in as reasonable a tone as she could manage. "The *te-Ketav* teaches us that all human life is sacred and commands us to preserve it regardless of our own convenience, considerations of rank or nationality or property, does it not?"

How can there ever be peace between our peoples if we harden our hearts and turn away from those in need? Might one act of kindness create ripples through the temper of the times? How could she make Marvenion understand? And yet, she thought in a moment of understanding, the physician had every right to feel angry. Tsorreh sent a silent prayer to the Source of Blessings that she might find a way beyond that animosity.

"Whatever his family connections, this patient is not our enemy," Tsorreh tried again.

Marvenion began pacing. "Even if I have been summoned, even if I am successful. . . . How can I explain the risk to you?" He turned away from her, facing the wall of medicine bottles. His voice hushed, hoarse with emotion. "If I am too late, or if I diagnose incorrectly, or if he does not respond to treatment—"

"Then it will not be your responsibility! I will swear by the One we both serve that you were bid to come, that the patient consented. That he sought your care!" In another moment, she thought, she would have no choice. She would have to reveal her identity and command him, as his *teravah*, to accompany her. "Or are you afraid because your skill is inadequate? Are you truly what you seem or an impostor in physician's robes?"

"I wear these robes honestly. I have brought healing to men and women with this condition. The uncertainty is not in my personal competence but in the limitations of all medicine."

Marvenion resumed his seat, his manner now somber. His voice lost the edge of agitation and shifted toward sorrow. "You have been in Aidon only a short time. You do not know the position of our people here or how precarious it has lately become. The risk is not merely to myself or even my family but to the entire Meklavaran community."

Stung, not entirely sure she had understood the implications of his statement, Tsorreh asked, "What do you mean? Surely, Cinath would not punish others—" She broke off, astonished at her own naïveté. Why should she expect fairness from Cinath? Why not use the death of his brother as an excuse to further tighten his hold on Meklavar?

"Once we were welcomed here," Marvenion went on. "We were valued for our industry and our learning. Nobles sought out our scholars to teach their sons. Merchants relied on the integrity of our money-changers. My own services were so much in demand, I could charge whatever I wished."

"You mean that now, since the fall of our city, we are seen as enemies and therefore suspect?" Tsorreh asked.

"Whenever there is fear, the ignorant blame those who are different. The powerful benefit by distracting attention from their own failures. We have always known this. We also know that these suspicions will pass with time. Those with whom we have dealt honestly will regain their senses." He shook his head, as if lamenting the follies of the world. "Sooner or later, the people of Aidon will realize we pose no threat to them. Then they will relent. In the meantime, we must do what we have always done: keep to ourselves and do nothing to attract attention."

"So you will allow a good man—a man who might be our friend—to die when you might have saved him?"

A ruddy flush rose to Marvenion's cheeks. The lines on either side of his mouth deepened, furrows of care etched into his flesh. "Will *you* bind me to my promise, knowing what it might cost our people here in Aidon? Think carefully before you answer. If I treat this lord, if I so much as pass the gates of his compound, and *anything* ill befalls him, then bloody retribution will fall on every Meklavaran in Aidon."

She could assume the risk for herself, and she could ask Marvenion to do so, but could she do it for *every Meklavaran* in the city? She no right—not even as *te-ravah*—to demand it of anyone else. She might inspire others with her own example, she might attempt to persuade, but she could not bring herself to compel such a thing.

"You must answer to your own conscience," she said quietly. "As for me, I cannot let him die, not if it lies within my power to save him. Will you tell me what to do?"

He stared at her, his expression unreadable. She could not tell if she had shamed him, or if her suggestion were so outrageous that he could not think of a suitable answer. Slowly, he nodded. "I will. The risk is low but acceptable."

"What risk is there, if I myself administer the treatment?"

"It may be that if the worst happens," he said, "the medicines I will give you may be traced back here."

"You must then claim that I obtained them by deceit, saying they were for one of our own people."

"Then I will teach you what to do, and may the Source of All Blessings watch over us all."

Tsorreh headed back to Jaxar's compound with a list of instructions and a parcel of medicines, tinctures of foxglove and hawthorn to ease the heart, horsetail, nettle, and Denariyan ginger to strengthen the kidneys. Before she left, they agreed that she would report back on the efficacy of these treatments and obtain new supplies as needed.

Chapter Twenty-one

WHEN Tsorreh and Astreya returned, the compound was buzzing with activity. Servants scurried about, performing all the tasks necessary to support a large household. Lycian's onager stood in the stable yard, being bathed and then rinsed with lemon water. Bees hummed among the planted flower beds. A pair of men in broad straw hats bent over to weed and tend the kitchen gardens. A boy, undoubtedly the same one Tsorreh had surprised on the stairs, chased birds away from tilled earth. A gaggle of maids chattered as they carried baskets of food and tubs of dishes between the house itself and the kitchen.

Astreya paused at the crossing of the kitchen and main paths. "I must go help my mother."

"Of course." Tsorreh tightened her grip on the precious box. "And thank you."

Bobbing her head, Astreya hurried away.

In Jaxar's chamber, Tsorreh found Danar sitting at his father's bedside. A book lay open across the boy's knees. Daylight streamed through the door on the far side, admitting a gentle breeze as well.

"Tsorreh!"

"I've brought medicines." *Real medicines*, she refrained from adding, *not priestly mumbles*.

"No one knew where you'd gone."

Ignoring Danar's comment, Tsorreh set the box on the table. She peered into the jar of parsley tea, to find it almost empty. To her eyes, Jaxar looked no better, but certainly no worse. "How does he fare?"

"He's been able to sleep. I think my reading soothed him."

"Yes, it would."

Danar looked as if he hadn't stopped for rest or meals but had ridden straight home. Dusky hollows shrouded his eyes, and a smear of dust marked one temple.

Tsorreh clucked, as she used to when Zevaron had stayed up too late. "Go to bed now and leave him in my care. Come back when you have eaten and slept. And bathed."

"But what if—"

"I will send word if there is any change. Go now, before I have two patients to look after!" She took Danar's elbow and propelled him toward the door.

Danar pulled away from her grasp. "You don't understand. If Lycian finds you alone with Father, she'll have you whipped. And if Father gets worse, she'll charge you with poisoning him. It won't matter that he's had these spells for years. She'll find a way to blame his illness entirely on you."

The room felt almost unnaturally still. Even the movement of the air through the opened door and the distant pattering of voices could not disturb the sense of waiting, of expectancy.

"Let me stay," Danar said quietly. "I won't get in the way. I may be useless at nursing, but if the worst should happen, I can be a witness to what happens here. I'm a member of the royal family, and my word means something. I'll challenge any charges my stepmother brings."

Greatly moved, Tsorreh nodded. Danar picked up the book and took a seat on the bench just inside the door.

Tsorreh opened the box, surprised to find her hands trembling. Marvenion had written out what she was to do on a paper tucked inside. She reviewed the instructions.

Jaxar might take hawthorn in quantity, and she was to prepare a fresh brew of horsetail and nettle, flavored with honey and ginger, to nourish his kidneys. This, too, he might drink freely.

Of all the medicines, foxglove infusion was the one most likely to cause harm if unwisely used, as well as the greatest potential for healing. Willing her fingers to be steady, she measured out the required number of drops of the liquid, mixed it with water in a cup, and gently shook Jaxar awake.

His eyes went wide, unseeing. She spoke to him, first in Gelone, then in her own tongue. Awareness returned gradually.

"No more potions," he mumbled. "Damned grass-tea, not fit for men to drink. Give it to the goats!"

Marvenion had said the parsley tea was mildly beneficial, certainly not dangerous, and that the patient should drink as much as he desired. "Perhaps it would taste better with a little mint and honey," she suggested. "I'll make you a soothing tea later. Drink this."

Tsorreh coaxed Jaxar to finish the entire cup, and then set about elevating his head and massaging his feet and lower legs as Marvenion had instructed her. The motions reminded her of how she used to care for Maharrad.

She bore with Jaxar's increasing complaints until it became clear that he was too restless to sleep, although Danar was snoring softly on his bench. There had been no improvement in Jaxar's breathing, although Marvenion had warned her not to expect it so soon. She picked up the book that had fallen from Danar's lap. It was a treatise on the care of onagers. Smiling, she took a seat and opened it at random to a section dealing with the fitting of bridle and harness. This seemed as tedious a place as any to begin.

Tsorreh read slowly, letting the syllables rise and fall in gentle waves. Jaxar's breathing slowed, and the creak and wheeze of his lungs seemed quieter. Closing the book and setting it beside the pitcher of parsley infusion, she got to her feet.

The door to the interior of the house had swung partway

open. Issios stood there, his face a mask. Tsorreh had no idea how long he had watched and listened. Unable to think of what to say, she closed the medicine box and picked it up. Issios did not move as she approached the door. Her heart beat faster and her palms sweated, but she kept a tight hold on the box. At the last moment, he turned his body to let her pass. Then he stepped on the dais and bent over Jaxar's sleeping form.

Tsorreh glanced back at the steward. The light from the opened outer door cast his face into shadow. She still could not read his expression, but it seemed softer, less critical, tinged with hope, or perhaps that was only her own heart speaking through her sight.

Since there was no sign of Lycian, Danar agreed to get some rest. Tsorreh spent the rest of the day brewing teas of hawthorn, nettle, and ginger, as Marvenion had instructed her, coaxing Jaxar to drink them, and reading to him. She exchanged the treatise on onagers for a history of Gelon by an unnamed scholar from Borrenth Springs. The flowery, overblown language was designed more to glorify the Ar-Kings than to accurately record events. Even so, she was able to glean enough to make the reading as informative to her as it was soothing to Jaxar.

Danar came into the bedchamber toward the end of the afternoon. He looked drowsy but he wore a clean tunic, and his face had been scrubbed and his hair neatly dressed. He offered to take Tsorreh's place. At first, she would not hear of it.

"When did *you* eat last?" Danar said in a slightly teasing tone.

"It doesn't matter—" she began, and then realized he was right.

One of Jaxar's personal servants arrived to take away the chamber pot. Jaxar had begun urinating frequently because of the diuretic herbs, just as Marvenion had predicted. From the antechamber came the alternating sounds of Lycian's high voice, the yapping of Precious Snow, and the indistinct answering rumble from Issios.

The outer door swung open. Danar jerked alert, quickly masking his reaction. Tsorreh's back stiffened. At least the box of medicines was nowhere in sight.

"And you must pay special heed to—" Lycian broke off in mid-sentence as she absorbed the scene, Tsorreh seated beside Jaxar's bed and Danar standing beside the door. Lycian's mouth dropped open and her face flushed, her fine brows drawing together. Three or four attendants, none of them pretty enough to give Lycian any cause for jealousy, clustered behind her. The white dog rushed at Tsorreh, barking and growling. One of Lycian's maids scooped up the trembling pet. Issios remained at the door. He nodded to Tsorreh, and she realized he'd delayed Lycian long enough to give a moment of warning.

Lycian glared at Tsorreh. "What do you mean by this intrusion into my husband's private chambers? You have no business here!"

"She's been helping me, Mother." Danar hesitated a fraction over the word *Mother*, but his tone was firm. He glanced pointedly at the table beside the bed. "Fetching and carrying, the sort of thing you wouldn't want me to do myself. Didn't you say Tsorreh must make herself useful?"

Responding to his cue, Tsorreh picked up the pitcher.

"On your way, then," Danar said to her. "Don't spill any on the way back."

Just then, Jaxar woke up. He drew in a deep, shuddering breath that shook the whole hulking mass of his body, but without any of the former wheezing. Lycian flew to his side, cooing with concern.

"Now I am back, dearest husband, and I will care for you myself. Do not tire yourself." She wiped his brow with one of the silk scarves that fluttered loose around her neck.

Tsorreh and Danar exchanged glances. Silently she headed for the door. Issios had not moved from his post there. As she slipped past him, he looked directly at her. His expression did not change, only the light in his eyes. With the slightest shift, the mere turning of his shoulders, he moved out of her way. She had to pass close to his body, but she now understood the subtle dance of his signals. He knew what she had done, and by moving into the space he created for her, she indicated her understanding, her acknowledgment of his thanks. He had just told her that he would do his best to find a way for her to continue with her treatment without Lycian's knowledge.

The kitchen was as busy as ever, not just with the preparation and sharing of food, but the thousand tiny acts of kindness and rage, pettiness and despair, that made up the lives of these servants. Tsorreh paused just inside the outer door, empty pitcher in hand, and let the sounds wash over her: voices, the clatter of metal implements, the rhythmic thud of knives chopping through vegetables, and the swish of water. As she crossed the main room, she inhaled the bruised-grass smell of greens, the tang of herbs, the sweetness of wine and of honey, of new-baked bread from the adjacent ovens, the savory smell of meat.

The pair of scullery girls nodded in shy greeting as Tsorreh entered. She found Breneya in the stone-walled distillery room, sorting and tying bunches of herbs to be dried. Strings of them hung from the rafters, and shelves filled with bins and baskets lined two walls of the chambers. The air was thick with the concentrated smells of herbs, vinegars, garlic, and powdered myrrh.

Breneya looked up as she hung a bunch of fresh herbs from a hook set in a rafter. She wore a spotless apron and matching head scarf. A short, curved knife hung from the ribbon around her neck. She wiped her hands and put away the knife, folding the ribbon around it and tucking it into one of the ample pockets in her apron.

"I've been sent to fetch more of the parsley tea," Tsorreh said, holding up the pitcher.

Breneya took it from her and filled it from a stoneware crock on one of the shelves. "There. That will do him good."

"Do you know this herb and its properties?" Tsorreh wondered if there were a second, hidden, network of healers in Gelon, women like this one who might pass on to their daughters the practical knowledge of medicinal plants.

The cook's mouth softened. "That I do. In the country where I was bred, we know many such things. We have no priests to tell us otherwise." She ran her hands over the round belly of the pitcher before handing it back to Tsorreh. "My grandmother always said that nothing else was so efficacious as a general tonic. When she was a girl, her own mother was near death. For three days, the old woman lay in bed, scarcely able to speak, and drank nothing but parsley tea."

"And did it help her?"

"Indeed, for on the fourth day, she sprang up, frisky as a kid goat, and lived another ten years!"

Tsorreh laughed. She couldn't imagine Jaxar frisky.

"It's good medicine, real medicine," Breneya murmured, thoughtful. Her gaze met Tsorreh's, and clearly she had made up her mind to speak.

"My Astreya told me where she'd gone with you, who you saw." She made the statement into an accusation.

"A physician of my own people, someone I trust," Tsorreh said.

Breneya went to the open door, glanced around, then closed it and turned back to Tsorreh. "Listen to me, foreign princess! I know nothing of the sorcerous folk! Nor do I care! But if your potions can help him—" Calming herself, shaking her head, Breneya lifted the latch and gestured for Tsorreh to leave. "There, I've already said more than I should. I should not have spoken to you. You are my lord's guest. Just . . . be careful."

When Tsorreh returned, Lycian's attendants were arranged about the opulent outer chamber of Jaxar's quarters. Fortunately, the white lap-terrier was nowhere to be seen. The attendants stared as Tsorreh crossed to the inner door. She wondered what they thought of her, what their mistress had said to them. What did it matter? None of them were going to become her friends, not in this house. She wondered what had happened to Menelaia, who was the closest to a woman-friend of her own age that she could remember.

As she neared the inner door, Tsorreh saw that the latch had not caught completely, leaving it slightly ajar. She heard Lycian's voice, no longer cloying and soothing, but raised, shrill.

"I will not be humiliated in this way! To be forced to shelter a harlot under my own roof! I am your wife! I have my rights!"

A rumbling answer from Jaxar blotted out her next words. Tsorreh hesitated, holding the pitcher close to her body. Heat suffused her cheeks. She was not sure she ought to go in, not sure she could force herself into Lycian's presence. Surely it would be better to wait out here, with the attendants.

"So you say!" Lycian shrieked. "All the more reason for you to be ashamed to so dishonor me, that you permit even a whisper of scandal to be spoken."

"The shame exists only in your own baseless fears." Jaxar's voice was now loud enough to be overheard. "Suspicion does you no credit. Of course, you have no proof. None exists."

"I have no proof yet. But I know what I know." After an instant's falter, Lycian continued with renewed ardor. "That is not my only objection to the chit. It is bad enough that you disgrace yourself with her, but she has been seen in the city. *Seen*, I tell you! If she is found at large, then we will be held responsible! The holy servants of Qr the Inexorable warned me of this danger. She will bring Cinath's wrath down on us with her running about with only a nitwit of a servant girl for her escort. Is that proper custody? Are we not answerable to the Ar-King for her behavior? What is to stop her from escaping? From consorting with criminals and insurrectionists? Even assassins? And who will believe she has not?"

A soft sound from the center of the room made Tsorreh turn. Her cheeks flamed and her hands trembled on the round belly of the pitcher. One of Lycian's attendants had risen. With a slight inclination of her head, the other woman glided to the inner door. She said nothing as she reached out to tap the door with her knuckles, but in the cant of her head and the expression in her pale eyes, Tsorreh read a wordless sympathy.

The maid rapped three times, a pause, and then three times more. From within the bedchamber, Lycian's voice halted in mid-sentence.

"What? What is it?" Lycian did not sound at all pleased.

"Gracious lady." The girl pitched her voice low and smooth, like cool silk. "The parsley tea, would it please you to receive it now?"

"Oh, very well! Bring it in. Jaxar, you must give serious thought to what I have said. For your sake—for all our sakes, promise me this."

"Set your mind at rest, my wife. I will consider it."

The door jerked open and Lycian bustled through. Tsorreh jumped out of the way, but Lycian gave her only the most cursory of glances. The attendant had already sunk into a graceful bow. Lycian swept through the outer chamber, trailing fluttering scarves and maids.

Tsorreh slipped through the inner door. Jaxar smiled at her from his bed, where he lay propped on layers of pillows. He looked weary but alert. A mixture of emotions touched her, relief and her own sudden yearning for a refuge. She wanted to go to his side and lay her face against his hand, as if she were a child and he, a kindly father. For his sake as well as her own, she dared not risk even the appearance of inappropriate intimacy. Instead, she poured out a goblet of the tea and brought it to him.

"I suppose I must drink this, if only to keep Issios happy," Jaxar said, wrinkling his nose at the taste.

"I doubt it will harm you, and it may do some good."

"Who says this? Where is it written?"

"Written nowhere that I have found. Yet." Tsorreh grinned. "But it comes from a very reliable source."

He took several large gulps of the infusion, then shoved

the goblet back at her. "Pah! Any more, and I will start lowing like a cow!"

Tsorreh put the goblet on the tray beside the pitcher. "Yes, it would be much preferable for you to bellow like a bull!"

Jaxar laughed aloud, then broke into coughing. When she bent over him, filled with sudden concern, he waved her away. She took her seat once more. The book Danar had been reading was still there. She picked it up and held it in her lap. "Shall I read to you?"

"Tsorreh, we must talk, and seriously. I see from your expression that you heard what Lycian said."

"A little of it," she admitted.

"Lycian finds much in life to upset her, but in this, she has reason. I know you went out into the city in search of medicine."

"I did not go alone. And I in no way dishonored my promise that I would not try to escape."

"I do not doubt your word, child. Nor should you underestimate the consequences if you behaved in any way that might be interpreted as escape." Jaxar paused, letting his words sink in. "I do not want to imprison you here, but the truth is that this house could become the only place in Aidon—perhaps in all Gelon—where you will be safe. I know the temper of my brother. In his heart, great courage contends for primacy with even greater fear. Do not inflame that fear."

"Why should he fear me, one single woman exile in this enormous city?" she burst out. "He has soldiers everywhere—city patrol, military, Elite Guards! How could I possibly pose a threat to him?"

Jaxar shook his head, sending a faint quivering through the loose skin at his neck. "I do not say these things are rational or fair, only that they exist. They were not always so, but ever since the conquest of your city, there has been a shift in power at court. It was subtle at first, and perhaps only someone with as many idle thoughts as fill my own mind would have noticed it."

Jaxar was no contender for the throne, even if he had

wanted it, not with his deformity and ill health, but he was a keen observer of courtly politics, of that she was sure.

"My brother has always been ambitious," he went on, "but now the Qr priests feed his every suspicion. Already they have far more influence than I would like, and I have yet to discern their motives. Beyond simple power, that is. They wish him to be in their debt, but to what purpose, I cannot say."

"What would you have me do?" Tsorreh said. "Remain forever within these walls?" *Who then will fetch the medicine the next time you are ill?*

"I told you that I have no wish to imprison you," he said, for the first time sounding irritated. "How can a mind be free to inquire, to explore, if the body is chained?" He sighed. "How, indeed?" It seemed to Tsorreh that until that moment, he had adapted so successfully to his limitations, using his books and instruments to expand his world, that he truly had not seen himself as disabled.

"I do wish to extend to you the freedom of the city," he went on, shaking off the moment of doubt, "but, as my wife informs me, all must be seen to be proper. Astreya is a good girl, if a bit flighty, and as good a guide as any, for she has been set loose from an early age to run errands everywhere. But no one, certainly not my brother, would consider her a suitable chaperone, let alone an effective custodian."

Tsorreh was forced to nod in agreement. Certainly, Danar went about with protection. If he, still at that headstrong, heedless stage of young manhood, could accept the necessity, then so could she. Maybe, she thought, Danar's escort could serve for both of them. Surely, such custody would satisfy Cinath's suspicions. She would not have to fear another incident with the city patrol, such as the one on her trip to the washery shortly after her arrival.

Jaxar happily agreed when Tsorreh suggested that Danar and his escort accompany her on any necessary errands. Besides, she added, Danar could show her much of the city and explain its history and customs, thereby contributing to his education as well.

On the other hand, Marvenion would refuse to admit a visitor who clearly belonged to a noble Gelonian household. Perhaps she could contrive to meet him in a public place, where the appearance of the guards would be less remarkable.

She would have to tread very, very carefully.

Chapter Twenty-two

OVER the next days and weeks, Jaxar continued to improve. Issios managed to deflect Lycian's interference, so that Tsorreh was able to maintain the prescribed medication schedule. When necessary, she consulted Marvenion in the marketplace. Danar would retreat a short distance, occupying his escort in order to give them a few relatively undisturbed minutes. Tsorreh had no idea what the two guards thought about these meetings, for their expressions were as unrevealing and their manner toward her as distantly courteous as ever.

In her fine dress, with the shoulder clasps of a well-to-do free woman, and accompanied by a noble youth and his escort, Tsorreh suffered no more confrontations with the city patrol. Besides obtaining more medicines for Jaxar, she located supplies and specimens for his laboratory, and found new books to occupy his convalescence and to enhance Danar's education. Occasionally Issios entrusted her with a small errand. Each time, she would ask Danar to take a different route so that gradually she became acquainted with a larger area of the city. As much as she dared, she struck up conversations with foreigners, not only her own people, but Denariyan traders and others. Her fluency in Gelone improved as she learned the rhythms and temper of Aidon.

Danar's bodyguards followed them everywhere, occasionally clearing the way through a crowd or intimidating pickpockets and beggars into keeping their distance. As the guards became accustomed to Tsorreh, they relaxed enough to respond to her conversational overtures. She learned their names and a little of their stories. Haslar was born to a family that farmed Jaxar's country estates, and Jonath was a third son of an impoverished noble family. Both were devoted to Jaxar and had no opinion on any political matter. At home, they practiced armed and unarmed sparring with Danar, but on the street, they observed strict formality.

On a cloudless morning, Tsorreh and Danar visited Sadhir, one of Jaxar's scientific colleagues, an elderly man whose withered, leathery complexion and accent were Denariyan, yet whose manners, dress, and abode all suggested a long and successful assimilation into Gelonian society. He was to lend Jaxar a book on the observation of celestial objects from different locations. Tsorreh looked forward to the visit with pleasure, for she had accompanied Danar here before and knew that a question or two, a slight indication of interest, would encourage the old scholar to hold forth on a variety of fascinating topics. In his long life, he had traveled to places she knew only from maps, from Denariya south to the fabled Firelands. In his youth, he had hunted strange beasts in the Fever Lands and emerged alive, had sailed the Western Sea past the Mearas and east to Occeldirin. He had looked upon the Sea of Desolation and ventured north to the country of the Azkhantian nomads.

Sadhir lived alone, except for a pair of elderly Xian servants. His collections filled room after room. The floor was hidden beneath overlapping carpets of intricately woven Denariyan patterns or Azkhantian camel's hair, upon which rested tables of carved sandalwood, statues of unknown gods and of women intertwined with two-headed snakes. Butterfly-silk tapestries and the stuffed heads of strange horned beasts hung on the walls. There were chests of carved camphor wood, cabinets with rows of tiny drawers, a massive chair that looked like sea-swirled granite, three-footed brass braziers, and much more.

For the better part of the morning, Tsorreh and Danar sipped the old man's tea, fragrant with dried jasmine blossoms, and listened to his rambling story of the sea monsters said to infest waters near the Firelands. Danar and Sadhir entered into a lively discussion about whether the beasts might be a form of long-necked whale or an entirely new species. Once, Tsorreh would have suspected such creatures to be the product of fear and the stress of a perilous journey working on superstitious minds. Now, for all she knew, they might be akin to the fire-spirits she had seen in the Sand Lands. The world was bigger and stranger than she had once imagined.

With reluctance, she and Danar took their leave, the promised book in hand. The street on which Sadhir lived was in one of those formerly fashionable districts that had since slid into graceful decay. The buildings had once been fine, and for the greater part, the carvings around door and roofline were clean, if eroded. Seasons of wind and weather had softened them almost past recognition. Overhead, the row of ancient trees had been pruned back so many times they appeared dead, except for the slender branches springing here and there from the scarred and knobbed trunks. The leaves cast faint dancing shadows against the brightness of the sky.

Tsorreh came away with a sense of the preciousness of this time, how much the old man had to say and how little of it might be preserved after his death. When Danar noticed her pensive mood, she spoke to him of her concerns.

"He doesn't look like he's in any imminent risk of dying," Danar pointed out with the optimism of the young.

Tsorreh shook her head. Danar's buoyant confidence struck her as naïve. Life was fragile, and words committed to paper or parchment only a little less so. Everything precious could be snatched away in a moment, by sword or fire or disease. She could remember only a fraction of the stories the old Denariyan explorer had told her. What would become of the rest when he was gone? Who would remember where he had found this artifact or that sculpture?

Some things, she added silently, brushing her fingertips over her breastbone, where the *te-alvar* pulsed gently, must never be forgotten.

On their way back to Cynar Hill, Tsorreh and Danar traversed the broad central boulevard that ran from the harbor to the King's Palace. Tsorreh had passed this way on her arrival in Aidon. Here she had walked with other slaves and captives, confused and frightened, still reeling from her sea voyage and the awakening of the *te-alvar*. Even then, she had been struck by the brilliance and richness of the city, the variety of costumes, the music, the flowers, the architecture. Now the streets seemed pallid, the more outlandish foreigners fewer and more subdued in their dress and manner. It was as if a veil had been drawn across a once vivid landscape. It seemed, too, that more than the usual number of city patrols moved among the crowd.

A crowd, yes . . .

As if reading her thought, Danar signaled for Jonath and Haslar to halt. "Something's going on. There." He jerked his chin in the direction of the harbor. Now she heard over the chatter of voices the shouted commands of the patrolmen and the muted clamor of an even greater throng. The brassy call of trumpets soared above the street noise.

"Make way!" a male voice thundered. Distance and the surging currents of traffic distorted but could not obliterate his words. "Make way for Ar-Thessar-Gelon, the Victorious, the Savior of Meklavar!"

Thessar? Tsorreh reeled with shock at hearing the name, at the unexpected nearness of the man who'd conquered her city.

Danar pulled Tsorreh back from the center of the street. They stood close together, flanked by his bodyguards and surrounded on three sides by ordinary folk, some in coarse workers' garb, others more richly dressed. Haslar and Jonath moved to protect them as onlookers strained for a better view. Soldiers wearing armor and plumed helmets joined city patrolmen in clearing the street. A few bystanders cheered in anticipation of the spectacle to come.

The trumpets drew nearer. Above the noise, Tsorreh caught the sound of men marching in unison and the clatter of shod hooves and wheels over pavement. She leaned forward to see the vanguard of the procession, more soldiers with their drawn swords gleaming as dusky-skinned boys scattered blue and purple flowers. Then came the trumpeters themselves, and row after row of men sporting plumed, polished steel helmets and breastplates.

Shock gave way to determination. If she had a weapon—a sword, a knife, a dagger—she could wait until the right moment. She could strike just as Thessar passed, this monster who had caused her people so much grief. The prince's guards would be slow to react to a well-dressed woman. They would pause for just a moment, trying to understand what was happening. In the end, they would capture her, and if there was any blessing in the world, they would kill her. What would her own death matter as long as she seized that single fateful opening? Shorrenon would be avenged, and Maharrad, and all the others, her people, her life.

An image rose up behind her eyes, so vivid it blinded her to the crowd and the approaching parade. When she had seen him at the fall of Meklavar, Thessar's fair features had been exultant, insolent, bloated with victory. Now her imagination washed those cheeks with blood, filled those pale eyes with horror at the true understanding of what he had done, the last realization he would ever have.

No one would mourn Thessar's passing. Certainly not the father who, from greed and ambition, had sent him to slaughter so many other father's sons. Cinath would rage, an insignificant and fleeting spasm of his shriveled heart, but it would be too late. It was already too late.

Her hands curled into fists and her nails dug into flesh. She trembled with the magnitude of her hatred.

Thessar's chariot came into view, embellished with stanchions bearing ostrich plumes dyed in royal blue and purple, trailing streamers of gold. The onagers were perfectly matched silver-grays, their haunches painted in spiral designs with Cinath's colors. They snorted and tossed their heads and rolled their eyes at the surge of noise from the crowd.

Moment by moment, the chariot drew nearer.

A city patrolman stood only a short way from her. He craned his neck to watch Thessar's approach, shifting his hands away from his sword. Tsorreh judged the distance, one long step or perhaps two, then a quick grab—and the hilt of the sword would slip into her hand. She would pivot, sweeping the sword free as she darted forward. The blade would swing in an arc, downward where it would be less visible, then up as she plunged through the rank of retainers and leapt on to the chariot. Thessar might realize his doom, but the sword would already be in his flesh, piercing his heart—

The patrolman turned his head and held his arms out to both sides, forming a barrier. "Stay back now! No shoving! Let everyone have a chance to see the Glorious Victor!"

Did his gaze linger for just a fraction on her face? Did her expression betray her intentions? Could he see the murderous rage in her eyes?

Gulping, trembling, she looked away. The slightest wrong move would draw his attention to her. She would lose her only chance.

No one would miss Thessar or weep over his corpse . . .

She wondered if it were possible to kill a man with her bare hands. If she were capable of it.

But someone would *miss him.* Like a whisper, like a feather's barely perceptible touch, the thought glided through her mind. *Someone—*

A mother, a comrade, perhaps a brother or sister or childhood nurse. Thessar had a younger brother, Chion, and a sister. Tsorreh didn't know her name, had never met her. Did they love him as Jaxar loved Cinath? As Zevaron had loved Shorrenon? Perhaps Thessar had a pet, one of those vile little lap-terriers like the one that followed Lycian everywhere, begging for attention.

A mother. Even Thessar had a mother although according to Jaxar, she was frail and reclusive, never appearing in public. Had she rocked him as a baby, held him in her arms, sung him to sleep? Had her heart filled with hope for him, as Tsorreh's had for Zevaron?

If by chance, Tsorreh managed to overcome Thessar's guards, what then? Even if she survived, even if she gained her freedom, Cinath would not let the matter rest. As Marvenion feared, the retribution would be fierce and bloody, directed against her entire people. Not only in Aidon but in Meklavar itself and in all the wide lands between.

He cannot destroy all of us.

Somewhere, here or at home, someone would strike back. Perhaps that someone would be Zevaron or a young man like him—hot-tempered, full of life and fury and bitter vengeance. And then Cinath would have another target for retaliation, another reason for brutal oppression. She had read in the histories by the unknown scholar of Borrenth Springs that the Gelon had burned at least one Isarran city to its foundations and then sown the charred fields with salt.

Through the crimson lens of her fury, she saw the future stretching out, flames and more flames, and fields running with blood. Gelonian blood, Meklavaran blood, Isarran blood, it did not matter. They were all the same color. The lamentations of the women were the same.

The *te-alvar* pulsed in her heart, a nudge only, a hint of gold against the blood-washed vision. Gentler this, not the shrill warning she had known before, but more like a whisper, like the small insight that someone must have loved Thessar once and perhaps still did.

That mote of light, of warmth, was bigger than the vastness of battle, of insurrection and conquest, of retaliation and revenge.

Tsorreh came to herself, jarred awake by the clatter of hooves and wheels, the surging cheers of the people around her. Their bodies jostled her.

"Thessar Victorious!" they cried. "Thessar! Thessar!"

Blinking, she fell back. Danar caught her with an arm around her shoulders. He spoke to her, but she could not distinguish his words above the roaring of the throng and the fading whispers in her mind.

At the edge of her vision, Tsorreh glimpsed a figure, robed and hooded, as it glided from a doorway and turned in her direction. She could not see its face, only the pale suggestion of a headband, but she had not the slightest doubt that the Qr priest had noticed her. *Recognized* her.

Closely fenced by his escort, Danar pulled Tsorreh away. Her legs would not work properly. She leaned gratefully into his strength.

Once they were well away from the procession, past the flow of latecomers who jammed the neighboring streets, Tsorreh breathed more easily. Her vision came back into focus. The streets around her, the buildings with their white stone walls and red tile roofs, were solid and familiar.

Several times, Tsorreh glanced back, half afraid that the hooded minion of the Scorpion god followed them. Although she caught no sight of him, her mind still flinched under their fleeting mental contact.

"I did not think—" Danar said, his mouth tight. "You should never have had to endure that. Forgive me, it's my fault."

"Fault?" Tsorreh's voice sounded hoarse to her own ears, as if she had been screaming. "No, why should you reproach yourself? You have done nothing to offend me. How could you have known Thessar would be here?"

They left the broad, flat avenues of the central city and headed for the base of Cynar Hill. The escort followed at their usual discreet distance, Danar striding ahead, restless and agitated, and Tsorreh moving as quickly as she could, given the lingering weakness in her legs.

"I *knew* he was returning. I *knew* there would be some kind of 'disgusting spectacle,' as Father calls it. I just didn't anticipate our running into it. It was unforgivable—"

"Danar, slow down," Tsorreh panted. "If you feel guilty

about anything, it should be for making me run to keep up with you!"

With a rueful quirk of his mouth, Danar moderated his pace. As they went on, the streets rose into switchbacks along the steepness of Cynar Hill. Above them, rows of ornamental dwarfed trees and walls topped with planters that overflowed their flowering vines, created the illusion of layer upon layer of terraced gardens.

"I would have found out sooner or later," she explained, trying to sound more rational than she felt. "There's no harm done, just a bit of excitement." She summoned a smile. "I'm sure that in a short time, we will look upon this as no more than a story to tell our—" she hesitated at the next word, which was to be *children*. She could not imagine telling Zevaron about today's events with pleasure.

Danar had fallen silent, but a tautness around his mouth and eyes betrayed his thoughts. He was still worried. "Tsorreh . . ." Danar looked away. His voice dropped in pitch, resonant with feeling. It was, she realized, no longer a boy's voice.

Gently she touched his arm. "Danar, what truly troubles you? Not this business with Thessar? Is it your stepmother again? Or do you fear for your father's health?"

At her words, he turned to face her. Light filled his sea-green eyes. She could not read the emotion there, only its intensity. The two of them stood very close and the sound of his breathing was quick and hard in her own ears.

"Forgive me—" A catch in his voice ended whatever he was going to say. He broke away, his cheeks flaming.

Understanding rushed through her. *Oh, my dear . . .*

She had no idea what to say to him. How could she tell him that she loved him as a brother, almost as a son, even as she loved Jaxar as a father? Danar would be humiliated at being regarded as a child when the passions stirring within him were clearly those of a young man.

They walked on in awkward silence. Tsorreh saved her breath for the exertion of the climb. Some people, she thought, were made for loving. Danar certainly was, and

Zevaron, she hoped. Shorrenon and Ediva. Jaxar, for all his ungainly physical appearance, must have loved Danar's mother, for he was a loving person. But she, herself . . . would any man ever see her as other than *King's wife*, exotic captive, *te-ravah?*

Tsorreh expected a round of festivities in Thessar's honor, an extravagance of praise for the near-godlike powers of the Ar-King. She was not disappointed. The entire city went mad with jubilation. The sounds of dancing, singing in the streets, and drunken uproar penetrated even the seclusion of the laboratory. The revelry continued well into the small hours of the morning. What she had not expected was a summons to the royal court.

Jaxar conveyed the command in his usual gentle, understated manner, but it was a command, no doubt of that. Jaxar and Lycian and Danar would attend as celebrants, basking in reflected triumph. All the royal family shared a measure of Cinath's glory. But Tsorreh's presence was to be one of subjugation, a public demonstration of the fate of all those who dared oppose the will of the Ar-King.

In Jaxar's eyes, she saw his dismay at what might transpire. She wanted to reassure him that dignity was too costly a luxury for one in her position. Cinath had slaughtered her husband and stepson, burned her city, turned her into a penniless exile, and then wrenched away the person most dear to her. What more could he do to her?

Strip her bare, spit on her, force her to prostrate herself at his feet? Lycian could devise far more degrading punishments. Beat her senseless, throw her to the barracks as he'd threatened to do to the black-skinned woman?

Kill her?

No, if Cinath meant to take her life, he would have done so already. Such a punitive action, inflicted so long after the actual defeat, would surely be seen as petty and spiteful. Whatever else he might be, Cinath was too canny a politician for that.

Jaxar stood just inside the laboratory door, leaning on his crutch. Tsorreh wished she could spare him this. She bowed her head, searching for any last shred of pride and finding none. "For myself, it is nothing," she said. Then realized, *But not for Danar.* He loved her with a boy's singular adoration. He must do nothing on her account, not even cast an accusing glance at his uncle.

He wants so badly to be a hero, but he has no idea how terrible a fate that is.

There was nothing she or anyone else could do to spare her from the spite of the Ar-King or his heir. She must endure it, but she would not see anyone else suffer on her account.

"Danar—" she wet her lips. "Will you tell him he must not interfere, must not try to protect me?"

A figure moved in the open doorway behind Jaxar's ungainly bulk. Danar slipped past his father. His face was set, giving him the look of an older, grimmer man. His eyes shone like ice.

"You know what will happen?" Tsorreh asked. "When I come before Cinath?"

Jaxar nodded. His breathing was so loud, it filled the room.

Tsorreh continued, "The last time I saw Thessar—before the parade, that is—my stepson pretended to surrender and then ..." She broke off. Although she had never told the story to either Danar or his father, some version must be common knowledge. "I dare not hope—I do not believe that Thessar will have forgotten the attack, or forgiven. He surely sees it as the most vile treachery. Now Shorrenon is beyond his reach." *But I am not.*

She paused, watching the dawning comprehension in Danar's face. He was Jaxar's son; he had grown up in a world of schemes and alliances, of nuances of power. Anything he said or did on her behalf would only multiply whatever agonies Thessar intended for her. That she had dared to make Danar into an ally, a champion—she could not imagine the retaliation for that offense.

"I will need your strength, Danar. Your silence. Can you do that for me—for your father? Will you?"

Jaxar's breathing shifted into a moan. Danar lifted his chin. She had his assent, but there must be more. He must say it aloud, like an oath.

He did: "I promise."

On the day of the royal audience, Jaxar was limping even more than usual. His health was much improved, but his deformed foot clearly pained him. He was forced to travel by litter, carried by four large men and accompanied by guards and servants. Danar and Lycian would ride as part of the cortège, but Tsorreh was consigned to walk with the servants. This latter, she surmised, was Lycian's idea.

Given her choice, Tsorreh would have walked. The fresh air and exercise would strengthen her mind. She would draw from the vitality of the streets, the gaudy mixture of color and texture, the reminders of a larger world beyond the compound walls. The city was more than the palace, just as Gelon was greater than Cinath.

While everyone else was attending to Jaxar and finishing preparations for travel, Tsorreh slipped down to the bath house. Lycian had already spent an hour there, most likely soaking in scented water and being massaged with costly fragrant oils.

Tsorreh eased herself into the servants' pool. The water, from an underground hot spring, was uncomfortably warm and smelled faintly of sulfur. No emollient oils or herbs had been added to sweeten its odor or leave her skin soft and glowing.

She touched her braids, looped together at the back of her neck. She still wore them in traditional Meklavaran style. One braid represented each of the seven brothers, each of the seven *alvara*, bound together as one, even as the Shield was one. They were a token of who she was, where she had come from, her dreams, her hopes, and, in a small way, her defiance against her captors.

As she unraveled the braids, Tsorreh hesitated. She had intended to comb out her hair and smooth it with oil before rebraiding. Then she would put on her fine dress with the ivory shoulder clasps, even as she had made herself beautiful when she'd overseen the surrender of her city.

She would hold herself royally and look Cinath in the eye. She would think, *You may have captured me, but you can never break the spirit of my people.*

Now, for the first time, she questioned the wisdom of her plan. She was not Shorrenon, to throw her life away for a gesture. Because of the *te-alvar*, she could not afford the luxury of martyrdom. If she defied the Ar-King and died as a result, her people might indeed rise up in protest, her murder fueling their rebellion. But at what cost?

Much more was at stake than the freedom of Meklavar, its political independence, and justice for its people. If she died, the *te-alvar*, the heart of the Shield, would be lost, and without it, there was no hope of regaining Khored's legacy. The *te-alvar* had dissuaded her from a suicidal attack on Thessar, but she dared not count on it in the upcoming ordeal.

What was it to be? A doomed, heroic challenge? Or submission—humiliation—in the service of an even greater cause?

Emerging from the bath, she finished combing her hair, stroking each wave as if it were a treasure. Unbound, it reached to her hips. She dressed and headed for the kitchen. Her hair swung gently, caressing her spine.

Breneya was at the back of the kitchen, inspecting and sharpening the knives. She had laid them in a row on the work table. She looked up when Tsorreh entered. Her mouth formed a question, then closed.

"I need a knife," Tsorreh said.

Breneya looked for an instant as if she would refuse, thinking Tsorreh meant to do herself or someone else harm. She picked up a knife, its short, curved blade and blunted tip meant for chopping nuts, rendering it unlikely as a weapon.

She watched in silence as Tsorreh hacked away at the mass of her hair, one handful after another. This took longer than Tsorreh had anticipated, for her hair was strong and resilient. It resisted her efforts. The edges came out jagged, falling just below her shoulders.

When Tsorreh looked up, she saw tears streaking Breneya's eyes. Breneya knelt at her feet, gathered up the glossy strands, and took them away.

No one took any notice as Tsorreh slipped through the back way and up to the laboratory. She looked around the familiar room as if seeing it through new eyes. *Captive's eyes, slave's eyes.* The eyes of one whose only aim is survival, in whom every other hope is so deeply buried that no temptation could stir it. Shuddering, she cast the thought aside.

The slave's dress she'd worn on her arrival at Jaxar's house now felt stiff and coarse against her skin. Emptiness replaced the weight of the clasps on her shoulders. Finally she knelt, removed her soft suede boots, and pulled on the sandals. The heavy ropes had stiffened since she last wore them, and she sighed as they scraped her skin. There was nothing to do but endure or go barefoot. *Let them see me as they sent me forth, as they would have me be.*

Just as she reached the door, she heard Lycian's voice from the corridor outside. "Where is she? Hiding as usual? Hiding and shirking! I want to see her before you leave. She shall not shame us with her insolent pride!"

Tsorreh jerked the door open. Lycian's maid, almost upon the threshold, startled and took a step back. Lycian pushed forward, Danar a step behind.

If Lycian had appeared gorgeous before, she now rivaled the statues of the gods. Pleats of gleaming silk, iridescent in shades of gray-silver, blue-silver, and shimmering rose-silver had been draped and gathered to accent the sensuous curves of her body. The tiny white jewels and silver wires twined through her pale-gold hair created a moony halo, framing her flawless features. Her lips parted as she looked Tsorreh over, a quick glance from hair to feet. Her lips tightened, and she nodded. Tsorreh forced down an ironic laugh that she had at last met with Lycian's approval.

Danar remained motionless while Lycian swirled away. Once they were alone, he turned to Tsorreh with huge, dismayed eyes.

"Your hair! Oh, Tsorreh, your beautiful hair. You didn't need to do this."

Tsorreh permitted herself a faint smile. "Did I not? And what would the Ar-King and his son, the conqueror of Meklavar, think if I appeared proud and unbroken? What would they think of your father, who had permitted such insolence?" When he shook his head, still clearly appalled, she added, "It is of no great matter. Do you think I am Lycian?"

At that, he smiled.

"Go now," she told him, forcing her voice to sound braver than she felt. "Attend your father. I would not have him fall ill because of this ridiculous spectacle."

When they arrived at the Palace, Jaxar and his family were conducted inside with a good deal of bowing and strewing of flower petals. Lycian was radiant from the adulation. A pair of guards took Tsorreh around to the side and through a maze of narrow corridors, up stairs and then down, until she'd lost all sense of direction. They encountered no servants or courtiers, not even a scullion, only an occasional guard wearing Cinath's colors. The guards went on in silence, as if Tsorreh were deaf and mute. They were tall and muscular; even without their weapons, either could have broken her like a twig. If they feared her "Meklavaran sorcery," they gave no sign.

She, on the other hand, felt a growing sense of unease that increased the deeper she went into the Palace. At first, she attributed it to her own very natural anxiety. Despite her brave intentions to endure whatever waited for her, she did not feel in the least stalwart. She might well break down under physical torment, but she had no warrior's pride to armor her against weakness. Women were expected to be delicate, were they not? If screams and tears would satisfy Cinath, then screams and tears he would have. If screams would keep her alive — and she *must* stay alive, she who was the guardian of the *te-alvar*.

As she thought this, she stumbled on an irregularity in the stone floor. The guard following her gave a sound like a wolf's growl as he shoved her forward. She scrambled to regain her balance. The *te-alvar* ignited in her chest, not in reassurance but in warning.

She felt a cold prickling along her spine and the hairs on her arms stood on end.

Qr.

The noxious trace vanished as abruptly and as completely as if someone had dropped a smothering cloak over it. Without thinking, Tsorreh lifted one hand to her breastbone. Warmth flared under her touch, then subsided.

They passed not to the audience chamber where Tsorreh had undergone her first interview, but to a far larger hall. She had not known the palace contained such a vast space. It was bigger and its painted ceiling far higher than anything in Meklavar. She recognized many of the gods portrayed by the statues, art from this conquered province or that. Wine cascaded from multi-tiered fountains. Half the courtiers filling the hall were already drunk, but not the watchful-eyed guards.

Drums and flutes and man-high lyres poured forth music, but she could barely make out the melodies above the cacophony of voices, some raised in song or laughter, many more in excited chatter. Where in all this riot of color and sound was Jaxar? Danar? The guards pressed close around her, preventing any contact with the throng.

At a signal she could not make out, the chatter died, as did the music. The revelers drew back and the foremost guard led the way deeper into the hall. The crowd thinned even further.

Ahead, Tsorreh recognized Cinath, tall and broad-shouldered, attired in elaborate, blindingly white robes and crowned with a garland of amethysts and blue topazes. He spoke with a man much more simply dressed, bald head bowed, no ornaments. The courtier straightened, and Tsorreh saw the scorpion emblazoned on his headband.

For a terrible moment, the world froze. She went deaf and blind to everything but that black shape against the white cloth.

A muted thud broke the silence and then another, a distant two-part rhythm. Was it her own heart? As if in response, warmth blossomed between her breasts, spreading outward. Movement and color returned. She felt her own limbs and heard the murmurs of the courtiers.

Cinath raised one hand, a careless flicker of a gesture, and the Qr priest took a step back. Now Tsorreh saw the priest's face, the rounded cheeks that spoke of ease and rich food, the mouth with its hint of a smirk; satisfied, confident, and greedy. The priest's gaze slipped across her but did not linger. He saw her only as a slave, of no importance to his own designs. Cinath, however, glared at her. She dropped her gaze as a slave would, but in that fractional moment, she got a good look at him. When she had seen him before, his eyes did not have that tautness, as if he had not slept well for fear of his slain enemies returning in his dreams.

Thessar, his cheeks flushed with drink, was surrounded by women in richly colored, bejeweled costumes, some of them so diaphanous and clinging they bared as much as they concealed. He threw his head back and laughed at something one of them said.

Tsorreh glanced back at Cinath just as recognition lit his eyes. She hunched over even further, although it impaired her view. She had not seen Jaxar or Danar, and it would be far too risky to search for them now. Lycian was undoubtedly nearby, eager to witness every unpleasant moment.

She heard the clink of metal ornaments—a chain, perhaps—and the tread of leather on stone. The guard in front of her stiffened and bowed. His attention was momentarily diverted from her. She remembered, with sardonic half-humor, how she had imagined snatching up a weapon and attacking Thessar during his victory parade. She knew now that she could not have done it. Taken a knife, maybe, but never used it on a living man. Thessar was a braggart and a bully, but Cinath—and here she dared to lift her gaze, in an instant taking in his face and bearing, the hovering priest, Lycian in her finery at the forefront of the audience— Cinath was a man on the brink of something she dared not name.

"Well, Thessar, here she is." Cinath's voice fractured her thought. "Your Meklavaran queen."

"Not mine, Father. Her dusty little city's mine, certainly. But *her* . . . who would want such a scrawny, dark little thing? I mean, look at her! I've seen ham-handsomer slaves every say. Every day!"

Good, she thought. *Let him gloat.* But he was intoxicated, and that made men unpredictable.

Danar, hold your peace.

They were talking again, Cinath and his son and someone else she could not see, but not the priest. Someone was mouthing words about *providing amusement* and someone else uttered a petulant complaint, something about the Xian wrestlers and raising a bet.

"By The Guardian of Soldiers!" That was Thessar again, slurring his words. "What can she do against us?"

Footsteps approached, the guards sprang back, and Tsorreh found her jaw in the grip of a man's large, powerful hand. Thessar wrenched her head back, turning her face from side to side. His fingers dug into her flesh, pressing her cheeks into her teeth. She tasted blood. Tears sprang to her eyes, but she made no effort to hold them back. Let him see how much he was hurting her. Let him think her weak.

"Bah! Look at her. Sc-scared as a rabbit! I told you before, Father, their women don't fight, don't rule. They're good for nothing but popping out sons for us to kill."

For the first time, real fear sank talons into Tsorreh's gut. *Don't think of Zevaron, don't remember him.*

The next moment, with her head still clamped at a punishing angle, Thessar ran his free hand over her body. He groped her breasts through the coarse fabric of her slave's dress, then slid down her belly and between her thighs. She shuddered and almost retched. No man had ever touched her in such a callously brutal manner.

Thessar gave a snort of disgust. He pushed her away, hard enough to send her sprawling. The mosaic floor was hard and cold. A burst of laughter, Lycian's foremost among them, covered his next words. Someone cried, "Thessar Victorious!" to a round of cheers.

"Celebrate!" Thessar shouted, and people began moving away in his wake.

Tsorreh curled into a ball, drawing in her legs and covering her head with her arms in case one of those elegantly garbed courtiers might think it amusing to step on her. A flurry of light blows landed on her shoulders. Just as she dared to hope she'd escaped the worst, a savage kick slammed into her lower spine. White pain seared her. She glimpsed the edge of Lycian's gown as the woman glided away.

Moments passed, marked by the galloping pace of her heart.

By the sounds, the chamber was roughly half-empty. A booted foot nudged Tsorreh's hip, but not hard enough to hurt. It was an attempt to attract her attention, not to inflict pain. She uncurled enough to lift her head. One of the guards gestured for her to get up. She did so, moving carefully because of the throbbing in her back. She did not think her kidneys had been damaged, but it was not going to be easy to walk.

The guards made no move to help her, as if a touch might contaminate them. They led her limping from the hall and along another confusing series of corridors and then, surprisingly, to a narrow room lined with cots of the barest, most meager sort. A slave dormitory, she thought.

Slowly she lowered herself to the nearest cot. When the door closed, leaving her in darkness, trembling shook her. She thought her muscles might wrench themselves from her bones. Her teeth clattered against each other. She felt sick and numb, all at once.

It's over, she tried to tell herself. *I'm safe.*

But it wasn't over, and she wasn't safe, insisted another part of her.

She lay there, racked by wave after shuddering wave until the spasm had run its course. At last, lassitude crept over her, a weariness so deep, she could not resist.

She ought not to sleep, here in the stronghold of her enemies. Here where she had no defenses, no protection, where at any moment someone—a guard, a courtier, Lycian, Thessar—*Cinath himself!*—might come through the door. Her body seemed to think otherwise as a soothing, gold-edged warmth pulsed gently between her breasts. Just as she lost consciousness, a thought came to her.

It is not over. It is only beginning.

Chapter Twenty-three

AS the mild Gelonian winter faded, a flurry of rainstorms passed over the city. The sky turned to patterns of white and gray, with only fleeting patches of blue. Between squalls, a light, persistent drizzle misted the air. It became impossible to stay really dry, and the older servants complained of pain in their joints.

Tsorreh felt cold all the time. The damp penetrated her bones. She never mentioned it, for she knew she was not ill, merely uncomfortable. Jaxar, for all his reticence on the subject of his physical ailments, was clearly suffering. He left the compound infrequently and then he was forced to use a litter. Even Lycian, who normally preferred to display herself on her elaborately caparisoned onager, called for a curtained sedan chair.

Danar cheerfully summoned his bodyguards to accompany Tsorreh wherever she wished to go, which was usually to fetch more medicines or to consult Marvenion on the adjustment of dosages. Jaxar suffered only one minor attack, which was quickly resolved.

Finally the storms ended and the days lengthened. The air turned sweet and mild. Flowers burst forth in every garden, every planter along the boulevards, and in pots atop every balcony. Bright new streamers replaced old, rain-faded decorations. The streets filled with people, abroad for no purpose but their own enjoyment.

Jaxar spent more time outside, often taking his midday meal in the garden courtyard. Danar could not stand to be indoors for long, so Tsorreh found ways to incorporate his language lessons as part of forays into the city.

Despite the increasingly fine weather, the washed-clean brightness of the buildings, the heady smell of the flowers, and the air of general jollity, she often felt a shadowy sense of threat. In Jaxar's compound, particularly in the quiet solitude of the laboratory, her sense of unease lessened, but it never completely vanished.

Although by now Tsorreh was familiar with the city, its districts and avenues, she felt even more anxious than when she had arrived the year before. She could not shake the feeling that somewhere, just beyond the limit of her physical senses, something had changed. Something was gathering. She tried to rationalize her feeling, for it made no sense. Surely, the threat to her, as a royal captive from Meklavar, was no greater. Thessar had returned, triumphant. She had placated him and thought it unlikely the Ar-King would bother himself with her again. Rumors of resistance to Gelonian rule in Meklavar were just that, talk of complaints and festering resentment, not widespread violence.

After the quietness of the winter, the whole city embarked on a round of spring festivities. Since the Gelon worshiped so many gods, a festival to one or another occurred almost every day. Only the Scorpion god received no public adulation, although it seemed to Tsorreh the priests of Qr were more numerous than before. They looked intent, almost grim, as they hurried about their business or stood in twos or threes at intersections and marketplaces, peering at everyone who passed.

Jaxar attended official ceremonies whenever his presence was required at the palace, along with Danar and a clearly delighted Lycian. Jaxar rarely showed any interest in public celebrations, although he had no objection to other members of his household enjoying themselves. Tsorreh went with Danar, at his urging, to the temple of The One Who Brings Forth Flowers, and again to The Bounteous Giver of Wine, but shrank from the spectacle of public drunkenness. The chants and dances would be interesting, were it not for that faint, pervasive sense of peril.

Jaxar also received guests at home. During the winter, and before that, when he had been so ill, guests were few. With the increasingly clement weather, there were more frequent social and political visits. Tsorreh was rarely invited. Lycian had cornered her in a hallway early in the season and let her know in no uncertain terms that she was not to draw attention to herself.

Lycian clearly wished to be the center of attention, admired by all. Tsorreh had great difficulty imagining how Lycian, with her fine clothing, extravagant jewels, and golden hair, could possibly see a penniless hostage as a rival. Yet on more than one occasion, she had overheard a snatch of servants' conversation to the effect that Lycian still suspected Tsorreh of being Jaxar's mistress. Tsorreh was as horrified as if she had been accused of sleeping with her own father, but she saw no way of denying the charge without raising the issue for renewed scrutiny of either herself or her protector. Lycian had no idea what her husband and Tsorreh did in the laboratory or why they would spend days at a time there, and nights, too—not understanding the opportunity offered them when the sky was clear and the far-seeing lenses opened the heavens' new and glorious vistas.

Jaxar would sometimes shut himself and his guests in the outer room of his chambers. No one except Danar and, on occasion, Issios, would be admitted. These special visitors were often, though not always, men of rank and importance. At first, Tsorreh thought that Jaxar chose the impressive formal chamber to subtly remind them of his status as the Ar-King's brother. She noticed, however, that he emerged from these meetings somber and weary. Often he would rest afterward, rather than return to the work he loved. The other advantage of this location was that, because the only access to the rest of the house was through the little entry hall, it could be easily protected from eavesdroppers with a single guard placed outside the door. No one, not even Lycian, dared disturb Jaxar and his guests.

One afternoon, Tsorreh finished the notations from the previous night's astronomical observations, cleared a portion of one of the work tables for a desk, and took out the book she had been attempting to translate. The ink had faded so badly that, in many places, the writing was impossible to make out. She had tried to decipher its contents on her very first day. Since then, in her spare time, she had begun to transcribe those sections she could understand, a few phrases in Gelone and in archaic Isarran, and figures she thought were numbers, perhaps a form of Denariyan notation. Taking out several volumes written in various Denariyan scripts, she searched for similar symbols, anything that might give her a clue. The scholarly work reminded her of home and brought a small measure of comfort. Her results also diverted Jaxar from whatever was distressing him, probably the Ar-King's renewed territorial ambitions in Azkhantia.

A tap at the laboratory door interrupted her. She straightened up, feeling the stiffness in her neck and shoulders after having bent over the table for so long. It was one of the boy servants, the same one she had frightened half out of his wits when Jaxar had been so ill. He still looked as if the slightest frown would send him bolting for safety. She gave him an encouraging smile and waited for him to speak.

The boy stammered that she was to come to Lord Jaxar in his own chambers. "At once," he added. Tsorreh thanked him, carefully closed the books in order to protect the fragile pages from dust, and hurried out of the laboratory.

As she strode down the corridor leading to Jaxar's suite, she heard the frenzied yapping of the lap-terrier and saw Lycian about to descend the main staircase. Lycian was wearing spring green today, cascades of silk dyed in subtly different shades and sewn with tiny bangles to give the effect of sunlight dancing through lacy branches.

For an instant their eyes met, and then Lycian whirled away, chin lifted, and swept down the stairs, with three or four of her attendants scurrying behind her. The dog gave a last yip and scampered after its mistress. In that moment, Tsorreh caught a flash of triumph in the other woman's face.

Tsorreh paused in the entry hall and tried to settle her nerves. She thought she had seen the worst of Lycian's temperament: jealousy, pettiness, and vanity. Never before had she observed this gloating satisfaction and ill will that ran deeper than mere spite. Lycian was more than a pretty figurehead. Driven by such emotions, she could be capable of great malice.

Tsorreh could break her promise to not escape. She could lose herself in the city. By now, she was no longer friendless, although she knew better than to put her faith in Marvenion's courage. No, for the moment it was better to trust Jaxar's integrity and his control over his household. He had never given her cause to do otherwise. With a deep breath, she knocked on the far door and stepped inside.

"There you are, child. Come here. We must talk."

Jaxar rested on one of the divans, his crippled foot elevated on a cushion-laden stool. A folding table of ebony inlaid with mother-of-pearl and silver wire held the remains of elegant refreshments, bits of delicate honey-pastries and fruits carved like flowers, a decanter half-full of pale golden wine, and three goblets.

Following Jaxar's gesture, Tsorreh seated herself on the nearest chair. The dress that she had once thought so fine, compared to the rough-woven slave's garment, seemed coarse when set against the silk brocade of the pillows, the exquisite carving of the wood, and the opulence of the mosaic murals.

"I wished I could spare you this," he said, his voice heavy.

Never had Tsorreh heard him so weary, never so discouraged, not even when he had been so ill.

"I had hoped—" he went on, "I had believed—that after the last interview, my brother would forget about you, or think you of such small consequence as to be unworthy of his attention."

As did I, she thought, her mouth going dry.

"When my nephew returned and the whole city buzzed with speculation about the future of Meklavar, I feared attention might be drawn to a living royal claimant. When there was no investigation and you comported yourself so well, I believed the worst had passed."

Tsorreh kept her gaze level, hardly daring to breathe. "Please. Please tell me what more has happened. Has—"

Has my son been captured? Has he—O Most Holy!—has he been killed?

"Of late, there have been certain . . ." Jaxar hesitated over his next words, "certain suspicions of your people. Fears of assassination plots. Accusations of sorcery. The ignorant often fear what they do not understand, and it is too easy to blame the stranger when misfortune strikes. It need not be anything significant, only the small reversals of daily life, the frustrations and bad luck. Now, for some reason, my brother has taken it into his thoughts that there is a conspiracy against him, against the Lion Throne, against Gelon—against the King's-god, for all I know."

Jaxar broke off into spasmodic coughing. After a few sips of wine, he was able to continue. "It's as if—but I cannot believe it of my brother. He has always been so strong of mind, so impervious to persuasion—as if someone were pouring a subtle poison into his ears, making him doubt where he once trusted. And to believe that even the least of his enemies now plots against him—no, he never would have, not for a moment!"

"Does he think *I* have something to do with this plot?" Tsorreh poured a little wine from the decanter and held it out to Jaxar. She would have preferred to give him water, but there was none.

Jaxar nodded. "There is no kind way to say this or to make it any less horrendous."

"You have always been honest with me."

"Well, then, here it is. He has commanded me to deliver

you to a court of inquiry, so that you may be questioned about your activities."

"What are the charges against me? Am I to know what I am accused of, so that I may defend myself?"

Jaxar shook his head. "It is the king's court, the king's justice."

"Am I already condemned?" Tsorreh struggled to control her rising panic. "Is this 'court of inquiry' genuine, or an excuse to make sure that in the future, I never become a threat?"

"It may well be that he believes you are yourself innocent of any action and only seeks to learn what you know of the schemes of others. I cannot tell from the summons. I know only that neither of us has any choice in this matter. I will go with you and I will speak to my friends in court. You will not go alone. But go you must."

I would spare you this, his eyes spoke, sad within the homely contours of his face. *I would protect you if I could. But against a direct order from the Ar-King, I have no defense.*

My dear friend, she thought, *I do not hold you responsible for the actions of your brother. I know you to be a good man, a righteous man. Your kindness must be my shield and armor.*

The hearing took place in the Hall of Judgment, in a different building from before, one that was new to Tsorreh. As before, she wore her slave's dress, although this time she kept her boots. Let her judges think what they might, it was hardly an act of treason to prefer comfortable feet.

The main doors of the Hall were massive, carved from seamless pieces of deep red wood. Tsorreh could not imagine the trees that had been used, for none of that size had ever grown in Meklavar. The doors bore the likenesses of two immense male figures, facing one another with grim, resolute expressions. One wore the pelt of a lion as his cloak, the mane of the great beast rippling down his back.

The other carried a sort of halberd, part axe, part spear. Monstrous sea creatures twined their tentacles around the long staff. From the richness of their apparel and the lavish gilding, she supposed them to be gods or perhaps god-like kings. Had Danar not referred to the rulers of Gelon as *god-begotten*? Whatever their ancestry, they clearly represented Gelon's power over both sea and land.

Tsorreh was not allowed to enter the Hall through the main doors. Four Elite Guards took her into custody and escorted her around to the side. They looked like ordinary military, except for their almost preternatural vigilance. Ribbons in the colors of the Ar-King twined around their left shoulder guards. They treated her with an absence of rudeness rather than with any civility, as if she were an inanimate object to be transported from one place to the other. She had not the slightest doubt that if she spoke or behaved out of turn, their response would be swift, decisive, and painful.

The guards took her to a small room, furnished with benches along each wall. A single high window admitted the hint of a breeze. She could not guess the original function of the room, but the temperature, lighting, and air circulation were not uncomfortable. One stationed himself outside the door and another inside, then indicated that she was to sit.

Tsorreh settled herself on the bench opposite him and rested her back against the wall. It felt pleasantly cool, if a little rough. She folded her hands on her lap and composed her thoughts by silently reciting whatever came to mind, passages from the Book of Hosarion, verses from the *Shirah Kohav*, childhood counting rhymes.

The guard watched her the entire time, unmoving except for a slight, rhythmic flexing of his muscles. She found herself fascinated by the pattern: calves, thighs, a minute swaying that might have been belly or back, a tensing of the shoulders, then upper arms and hands. In between each muscular contraction, his vision seemed to sharpen upon her.

When she entered, the Hall had seemed quiet, but now, sounds filtered through door and window. She heard the pattering of shod or sandaled feet, voices soft and shrill, close and distant. None of this seemed to affect the guard, but it afforded Tsorreh a degree of distraction. Just as she collected herself to return to mental exercise, counting from one to ten in every language she knew, the guard came alert. She had not heard any change in the noise outside, but apparently he had. He opened the door. Two of his fellows entered, with a prisoner between them.

Prisoner was the only word she could think of to describe this man. He was young and slight, undeniably Meklavaran by the color of his skin and the proud arch of his cheekbones. He sagged in the grip of the guards. One eye was blackening and a crusted abrasion marked one swollen cheek. The guards threw him onto the nearest bench.

Tsorreh scrambled to her feet, drawing breath to protest, but the guard at the door intensified his focus on her. She lowered herself back to the bench and sat with her gaze downcast. One of the two escort guards remained, so now there was one for each prisoner, two near-statues bracketing the door. Nothing more happened.

Gathering herself, Tsorreh hazarded a glance at the young Meklavaran. He appeared to be a few years older than Zevaron, with the soft hands and thin shoulders of a scholar. His wounds looked recent, at best a day old. He sat hunched over, head lowered. From time to time, a spasm shook his thin frame. Terror, she thought, rather than physical injury. She wished she could speak to him, at least learn his name and family.

What had he done to become the subject of such rough treatment? Surely, he could not be guilty of anything beyond his birth or a few incautious but true words. He was clearly a student, not a warrior—no threat to anyone!

After a time, the young man was taken away and two more male prisoners brought in, one of middle years, the other young and strongly built, with wind-roughened cheeks and livid scars lacing his exposed skin.

Tsorreh wondered why they had not been kept in different rooms. Perhaps the presence of these others, men who had evidently received harsh treatment, was designed to generate confusion and fear, to impress her with the fate that might be hers. The longer she waited, the more thoughts came to her, of Marvenion's story, of his fears.

After several hours, she was offered water and privacy to relieve herself and then taken to the inner chamber.

Head held high, flanked by her guards, Tsorreh walked through the door. The moment she entered the Hall, her chest constricted. She tried to sense the *te-alvar*, expecting it to flare up at any moment. It had gone quiescent, though not inert. Instead, it felt poised, as if waiting.

The Hall itself was long and narrow, with airy vaulted ceilings, lined with columns of green-veined marble. Row upon row of candles filled the chamber with golden brilliance. At the far end, a single enormous chair dominated the raised platform. Fish and seaweed had been carved into the chair. Some of the fish were very strange, with bizarrely distorted heads, parrot beaks, and tentacles for hair. By some artistic conceit, the arms and back of the throne bore the likeness of a stately man—at least, in the torso and head. Seated on the throne, as he was now, Cinath appeared to rest in the sustaining embrace of a sea god. Cinath's demeanor was gravely dignified and stern, yet his fingers moved restlessly on the carved arm rests.

To either side of the throne, below the dais, ranged a half-dozen lesser chairs. Jaxar occupied one of them, and Thessar as well. Tsorreh did not know the other men, although one or two looked vaguely familiar, perhaps from her arrival in Gelon. The youngest one was probably Chion, Cinath's second son.

Tsorreh felt the intense scrutiny directed at her, although she tried not to stare in return. From the edge of her vision, she noticed Thessar's frown. She had not observed him closely at his victory parade or at that ghastly drunken encounter at the palace, and her memory of him after the fall of Meklavar was colored by other events. He had aged greatly since that time. She remembered him as vigorous and confident. Hollows now circled his eyes, giving them a haunted look.

A few benches, occupied by more nobles, formed a gallery to either side of the central aisle. Several men, scribes among them, sat behind a long table to the right. Besides the dignitaries to either side of Cinath on his throne-chair, a variety of courtiers stood about the chamber, singly or in groups, turning to stare at her as she was brought in. Very few of them, she noticed, were women. Danar was there, without his bodyguards, watching her with a face as calm and set as marble.

As she passed him, Tsorreh recognized Lord Mortan, who'd brought her to Gelon on the *Silver Gull*, as well as a number of men in the garb of priests. The tallest wore a hood covering his face. Her spine stiffened when she saw the scorpion emblem on the headbands of those who stood closest to Cinath.

The guards halted well away from the throne, saluted the Ar-King, and then withdrew slightly from Tsorreh, but she was not beyond the reach of their swords.

Lord Mortan rose from where he had been sitting beside the scribes at the table. He stalked toward Tsorreh, his eyes glittering.

She held herself still, betraying nothing of what she felt. The Qr priests unnerved her, but they did not rule here or sit in judgment, and neither did Mortan. Cinath was the one she must appease.

"The Queen of Meklavar," Lord Mortan drawled. "She certainly doesn't look like much. But then, who would have thought such an insignificant city, one hardly worth the bother of conquest, would cause us such so much trouble?"

"Then you had better have stayed at home!" Stung by Mortan's insolence, she spoke without thinking and instantly regretted it. What had gotten into her, to indulge in such a rash, fruitless gesture? When she'd first come here as a prisoner, she would never have spoken so brazenly. She had made her submission to Thessar without wavering. But the months and seasons had restored her confidence and a measure of her pride, not just in herself but in what she stood for: Meklavar's heritage.

Several of the nobles gasped aloud at Tsorreh's challenge. One lord, standing near the dais, scowled at her. He held an ornate staff, and she supposed he had an official rank in the proceedings. "You will address his Glorious Majesty, Protector of the One True Land, may-his-splendor-ever-increase, with proper reverence!"

Tsorreh brought one hand to her chest and pressed it over the aching knot. It was not the *te-alvar* that she sought, she realized, but her own heart. Her own pride. If she bowed to this tyrant, this conqueror and his sycophants, would all of Meklavar bow as well? She shrugged away the notion. She was no ruler, for all her royal marriage. It would cost her nothing to yield. She might even undo a morsel of the insult she had just offered.

She forced out the words, "Your Majesty, forgive me."

One leg at a time, she knelt down. The floor, closely fitted slate tiles, felt cool and hard. Her unbound hair, which had grown out since she'd hacked it off, fell forward around her face like a mourner's veil. She bent over until it brushed the floor. A ripple spread, almost invisibly, through the hall. Tsorreh sensed surprise, anticipation, an almost gloating exultation. She heard whispers from behind her, around the room, Thessar's satiated chuckle, a deep silence from where Jaxar sat. From the audience behind her, she imagined Danar's anguish.

Do not grieve for me, she thought, wishing he could hear. *It is only my pride at stake, nothing of any importance.*

The Elite Guards reacted to her movement, shifting closer to her. She lifted her eyes. From the gleam in the Ar-King's eyes, he thought little of her concession.

"Enough!" Cinath said. "If I wanted groveling, I would have had her scourged and her legs broken before appearing before me. Mortan, proceed with the questioning."

Mortan waited until the guards had hauled Tsorreh to her feet and pulled her back to her original place. He approached her. "You are an enemy of Gelon, yet your life was spared by the munificent grace of the Ar-King, the Jewel of the Golden Land."

He paused, clearly expecting a response. Tsorreh did not know how to answer. She tried to look contrite.

"Tell us how you repay this generosity," he said.

She blinked, wondering if she were expected to express gratitude. Before she could think of an appropriately submissive response, Mortan smiled, or rather, the corners of his mouth drew apart, revealing even, slightly yellowed teeth. Nothing else in his face changed, not his eyes, not the tension in his jaw.

"For example, how do you occupy your time? What benefits do you bring to those to whom you owe your very existence?"

"I serve Lord Jaxar, as the Ar-King commanded." Even as the name of her friend passed her lips, she felt a shiver of trepidation. A couple of the lords glanced at Jaxar, who returned their regard with his usual tranquil detachment. Thessar looked bored. Danar's face turned white.

"Indeed." Mortan drew closer. "Exactly what do you do for him? How closely do you work with him? Does he confide in you, make you privy to his secrets?"

"I help him in the laboratory," she said firmly. "If by *secrets*, you mean his researches into the nature of light and the movement of stars, then yes, I suppose that is true. I take notes as he dictates, I translate texts into Gelone, I fetch supplies—"

"You fetch supplies—from where?"

"From various places. Sometimes a colleague will have a book or a specimen that Lord Jaxar directs me to fetch, or he may ask me—I mean, *tell me*—to purchase things in the market."

"What things?" Mortan strolled over to the table and bent over to make notes.

"Herbs," she answered, searching her memory for the most innocuous-sounding items, "incense, resins, small brass dishes."

"Ah, I see. And how often do you leave his compound on these errands?"

"I cannot say. It varies."

"No matter. Where did you say you went?" Mortan did not look up, but continued writing.

"Wherever I am bid."

"Who goes with you?"

Tsorreh's gaze flew again to Danar's bloodless face and then to Jaxar's. She sensed questions within questions, traps disguised as inquiries. "I—I am usually escorted by Lord Danar and his bodyguards."

"That sounds most appropriate. But you said, *usually*. Not *always*? Are you then sometimes alone in the city?"

Tsorreh swallowed. "How can one be alone in such a great—"

"Do not dare to insult this court of inquiry!" Mortan covered the distance between them in an instant. She could smell the surge of fierce, hot anger in him. "You *have* been alone then, by your own admission. Alone and unattended, unobserved, free to make contact with any manner of persons. Who do you meet when no one is watching?"

"I go where I am sent and do what I am told." Did they know about Marvenion? If they did not, she was not going to tell them.

"Who do you speak to?" Mortan's breath hissed over her cheeks. "Give me their names!"

"I—I don't know!" she stammered, trying to think. He would not accept a simple *no*. She wished she knew what testimony he had already heard. Had Marvenion been brought before them? Czi-sotal? The shoemaker's apprentice? Astreya's sweetheart—or had he been one of her accusers?

"You don't know? In all the time you have been in Aidon, you have spoken to *no one* outside the household of Lord Jaxar? And you expect us to believe such patent nonsense?"

"Of course, I have spoken to people—shopkeepers, beggars, servants of the houses. I don't know their names!"

Tsorreh made no effort to disguise the note of rising panic in her voice. Let him think her cowed into terror, if it would buy her time to think.

He straightened up, his expression moderating. "Perhaps we can refresh your memory. Have you ever spoken to Werenth?"

Tsorreh had no need to feign a blink of surprise. If she said *no* to a name she did not know, how would she respond to one she did?

She lifted her chin. "I have said, I do not know their names. The persons I spoke with were of no importance, nor did we discuss anything beyond the price of salt."

"Tagetor? Rithan? The Denariyan trader, Aswathan?"

"I have already told you—"

"What about Sadhir?"

Sadhir? The old scholar—no, she would not implicate him! She hesitated for only a moment, but it was enough.

"You were observed entering his dwelling on more than one occasion. Can you deny it? I have dates, witnesses, sworn testimony."

Tsorreh's belly clenched around a shard of ice. She and Danar had gone to Sadhir's house openly and at Jaxar's request. What was Mortan trying to do? How wide was he casting the net? With an effort, she kept her eyes on her questioner. She must think only of him, not Sadhir, not Marvenion. Not Jaxar. The murmur of conversation had died away, so that it seemed every ear was bent toward her.

With only a slight lessening of control, Tsorreh allowed her voice to tremble. "I did go to the house of Sadhir. I went to obtain specimens and to consult his library. Was that wrong?"

Mortan paused, barely masking the smirk of exultation. "So you have decided to cooperate. What did you and this Sadhir speak of?"

"Of the items I had been sent to fetch, of his travels long ago. Commonplace things, the usual courtesies."

"You are sure that's *all* you discussed? Not the weather, not the *price of salt*? Not the state of affairs in Meklavar?

Do you expect us to believe that you did not *once* mention the fall of your city? Was he not in the least curious who you were and how you came to be here in Aidon?"

"He does not know who I am!"

"Just one more Meklavaran slave?"

Tsorreh opened her mouth to cry out that she was not a slave, but held back at the last moment. Meekly, she hung her head.

"Did anyone else ever participate in these ... discussions? His servant, perhaps? Another Meklavaran exile? A visitor from your country?"

"No, no one."

"You never spoke of how you came to Aidon? Of the conquest of Meklavar? Of conditions in your country?"

"No!"

"You testify that Sadhir never mentioned a plot against the Lion Throne? Any wish or scheme to raise arms against His Glory?"

Panic curled through Tsorreh's breast. Would the harmless old man soon suffer the same treatment as the other prisoners she had seen? Was he even now the target of Cinath's suspicion? Why? What sense did it make?

She choked back a protest, rather than risk provoking Mortan further. "We spoke only of scholarly things. So far as I know, he has no political opinions whatsoever."

Mortan, however, would not be diverted. His questions rolled on, propelled by their own momentum. "Had any ill will been expressed toward Prince Thessar? How about Prince Chion? Lord Jaxar?"

"No. They are friends, colleagues!" Tsorreh managed to interject in the torrent of questions.

"Did Sadhir ever utter a spell or incantation?"

"What?"

"Did he use magic, even the most innocuous-seeming? Did he ever criticize the actions or policies of the Ar-King, may-his-justice-grind-the-unworthy-into-dust?"

"No!"

"Have you, yourself, ever plotted harm against any

member of the royal family? Have you heard even a breath
of rumor or a snatch of conversation plotting against the
throne?"

"No, again, no!"

Mortan was shouting at her now, his face suffused with
blood. Rage flowed through him, rage and fear. Tsorreh's
body flinched with each blast. He was searching, grasping,
trying to intimidate her into giving him—

"Has anyone ever asked you to deliver a package? A
sealed message? A note? To say or do anything to be kept
from Lord Jaxar? Has Lord Jaxar ever received private
visitors?"

"Well, yes—"

"Who? When? What did they say? Names! I want their
names!"

She stared at him, unable to suppress the quivering in
her muscles. A long moment went by. What did he expect
her to say? Did he think she listened outside the door? Or
was he hoping to so terrify her that she would say anything,
invent anything just to appease him? No, not just him.
Cinath, too, who sat, face dusky with unreadable emotion,
like a misshapen ogre on his sea-throne. And hovering behind him, the phantasmic many-legged shape of a scorpion.
The questions and the consuming hunger behind them were
not Mortan's, not Cinath's.

She searched within herself for a pulse of sustaining
warmth from the *te-alvar*, but felt nothing except the hard
core of her own anger.

You may cage me, she thought, glaring at her tormentor,
*you may scream curses at me. You may beat me, torture me.
But I will never serve you! I will never consent to be part of
this vile persecution!*

"Oh, leave off, Mortan!" Chion, Cinath's younger son,
drawled. "You've frightened the poor thing out of what little wits she had to begin with."

Mortan, his jaw muscles clenching visibly, turned and
bowed. "As the young prince wishes."

He turned back to Tsorreh, his mouth stretched in an

oily smile, his eyes as hard as ever. "Your loyalty to your comrades is admirable, if misplaced. Perhaps you will be more willing to discuss your own opinions. You are unhappy that Meklavar is now under Gelonian rule, are you not? Do not attempt to deceive us. In particular, it cannot please you to see Ar-Thessar-Gelon alive and well. You were present at the attempted assassination of the Prince. For all we know, you yourself planned it."

Tsorreh caught the faint movement as Jaxar shifted in his chair. Mortan might be arrogant, but he was no fool.

"I have never sought the death of anyone, man or woman." She was surprised at how thin and weak her voice sounded. "Our sacred texts command us to protect life, not destroy it." By the grace of the Holy One, she could say that much in truth. She lifted her gaze to Cinath. "Your Majesty spared my life and placed me in greater comfort than I had any right to expect. I have never dishonored that kindness."

"So you say." Cinath murmured, clearly disbelieving her.

Mortan resumed his questions, his voice silky. "You have been accorded a certain freedom of the city, by your own admission. You are not chained, day and night? You have adequate food, a roof at night? You have had ample opportunity to walk the streets of Aidon. And in these outings, you must have heard news of Meklavar. Of the insurrection there?"

"I was in the crowd that welcomed Prince Thessar back to Aidon. Perhaps one of your agents noticed me there." Tsorreh turned her head to look directly at Mortan. "If so, he would have also seen that I was escorted by Lord Jaxar's own son and his personal bodyguard." A daredevil impulse prompted her to add, "I could hardly have engaged in subversive activities in such a public place, with such witnesses."

"What you are capable of remains to be seen," Mortan retorted, moving closer. "You know nothing? *Nothing?* You cannot seriously expect us to believe that you have had no contact *at all* with your countrymen?"

Tsorreh glanced at Jaxar and quickly looked away. Had he told Cinath of her visits to Marvenion? Would Cinath or any of his court believe that her only purpose was to help her friend and mentor, without any political motive?

Carefully, she selected her next words. "I have had no dealings with any Meklavaran rebel."

"Then you admit to having knowledge of them?"

"No."

"We know that you have. You were seen. You were *overheard*. Come now, don't insult us by this ridiculous and transparent pretense. We know that you Meklavarans have secret ways of contacting one another. There's a colony here that's as old as the city itself. Your countrymen must know who you are and where you are kept. Who has approached you? When and where?"

"No, they haven't. It's not like that. I—"

"You've been given the freedom to come and go as you please! You've said so yourself—we all heard you. Do you deny you sought them out? Do you still cling to the ridiculous assertion that not a single word passed between you about the fall of Meklavar and plans to free it?"

"I told you," Tsorreh replied, fighting to keep rising desperation from her voice, "I know only what you yourself just said. I was never alone—"

"Who knows how you may have influenced even the most virtuous bodyguard with your black arts? You are Meklavaran, learned in all the secrets of your race. A potion here, an enchantment there, a spell whispered in the dark, and most men will see, or do, anything."

Tsorreh wanted to stamp her foot at the idiocy of Mortan's claim. The gleam in his eyes and the sincerity of his words held her fast. Did he truly believe her capable of bending a man's will to hers?

No, she decided, he did not. But he did believe her to be a threat.

"This line of questioning is pointless," Jaxar broke in, his voice a rumble. "It is an insult to the intelligence and dignity of this court, and more than that, to the judgment of my royal and most puissant brother. Cinath, it was on your own orders that I took this woman into my household over a year ago. I have observed her carefully, and I have questioned her numerous times. She is educated, to be sure, but no more so than any other noblewoman of her people. Not only that, she has almost no knowledge of matters beyond her scrolls and books. She's quiet and modest, useful enough as a clerk, but as to the notion of her possessing any supernatural abilities? Please, do not strain all rationality with such blabber! Do you think she could be a sorceress and *I* would not detect it?"

"I agree," Cinath said, shifting in his chair. The unhealthy flush had drained from his face, leaving him looking weary but rational and in control of himself. The Qr priests sagged in their seats. Jaxar's words appeared to have broken their hold over the Ar-King, at least temporarily.

"You may be many things, my brother," Cinath said, "but I have never known you to be unobservant. I also find it difficult to believe that anyone who did have such sorcery at their command would permit themselves be held captive."

"Not to mention being forced to wear such hideously unfashionable garments," Chion giggled.

"Unless their goal was to lull our suspicions, to plant treachery in the very heart of our great city," Mortan said, but with less vehemence than before.

Cinath scowled, looking impatient. Mortan hesitated, but only for a moment. Tsorreh caught the look that passed between him and the Qr priests.

"Tell us," Mortan said, shifting topic, "about this new prophet who has arisen in Meklavar."

"Prophet?" She shook her head. "I don't know what you're talking about."

"Is that not exactly what we would expect her to say?" Thessar grumbled.

One of the nobles sitting beside Cinath spoke up. "Meklavar is full of prophets," he said loudly. "The land there is too poor to grow anything else."

"Prophets and goats," Chion quipped from his chair.

The assembly laughed, some of them with nervous

glances at the throne. Even Cinath smiled. Heat rose to Tsorreh's cheeks.

As the laugher died down, Thessar shifted forward in his seat. "This prophet is no more a threat than any other, full of bluster and portents. Of course, he predicts the end of Gelonian rule. It's what the people expect of him."

"Why should we permit even a single word of sedition?" Cinath sat back, resting his elbows on the arm rests and steepling the fingers of his joined hands. He did not look at all pleased with his eldest son.

"Because it is not worth the trouble to suppress it," Thessar answered, "and because it keeps the people divided and therefore, malleable. Father, there is nothing special about this prophet . . . what is he called? Iskarnon? A dozen similar blowhards go about the land, saying very much the same thing. The people argue ceaselessly over who is their true savior. They have no focus, no discipline. They squander their energies on useless bickering, struggling for influence among themselves. Disorderly and chaotic, they break upon us like misty waves against a promontory of adamant."

"By your standard, O Most Sagacious Prince, we should encourage a thousand more such prophets!" one of the courtiers said, and there was more laughter.

"Majesty," the senior Qr priest took a gliding step, his feet hidden beneath the hem of his robe, "is it wise to discuss policy before such a witness?" He indicated Tsorreh with a dip of his head.

"Come now!" Thessar gave a nervous laugh. "You cannot seriously think we are saying something she does not already know! And even if she did not, what use could she make of the tendency of Meklavar to spawn prophets? Not even the most inspired general could weave them into an effective fighting force, let alone one ignorant, inexperienced woman. Just look at her! She could no more lift a spear against us than could my song-finch!"

Of course, Tsorreh thought, Thessar could not admit she posed a threat. To do so would be to admit his own weakness. He had already been attacked by an enemy he believed to be conquered. That lapse of judgment had almost cost him his life. For his honor to be restored, Meklavar must be seen to have once been mighty and now utterly powerless.

"Father, I told you this interview was useless," Thessar said to Cinath. "There is no one left in Meklavar capable of opposing us. They will grumble, yes, and bleat out prophesy on every street corner. If a nest of rebels gets out of line, more than that old governor can handle, a few decently trained soldiers will soon put them down."

The courtier beside Thessar had been listening to the discussion with a grave expression, occasionally running one hand over his chin and mouth as if to prevent himself from speaking. Tsorreh remembered him from her arrival at Aidon, his features so like Cinath's. "Your Majesty, if I may speak?"

"Do so, Veramar. I welcome your counsel."

"Everything that has been said is true. One woman hardly poses a threat in herself. Meklavar has been overcome, her leaders dead or scattered. The governor you have set in place bows to your will. Yet the influence of such an ancient people ought not to be lightly dismissed, nor their subtle power. We know—" and here, the lord's gaze flickered for just an instant toward the Qr priest.

Tsorreh felt a shiver, a tracery of ice, along the back of her neck. Mortan was a harrier, trained to lead the attack, to poke and prod and intimidate, but this man's careful approach terrified her far more.

"We know," Veramar continued, "that there are other forces at work in the world beyond the movement of armies, whether they are great or small or merely ragtag bands. Before we dismiss this woman, we must be very sure that she is not a nexus point for our enemies."

"You mean, her people might rally around her?" Mortan asked. "I concede your point, Lord Veramar. Even if she herself does not lead them, she is still the only surviving member of their royal house. Her very presence here might inspire them."

The discussion wound on, with various courtiers advancing their opinions. Cinath listened, his eyes narrowing from time to time. Otherwise, he gave no sign of his thoughts. One of the Qr priests glided to his side and whispered to him. Cinath listened for a moment, then shook his head and waved the man away.

"Should we not simply eliminate that threat?" one of the other courtiers asked.

"What, and make her into a martyr?" Thessar snapped. "That's just the thing that *would* unite these people!"

"Cinath," Jaxar cut in, with far more assertiveness than before, "this haggling is beneath us. Petty cruelty, such as taunting a helpless prisoner with possible execution, only diminishes our moral authority. We have agreed that Lady Tsorreh represents no threat to Gelon. She is neither a military leader nor a political one, but a quiet scholar who has rarely had contact with anyone beyond my household. Or have we drunk so deeply of the well of unreason that you think she could subvert even *me*? Do I look like a dangerous insurrectionist? Have I ever acted or spoken against your sovereignty?"

"I have no doubts of your loyalty, my brother, and I trust your judgment better than that of some," Cinath replied. "I see no point in continuing these proceedings. This woman has made her submission, she clearly knows nothing, and we have more important matters to attend to. I'm glad she is of use to you, brother, for she's of no value to me."

When Jaxar drew in his breath to protest, Cinath laughed. "Don't be afraid, Jaxar. I'm not proposing to execute her. It's not worth the risk of martyrdom. No, she's safe with you for the moment, provided you prevent her from becoming a focus for conspiracy in the future."

"That I will gladly undertake to do," Jaxar replied with obvious sincerity. He inclined his head. "Once more, your wisdom and right judgment have prevailed."

"Hmmm." Cinath frowned slightly. He looked about the room, sighing, and paused at Lord Veramar. "All right, you clearly have something more to say. What is it?"

"Your Glorious Majesty, we've already established that not all power is military. There is political influence as well as those strange talents we do not yet understand."

"You mean this business of Meklavaran sorcery, I suppose." From his tone, Cinath meant the comment disparagingly, but something in his eyes, a fleeting shadow, told Tsorreh that suspicion had once more crept into his mind.

Veramar's momentary pause imbued the moment with heightened expectancy. "As always, Your Majesty is correct."

The tallest of the Qr priests, the one whose hood hid his face, glided forward. Tsorreh had the impression he did not walk as other men did, swaying from one foot to the next, but in a nonhuman fashion. A snake's writhing coils came to mind, or the articulated movement of an insect.

"Most Sagacious and Radiant Monarch." The priest's voice issued from within his hood with an odd echo. "If we are to arm ourselves against infernal enemies, or even prove their existence, we must understand their nature. Not even the most learned of your scholars would deny this, for why else would they seek out texts in ancient languages, if not to glean the knowledge of things the world has forgotten?"

With these words, the shadowed head swung toward Jaxar, who gave no visible reaction. What could Jaxar say? It was impossible for him to argue that research and scholarship were without value.

"This woman may have no sorcerous talent herself," the priest went on, "or it may lie dormant, beneath the level of her own awareness, hidden from even the most strenuous interrogation. Surely, if there is even a remote chance that it exists, we dare not allow its presence so close to the throne." Again, the cowled head swiveled in Jaxar's direction.

"So it has been argued," Cinath said. "Yet, short of doing away with her completely, I do not see how such a hypothetical threat can be dealt with."

"We—my brother priests and I—under the guidance of

Qr the Inexorable, have achieved some small skill in such matters," the priest said. "If it pleases the Glory of the Golden Land, may-his-wisdom-never-fail, to entrust us with this investigation, we propose to study this woman, using our own methods. Perhaps she is truly as innocent as she claims," he said, his tone clearly indicating he believed otherwise. "Or she may unconsciously harbor a threat, hidden as deep as the marrow of her bones. Whatever it is, we will ferret it out. We will do this for the protection of Gelon and the glorification of your reign, may-it-endure-to-the-end-of-time."

Tsorreh listened to the priest's words in growing panic. No, not panic, outright terror. Her brief contact with the Qr priest in Gatacinne still horrified her. She wanted to scream that it was they, not she, who possessed unnatural powers.

All too well, she remembered the interrogation at Gatacinne, the insidious pressure from the Qr priest's mind tightening around her own, sharp and insistent.

"You will tell us," he had hissed, *"yes, you will . . ."*

In supplication, Tsorreh brought her hands in front of her chest, palms pressed tightly together. She reached within herself, to the place where the petal gem rested.

O Most Holy, be with me now! Strengthen me, throw your protection over me, that this evil might pass!

No pulse of light, of power or clarity, answered her. The stone had gone inert, quenched. It could not shield her without revealing itself. She was alone in the grip of her enemies.

The moment moved on. Cinath was speaking again. Tsorreh was so overcome with fear, she could not understand his words. She forced herself to concentrate. She had been speaking Gelone almost exclusively for over a year, even dreaming in it. Now the intensity of the moment left her so dazed, so numb that she could not understand even a few simple phrases.

With an effort, Tsorreh understood Cinath to say that he

would consider the priest's petition. Through her suddenly blurred vision, she sought Jaxar. He had leaned over to speak to Cinath in such a way that they could not be easily overheard. For the moment, she had a tiny reprieve. She forced herself to breathe as Cinath's gaze went unfocused, his attention on his brother's words. He nodded, then stood with a brisk, powerful motion. "Out, all of you. Take the prisoner—the witness—back to the detention room. I will decide what to do with her later."

The nobles scrambled to their feet when the Ar-King rose. With only a few murmurs, more of surprise than of dissent, they hurried to disperse. Only Jaxar kept his seat. He gestured for Danar to leave with the others.

The Elite Guards closed in around Tsorreh. The senior officer motioned for her to follow him, but with a shade more courtesy than he had shown her before. In the detention room, she found herself alone except for the guard stationed inside the door. What he expected her to do, she had no idea. She couldn't read anything in his expression beyond a tinge of bored superiority. Closing her eyes, she tried to pretend he wasn't there.

As her heartbeat calmed, it came to her that this respite was a gift. It would be easy to work herself into a frenzy of worry, of feeling defenseless and trapped, convincing herself there was nothing she could do, no avenue of escape. For the moment, she was safe, she was whole, and she was mistress of her wits.

She realized, as the moments ticked by, that woven through the feelings of helplessness, of grief and despair, she felt angry. It seemed that all her life had been leading up to this moment, all the years of being told what to do, what to be. A dutiful daughter, a subordinate second wife, a mother whose only thought must be of her son, a captive, a helper, and now an accused prisoner.

Prisoner, yes! That was it. Always serving someone or something greater than herself! She had not been entrusted with the most precious responsibility of her people, she had become *enslaved* to it. No one had asked her if she wanted to carry the *te-alvar*, any more than she'd had a say in when or whom to marry, when and whether to bear a son, or in the fate of her city. On the fateful day she had stepped into the Treasury and taken the *te-Ketav* into her hands, she had also started down a path quite different from the one planned for her. And it had brought her here.

To what purpose? she stormed inwardly. To wait while men who cared nothing about her decided her fate? To find herself trapped between one doom and another? To discover that just at the moment when she most needed the magical gem to protect her against the insidious priests of Qr, it had deserted her?

Or had it?

The thought took her aback. She had assumed that the worst possible thing had already happened: the heart of the Shield taken out of Meklavar, the Shield itself scattered as in her vision on Victory Hill, herself as its guardian encircled by enemies that grew ever more strong, more resourceful.

But what if that were not, indeed, the worst fate?

Maybe she was *meant* to be here in the stronghold of her enemies, in Aidon, in Cinath's Palace, in the very center of Gelonian power. Could it be possible that the *te-alvar* had not abandoned her but had *guided* her here?

Tsorreh took a deep breath and forced herself to think.

The Shield was no longer intact, that much was undeniable. Over the ages, its power had diminished. Knowledge had faded into myth. History had become a luxury, a thing for scholars, not practical men. One by one, the heirs of Khored had drifted away, along with their precious burdens. Two were certainly lost, Eriseth in far Denariya, the other—Benerod—when his descendants disappeared.

On the other hand, the chaotic embodiment of Fire and Ice would never have given up the struggle. It would have persisted against the unwavering might of the Shield, always testing, always probing, searching for a way in, a way to return. It could not yet take physical form, so it worked through the agency of others, others it could shape and influence.

What if the *alvara* possessed their own foresight, their own wisdom? They had been created to defeat the armies of Fire and Ice, but afterward, Khored and his brothers had hidden them, preserved them against a time when the monstrous evil might rise again. Through the ancient magic, she had glimpsed shadows of chilling cold, of infernal flame, long slumbering but now rising from its prison, gathering strength.

The jointed limbs of Qr, agent of Fire and Ice, stretched across the Golden Land. Something moved in the world, something of frozen fire and shadow. In his greed, Cinath had become its pawn, its unknowing ally.

Could one woman succeed when so many strong men had failed? But she had no choice. She alone bore the heart of the Shield.

Tsorreh opened her eyes and the world leapt into focus. Calm settled over her like a mantle. Something akin to a thrill danced up her spine, and her heart sped up, as if she were preparing to flee. No, not to flee. To stand firm. To witness and remember. To endure until the time came to act.

There was a commotion at the door. The guard opened it a crack and spoke to someone outside.

"Come on, then," he said, turning back to her.

Tsorreh went with him, trying to prepare herself for the worst. She did not know how she would find the strength to resist the questioning of the Qr priests, having tasted their mental powers at Gatacinne. There was no point in wasting her energy on worry. She would simply find a way. There was no other choice.

To her surprise, the guard proceeded along the spacious corridor leading back to the Justice Hall. He led her back through a series of public chambers. Nobles and courtiers stood talking or moving about on their own business. A few turned to stare as she passed, with an impersonal disapproval directed more at her slave's dress than herself personally. Neither Lord Mortan nor the Qr priests were in sight.

At a side entrance, the guard turned her over to another man, obviously of lesser rank, who was positioned by the door. Tsorreh listened in amazement as the senior guard gave orders to take her back to Lord Jaxar's compound.

Chapter Twenty-four

FOR the rest of the day, Tsorreh waited anxiously for Jaxar to return from the Hall of Justice. She wanted to know why she had been released, but more than that, she fretted for the safety of her friend and protector. Had she compromised him? Would Cinath, volatile and headstrong, turn against his own brother? And what was the role of the Qr priests in the investigation? She paced the laboratory, moving restlessly between the work tables and bookshelves, and tried to concentrate.

Hoping to divert herself, she turned to the laboratory equipment. They had lost an entire day on Jaxar's latest project, compiling measurements of the Dawn Star's rising and setting. Jaxar had entertained the notion that the bright, constant body was a species of stationary comet. Now Tsorreh spread the charts and notes across one of the tables and stared at them. Even her own script looked alien, as if it had been penned by someone else.

As the hours passed without a sign of Jaxar, she feared the worst. Even if the Ar-King had not detained him, the day might have overtaxed Jaxar and caused a relapse. Hunger stirred, heightening her fatigue. She went down to the kitchen long enough to gulp down a bowl of cold barley stew and learn that Jaxar had returned to the compound as he had left it, in a litter.

Danar came into the laboratory just past sunset. As he closed the door behind him, she leapt to her feet.

"Your father? How is he?"

"He's resting. Asleep, I think. Oh, Tsorreh!" Danar looked stricken. "I'm sorry. I didn't think to send word to you. I'm a graceless lout to have caused you even a moment of worry!"

Tsorreh's legs threatened to give way under her. She lowered herself to the nearest bench. "Tell me, what happened after I was taken away?"

Danar hung his head, shaking it like a whipped dog. "I know no more than you do. Father said only that you are free. Well, as free as you were before."

"And he is well? He has not had another episode? A seizure of the heart?"

"No, no, he is only tired. He says that he will speak with you tomorrow morning, if you will have breakfast with him in the garden."

Tsorreh would much rather have gone to Jaxar immediately, but her own anxiety was hardly reason enough to disturb the rest of a friend, ill and exhausted. At least, he was safe. One night of waiting for further details was a small enough burden.

She arose the next morning as light spread across the eastern sky. By the time she entered the garden, birds were singing. Dew sat lightly on grass and vine. A sweet cool freshness filled the air. It would not last long, giving way to the heat of the day. Alone in the garden, she stretched her arms out, wishing she could draw the moment inside herself. She saw, as if for the first time, the care with which the garden had been designed, how the benches and tables were placed, how the trees had been pruned to maintain the illusion of naturalness. She wondered at finding such a haven anywhere in Gelon.

Gelon was not the enemy, this land of builders and engineers, of gardens crafted with artistic sensibility, of hodgepodge riches. Was it Cinath's own ambition that allowed Qr to gain a foothold? Or had these events been set in motion by the gradual dispersal of the *alvara*?

She doubted she would ever know the answer. Did it matter? She was here, in Aidon, in this jewel-perfect garden on a fresh morning, graced by a moment of joy.

With a pleasant chattering, Astreya and one of the kitchen maids bustled into the garden, bowed to Tsorreh, and began to set one of the tables for breakfast. Tsorreh watched, struck by their cheerful energy. Their voices harmonized with the cries of the birds.

Jaxar shuffled into the garden, leaning heavily on his crutch. Tsorreh ran to his side. He smiled and patted her arm as she settled him in his favorite chair, one with arm rests that made it easier for him to get up again.

Tsorreh took her own place beside him. A look passed between them, a shared concern, each for the other. As Danar had said, Jaxar looked weary but not ill. Tsorreh had not thought how she herself appeared, for she had spared little attention for her dress or hair, beyond tying her hair back with a twist of string. Too miserable with worry to consider, she had put on the slave dress again. Jaxar said nothing, but she caught the fleeting moment of sadness in his eyes and resolved to wear the better gown and find a more becoming style for her hair until it grew out fully.

Before they could exchange more than a few courtesies, the girls came back with trays of food and drink. Tsorreh felt uneasy as a plate of bread, hard-cooked eggs, and sliced peaches drizzled with honey was set before her. They had shared many such meals in the laboratory, his private space and her sanctuary, but never here in the family garden. Lycian would not be pleased.

Lycian, she reminded herself, was not here. She raised her goblet of watered apple wine in a silent toast to Lycian's absence, and drank deeply.

Jaxar sipped his parsley tea, nibbled a little fruit, and

shoved bread crumbs from one side of his plate to the other. Around the periphery of the garden, behind walls of tree and trellised flowering vines, the noises of the morning household work died down.

"Now we will have a modicum of privacy," Jaxar commented. "It's taken me years to train them to leave me in peaceful meditation at this hour. Let's not waste it. I'm sure you want to know about my meeting with Cinath."

"Yes, I had wondered. It seemed as if he were ready to hand me over to the priests of—" she stumbled over the name, "of Qr."

"They're an eerie lot, I agree. Full of superstitious nonsense."

"Not entirely nonsense, if the Ar-King listens to them," Tsorreh pointed out.

Jaxar nodded. "Years ago, the Scorpion god had no name. It was one among many nature spirits. I'm glad you don't shudder and scream at the very mention of scorpions, like Lycian."

"Even scorpions have their place, even if it is inconvenient for the people who want to live there. I've seen them in my own country, and in the Sand Lands as well. Yes, they have venomous stingers, but they use them only to defend themselves and to kill for food. I don't believe they have any malice in them. But these things depicted on the brow bands of the priests—*these* are not natural creatures."

"I am not easy at how their power has grown, especially over my brother," Jaxar said, clearly meaning the priests, not the scorpions. "It's one thing for silly women to pray to whatever god they think will preserve their figures or give them sons, but quite another when the Ar-King himself, responsible for Gelon and all its increasingly numerous provinces, lends an ear to ambition and superstition. I told him so."

Tsorreh blinked, for a moment unable to think of what to say. Behind his gentle tones, Jaxar was furious. And frightened.

"You must—" she struggled for words. "You must have been very persuasive."

"Hmmph. If I don't speak plainly to him, who will? Cinath boasts that he makes his own decisions. He has always been wary of letting anyone influence him unduly. So he denied their request to turn you over to them. For this time, at least."

"And next time?"

"What happens next time will depend upon what they offer him and what he believes they can actually deliver." He paused, running one hand over his face, rubbing the folds of loose skin.

Tsorreh remembered his eyes when he told her of the summons. *I would spare you this. I would protect you if I could.* But flesh and steel and worldly influence could accomplish only so much. Khored had understood this well, which was why he had relied not only on his armies but also on the Shield.

"I am grateful for everything you have done on my behalf," she said in a voice that quavered a little. "You have been my true friend."

"And will continue to be so," Jaxar replied. "Together we will face whatever comes. I have as much at stake here as you do, child. He is my brother, after all, and I love him. I also love my country, and my family and friends, all of whom will suffer grievously if Cinath succumbs to this nonsense."

He may not have a choice. The thought flitted through Tsorreh's mind. For just an instant, she saw Cinath, whom she once hated, as a victim, even as she was. *But he is still responsible for his crimes. He has caused so much pain, so much death and destruction!* she thought. *It goes on, even today, in Meklavar and here in Aidon.*

"In the meantime," Jaxar went on, "we must do nothing to provoke him. I'm sorry I could not protect the other suspects. I have only so much influence over my brother when he has set his mind on a course of action. I must choose wisely what is important and which arguments to make."

From somewhere in the compound, a lone bird called. Jaxar drew a shallow, wheezing breath. "We must not risk your leaving the compound, even escorted, not until this furor dies down."

So she was to be a prisoner after all. Longing pierced her, to hear her own language, to see faces of the same golden color as hers, to catch the familiar smells of cedar and cinnamon and myrrh. How could Jaxar understand? He would have been content to never leave his precious laboratory except to observe the stars from the roof. He meant well and would doubtless do whatever he could to make her confinement pleasant. Besides, a prisoner was what she was. What right had she to expect anything different?

Self-pity rang hollow in her mind. It reminded her of the whining of locusts, petty and paltry, yet corrosive.

"If I cannot leave the compound," she said, frowning, "then how will I get medicine for you—" *the next time you fall ill?*

Would he agree to send Danar? Or Astreya? Would Breneya allow it, when anyone seen entering the residence of a Meklavaran might become a suspect herself?

Jaxar laid one hand on hers and gave her a fatherly smile. "I shall take great care to remain in good health."

There was a second reason why Tsorreh must seek out Marvenion, one she dared not even consider in Jaxar's presence, lest he, with his perceptiveness, suspect. She must find a way to warn Marvenion of what had happened at the interrogation, that he and every other Meklavaran in the city were now in even greater danger.

Tsorreh waited another two days, two days of quiet work in the laboratory, venturing out into the main part of the compound for only the briefest and most necessary reasons. Jaxar made no remark about her subdued disposition, yet she was certain he had noticed it.

A general relaxation of discipline heralded the approach of the Festival of The Bounteous Giver of Wine. As twilight seeped across the sky, Tsorreh persuaded Jaxar to rest, for they had been working since breakfast on an experiment

concerning the refractive qualities of glass. For once, she
had no further responsibilities. Danar had finished his reading assignments and gone off to visit friends, who would
probably then attempt to elude their bodyguards and go
tavern crawling. On this warm evening, many of the servants had been given time off to attend the festivities, according to tradition.

It was not difficult to creep out the gate and make her
way down the hill. People thronged the major streets. Many
of them were already drunk, and no one took notice of one
more celebrant. She wore the fine dress Jaxar had given her,
but without the distinctive ivory clasps.

Bonfires burned in the plazas. Amid the dancing and music, a small crowd carried a crude wicker platform on their
shoulders. On it crouched a man in the mask of a monkey,
naked except for an elaborate, garishly colorful wrapping
that enlarged his penis to elephantine size. Revelers tossed
handfuls of flower petals and garlands of ribbons at him,
and he replied with chittering cries and obscene sugges-
tions. City patrol nodded tolerantly at the antics.

The air was filled with the mingled, heady smells of wine
and sex, of perfume and burning torches. Here and there,
couples embraced openly, fumbling with each other's clothing, some of them pairs of men. Tsorreh stared, caught between fascination and embarrassment at the public display.
She had heard of such things, but never before found herself amidst frankly orgiastic abandon.

Tsorreh felt an instant of apprehension as a party of men
in ragged clothes, laughing and guzzling from wineskins,
gestured for her to join them. She tossed her head as Astreya did and went on her way with no greater harm than a
few blurred compliments. From time to time, she peered
into the shadows, fearful that she might spy a cloaked figure
gliding after her. If there were such a lurker, however, the
confusion of the festival disguised him well.

The merrymaking diminished as Tsorreh approached
Bathar Hill, but did not end. Even in the usually quiet
neighborhood, singers and dancers caroused here and there.

When she arrived at Marvenion's house, his daughter, Rebah, welcomed her with a shy smile. Instead of conducting Tsorreh inside, Rebah asked her to wait in the antechamber.

The chamber was decorated in a subdued style, yet every strand of the woven wall hangings, every detail of the little side table, reminded Tsorreh of home. She closed her eyes and drew in a deep breath, savoring the quiet and the faint odors of fragrant wood and incense.

A few moments later, Marvenion came through the inner door. Concern furrowed his brow, so Tsorreh quickly reassured him that Lord Jaxar was well enough. "I have come on quite a different matter. Our people are in danger—"

"Yes, I know. Come inside." Marvenion led her not to the room he used as his clinical office and study, but to a more intimate chamber. Passing through the door was like stepping into the past and across many miles. If the antechamber had suggested home, this room was saturated with memory. Tsorreh drank in the colors of the cushions and carpet, even the enamel plate of dates rolled in crushed almonds. She wanted to cradle the round-bellied oil lamp, to stroke the plush fur of the gray tabby cat that yawned and stretched on its cushion, to sink to her knees and weep.

As her eyes adjusted to the soft orange light from the lamp, she made out two men on the far side of the room, now rising from the low couch. Bearded and dressed as prosperous Meklavaran traders, they could have stepped right off the *meklat*.

"This is Tsorreh, a countrywoman." Marvenion's voice carried an edge of warning.

Before she could say anything, one of the visitors moved closer. "Tsorreh . . . Tsorreh *san-Khored*? Can it be?"

"I know you," she said, searching her memory for names. "I know both of you. Your father—no, both your fathers— counseled my husband. You are Harellon, of the trading house of Deneroth." She paused, remembering how Harellon's father had disapproved of her half-Isarran blood.

Courtesies between them had been chilly and polite. To the other man, she said, "I'm sorry, I don't remember your name. Your father is Viridon san-Cassarod, is he not?"

"*Te-ravah.*" The second of the visitors bowed to her, followed an instant later by his companion and a deeply astonished Marvenion.

Tsorreh wanted to scream at them to stop this obsequious nonsense. She was an exile, cut off from her city, her people, her only son, desperately lonely and often terrified, subject to the same whims of the Ar-King as the lowest of them.

The words choked in her throat. She could never be solely who she was. These men *needed* her to be something else—a queen, a rock, a beacon. So she waited while they finished their reverences and her aching heart went numb. Then she persuaded them all to sit down while Marvenion's daughter, more shy than ever, served them mint-infused tea and honey-nut pastries.

Harellon, she knew slightly from some courtly event or another. She remembered him as being younger, but the fall of Meklavar and hard travel had weathered his face. The other named himself Setherod, the younger of two remaining sons of Viridon.

"You have not heard, then?" Setherod said in response to her inquiry. "My father died shortly after we surrendered."

"I'm sorry to hear that," she said. "I didn't know. I have had so little news from home. It must have been very difficult for you."

Setherod lowered his eyes, but not before she read the flash of anger. "Yes, you might say *difficult*. The city was in chaos. The *te-ravot* was dead, and *ravot* Shorrenon as well. You and *ravot* Zevaron had disappeared, slain for all we knew. Every day, there were new reports about Ar-Thessar-Gelon. Half of them said he was dying, the other that he had recovered and was preparing lists of names for execution. His soldiers were everywhere. There were hangings and floggings on every corner. The *meklat* was empty. People were terrified to leave their homes. But," he paused, glanced at her, and then quickly looked away, "life must go on."

"Yes, it must." Her lips formed the words while images dissolved behind her eyes. She remembered her city the last time she had seen it, the massive gates in ruin, streaked with oil and soot, and the slow procession of soldiers bearing Maharrad's white-shrouded body. Shorrenon on the throne that had been his father's, sitting tall and straight, his sword bare across his knees. The long dark flight through the tunnels into the Sand Lands and beyond.

Marvenion shifted, uneasy. "We heard rumors, of course, but could not believe things were really that bad in Meklavar."

Harellon said to Tsorreh, "You left the city in the chaos of the early days." His words were perfectly polite yet carried a hint of censure. "The general was taking no chances on an uprising, and no one knew if Thessar would live or . . ."

Or what Cinath would do if his son died, Tsorreh finished silently.

Setherod shot a hard look at his companion. "I didn't desert my people, if that's what you're implying! It wasn't my choice to leave. After my father died and my brother took up the leadership of Cassarod, it became imperative that one of us remain free in case the worst happened."

Tsorreh remembered what Shorrenon had said in the war council, that the Gelon would execute or exile all the noble houses.

"When I left, there had been a certain amount of confusion, of displacement," Harellon said. "Some people were trying to leave Meklavar, others from the outlying areas were trying to get in, Gelonian forces were putting down outbreaks of rebellion. Of course, the heads of all the important families were closely watched." He paused, pressing his lips together with an expression of disapproval that reminded Tsorreh very much of her father. "With the royal family dead or disappeared, who knew where, and the

Council in disarray, the Gelon suspected anyone who might be able to raise a following."

Tsorreh caught the flicker of hostility between the two men. Each saw himself as the man destined to lead a Meklavaran uprising. They would never agree, that much was clear. Setherod would not give up the privilege of rank granted by his Cassarod lineage, descended from one of Khored's own brothers. Harellon lacked the personal charisma that might make up for his more common origins. Behind their rivalry, she sensed their yearning, the shared dream of a free Meklavar. If Shorrenon were alive, they would have followed him without question.

The discussion continued, recounting the struggles of a city under occupation, the cycles of revenge and retaliation, of fear and power and grief. The Gelon did not mean to destroy Meklavar, at least they had not at first, not like the Isarran city that a previous Ar-King had ordered burned to the ground and the charred earth sown with salt. Meklavar had too much value as a fortress along the trade route to Denariya. Cinath could not replace its entire population. He needed merchants and bankers, crafts people and caravaneers. Most of all, he needed a secure and peaceful city. A city bowed but still productive, not in ruins.

The Gelon were not mere brutes; they had centuries of experience in governing conquered lands. If the only thing at stake were the welfare of her city, Tsorreh might have conceded the throne to the Gelon. It held no attraction for her. She had seen what the long years of responsibility had done to Maharrad, how leadership had turned Shorrenon into a martyr, how Zevaron could never have led a normal life. Was it worth so many lives to elevate one man in place of another? Was it not better to have order and peace and justice, even if the laws were made elsewhere? The people of Aidon, what she had seen of them, were not oppressed, nor were they monsters.

But ever since Tenereth had placed the *te-alvar* within her body, since its power had brought her visions of the past, she no longer thought of the Book of Khored as a poetic legend. Now she knew there was more at stake than the comfort and security of one city. Invisible forces moved in Gelon, the shadowy reach of the Scorpion god. Images sprang to her mind: *Ashes and frost, things ancient beyond imagining, things subtle and patient.*

As Setherod talked, Tsorreh studied him, not only with her eyes but with the strange senses of the *te-alvar*. Cassarod was one of the lineages of the Shield, the red gem that embodied courage. Yet she could sense nothing of its presence in him. He was no coward, but his bravery was personal, not the transcendent incarnation of the virtue. It must be his older brother, Ganneron, who bore the *alvar*. And Ganneron was still in Meklavar.

"We have no leader to unite us," Marvenion was saying. "We are scattered, adrift. The Gelon pick us off at their whim."

"For the moment," Setherod conceded. "But it's early yet. Order is being restored in Meklavar. Surely, when the Gelon see there is no effective resistance, they will relax their hold. Eventually, it will be safe to return."

"There is the Prophet," Harellon said thoughtfully. "Under the right circumstances, the people would rally to him."

"The Prophet? I have not heard of him," Marvenion said.

"Cinath has," Tsorreh murmured.

"He is hearsay, a legend," Setherod said. "I doubt he even exists."

"He exists," Harellon insisted, "but I fear he cannot help us. One story is that he fled the city just before the fall, moving like smoke through the lines. Another is that he walked out of the Sand Lands one day, preaching about the return of Khored and the end of times. He says we must prepare for a battle even greater than defeating the Gelon."

A battle even greater. Ashes and frost . . . subtle, patient, coming closer.

"Understandably, the Gelon do not like this kind of talk," Harellon continued. "Even less so because when they send soldiers after him, he vanishes."

Setherod shook his head. "That only proves my point. How can such a man be anything but a fabrication? For all we know, Cinath's ministers invented him as an excuse to oppress us even further."

"Do you accuse me of lying? Or of being stupid?" Harellon said, plainly angry.

In Tsorreh's memory, she relived the moment during the war council when accusations of treason had burst forth. Maharrad had quelled them, saying, *"Shall we do the work of the Gelon for them?"*

"Enough!" she exclaimed. "How can we stand against our enemies if we turn on each other? If we let our differences become more important than what we hold in common? If we lash out at the friend in front of us, instead of the enemy we cannot reach?"

Suddenly, Tsorreh could not contain the energy that surged up in her. She sprang to her feet. In the corner, Marvenion's daughter lifted her head and watched, her eyes shining.

"What is truly important? What will it take to stand against a conqueror who is both powerful and disciplined? If we are to succeed, I tell you, then Meklavar will need *all* of us. Working together, not at each other's throats like savage beasts!"

As one, they turned to look at her. She raked them with her glare.

For a long moment, they sat as if stunned. No one moved. They seemed not even to breathe. Tsorreh wondered if she had said something foolish, or if they simply had not expected such zeal from a woman.

Let them think what they like, so long as they listen!

Harellon lowered his eyes, his shoulders sagging. Setherod stared at her, as if she were no merely human woman who had just lectured him, but something more.

The next moment, she thought in disgust, *they will start treating me like a hero out of legend and forget all about what I just said.*

Slowly, reverently, Setherod knelt at her feet. His voice

rasped with emotion. "*You* will lead our people to freedom."

Tsorreh did not want such adulation. She had never seen herself as a leader, rebel or otherwise, certainly not a ruler in her own right. She had been the inexperienced second wife, the mother, the comforter of an old man—

The woman who stormed off to preserve the library, she reminded herself.

The woman who had gotten Zevaron out of Meklavar, kept him alive and free.

The one who had taken Lycian's blow, meant for a helpless servant girl. The one who had found a way to save Jaxar, regardless of the risk.

The one who now bore the heart of the Shield, the clear glowing petal of unity. The only one.

Tsorreh laid her fingertips on the back of his bowed neck. "I thank you for your loyalty. I—"

She broke off at a sudden rush of energy from the *te-alvar*. It came alive, hot enough to sear her from the inside. Its power stole her breath for a moment. Then, as if she had passed from shadow into daylight, her inner vision cleared. She sensed the distinctive presence of the minions of Qr, that hint of frozen fire.

They were very near, searching. Searching for *her*.

Between one heartbeat and the next, the air was rent by the noise of pounding at the outside door, muffled by the intervening walls but unmistakable. Rebah let out a shriek.

The men reacted quickly. Setherod scrambled to his feet. Harellon's hand reached for the hilt of the short sword hanging from his belt.

"Quickly! Follow me!" Marvenion cried. "This way!"

The physician snatched up the round-bellied oil lamp and darted to the back of the room. He jerked aside the tapestry that ran from a rod just below the ceiling to the floor. A narrow door lay behind it. Flinging it open, he gestured to the others.

"Rebah, you first. Take the lamp. Lead the others—just as we practiced."

"Papa!" Rebah moved quickly to obey. She disappeared into the darkness beyond the door, with Setherod following close. Harellon paused to look back at Tsorreh.

"Go on!" she urged.

Harellon dashed after the girl and Setherod.

"You must not be taken!" Marvenion grabbed Tsorreh and shoved her bodily through the opening.

The door slammed behind her. She heard the metallic clink of a lock closing. Then Marvenion said, speaking low from the other side, "I will delay them as long as I can. With the blessing of the Holy One, they will arrest me and not look further. *Go!*"

The passageway behind the door was narrow, barely wide enough to slide through. No attempt had been made to smooth the stone. The rough edges caught Tsorreh's dress and scraped her elbow as she fitted herself into the opening.

Ahead bobbed a sphere of light. She glimpsed Rebah's face, starkly shadowed, before the bulk of Harellon's body blocked it.

"Quickly!" Harellon's voice filled the narrow space.

"No, you go on." the girl's reply came in an urgent whisper. For all her previous shyness, she now spoke with authority. This was her house, Tsorreh thought. Her world. Her father.

"Take the lamp," Rebah said. "The passage bends twice. Stay to the right. You'll come out in the alley behind the next row of houses. And *be quiet!*"

With a great deal of shoving, Harellon pushed past Rebah.

Tsorreh reached the girl in a few steps. "What about you?"

"I can find my way in the dark well enough. Papa made me practice. But I'm staying here. It's as safe as anyplace, and if anything happens—"

Rebah broke off at the sound of men's voices from beyond the door. Until that moment, Tsorreh had not realized how thin the wooden barrier was and how readily sound penetrated. She held her breath, afraid that even the slightest noise might be overheard.

"Nothing—" said one man's voice.

"Where is she?" asked another.

"As you see, I am alone." Marvenion's voice rose above the sounds of furniture being overturned, and other noises Tsorreh could not identify, but clearly, the room was being thoroughly searched. "What do you hope to find here? Is this rummaging about really necessary?"

"She was here . . ." came a slightly hollow voice, resonating eerily through Tsorreh's skull. It seemed to fill the narrow, lightless passage. She quivered like a wild thing caught in an iron trap, waiting to be discovered.

More voices came through the door, voices raised now in argument. The hollow voice—a Qr priest?—insisted that their quarry was very near, but the strongest of the other voices sounded tight with suppressed resentment.

"We've wasted enough time here." The clipped speech reminded Tsorreh of the Elite Guard at the Hall of Justice. "We have more pressing responsibilities this night."

"No, we must not leave yet! I command you to search further!"

"Search where? Do you think this woman is hiding in the mortar between the floor stones? Or in the stuffing of one of these pillows?"

"She was here, I tell you . . . *is* still near . . ."

Tsorreh could almost hear the whispered sweep of the priest's long robe as he glided nearer.

Another man's voice, edged with impatience: "Captain, shall we arrest the man and be done with it?"

"On what charges?" Marvenion demanded. From his voice, he was standing on the opposite side of the room, beside the outer door.

"Harboring a treasonous witch," the priest hissed.

"Not without evidence she was actually here," the captain snapped. At any other time, Tsorreh thought, he would simply have taken Marvenion and anyone else within the house for questioning. But the priest had antagonized him, challenging his authority, and he was angry.

Strong, slender fingers closed around Tsorreh's arm.

Grasping Rebah's hand, she let the girl's steady presence flow into her. The *te-alvar* was quiescent, and yet she knew it had not abandoned her. It was, in a way she could not understand, sheltering her, placing her beyond the priest's powers of detection. She could feel him, standing before the wall hanging. Searching for her.

By some miracle, he moved away, still probing. Catching her scent in the chamber, perhaps, but nothing more.

What if the guard captain became suspicious? What if he lifted the tapestry to reveal the door? Should she make her escape now, while she still could? Or would an inadvertent sound, or perhaps the very sensation of motion, alert the priest? She felt sure that the petal gem could not protect her against physical discovery.

Rebah gestured with their joined hands to move down the passage. Tsorreh followed and tried not to think about even a single misstep.

The sounds from behind the door fell away. They went on, one careful step after another. Their progress was slow, too slow. At any moment, Tsorreh expected the door to be flung open and to hear the shouted command to halt.

With a creak, the door did swing open. Tsorreh glanced back, her muscles tensing for a useless sprint down the passage. A bar of light fell across the narrow space, revealing the silhouette of a man.

"It's all right, they've gone," Marvenion called out, his voice tremulous, almost quavering.

"Papa!" Rebah hurled herself into his arms.

Tsorreh followed, shaken with astonishment. The next moment, Marvenion led them both out of the passage. Tsorreh crumpled into one of the chairs. Her heart was beating so hard, she could not speak.

With a child's unshakeable confidence, Rebah accepted the miracle of their escape. Smiling, she went in search of restoratives, and returned only a few minutes later with a tray of fresh mint-tea and almonds crusted with crystallized honey. The maid servant had fainted after being summarily shoved aside by the guards, but was recovering well.

Tsorreh cradled her cup of tea in her hands and tried to stop trembling. Marvenion kissed Rebah on the brow. "You carried yourself with the valor of our race. I am proud to call you daughter. However, should there be another time, you are not to linger. You must do as I bid you."

Rebah lifted her chin. "I will do as I see fit. Who can know ahead of time what will be best?"

Listening, Tsorreh wanted to laugh and weep, all at once. She supposed that fathers had been cautioning their children in this manner since the beginning of time. She thought of Jaxar and what he might say of this night's misadventure. He would rail at her for the risk she had taken. More than that, he would be hurt and disappointed that she had broken her word. She must find a way to keep it from him.

Chapter Twenty-five

AFTER a brief rest, Tsorreh gathered up the courage for her return. She dared not delay too long, lest someone in Jaxar's household, perhaps Jaxar himself, realize she was gone. For all she knew, the Qr priest and his fellows, aided by the Elite Guard, were still searching for her.

Once again, she was able to lose herself in the celebration. Merrymaking continued throughout the city at an even higher pitch of frenzy than before. From the greater size of the gatherings, she concluded these people meant to carouse until dawn. By the time she reached the foot of Bathar Hill, every nerve in her body quivered with strain. Every few moments, she glanced behind her or peered into the shadows at the edge of the light cast by bonfire and torch, or searched the crowds for hooded figures. The drunken caresses of strangers held no terror for her now. By comparison to her pursuers, the revelers seemed benign, clumsy but not malicious.

Tsorreh found the compound gate as she had left it, closed and unbarred. The house was dark and quiet. She was able to slip inside and up to the laboratory without notice.

The next days passed slowly. She alternated between restlessness on one hand—craving news and sights beyond the compound walls, and most especially, contact with her countrymen—and apprehension on the other. What was happening in the city, in the court, in Cinath's mind? What were the Qr priests whispering in his ears? Or in the ears of his foppish son, Chion, since Thessar apparently wanted nothing to do with them? Had Thessar become their enemy because he would not be their puppet? What were Mortan and that hideous Veramar scheming?

She tried to convince herself that the Elite Guards would soon be assigned to other duties, just as the attention of the Ar-King would be diverted, perhaps to a military action or courtly intrigue. Yet in her belly, she knew that the minions of Qr would not tire in their search for her. Her only hope of safety, a fragile one at best, lay within the confines of Jaxar's domain. Until she could be sure of a secure passage beyond the Ar-King's reach, she dared not risk arrest.

During those next days and weeks, she greeted each morning with the certainty that today, the Ar-King would summon her again, and this time Jaxar would not be able to protect her. Despite Jaxar's confidence in his own position, Tsorreh worried that he might have pushed his brother too far. The priests of Qr might create enough suspicion in the Ar-King's mind to overcome the ties of blood and the bounds of reason. Then, not only would she be vulnerable to the growing influence of Qr upon Cinath, but Jaxar might suffer as well.

In her nightmares, she envisioned terrible fates for the men she had seen in the holding cell. Her imagination roiled with images of Qr temples becoming so tall and numerous they blotted out the bright marble palaces. Faceless priests in their hooded robes glided through twilit streets, leaving trails of condensing darkness in which disturbing shapes slowly began to take substance.

Jaxar tried to be patient with her during this time. Besides their usual work together, he arranged for musicians and poets to give performances in the privacy of his compound. Lycian was delighted, even if Jaxar insisted that she invite no more than a handful of friends. The intimacy of the events lent them even greater glamour in Lycian's eyes and enhanced her social standing. Although Tsorreh was not permitted to sit with the family, Jaxar directed Issios to provide her with a comfortable seat, shielded from the prying curiosity of Lycian's friends, so that she might enjoy the music.

Danar, too, did his best to divert Tsorreh. Together they read aloud and memorized her favorite selections from the Cilician *Odes*, and explored the work of the poets who participated in the evening performances.

Months passed. The seasonal rainstorms turned the skies dark and turbulent gray rivers ran down the paved streets. With the return of warmer weather and sunshine came a sense that the storms had passed in more ways than one. Cinath, who had moved his court to a more pleasant location during the winter, returned to Aidon, and still had issued no further summonses.

Cinath now divided his military ventures between Isarre and Azkhantia. The situation in Meklavar had apparently settled down after a series of arrests. The prophet everyone had spoken of had apparently fled to the mountains. After the first flurry of anxieties, watching daily for new developments, life in Jaxar's compound resumed its own rhythm of meals and rituals and daily work in the laboratory. Astreya married the young oil merchant. Danar spent more time away from home, both at court and training in various weapons and military skills expected of any young nobleman. Tsorreh missed his company, but felt relieved that his infatuation with her seemed to be maturing into friendship.

Three years after Tsorreh's arrival in Aidon, the city was thrown into mourning by news of the death of Prince Thessar. Cinath had dispatched his elder son to lead the Azkhantian expedition, and things had gone badly. Rumors abounded as to whether Thessar had made a last glorious stand against the bloodthirsty nomads, or whether one of his own officers, most likely in the pay of Isarre, had stabbed him in the back during a battle, or whether he had perished as a result of black Meklavaran sorcery.

Jaxar and his family attended the official state funeral. Afterward he said little beyond that Prince Chion had taken his brother's place as heir to the throne. Jaxar sounded so grim that Tsorreh hesitated to question him for further details. Danar's opinion was that Chion might very well have conspired against his own brother, a notion that Tsorreh found appallingly possible.

During the warm summer nights of Tsorreh's fourth year in Aidon, she and Jaxar concentrated their efforts on nightly astronomical observations. Jaxar had long been fascinated with the study of comets, comparing historical records with current sightings. A new comet, not mentioned in any of his texts, had recently appeared. Tsorreh helped him to track its course as it moved through the heavens. Jaxar's enthusiasm grew with the increasing brightness of the celestial object.

They had first observed the comet as a single ice-pale mote at the limit of the focusing capability of the telescope. Instead of waxing and waning, it grew steadily in size. Through Jaxar's best lenses, Tsorreh saw its filmy tail for the first time, like a smear of chalk against the deepness of the sky. Its growth seemed to accelerate, as if it were rushing headlong toward the earth.

At last, Tsorreh could see it without the lensed apparatus, although for a time, Jaxar's eyesight was not keen enough. Then even he could make it out. He commented that if the comet continued on its present course, it would soon be visible during the day.

Tsorreh had seen enough of the temper of the city to worry how the people would respond. They would think it an omen and would rush to the priests of whatever gods they worshipped. She reflected that the priests knew no more of the nature of such phenomena than did anyone else, but that would not stop them from making pronouncements and prophecies, or selling protective amulets for as much as their devotees could afford.

As afternoon drifted into twilight, heat hung in the air like an invisible blanket. The city drowsed, the people moving languidly about their tasks. Only Jaxar, fired by the passions of his scientific curiosity, seemed immune to the pervasive lethargy. When he noticed Tsorreh yawning over her notebook, he sent her off to bed. At first, she resisted sleep, but she had been up late for several nights in a row. Her body craved rest, and her eyelids burned with fatigue.

She awoke with a start hours later. The air was cooler but very still, expectant. A dim light bathed the laboratory. The door leading to the observatory was open. She went to the bottom of the ladder.

"Jaxar? Are you up there?"

A rustle of footsteps answered her. "Tsorreh! You're awake? Splendid! You must see this. Come up at once."

Tsorreh had never heard Jaxar so excited. Wonder infused his voice. She scrambled up as quickly as she could. For an instant, she wondered if she had slept through until dawn, the sky was so bright. As she took in the sight, she staggered, for a moment too struck with awe to speak. Jaxar sat on his stool, equally transfixed.

A brilliant sphere blazed in the west, moving slowly toward the east along the northern horizon. It pierced the night, casting off shards of light like trails of falling stars. As if, Tsorreh thought, it had been composed of fire and ice, now shattered into a hundred fragments, plunging toward the arctic dawn.

It was both beautiful and terrifying.

Behind Tsorreh's breastbone, the *te-alvar* flared. So sudden was its awakening and after so long a slumber that she cried out and pressed both hands over it. Its invisible light pulsed through her fingers, filled her chest, and streamed through her entire body. Her bones vibrated with its power.

The heart of the Shield had been waiting, watching for this very moment.

"Tsorreh, my dear? Are you ill?"

"I am well," she managed to gasp. "Only . . . overcome for a moment."

"Ah, you might well be," Jaxar sounded both wistful and awed by what he had seen. "A phenomenon like this comes to us but rarely. Most men live their entire lives without beholding such a sight. We shall not see its like again."

Tsorreh lifted her face once more to the sky just as the fiery-white comet disappeared behind the northeast ridge of house tops. She felt herself half in the world, half in a dream. The *te-alvar* hummed through her bones and colored her vision. With a breath, she might stand again with Khored under the ice-raptured sky.

Although she could no longer see the comet, she felt it still—racing, falling, hurling itself earthward. Her vision went gray and opaque. She sensed the screaming speed and momentum of the thing and its desperate *need*.

Something pulled it, commanded it, something fed by the very place in which she stood.

Qr? Reaching out to the shadowed evil of ancient days? To Khored's enemy?

Far, far to the north, beyond the limit of her physical vision, she saw light surge up into the sky, blotting out the stars. Bedrock trembled. Mountains fractured. Echoes slapped back from one cliff face to the next, and blood-colored light limned the jagged line of peaks. And from deep within the earth, deeper and darker than even the tunnels of Meklavar, something stirred. Something reached out with slow and terrible sentience.

Tsorreh wrenched her awareness back to the rooftop in Aidon. She trembled in every muscle. Her heart stuttered, then grew steadier, bathed in the power of the petal gem. Slowly, her breath softened, and her pulse slowed toward normal. She felt herself once more in her body.

They sat for what seemed an eternity, as night wrapped itself around the compound once more. Jaxar gave a deep, satisfied sigh.

"What a sight." His voice was hushed, almost prayerful. "I never thought to witness such a thing. A comet falling to earth."

Tsorreh swallowed. Her throat was hard and dry. "Where? Where did it strike?"

"Let us see what we can determine. I will need a map." Jaxar gathered himself, moving with his usual awkward stiffness. Together they went down into the laboratory. While Tsorreh lit the oil lamps, Jaxar spread out his charts. Consulting the notes he had taken of the comet's approach and descent, he made calculations, measuring out distances on the maps.

"There, more or less." He jabbed a stubby finger somewhere in the northeast region of the Azkhantian steppe. "Alas, it's unlikely that any Gelon will be permitted that far within the nomads' territory. It would be—" he sighed again, wistful now, "an amazing thing to study whatever is left of the comet."

Tsorreh shivered inside. The last thing she wanted was to stand before that frozen, fiery brilliance. She bent over the map. "These markings indicate mountains, I believe."

"Yes, so far as we know. The map is old, pieced together from traders' reports that go back to times when relations between the Azkhantians and ourselves were less contentious. My old friend Sadhir, may-his-spirit-rest-in-peace— whom you and Danar were so kind to visit—created some of these maps, based on his own travels. The distances may be in error, but I believe we can reliably say that a range of mountains borders the northern steppe in that location."

Tsorreh went to the bookshelf where she had arranged the small collection of Meklavaran texts. Jaxar did not possess a copy of the *te-Ketav*, but some of the historical works in his collection made reference to it. Gelonian scholars were notorious for quoting the scriptures of other races. She paged through several volumes while Jaxar once more bent over the map, muttering under his breath about trade routes.

The third book yielded what she sought.

"And it came to pass," she read, moving her lips with the words, "that Khored and his brothers defeated Fire and Ice and exiled it to the far regions of the world, to the ring of glacier mountains of the north, and then beyond the veil between the worlds."

To the glacier mountains of the north ...

She felt dizzy, thinking about the comet smashing down into those mountains, freeing what lay there. The *te-alvar* was summoning her, bidding her act after all these years of watchful waiting.

But what was she to do? Given her status as a prisoner and the increasing influence of the priests of Qr and their tenacious watch over her, what *could* she do?

Tsorreh realized, then, that she was trembling as much from fury as from fear. She was tired of secrets, tired of waiting, tired of hiding like a hunted animal, tired of her very existence being dependent on powerful men.

She had been given a burden, a guide, a treasure beyond measure, but for what purpose? To flee and sneak and keep it hidden while the world crumbled around her? Why had she been the one to receive the *te-alvar* if she were not also meant to use it?

PART IV:

Zevaron's Search

Chapter Twenty-six

To the west, beyond the Mearas, a storm was brewing. Zevaron tasted it on the air, though as yet, only a darkening haze marred the perfect sky. Heat drenched the air, a stillness he had learned to never trust. The canvas sails of the *Wave Dancer* hung almost limp, and the ship, usually responsive to his hand on the tiller, moved sluggishly.

Chalil came to stand beside him, wiping sweat from his forehead. The last four years had worn hard on the pirate captain. Gray streaked his night-dark hair, and his skin was as creased and weathered as old leather.

Zevaron turned to glance at his friend and captain, a smile tugging at the corners of his mouth. In another decade on the *Wave Dancer*, he would look just as sea-worn. With his long hair tied back, his curved mustache, and his skin darkly tanned, he could easily pass for Denariyan. His command of the language would never fool a native but did well enough for outlanders.

"Curse this calm!" Zevaron said, but with good temper. "It will hold us here until the storm catches us."

"And so?" Chalil's eyes narrowed as he scanned the horizon, and Zevaron knew what he was thinking. *Better to face a storm than a warship.*

Chalil and his crew wanted no part in the ongoing naval

conflict between Gelon and Isarre. War was bad for trade and worse for a pirate who depended on the availability of rich merchant ships. The situation had become even more dangerous when Gelon determined to put an end to piracy. They had paid Lord Haran's ransom grudgingly, and then had come after Chalil with an astonishing show of force, bent on striking terror into any who dared prey upon one of their own. Two narrow escapes, achieved by luck and seamanship, had convinced Chalil to seek safer waters. So they took what was left of the treasure through the long, difficult passage via the straits of the Firelands and beyond, to the free trader haven of Pirion, and then to Denariya itself.

Chalil had been right, Zevaron thought. The sea was filled with gifts, not the least of which was forgetfulness. Zevaron had never dreamed of such countries, such rich colors, such tastes and sounds and smells. Such voluptuous women.

As part of Chalil's crew, Zevaron had spent seasons in Denariya, even venturing into the Fever Lands for ivory and gold. The strange constellations became familiar, and he had grown accustomed to eating rice instead of wheat, to fish and fiery peppers.

Now they were embarking upon what Chalil called "a different type of thievery." The *Wave Dancer's* hold was filled with fine embroidered silk, sandalwood incense, myrrh and peppercorns, barrels of exotic wines, pots of kohl and cinnabark, rose tincture and dried mango; all goods that brought a hundred times their purchase price or more. The passage had been uneventful thus far, the Firelands Straits no worse than usual.

The wind picked up, filling the sails, and the *Wave Dancer* moved easily under Zevaron's hands. They meant to travel east, then north to Gelon and the port city of Roramenth. Chalil had chosen Roramenth because it was large enough to trade in luxury goods yet not as well-garrisoned as Verenzza. Chalil might have repainted the *Wave Dancer* and donned the coat of an honest merchant, but there was still a bounty on his head. Even now, years later, some might recognize him.

They had stopped at the Mearas, the cluster of desolate rocky islands that formed the gateway to the Endless Sea, to trade their spices for fresh water, meat, bread, and more dried fruits. In a smoky tavern, Zevaron had listened while Tamir and Chalil bought an extra round of bitter ale and exchanged news with the crew of a ship bound out of Durinthe in Isarre. Gatacinne remained in Gelonian hands, they said, as did Valoni-Erreth, the city the Gelon built for themselves. But they were quick to add that the Isarran King still ruled in Durinthe. Ar-Cinath-Gelon, perhaps frustrated with the stalemate, had sent his son, Thessar, off to "subdue the savage nomads of Azkhantia."

So the Gelonian prince survived Shorrenon's attack, Zevaron thought, but said nothing.

Chalil commented that Thessar's current mission sounded more like a punishment than an opportunity for glory.

"Ah, but if he takes any territory at all, he can return home with his honor restored," the Isarran captain said dryly.

"Territory? From the Azkhantians? He'll be lucky to escape with his hide," was Omri's comment.

There was no talk of Meklavar beyond what Zevaron already knew, that Gelon now ruled there with an iron fist, that many of the old noble families were dead or scattered.

Chalil had taken him to Denariya to prevent him from getting himself killed, that much he now understood. As long as he was half a world away, there was nothing he could do and no revenge he could seek. He had set aside those memories for a time. Now each passing hour brought him closer to Gelon and to uneasy dreams of vengeance.

"He saw that you knew the woman and aimed his words like a spear point at your heart," Chalil had said, sure the Gelonian slave-master Haran had lied about Tsorreh's death out of sheer malice. Could she have been taken on that first ship to Gelon and still be alive?

Now, with the Mearas behind them, Zevaron was no closer to an answer than when he had last sailed these waters. His hands clenched the tiller hard enough to turn his knuckles white.

"You've stood here too long," Chalil said. "That's what ails you. Go below, check that everything is secure."

Zevaron did as he was told. He had learned seamanship as well as fighting and trading in the last four years, but he was not eager to be at the tiller in bad weather.

By the time Zevaron returned to deck, the storm was bearing down on them like a sea-hawk plunging to seize a fish. The waters crashed and rose. The deck heaved under his feet. He braced himself, holding fast to the railing.

The winds grew every moment in strength, sending the *Wave Dancer* pitching. Wind-whipped spray blanketed the view. With sail and oars, the crew struggled to keep the ship on a steady course, to turn her so that her bows were to the waves and she might ride the storm at the best angle.

Then the rain came, pelting them from behind. Waves surged higher, fresh water mixing with salt. The sea rose to meet the fury of the heavens. Ridge after ridge of gray-green water raced toward the ship. She lifted to meet them, plunging and bucking like a wild thing. The waves broke over her sides, flooding the deck. Chalil shouted orders, but the gale tore away his words.

Time swallowed them up. The day, which had begun so warm and still, grew colder by the minute. The crew rowed and climbed and spliced and cut. All the while, the sea roared about them.

Zevaron took his turn on the oars. He rowed until his muscles burned and then went numb. Thirst clawed at him. Sometimes he thought his hands shook, or perhaps it was the fury of the storm pounding the ship.

Omri thrust a cup at him. It was rainwater, somehow gathered in the confusion. The water cooled his burning throat and renewed his strength.

When Zevaron came back on deck, it took all his sea training to keep his feet. He peered through the slashing rain. Water sheeted from the sky. Waves that were more froth than water shot upward.

In the howling tempest, an immense shape took form. At first, Zevaron thought it a trick of the rain, a sea-mirage. But no, something *was* there, insubstantial and wavering, mist condensing against the maelstrom of white and gray. He felt the thing in the sea, as if an unknown part of him, a sense that had lain sleeping all these years, now stirred.

The water around the shape churned and boiled, adding steam to the tattered, whirling whiteness of the storm. Voices echoed on the wind. The ship's timbers groaned.

The upper part of the figure rose above the plunging waves, human and dragon and sea-beast all in one. The massive head lifted, a mane like tangled kelp streaming over the shoulders. A crest of knobbed, interlaced coral sprang from the overhanging brow, arching over the domed skull and down the spine. The skin, what Zevaron could see of it through the foam, was green and mottled gray, patterned with pale incrustations and plated scales that shone like mother-of-pearl. Its eyes were huge and lidless, made for peering through lightless depths.

The apparition sank down, as if gathering itself. Arms— two or three or even five, Zevaron couldn't tell—burst from the water, lashing it to even greater heights.

O Most Holy One, if ever you loved your children, save us now!

The words poured from the innermost core of Zevaron's heart. From the depths of his soul. An image sprang up behind his eyes, of Chalil, who had been as a father to him, of Tamir and stolid Omri. He saw them sink beneath the water, bodies like sodden petals drifting downward, drawn into the inexorable, swirling currents. In the frozen dark, they settled among the bones of monstrous benthic creatures, where no one knew their names or sang their lineage. Bereft of light, of warmth, of memory, they perished as if they had never existed, never loved, never known a moment's joy.

The monstrous fist descended, missing the *Wave Dancer*

and passing instead through the maelstrom. A wall of water slammed into the ship. It surged over the deck. Timbers shrieked. The prow lifted, shuddering, reaching for the light. Zevaron staggered, thrown to his knees. Then the ship began to slip downward.

Zevaron scrambled to his feet on the tilting deck. He raised his own fist, filled his lungs with fury and hurled it out.

"NO!" he screamed. *"YOU SHALL NOT HAVE THEM!"*

For an instant, time itself seemed to pause. Although the wind and rain continued, the sea scarcely moved, as if the waves were mere painted images. The ship hung suspended in its descent.

The immense, distorted head swung around. This time, the eyes were not blind, pallid orbs, but lit from within. Zevaron reeled under their weight. The apparition's watery breath enveloped him. He felt its awareness, the leap of curiosity.

The thing was in his mind now, ringing through the caverns of his skull. Thoughts reverberated, overlapping and rippling, so that he could not tell which were his own and which came from this strange creature. He no longer feared for himself, the watery death it brought. He feared only for the others—his shipmates, his friends.

Once, in Tomarzha Varya, he had heard from afar the pealing of bells for some Denariyan religious celebration or other. He remembered the cacophony of sound and how it fell away at the end, leaving a single melody, so pure and clear it stirred him to tears. Now the jumble of thoughts within his mind also faded. The storm quieted. The winds shifted and the apparition before him dwindled. He no longer looked upon a grotesque colossus, half sea-dragon, half parody of a man, but upon a much smaller figure.

A waterspout of deepest blue bore the sea king up, covering the lower part of the naked form. It lifted him so that his gaze was level with Zevaron's. The creature seemed to be standing utterly still, yet in constant motion.

He bore the aspect of a bearded man, broad of chest and heavily muscled, yet with a sleekness that reminded Zevaron of dolphins. Seaweed twisted with strands of pearls fell across his shoulders in a mane. The light around his body shimmered like opals. His eyes reflected the same radiance, but Zevaron sensed a darkness behind them, slow brooding ferocity and intelligence.

As they gazed upon one another, the storm itself fell away. One enormous hand lifted in a salute.

Hail to thee, O Khored's heir!

Zevaron was too stunned by the thoughts reverberating through his mind to make an immediate answer.

Khored's heir, the sea-creature called him. Zevaron could not imagine how he could have known. The *te-Ketav* spoke of ancient magic, of a time before time when the world was formed in Fire and Ice, Stone and Water, when light and shadow, death and life had sprung into being. He had thought the whole business mythical, unreal. Yet now, as he faced this spirit of the sea, a new understanding shivered through his bones and sang along his nerves.

"I greet you, elemental form of the sea!" Zevaron leaned over the railing, calling out in the ancient, formal tongue.

Laughter, dark as the lightless depths, bright as foam, welled up from the massive shape. Zevaron remembered the old stories where the hero gained power over his enemy by learning its true name. That much must be true. He wondered if he had offended the creature, yet what did it matter what he called it? What did it want with him?

As if sensing his thought, the sea king nodded his head. The strands of his mane and beard undulated like sea-grass. The tiny pearls woven into his hair chimed like bells.

> *"When the shadow of the scorpion*
> *Dims the Golden Land*
> *And heaven's spear to the mountain falls,*
>
> *One shall come from the sand, from the sea,*
> *Heir to the ancient shield,*
> *Son of a mother twice reborn,*
> *Servant of the Frozen Fire.*

> *Then shall the prophet weep,*
> *And the lion lie down with the deer,*
> *Gladness will lighten every heart,*
> *And peace will return to the land."*

The sea king's prophecy bore down on Zevaron as if he had suddenly slipped beneath the waves and plunged to the uttermost depths. For an eternity between one heartbeat and the next, Zevaron could only stare at the moon-pale eyes.

... from the sand, from the sea, Heir to the ancient shield ... That must mean him and the Shield of Khored that was the symbol of his race.

The creature began to sink beneath the waves. In an instant, he would be gone.

"No!" Zevaron cried. "Wait! What do you see ahead for me? What must I do?"

Son of a mother twice reborn. The words echoed in his mind.

"My mother! What do you know of my mother? What does the prophecy mean?"

The prophecy, O Heir of Khored, was written at the beginning of time. Yet some turnings ago of tide and moon did pass a woman of your people, bearing your blood and the sacred treasure of your race. She spoke of kindness and the singing of the stars. I drew nigh, to taste the perfume of her words.

"Where did she go? Where set ashore?"

The waters were already closing over the immense form. Zevaron almost screamed with frustration. Then came a last ghostly whisper.

The Port of Tears.

The wind settled, a constant, easy push from the west. There was no longer need for oar power. Under Chalil's direction, the crew began repairs. They stopped that night at a cove, a day's sailing out of Roramenth. Zevaron went ashore and sat staring into the fire, turning over the words of the sea king.

> *One shall come from the sand, from the sea,*
> *Heir to the ancient shield,*
> *Son of a mother twice reborn ...*

Too close, the phrase was too agonizingly close to the facts. He was of the lineage of Khored of the Seven-Petaled Shield, and he had come to Gelon across the Sand Lands, and now over the sea. *Twice reborn.* Alive?

Chalil came to sit beside him. "Something troubles you. Your old enemy?"

Zevaron shook his head. He had hardly spared a thought for the brutal slave-master.

"Your mother, then. You think of her?"

"The sea king spoke to me, he made words in my mind. He said she'd passed over these waters and gone to the Port of Tears. Chalil, I can't think. Was it all lies and fancy words?"

"A man can see and hear many things in such a storm."

"You saw it, too. You must have!"

"I saw a water spout, and waves as high as our mast, and much rain." Chalil's dark eyes reflected the firelight.

"But no monster, half-fish half-man, all bedecked with seaweed and strands of pearl?"

"I saw you were nearly swept away."

Zevaron bit off an exclamation. Had he imagined the encounter and the mystifying verse or concocted it from his own uneasy dreams, his uncertainty about his mother? Or were there certain truths that could not be seen by everyone? In the unimaginable past, had Khored lifted up the Seven-Petaled Shield, only to have the very people it would save declare they could not see it?

"Zev, you have been brooding about your mother and whether that Gelon lied about her death, on and off these past four years," Chalil said earnestly. "If you go on in this manner, it will drive you mad. You must put the matter to rest."

That officer, Haran was his name, could have lied. The creature from the sea—if there even had been one—could also have lied. But something had roused inside Zevaron, a kernel of hope.

"The Port of Tears," Zevaron repeated. "Do you know of such a place?"

"Why, lad, it was the old name for Verenzza, before the Gelon took it for their own. It was once the home of a fisher folk, but one day, or so the story goes, all the men went to sea in their reed boats, as they always did, and none returned. Some said the leviathan of the deep swallowed them up. The women waded out and watered the sea with their tears, and some say they found their husbands below, in castles of pearl and coral. For myself, it is naught but a pretty story. Most like, they starved or went away to find new husbands elsewhere. Then the Gelon built a city in that place, and through the gates pass many slaves, so once again it is a port of tears."

They put ashore at Roramenth. Zevaron wandered through the merchant district with Tamir, looking for buyers for their cargo, although Chalil handled the actual bargaining. To Zevaron, the city was very different from Meklavar and yet the same. There were markets and shops, fountains where women dipped their buckets, and corners where old men sat drinking tea and gossiping in the sun.

Shadows lengthened and the heat of the afternoon rose like a sigh from the city. The day had gone well, bringing enthusiastic customers. Tamir suggested a drink at one of the open-air taverns, preferably one that dispensed the favors of ladies as well, and Zevaron readily agreed. He welcomed the opportunity to sit down. His feet had grown accustomed to a wooden deck, not hard stone and dirt.

They took their places around a table under a lattice awning and sipped the local brew, frothy and pleasantly bitter. At this hour, there were still plenty of people to watch. The street was broad, paved in Gelonian style with flat stones and lined with planters of flowers.

They sat in amicable silence, savoring the mild exhilaration of the brew. Zevaron noticed a number of people, mostly women, entering and leaving a newish building a little ways down the street. Tamir shrugged and said it must be a temple of some sort, although what kind he did not know. Like other Denariyans, he took no interest in any religion besides his own.

Zevaron could not keep from staring. Certainly, the women were pleasant to look at. Yet something about the building drew and repelled him, although he could discern no difference between it and any other. It was newer and larger, with a geometric frieze running just below the roof line. He motioned to the tavern keeper. When the man approached to refill their mugs, Zevaron asked in Gelone, "What temple is that?"

"Qr."

"It seems to be very popular."

"When I was young, it was just another minor cult. We kept to the proper gods of our families. Now the influence of the priests of Qr seems to grow with every passing day. Even the Ar-King, may-his-glory-shine-forever, consults them. Some say the high priest warned Cinath not to sent his son off to Azkhantia to fight the bloodthirsty savages. Ah, a bad business, that."

"What do you mean? Did he not triumph?" Zevaron asked, keeping his voice carefully neutral.

The man shook his head and made a gesture that Zevaron assumed was a warding against evil. "You have not heard the news, being strangers? Do not speak of it where you may be overheard and questioned."

"Why, what happened?" Zevaron whispered.

"He was betrayed and killed. A foul affair if ever there was one."

Zevaron, remembered Omri's comment that Prince Thessar would be lucky to escape with his life. From all accounts, the Azkhantian nomads were ruthless, indomitable warriors. Certainly, they had held their borders against Gelonian forces since before Cinath came to the throne.

"They say," the tavern keeper lowered his voice even further and bent down so that they could not be overheard, "that *Meklavar* had a hand in it. That it was revenge against the Prince for the sack of their city. They say it was sorcery, black and terrible."

Zevaron's skin went cold. He took a gulp of his brew.

"It seems to me," Tamir said in a mild tone, "that the Meklavarans could not be such powerful sorcerers, or they would have defended their own city better."

The tavern keeper blinked. "That is as it may be. I'm only telling you what any man may hear in the marketplace. Will you be wanting dinner, good sirs? Or another round of brew?"

"Thank you, no," Tamir said. "I believe we've had enough."

They drained their mugs and paid their bill. Shadows deepened between the buildings. The street, which had seemed so peaceful and innocuous, took on a faintly sinister air. Zevaron did not know what he expected to find in Gelon. Arrogance on the part of officials, soldiers, nobles? The sense of order and disciplined intellect he had seen on the battlefield? Yet another exotic country?

An undercurrent of hatred directed at Meklavar?

"I did not know Gelon was such an enemy to my people," he said to Tamir.

"I do not say this as an insult, my friend, but Meklavar is widely thought to be a land of ancient magic. Aside from their household idols, I have never seen any such thing here in Gelon. It is natural, I suppose, that the Gelon would fear such an enemy, even in defeat."

Zevaron made a gesture of exasperation. "Meklavar is ancient, yes, and learned. But a *hotbed of sorcery*?" He snorted. The idea was so ridiculous as to be unworthy of further comment.

Yet how else could he account for the sea king, who had risen from the storm, who only he had been able to see and hear, who had spoken prophecies to him? Was it only a vision sprung from his own mind, woven of the shapes of wind and wave, and the fantastical tales from his childhood?

No, the sea king and his words had been real enough. If they were magical, then magic must be as real as anything a man could touch or taste.

As Zevaron and Tamir talked, their path carried them in the direction of the Qr temple. A young man in white robes, his head bound with a cloth bearing a symbol of some sort, came out on the steps. He carried a barred staff from which hung three brass bells, each the size of a man's head. Setting the tip against the paving, he tapped the bells in sequence.

The reverberating tones built on one another, clashing to a peak and then dying down. Zevaron wanted to clap his hands over his ears to shut out the discordant, strangely compelling sound.

"Come, all you who hunger, who thirst, who mourn," the young priest called in a ringing voice. "Bring your sorrows to Qr, and you will know peace! Enter, enter! Qr welcomes you all!"

A trio of women, their faces hidden behind veils of silk embroidered in threads of gold and silver, hurried past. One of them dragged a half-grown boy by the hand.

"—mustn't be late for the service."

"—waited all day for this—my cousin ..."

"Yes, you told me, the one who was barren—"

"The midwives swear it will be a son ..."

Their voices faded as they passed within the temple. Other women joined them, some carrying baskets of spun, dyed wool, and wine jars. One led a pure white lamb and another carried a cage of doves.

Tamir, who had not reacted visibly to the clamor of the gongs, said, "Shall we witness these wonders?"

No. But Zevaron actually said, "Why not?" trying to sound indifferent. He followed Tamir up the steps, seeing now that the emblem on the priest's forehead was a scorpion. He drew a breath, hesitating. The scorpions of Mekla-

var, and their smaller Sand Lands cousins, were deadly to
cats and small children. When he was a boy, Tsorreh had
killed one in his bedroom with her slipper. He still remembered the expression on her face, the single-minded, protective rage. She would have attacked anything that threatened
him with equal fervor.

*The scorpion did no wrong, defending itself. Most likely,
it had wandered into the palace in search of water. It was a
natural creature, following its own nature.* Then why did the
stylized image on the priest's brow raise the hairs on the
back of his neck?

The priest with the bells went inside, but two others,
stolid older men, greeted the congregation as they passed
through the open doors. They indicated where the various
offerings were to be taken. One of them frowned when he
saw that neither Zevaron nor Tamir had brought anything.

"You are new to the ways of Qr. Nevertheless, the great
god offers his blessings to all, and from their gratitude, this
holy work is continued." The priest stood back for them to
enter.

Caught up in the movement of the crowd, they passed
through an entrance hall, lined by torches on either side
despite the early hour, and then under the arch of an interior door. The torchlight flickered across paintings of giant
many-legged figures, giving them a semblance of animation.
Walking below and between the wavering images, Zevaron
felt as if he were entering a nest of giant scorpions. Within
the darkness of the sanctuary, a gust of air, cold and hot at
once, brushed the back of his neck. The shadows no longer
suggested a nest of tiny creatures, but a single, overarching
shape, like a scorpion and yet more.

The moment passed, the shadows fell away, and he stood
in the center of a crowd. At the front of the chamber, the
young priest with the bells and another, this one hooded,
bent to receive offerings of fruit and flowers, cloth and wine,
and other goods. The altar itself was shrouded in layers of
dark gauze, so that Zevaron could not guess what lay beneath. Around him, people began singing and swaying.

"Aaahhh, oooaaahhh,
  O Spirit that walks between the worlds,
  Wonder of wonders,
  Beyond life, beyond death!
  Come speedily into the world
  Across flame, across ice,
  Come to us! Come to us!"

The force of the concentrated prayers, the immense drawing *pull* of their power, swept through Zevaron. He felt as if he were standing in the midst of a gigantic lodestone, fueled by the temple and its worshipers. They reached out, spanning unimaginable distances. Wordlessly, he sensed the same ritual repeated in a hundred other such congregations. Each one merged into an irresistible singleness of purpose.

The chant repeated, swelling until the last *"Come to us! Come to us!"* rose in a single roar. Beside the altar, white-clad figures swung pots of incense. Caustic smoke billowed into the air. Zevaron's lungs burned.

Zevaron glanced around, feeling increasingly uneasy. To every side, people lifted their hands, rocking from side to side, heads thrown back, eyes closed or rolled up in their skulls. Even Tamir seemed caught in the waves of impassioned cries. A man—one of the merchants they had bargained with earlier that very day—bumped into Zevaron, who was not moving in rhythm with the others.

The hooded priest lifted his hands, turning slowly as if he were reaching out to every person in the congregation. A feeling grew in Zevaron's mind, that the priest was drawing something from the assembly and funneling it. Where? To whatever lay beneath the gauzy wrappings? Or—no, it was impossible!—to the heavens themselves?

The priest's focus moved across the room, drawing ever nearer to Zevaron. Zevaron felt he must leave immediately, before the priest realized that not everyone was in the thrall of chant and smoke. He grabbed Tamir's arm and pulled, knowing his voice could not be heard above the undulating cries.

Tamir responded sluggishly, resisting as they stumbled back through the entrance hall. One of the older priests, holding a staff tipped with a sharp brass hook, barred their path.

"You would leave *now*, before the holy presence descends?" the priest asked.

"My friend is ill," Zevaron improvised. "I must take him home."

"Where else should he be, but in this place of healing? Who else has the power to aid him, except for Qr?"

"We brought no offering," Zevaron improvised. "Therefore we are unworthy to receive a blessing. We must return with a suitable sacrifice."

At that, the priest grunted and stood aside. Zevaron half-dragged, half-carried his friend down the steps. Only when they were well clear of the temple did Tamir cease struggling. He bent over, coughing.

"What—what happened? By the leviathan, I feel sick."

Zevaron glanced back at the temple. "The incense, I suppose. It smelled foul enough. You were dancing and singing with the rest of them."

"My thanks, then, for getting me out of there. Ach! My mouth tastes like bilge water!" Tamir turned his head and spat.

Zevaron chuckled. "That was the tavern brew, as like as not. Come on, the sooner we're back aboard the *Wave Dancer*, the better you'll feel."

Tamir trudged beside Zevaron. "How is it you were not also made sick? Don't tell me it was Meklavaran magic!"

"Shh, I don't think it's safe for anyone here to speak that name. It's hardly magic when one man drinks twice as much brew as another and then faints like a girl from smoke and singing."

"Aye, likely that's it. One thing's sure, I'll feel better with a ship beneath my feet and not this cursed solid land."

Suppressing a shudder, Zevaron agreed with him. The sooner they were back on the open seas, the better.

Chapter Twenty-seven

THE next week passed smoothly, as the *Wave Dancer*'s hold emptied and her treasury filled. Returning to the docks with Tamir after helping with the delivery of the last of the cinnabark, Zevaron spied Chalil in earnest talk with two men in long robes. Although he had not seen another of his people in the last four years in Denariya, Zevaron recognized them instantly. It was not the honey-dark skin and black hair nor their dress that gave them away, for they seemed indistinguishable from any other somber, conservatively dressed men. Rather, something in the intent way they bent close to Chalil, their gestures, the rhythm of their speech, all struck a resonant chord.

The younger of the two glanced up nervously as Zevaron and Tamir approached. The conversation stopped abruptly. Chalil gestured, *Back off, return later.* Zevaron stared, astonished, but Tamir pulled him away, down the next pier and rapidly out of sight.

"Best to let the captain handle business as he sees fit," Tamir said, "though why he didn't meet in a more private place, I don't know. Most likely, it's no mystery at all, only rivalry, traders come to offer a better deal."

The Meklavarans looked like any other merchants, but

Zevaron knew, somehow, that their business was not about selling sandalwood incense or brocades.

When Zevaron and Tamir returned to the ship a short time later, the two Meklavarans had gone. Chalil looked immensely pleased. Instead of the risk of remaining in a Gelonian port and sorting through which Gelonian goods might turn a profit back in Denariya, with each passing day increasing the chance of being recognized as pirates, they were to leave on the morning tide. Their cargo this time was human, a collection of Meklavaran families, along with whatever goods they could carry. The *Wave Dancer* would take them to Durinthe, in Isarre, and from there would continue south around the Fever Lands to the Firelands Straits and home, her treasury enriched doubly from the sale of the Denariyan goods and the passage fees.

Only a few hours later, the two Meklavarans returned, along with an old grandfather barely able to walk, their respective wives and three sisters (two of whom had husbands and children) and a collection of cousins, thirty in all. They arrived in separate groups, mostly likely having taken different routes through the city. Their faces looked drawn, even the young ones pinched and silent. Each carried as much as he could manage, except for the old man, who bore only a single item wrapped in thick, undyed silk. He held it carefully, as if it were more precious than his life. The boarding plank was almost more than he could manage, inching along with his eyes fixed upon the wood beneath his feet, but he would not let any of the others take his burden. Zevaron, aboard the *Wave Dancer*, reached out to steady him. The old man mumbled his thanks in heavily accented Gelone.

"'Reverence for wisdom is twice blessed,'" Zevaron said, quoting the *te-Ketav*. "'It brings grace to him who gives and him who receives.'"

The old man looked up, his eyes glittering in the light from the *Wave Dancer's* lanterns. "You—you are Meklavaran," he said in that tongue.

"Come this way, grandfather," Zevaron said. "Let me

take you to the captain's cabin, where you may rest before going below. And tell me," he added, lowering his voice, "why you must leave Roramenth in such haste, under cover of darkness."

"You have not heard?" The old man's reply was interrupted by the process of maneuvering to the little cabin, settling him in Chalil's single chair, and securing the door.

"No, I have had no news of home since . . . for a long time."

"It was bad enough when we left Meklavar thirty years ago," the old man said. "Such a sadness to go, but business was poor and my wife with child. We had to eat and Gelon was rich in trade. It was a civilized land, we thought, and so it was under the old Ar-King, he who was father to this Cinath. But now . . . we have word from my son in Aidon that Cinath believes there is a Meklavaran conspiracy against his throne. Conspiracy! Why would he think such a thing, when we have been good citizens for these many years? The man has gone mad. I heard he has been executing or enslaving our people in the capital city."

He paused only an instant to draw breath. "Cinath's decree will soon reach Verenzza and all the provinces around. We must leave while we can, while I still have the strength. Your captain, this Chalil, he has a face both honest and wild. Tell me, by the Shield of Khored that saved our people in times gone by, can he be trusted? Will he betray us, sell us into slavery and take our money?"

"You may rest assured that once Chalil has made a bargain, he will keep it," Zevaron said. Even as a pirate, even negotiating the ransom for the Gelonian captives, Chalil had never broken his word. "If he says he will take you to Durinthe, then to Durinthe you will go."

The old man closed his eyes in relief. "Thank you, my child. This place has been a good home to us and it grieves me to leave it. Yet wherever we go, our hearts remain in Meklavar. We will have one another, and word will come of our brothers throughout the wide world."

Zevaron nodded. Although he had little contact with

them, spending much of his time at sea or in the company of Chalil and his crew, he knew of the far-flung network of Meklavaran merchants, craftsmen, and money-changers. They exchanged news and helped one another in trade. He had been too young to care about such arrangements when he and Tsorreh fled.

"Have you—?" He paused, searching for the right words. "Do you know of others here in Gelon? Perhaps those taken as hostage after the fall of Gatacinne?"

"Yes, we all heard that Isarran slaves were brought back as part of the looted riches." The old man shook his head. Meklavarans had never considered human beings as chattel, a means of wealth.

"There was a Meklavaran lady in Gatacinne at that time. She could have been seized with the others."

The old man paused, the wrinkles between his brows deepening. "There was talk about that time of a member of the royal household being held hostage in Gelon. A woman, I believe, although I do not know if she was ever at Gatacinne. For all I know, she is still in Aidon."

"In the prisons of the Ar-King?" Zevaron trembled with outrage and excitement.

"If she were truly of the lineage of Khored, I doubt even Cinath would treat her so. The Gelon may be barbaric in many ways, but they have a long tradition regarding the proper treatment of hostages. In their own history, the exchange of prisoners, often children, was an honored way to ensure peace between quarreling families. If one of them were mistreated, that would set an unfortunate precedent, do you see?"

Zevaron excused himself, leaving the old man to a little more rest. He found Chalil and drew him to a relatively quiet place, out by the *Wave Dancer's* curved prow.

"You were right about my mother still being alive and in Gelonian hands," he said. "I have just spoken with the elder. In all likelihood, she was sent to Aidon and placed in custody befitting a noble lady."

Chalil was silent for a moment, his face unreadable in

the near darkness. "Four years is a long time. Much could have happened."

"You may be right," Zevaron admitted. The prophecy spoken by the sea king might have been no more than a vision born of the storm. "But I feel—I believe—she is still alive. And if she is, who knows what may become of her in this madness? I must find her and take her away to safety."

Chalil looked into the night and sighed. "I knew this time would come. You were destined to leave us from the moment you came. Still, we had a good long run of it, and I am thinking this will be the last time I sail these unhappy shores. I will miss you."

Zevaron did not know how to answer. Chalil had been like a father to him, but that was not enough reason to turn away from the demands of family and conscience.

"You cannot go wandering around Gelon, asking questions about royal hostages, even if Cinath had not taken it into his mind to persecute your people," Chalil said with a thoughtful expression.

"I can pass as Denariyan well enough."

"Until you encounter one of us. One word in your atrocious accent will betray you. I am thinking that while a lone traveler may be suspect, no one looks closely at a servant or a bodyguard. You remember Ranath, the fat cloth-merchant who bought up the cheapest of our silks? He let slip, by way of bragging, that he could get a better price for them in Aidon than in Verenzza."

"Are you suggesting I disguise myself as a cloth-seller?" The idea was risky. A hundred things might go wrong.

"I am thinking that the longer journey provides more opportunities for thieves, and therefore greater need for protection."

"A bodyguard?"

"You fight well and you keep your wits about you."

"This merchant might remember me as a sailor. Why would he hire me as a bodyguard?" Zevaron asked.

Through the gathering dark, he felt Chalil's smile. "Leave that to us."

*   *   *

It was a simple enough matter for a man of Chalil's resources to set up a faked ambush and rescue just outside of Roramenth. It meant delaying the *Wave Dancer's* departure for another day, but Chalil smoothed things over with his Meklavaran passengers, kept them hidden onboard, and guaranteed their safety.

Tamir and Omri played the thugs with gleeful abandon, bearing down on the cloth-merchant in his onager-drawn wagon. They burst from their hiding place in a turn in the road, drew their flashy but useless trophy swords, and rushed forward. Omri seized the reins of the onagers and shouted at the merchant to get down if he valued his life. Protesting weakly, the merchant complied. At the same time, Tamir lunged for the single servant, a hulking, clumsy boy who was clearly befuddled by the speed and apparent ferocity of the attack.

Zevaron let the sham fighting proceed just long enough, then ran up, brandishing his own sword. Tamir dashed back to the Roramenth road while Omri put up enough of a fight to appear realistic and to make Zevaron look good. They fenced for a few moments and then Omri turned tail as well.

Watching Omri go, Zevaron silently wished both of them a smooth voyage and a safe harbor. He did not think he would ever see them again. Then he turned back to the merchant, who stood clutching the halter of one of the onagers. He caught no hint of recognition in the man's eyes. That was not surprising, for such men rarely paid much attention to anyone but the owners of the goods they bought, not the hired help, not the porters and lackeys.

Smiling, he sheathed his sword. "Are you hurt, my lord?"

"No, no. I was just caught unprepared. This road has always been safe before."

"These are unsettled times," Zevaron said. "It's a good thing I came along when I did."

The merchant started to climb back up into the wagon,

then paused. "You speak good Gelone, but you're not one of us. Denariyan, I'd guess?"

Zevaron smiled.

"Where are you bound?" the cloth-merchant asked.

"Wherever there is honest work for me. As you see, I have a measure of skill with a blade."

"Indeed, to my good fortune."

From there, it was but a small matter to agree on a fee for protecting the merchant and his wares on their journey. Zevaron bargained enough to sound realistic, but not too high. He wanted the merchant to think he'd got the better of the deal. In addition, he made sure to practice his sword moves every night where the merchant could see him. Some techniques he remembered from his boyhood training, although the thick-bladed Gelonian sword was ill-suited to that style. Other exercises, designed to strengthen muscles as well as hone reflexes, he had learned from his fellow pirates. They fought with whatever weapons came to hand, curved or straight, short or long, Denariyan or Gelonian, or even the rough bronze blades of the tribes who roved the barren lands north of the Mearas.

They went by road to Verenzza, stayed at the home of the merchant's cousin for two days, and then took a barge upriver to Aidon. Twice along the road, they were eyed by fellow travelers whose ragged clothing and haggard expressions suggested desperation. But when Zevaron displayed his sword, handling it to best display his skill, they backed off, and there were no incidents.

He sat on the barge, watching the sleepy landscape slip by, the green-silver ripples of the Serpan River, wondering if Tsorreh had come this way. Had she looked out over these fields, these trees with their long, supple branches trailing in the shallows, and had she seen the light on these waters, iridescent in the twilight? Where was she now? Was she safe?

Aidon was like nothing he'd imagined, an immense, sprawling city. An enemy would dash his force against its complex heights and subside, like waves against the rocky beaches of the *Mher Seshola*. The thought came to him that Gelon, like Aidon itself, would fall from within, from rot at its heart, not from any outside invasion.

All things have their season; all things pass away.

He had not thought of the holy scripts since that terrible time when he first believed Tsorreh was dead. How could he pray to a god, any god, who would let such a thing happen? Now hope had arisen, and everything he'd clung to during those four years of exile had been shaken by the appearance of the sea king.

What should he believe? What *could* he believe? The gentle currents of the river and the towers of Aidon gave him no answer.

The barge docked at one of the many wharves, and laborers offloaded the wagon, along with carts and draft animals, passengers and baggage. The cloth-merchant hired one of the wharf boys as a guide, and together they made a little procession up into the city.

As they passed through a riot of different colors, garments, and aromas, Zevaron could well believe that exiled Meklavarans had made their home here. There must be a dozen different races living as neighbors. Some of them he recognized: Gelon with their pale skins and red-tinted hair, huge Xians, and Sand Lands tribesmen in their striped robes and head-cloths, leading fine-boned horses. Others seemed strange, even in this jumbled crowd.

Once or twice, Zevaron spotted figures in the robes of Gelonian priests, and although he looked, he could not tell if the emblems on their robes had jointed legs and curving stingers. He had no chance to speak to any of them.

They passed by taverns and nautical businesses and into a district of warehouses and stables. After a bit of lively negotiation, the merchant found a place to board his onagers and his wagon.

Eager to begin his search, Zevaron waited impatiently for Ranath to conclude his business. Ranath, however, required Zevaron's services in accompanying him to the house of another of his cousins. By this time, Zevaron was very close to declaring his obligation fulfilled, although the extra money would be useful. Now that he had seen Aidon, he realized it would take time to find Tsorreh. Among other things, he needed a meal, a bath, and a relatively safe place to sleep.

The cousin's house was a little ways up one of the hills, a compact walled compound. Brass-bound wooden gates led to a garden and a modest one-story house built around a little courtyard with a fountain. Here Ranath sat with his cousin, eating seed cakes brought to them by an elderly Xian woman-servant, while Zevaron stood behind his employer's seat.

The cousin, Ottoren, bore a strong family resemblance to Ranath, stocky and going to softness but possessing keen, restless eyes. When Ranath proposed to engage Zevaron's services again in several months' time, for protection during his next trading venture, Zevaron demurred, saying that he could not wait that long.

"I could use a competent guard for my warehouses here, or for personal security," Ottoren suggested, "My cousin's praise is recommendation enough."

A position with a respectable merchant might give him a legitimate reason to be in Aidon. Bowing, Zevaron replied that he was honored by the offer and would consider it. He had personal business to attend to first. The merchant cousin seemed to think this entirely reasonable. Zevaron accepted his pay and stayed to take a meal with the servants. The household steward suggested a nearby inn.

Zevaron located the inn without too many wrong turns. It was farther from the harbor than he liked and not in the safest district for the unwary, but he was familiar with such dangers. He settled his few belongings in his upstairs room, leaving behind only those items he could afford to lose, made sure that not all his weapons were visible, and went down to begin his exploration.

The sun had swung past its zenith and begun a slow descent in the west. Zevaron paused outside the inn's door,

watching the street outside. Men passed, drawing handcarts
or laden under sacks or wicker panniers. A barefoot boy led
two of the slow massive barge-oxen. Within a short time,
Zevaron got a pretty good idea of the people and their business. As he studied the scene, he formulated his next step.
His first problem was not knowing if Tsorreh's identity had
been discovered. Had she come to Aidon as an ordinary
slave or as the Meklavaran *te-ravah*? Surely, there would be
a record of prisoners of importance.

As shadows deepened, the tavern owner lit the outside
lanterns. Men wandered in, calling to one another.

As the common room of the inn began to fill, Zevaron
took a place at one of the larger tables. Ordinarily, he would
be happy to spend a few coins with such women as were
willing and reasonably clean, for an hour's companionship
and pleasure, but not tonight. As he sipped his watered
wine, careful to not drink it too quickly lest it dull his wits,
he listened to the conversations around him. Sensing the
rhythms, he searched out which men talked too readily,
which ones not at all, and which spoke with a careful balance of camaraderie and discretion. A few oblique inquiries
about how slaves were brought into Aidon, and also what
hostages might be held here in the city, brought no useful
information. Yet Zevaron was satisfied that he had not elic-
ited any undue suspicion.

The night was still early, so he left the inn to try another.
He headed in the direction of the river, for water-rats and
sailors had much in common, and he knew their ways.
Gradually, he worked his way through successively more
disreputable areas of the city. His senses sharpened reflexively, and without conscious thought, he shifted his posture.
His walk took on the sure, elastic stride of a skilled swordsman. His eyes narrowed, and the supple tension in his
shoulders conveyed deadly alertness. Even drunken men
swerved from his path.

The night wore on. The moon set, and pools of darkness
swathed the narrow, ill-smelling streets. Even the most stalwart ale-sellers nudged their inebriated customers out.

Tired, yet too wrought up to sleep, Zevaron returned to his inn. He stretched out on the hard cot, stared at the ceiling, and tried to make sense out of inconclusive information.

Over the nights that followed, he pieced together what generally happened to slaves or hostages brought into the city. Slaves taken by Ar-Cinath's forces, usually in conquest but also as tribute, were considered the property of the Ar-King and were usually sold to enrich his coffers. Doubtless, Zevaron concluded, the proceeds helped to pay for his next war. Records might be kept of the numbers—so many male slaves from such-and-such a province—but none of the men Zevaron talked to had any interest in their names. Most likely, his drinking mates advised him, anyone taken captive four years ago was either dead or long since shipped off to work in the countryside. The Ar-King took care to avoid a concentration of enemies within the boundaries of his capital city, even if they were slaves.

One old sot remembered something about a foreign queen's arrival in Aidon; a sorceress, everyone said. His wits were so addled with chronic drink that he couldn't recall more than that or even how long ago it had happened.

Zevaron planted a few hints of a reward for information about the sister of a patron, a woman of mixed Isarran and Sand Lands blood, he said to explain her coloring and in case Tsorreh had hidden her Meklavaran origin. Then he turned his back on the wharves.

The closer he got to the center of the city and Cinath's palace in particular, the more armed guards he saw. Plumed helmets, bright armor, and sashes in the colors of the Ar-King were in evidence everywhere. At almost every major intersection and along some of the boulevards, patrols stopped anyone who did not look rich or did not look Gelon. Zevaron was not ready to test his ruse, not yet. The patrolmen reminded him too much of Gatacinne.

By the end of a week, Zevaron became increasingly frustrated. Perhaps the best way through the blockades was the

patronage of someone like Ranath's cousin. The cousin—
what was his name, Ottomar? Ottoren?—might have forgotten his offer, but Zevaron retraced his steps to the
cousin's compound not even knowing if Ranath was still in
the city.

When Zevaron was ushered into the cousin's garden,
which was apparently where he preferred to conduct his
interviews, the merchant shook his head.

"I'm sorry, but I've hired someone else for the job." Ottoren sounded genuinely regretful. "I would have liked to
oblige my cousin with patronage of one who did him such a
service, but . . ." He shrugged his fleshy shoulders, meaning,
business is business. "You should not have waited so long.
What were you about, if I may ask?"

"I was—and still am—looking for the kinswoman of a
friend," Zevaron said. "He traced her here to Aidon, but
cannot find her."

Ottoren gave a mild snort. "This is a big city. A woman
could be swallowed up and leave no trace, or a man as well."
His eyes narrowed. "She's Gelon?"

"No, dark like me, but not Denariyan. Isarran and Sand
Lands blood."

"Not Meklavaran?"

Zevaron gave his stoniest look of incomprehension.
"Why do you ask?"

Ottoren shook his head again. "I have nothing personal
against them, mind you. I've traded with them for years and
found them honest if not exactly affable. But if your—ah,
friend's—kinswoman has been taken as Meklavaran, I
doubt there's much chance you'll find her alive. A few years
back, right after Prince Thessar, may-his-soul-find-eternal-
delight, conquered their city, things were different. People
felt a certain—ah, sympathy, you might say—for them.
Even those taken as slaves. Now . . ." He shrugged again.

"Were there any noble ladies captured and brought to
Aidon at that time?"

"Let me see." Ottoren rubbed his chin. "I remember
hearing of one, but if you're thinking it might be the one

you seek, I doubt it. One of my patrons mentioned attending a concert at the compound of one of the Ar-King's own family—cousin or daughter's husband, I can't recall. Could have been his brother for all I know. He mentioned that he'd caught sight of an important Meklavaran hostage, as if she were one of the attractions of the evening. Poor thing, I can't imagine what's become of her. It's not likely Cinath let her live."

It took all of Zevaron's self-control to remain still. He reminded himself that this merchant didn't *know*, he was only guessing. He counted heartbeats, so loud they rocked his chest. *One, two* . . .

The merchant was staring at him with a slightly suspicious expression.

"An interesting story," Zevaron said carefully, "but I do take your meaning. I thank you for your hospitality."

Ottoren signaled for his servant to escort Zevaron to the gate. "I'll keep my ears open for another position."

"Thank you, and good day." Zevaron bowed and took his leave.

For the rest of the day, Zevaron strode through the city, trying to wrestle his feelings under control. Although he kept to the poorer areas, his gaze often lifted to the gleaming houses on the hills, wondering if Tsorreh had lived—and died—in one of them. But he did not trust his temper enough to approach them. Not yet.

The woman Ottoren mentioned could have been Tsorreh, but she might also have been a lady of another noble house. Many of the great families had been scattered after the fall of Meklavar. And if it were Tsorreh, she might well have been spared the current persecution. He would have to find out more about Cinath's relatives and where they lived, and a way around those patrols. So far, he had encountered no difficulty in passing as Denariyan, and any of a dozen stories might gain him access to the hills.

He headed back to the inn with brightened spirits. The

day was ending and he found himself surprisingly hungry. He stopped at an open cook stall for a tankard of barley-ale and a platter of savory pastries, dough stuffed with minced fish, herbs, and onions, then fried to crispness. The food was surprisingly good, and the stall owner did a brisk business as evening drew on.

It was almost dark when Zevaron returned to the inn. As he approached, he noticed several men lounging nearby. They looked no different from any of the other casual laborers of the neighborhood. Despite their air of indifference, he felt them come alert at his approach.

One man, who had been leaning against the side of the inn, straightened up and came toward Zevaron. His age was difficult to tell beneath the scarred, weathered skin, but his clothing looked too well-made for a gutter rat.

"Were you waiting for me?" Zevaron kept his voice soft, easy.

The man's eyes flickered in response. "If you're the one who's been asking about a Sand Lands woman, came here three-four year ago. And offerin' a reward."

Zevaron hesitated. Until he was certain, he could not afford to pass up any possible trail.

"Interested?" the man asked.

"Could be. Depends on what you have. If it's good . . ."

The man grinned, showing two missing teeth and the rest dark with decay. "Maybe it's the one you're lookin' for, maybe not, price is the same. But this woman, my brother bought her as a slave to cook and clean, y'know. He treats her all right. If her family were to reimburse him, he'd sell her back, he's got such a soft heart."

That much, Zevaron did not believe. The brother would want a good deal more than what he'd paid. Zevaron would deal with that problem once he had found her. "Fair enough," he said. "You'll get your fee whether she's the one or not. But you'll get it once I've seen her for myself."

The man shrugged, "Come on, then," and led the way.

Chapter Twenty-eight

ZEVARON watched carefully to see if the other men loitering outside the inn might follow, but they remained behind, continuing their desultory conversations. Of course, they might trail him once he was out of sight. If they did, however, they would be too far behind to take him by surprise.

At first, Zevaron's guide kept to the open streets. Only a few men were about at this hour, making their way by the light of the occasional lantern hung over the lintel of a tavern. Soon they passed beyond the corners marked by inns and wine-shops. The buildings ran together, blocks of cracked stone walls and splintered eaves. The air turned stale, laden with the smells of unwashed bodies and garbage. At one corner, they surprised a dog pawing through a pile of refuse. The animal cringed and slunk away, but the man only laughed.

"What kind of work does your brother do?" Zevaron asked. If the man could afford to buy a slave, why was he living in this place?

"Tanner," the man replied. "Can't live among higher folk, not the way he smells."

Zevaron did not know enough about the trade to tell if this were reasonable or not. He touched the hilt of his sword, making sure he could draw it easily, and went on.

Shadows clung more thickly as full night closed in. Clouds veiled the half-moon. Outside lanterns were few and widely spaced. Here and there, usually on a second story, Zevaron spotted dim, wavering lights, the kind cast by small oil lamps. It would not be enough to read by, but was probably all these families could afford.

The thought diverted Zevaron's attention just as he and his guide entered a particularly dark corner. Zevaron's senses snapped back into focus as his fighting instincts roused. He'd heard no sound, caught no flicker of movement. Alarm, hot and silvery, danced through his veins. The little space, bounded by walls on two sides, was too still, too quiet.

His hand sped toward the hilt of his sword even as the first figure launched itself at him.

No light reflected off the assailant's knife, yet Zevaron gauged its size and length, knowing exactly where it would be in the next moment. His sword slid free as his body pivoted. The thrust missed him by a hair's breadth. Propelled by his own momentum, the attacker stumbled forward. Zevaron continued his spiral movement, weight balanced like a dancer's, sword curving through the air. The blade whispered through crude cloth and met flesh. He reversed the stroke into a sweet arc. A second attacker screamed.

Zevaron acted without thought, driven by years of drill and then more years of actual fighting. He whirled, blade singing, and felt the slight catch of skin, then the smooth liquid slash through muscle and sinew. Curses and ragged footsteps disappeared into the night.

Then he was standing alone in a pool of darkness, reeking of blood and piss and fear-sweat. Adrenaline shrilled along his nerves, and breath hissed between his teeth. His body shook with the pounding of his heart, the sudden dryness of his mouth, and most of all, with anger at himself.

Fool! Fool and pig-brained, slack-bellied son of a fool! He cursed himself silently in the manner of the gutter denizens of Tomarzha Varya.

All in all, he'd gotten off lightly. He might have a few

sore muscles in the morning, but he didn't think he'd been touched. He was too wrought up at the moment to be sure. His vision had sharpened, as it did in battle, and adapted to the dark. Though he searched the area, he found no bodies. He might have gut-cut one of them, which meant lingering putrefaction and death. There was nothing to be done about it.

Out of long practice, he wiped his sword on the tail of his shirt and sheathed the weapon. He was a distance from his inn, but the walk would do him good. He needed time to calm down and let the fever drain from his muscles. The chance of finding Tsorreh now seemed even more remote.

The street lay empty and quiet, except for the wavering voices from a tavern at the far left side. It was so dark, Zevaron could not make out the sign, although voices and flickering lights indicated the place was still doing business. A man emerged, pausing in the door. His form, slender under the typical Gelonian tunic and short cape, was silhouetted for a moment against the dimly lit interior before he passed into the darkness of the street.

Zevaron walked faster, aware that he had ended up in perhaps the worst district of the city. While he didn't fear a second attack, neither did he want to invite one.

Silent and swift, two figures broke from cover. They converged upon the man who had just left the tavern. They judged the distance nicely, just out of easy hearing for anyone inside. Zevaron heard a cry of alarm, quickly silenced, accompanied by the sounds of fists on flesh, scuffling, and a body thudding against stone wall.

This was none of his quarrel, Zevaron told himself. He'd had enough senseless fighting for one night. He did not have time to get involved, and the attack would be over in an instant. The thieves would soon be off with the victim's purse, leaving no lasting harm beyond a few bruises.

The attack did not break off as Zevaron had expected. The victim's cries turned to those of real pain, not just surprise. That settled the matter. Zevaron freed his sword and bolted in the direction of the fight. The two assailants had dragged their prey into an alley, very much like those Zevaron had darted down during the fight at Gatacinne. Both smelled of rotten food, stale wine, and urine.

Zevaron caught the sound of a body sliding along rough stone to the ground. He rounded the corner of the alley. By chance, the clouds parted at that instant. Moonlight revealed two bulky figures bending over a fallen third.

"You lift his shoulders," one muttered, "and we'll—"

"Riya! Riya!" Shouting the Denariyan war cry, Zevaron burst upon them. They whirled to face him.

Light gleamed on the edge of a long knife. Zevaron sent it spinning away. He sank into a fighting stance, sword lifted and ready.

"If you value your lives," he growled in Gelone, "you will depart while you still can."

They turned and ran. In that moment, Zevaron saw that they were masked.

The fallen man moaned, pawing at his chest. Zevaron secured his sword and knelt beside him. The light was too weak to see if the poor fellow was badly injured. From the noise he was making, he could breathe well enough.

"It's all right," Zevaron said. "I doubt they'll be coming back. We'd best leave this place. Can you walk?"

The stranger cursed mildly but, with Zevaron's help, clambered to unsteady feet. He bent over, twisting to face away, and vomited noisily.

"I'm afraid I must prevail on your good will for a little longer." His voice was pleasant, and Zevaron realized with surprise that the other man could not have been much older than he was. "Could you—if you could help me home, my father will give you a reward."

"I didn't help you for money," Zevaron said tightly. "But I can't leave you here for the next scavenger. I think a newborn kitten could have the better of you just now." He slipped the other man's arm over his shoulder. The other was a little taller, but slender. "Which way?"

"Turn right here, and then straight until Old Fountain

Street, then up along the Avenue of Bronze to Cynar Hill. The house of Jaxar."

"I'm a stranger here, as you see," Zevaron said as they limped along. "I don't know where that is."

"You don't know..." The other man sounded astonished. "You truly don't know who I am."

Zevaron felt a surge of irrational impatience. "You're the son of the Ar-King himself, for all I know. I told you I didn't chase those thugs for any hope of gain." *All I want now is to get you home and off my hands.*

"It's best not to make jokes about my uncle."

"That kick to your head must have been pretty nasty."

"As you wish. *Don't* believe me if it suits you."

They went on for a time in silence. Zevaron was mildly impressed when the patrol stepped aside to let them pass without a single question.

They reached the hilly area and began to climb. The compounds here were large and, even in the uncertain light, Zevaron noticed the smoothness and grace of the stone walls, the carvings, and the immaculately kept gardens.

"That one," the young man said, pointed to a long wall that gleamed as if moonlight had been woven into it. He fumbled with the latch and the gate swung open. An old man, bald and thick-bodied, stood there, lantern in hand.

"Blessings unto the gods! You are safe!"

The servant urged them inside and through a garden where sweet fragrances arose from the beds of night-darkened flowers. Beyond lay the house.

"My lord! He's home! He's safe!" the servant called as they made their way through an entrance hall. The interior courtyard was like a garden, lined with planters and open to the sky. Beyond it, they entered the main part of the house. The servant rushed ahead, craning his head toward the top of a flight of stairs.

A woman rushed through the largest of the doors, her peacock-bright gown in disarray, golden hair tumbled about her shoulders. In one arm, she held a mass of white fur, clearly a small shaggy dog.

"Danar?" A second, older man appeared at the top of the stairs, moving slowly with the assistance of a crutch. His form was shadowed, but relief resonated in his voice.

"Father, I'm s-sorry." The young man pulled himself upright and stepped away from Zevaron's support. "I behaved rashly, but I'm not hurt."

"Jaxar, I told you he would be all right." Behind the man at the top of the stairs, a woman appeared, slender and dark. The little white dog in the arms of the golden-haired woman began barking and struggling, quieting only when its mistress cuffed it about the head.

The second woman stepped forward, and the light from the steward's lantern burnished her features. Zevaron, glancing up, caught the honey-gold skin, the slightly tilted eyes, the braided midnight hair.

She cried out his name in a voice that shattered the air.

It was Tsorreh.

Chapter Twenty-nine

ZEVARON bolted up the stairs, taking them three at a time. Heart pounding, he wrapped his mother in his arms. She was smaller than he remembered, slim and wiry, yet her fingers closed around his shoulders with surprising strength. All the fear and grief he had buried inside himself during the last four years came surging up, washing away all other thought. He could not speak. He could barely breathe.

She laughed as they rocked one another. "Zevaron, it's you! It's really you!"

He found his voice. "You're alive!"

Tsorreh drew back, looking directly at him. He was struck at once by how young she was. Only a shadow below her eyes, a tautness in her arched brows and at the corners of her mouth betrayed a deeper feeling. Whether it was anxiety or sorrow, or both, he could not tell. That was only to be expected, here in the stronghold of her enemies. She did not look like a slave, in her well-made gown, clasps of ivory and pearls at her shoulders. He glanced at her wrists and saw no manacle scars.

She was *alive*, that was all that mattered. This Jaxar was clearly a man of consequence. The lady must be his wife, and the young man Zevaron had rescued, his son. Danar had mentioned a reward. Zevaron had little use for money, but now he fully intended to collect quite a different favor.

Meanwhile, at the bottom of the stairs, Danar was fending off the attentions of a servant, declaring that he was unharmed.

"You ungrateful child!" the richly-dressed lady shrieked, looking as if she would like to strike him. "You have given your father such a fright!"

"I heard you were captured." Ignoring the commotion below, Zevaron turned back to Tsorreh. "And then, someone—a Gelonian officer—said you were dead. He showed me your braid with the Arandel token." He pulled it out from where it lay hidden against his chest, slipped the cord over his head, and handed it to her. "They said—" His throat closed up.

"Hush, it's all right." Her fingers closed around the token. She touched her hair, as if remembering. It was shorter than when he'd last seen her.

"The Source of Blessings has preserved us through a terrible time and brought us together once again," she said.

Zevaron pressed his lips together. It was by his own efforts and a good deal of luck, and not supernatural intervention, that he had found her.

"What are you doing here? Are you a—" he stumbled over the word, "a slave in this house?"

"Officially, I am a prisoner, given into Jaxar's custody. I'll explain more about it later. Jaxar, this is my Zevaron."

Jaxar's puffy face spread into an expression of delight. "My boy, I cannot tell you how welcome you are. To be separated from you was a great sadness for your mother."

"*You* are Tsorreh's Zevaron?" Danar said. "Father, this man came to my rescue. Two thugs, down by *The Blind Pilot*—"

"Really, Danar, what do you expect if you go wandering about in such disreputable areas!" the lady broke in. The dog in her arms had stopped barking and subsided into an occasional growl.

"I'll go where I like!" he shot back at her. "I'm no longer a child!"

"Then stop behaving like one!" she replied, her voice becoming even more shrill.

Zevaron tightened his grip on Tsorreh. The animosity between son and mother scoured his nerves like salt.

"Father, they were lying in wait for me, I swear—" Danar said.

"And where were your bodyguards, to whom we pay a small fortune? You sent them off so you could go off on one of your little adventures, didn't you?" the lady snarled. "Then you deserve whatever happens to you!"

"Enough!" Jaxar interrupted her, then continued in a calmer tone. "Lycian, my dear, will you be so kind as to arrange a bed for our guest—"

"Father, I must tell you what happened," Danar persisted. "These were no ordinary thieves—"

"I suppose we can find him a place with the servants." Lycian glared at Jaxar.

"—and treat him," Jaxar continued, "with our most gracious hospitality."

Despite the late hour, Zevaron had no intention of remaining within these walls. But he would not leave without Tsorreh. Never again would he desert her. She had said she was Jaxar's prisoner. One way or the other, he would get her out of here.

"—a pallet in my chamber," Danar was saying. "We could—"

"Out of the question!" Lycian interrupted. She gave Zevaron a look that said she thought him little better than the thugs who had attacked her son. "It is—"

"It is too late to stand here arguing." Jaxar shifted his weight on his crutch. Gray tinged his jowls and the hollows around his eyes. "Just for tonight, put him in the guest quarters. We will make other arrangements, if need be, in the morning."

"Nothing would please me better," Lycian sniffed elegantly, "but the chambers are not adequately aired, and I cannot awaken the servants at this outrageous hour to make them ready." Setting the little shaggy dog on the floor, she reached out one graceful hand. "Come to bed, my husband, for you are weary and this pointless argument has tired you overmuch. The boy can sleep in the gardener's shed. It is better than he is accustomed to, I am sure."

Zevaron set his jaw to keep from shouting them all down. He didn't care where he slept, as long as it wasn't *here*. Yet he had learned from Chalil that demands, especially difficult or unpleasant ones, were best presented in a temperate manner. It would be prudent to wait the right opening, to emphasize the debt owed to him.

"Mother!" Danar said, "I will not have you insulting the man who just saved my life! Don't you understand? This wasn't just a little roughing-up and the loss of a purse. They didn't care about my money, they wanted *me*. They were about to drag me off when Zevaron came by."

"And do what to you?" Lycian asked. "Really, Danar, your imagination—"

Jaxar descended the stairs, a stiff, awkward maneuver. "Even if Zevaron had not done us a great service, he is Tsorreh's son and we cannot treat him with less courtesy than an honored guest."

"Please," Tsorreh said, her voice low and gentle. "Do not trouble yourselves on the account of either myself or my son. A second pallet in the laboratory will not, I hope, inconvenience any member of this household."

Lycian looked astonished, for the moment without a reply. The white dog whined.

Zevaron began, "That will not be necessary—"

Jaxar glanced up at Tsorreh. "Are you sure it will not discommode you? No?" He chuckled. "I suppose the two of you have much to say to one another. Lycian, will you at least have a meal sent up?"

"If I may be allowed," Tsorreh said, "I myself will tend to my son."

Everyone looked pleased with this, and in the momentary pause that followed, Zevaron saw his opportunity. He delivered a full Denariyan bow to Jaxar, along with his most charming smile.

"My gratitude for your hospitality, Lord Jaxar. However, there is an obligation between us. You say you are indebted to me for preserving your son's freedom, if not his life. How far does that gratitude extend? Does such a service not merit a reward?"

Jaxar's expression betrayed no hint of emotion. For a moment, only the sound of his breathing disturbed the silence. Zevaron realized that despite his best intentions, he had insulted the man.

"Men of honor repay debts with open hands," Jaxar said. "Surely the matter of a reward, whether it is a sum of money or a position in my household here with your mother, can wait until the morning. Then we can give the matter the careful consideration it deserves. You have my assurance that I will deal generously with you."

"Gratitude is best expressed in action," Zevaron said.

"What do you want?"

"My mother's freedom."

"Zevaron!" Tsorreh gasped at the same time Danar exclaimed, "What!"

Jaxar held up a swollen hand. "That is not possible. I am more sorry than I can say."

"Are your words of gratitude mere empty sounds then?" Zevaron demanded. "Where is your Gelonian honor now? Would you imprison her here, within reach of the Ar-King—"

"Zevaron, you know nothing about it!" Tsorreh cried.

Lycian recovered her voice. "My husband, this is an ideal solution, do you not see? This boy can take her away, and you can claim she escaped. The Ar-King, may-his-wisdom-never-fail, will be upset, of course, but that will soon pass. No one will blame you."

"Blame is *exactly* what will happen," Jaxar said to her, "and this entire family will suffer the full weight of my brother's anger. I don't need to tell you what that means, these days."

Lycian's already pale skin turned even whiter. She clasped her hands together between her breasts, shaking her head in silent negation. "I see that you will not listen to sense—"

"Go to bed, my wife. This late hour is hardly suitable for serious discussion. I promise you that nothing of any consequence will be decided tonight. In the morning, when we have all rested, I will hear your thoughts."

"And pay as little attention to them as you ever do! No, I am sorry, I did not mean that. Of course, you are right. I will obey you as a loving wife should. In the meantime, I will seek the eternal wisdom of Qr, may-its-power-guide-us-evermore." With the little dog scurrying to keep up, Lycian swept from the room.

Zevaron waited until Lycian was out of earshot. He faced Jaxar, curling his fingers around the hilt of his sword and making sure the motion was seen. The old man was a cripple, unarmed, and if Danar had a weapon, he'd lost it in the ambush.

"Now we *will* continue our discussion," Zevaron said, "and matters of consequence—as you put it—*will* be decided. I ask you again, will you free my mother? Or must I take her from this place by force?"

Danar, his face suddenly hard, stepped between Zevaron and Jaxar. "You are in no position to threaten my father or make any such demand, not even at sword's point! How would you like a taste of Cinath's prisons?"

"Danar, watch your words!" Jaxar said.

"I fear nothing from you," Zevaron said to Danar, "you who did not even have the wit to see the trap you walked into."

Tsorreh thrust herself between Zevaron and Danar. "Stop it, both of you! Shall we turn on one another and do Cinath's bloody work for him?"

A shudder passed through Zevaron. He had heard words very like those at the council meeting during the siege of Meklavar. His father had been alive then, and his brother, Shorrenon. The councillors had hurled accusations and almost come to blows.

Remembering, Zevaron removed his hand from his sword.

"Your son deserves an explanation, at least as good a one as I can offer," Jaxar said. "Lad, I don't know what you know of Gelonian politics. Affairs in Aidon are in precarious balance. The Ar-King, the military, the great nobles—"

"The temple of Qr," Tsorreh put in.

"That, too," Jaxar continued. "I do not know who was behind this attack on Danar or how serious a threat it represents. But to act precipitously is to court disaster. That much I do know."

"You will sit here while your ship burns around you, and not even allow your crew to save themselves!" Zevaron said. "Not even the meanest raft-rat in Tomarzha Varya would do so. And you still owe a debt to me, Lord Jaxar, worth the life of your son."

"Zevaron, please," Tsorreh said. "Do not do this. Do not insist."

Danar looked stricken. Jaxar, his face flushing with emotion, said, "I care for Tsorreh as if she were my own daughter. If only it were a simple matter of releasing her, I would gladly send her to safety and then deal with the political reprisals. But such a rash deed would have dire consequences for more than myself or even my family. I cannot say how far the repercussions might extend, but I greatly fear it would be wider than this household, even this city. Perhaps even all of Gelon."

With reluctance, Zevaron admitted to himself that he was not going to succeed. Not this night, at any rate. His best chance was to remain as Jaxar's guest until he understood the situation better. Even facing the difficult task of spiriting his mother out of the city and to a safe haven, he was not without resources. There might be other Meklavaran exiles in the city or Denariyans he could call on in Chalil's name.

Jaxar and Danar retreated to their respective chambers, leaving Zevaron alone with Tsorreh. It astonished him, after so many years, to be standing beside her.

"Are you hungry?" she said. "Tired?"

Zevaron shook his head. On more than one occasion, he had fought when he was far more weary than he was now. His nerves were so taut, he doubted he would be able to sleep.

Tsorreh smiled at his silence. "The Gelon are enthusiastic on the subject of cleanliness. Come, I'll take you to the bathhouse, and you can tell me what happened to you since we parted ways at Gatacinne."

Taking a lantern, she led him from the main building and along a neatly kept path. He could not see much in the darkness, only the arch of willowy trees. He tasted sulfur on the cool night air.

From here, they descended a short flight of stairs to the bathhouse itself. It was divided into two areas, presumably one for men and the other for women. Tsorreh indicated the left entrance. Inside, partitions separated private bathing areas. Each one contained an enormous basin set in the floor, easily large enough to accommodate a grown man. Pipes set in the wall carried a stream of sulfur-tinged water.

Setting the lantern on a shelf set in the wall, Tsorreh placed a cork plug in one of the basins. While the basin filled, she brought in a towel, a basket of soap chips, and a pile of clean clothing, undergarments and a soft white tunic of the sort Danar and Jaxar wore. Then she retreated behind the partition to give him privacy.

Zevaron placed his sword within easy reach, then stripped and immersed himself. The water was surprisingly hot. Curling vapors tickled his nose. He leaned back and sighed deeply as heat softened the muscles of his back and shoulders.

"Yes, I thought the same at first," Tsorreh's voice came from behind the partition. "These baths are one of the wonders of Aidon. In other cities, the water must be boiled and carried by slaves, but there are hot springs deep within these hills and when the city was first built, pipes were laid in. You'll get used to the smell in time."

Zevaron picked up one of the soap chips. At least, he

thought it was soap, but the texture was far smoother than the lye-and-oil chunks he'd used onboard the *Wave Dancer*. He began washing himself. The creamy lather stung the small cuts that were the inevitable result of travel. It took two of the palm-sized chips to clean both skin and hair.

At last he was warm and clean. As he lay back, relishing the feeling, Tsorreh spoke again. "Tell me of your last four years, my Zevaron."

Where to begin? "I tried to get to you back in Gatacinne. But there was fighting everywhere and I ended up—" *A slave, a rebel, a pirate.* "When I thought you were dead . . ."

The Gelonian officer's face, contorted with rage, the nights spent rocking with the Wave Dancer's *rhythm, too sick in soul and heart to care if he lived. Walking the streets of To-marzha Varya, drinking in the spice-laden sun, dancing with the girls in the market. The wavering scorpion shape at the entrance to the temple in Roramenth . . .*

How could he tell her about those things? How could he make her understand what his life had been like? "I spent a time in Denariya," he said.

"Did you, indeed?" She waited for him to go on, but he did not. "Later, I hope to hear more."

"When we are safe," he answered. The seductive warmth of the bath and the fine soap, the obscene luxuriousness of it all, suddenly sickened him. He yanked out the plug and began toweling himself dry. Twisting most of the water from his hair, he bound it in a sailor's knot.

"Mother, we have to get out of here. Aidon isn't safe for any Meklavaran and neither is anywhere else in Gelon. To-morrow I'll find us a ship for Isarre—not Gatacinne again but Durinthe by way of a neutral port, maybe in the Mearas."

"Zevaron, no. Cinath made Jaxar responsible for me, and I won't put him at risk. The political situation is much less stable now than when I first arrived. Even before Cinath sent his son Thessar off to Azkhantia on that suicide mission—you've heard what happened? Even before that, Cinath was apt to turn on those around him. Now he's gotten even more unpredictable and paranoid. You could say he's more than half mad. The priests of Qr are the only ones he'll listen to. They encourage his ambitions, as if the present size of his empire isn't enough. They—"

"That's exactly why we need to leave now." Zevaron ignored the clean clothing she'd left for him. He was damned if he'd look like a Gelon. His old Denariyan clothes, worn and travel-stained as they were, were good enough. He pulled them on and stepped around the partition.

Tsorreh was sitting on the wooden bench, her hands folded neatly on her lap. She'd braided the Arandel token into her hair.

"Let Cinath spew his venom on anyone he likes if it will divert him while we get away," he said.

"Jaxar has been my friend, my protector, and my teacher. I won't place him in danger."

"Danger? Just look at this place. He's a rich man. And wealth like this comes with power."

"He's Cinath's *brother*," she said pointedly. "Lately, Cinath has gotten the idea that everyone near to him is conspiring to usurp his throne. With Thessar dead, the succession's clouded between Chion, the next son, and Jaxar."

He didn't want to hear this. Why should she care? Hadn't Cinath and his kind burned her city, slaughtered her husband, scattered her people? What had happened to her in Jaxar's house, that she now cared what happened to him?

"Jaxar is still kin to the Ar-King, so he deserves what he gets," Zevaron said, his voice cold with anger. "They're killing or enslaving every Meklavaran they can get their hands on, or haven't you heard? Do you think Jaxar will protect you if Cinath's men come for you?"

"Yes, I do, and yes, he has!"

Zevaron remembered in a flash of understanding that Tsorreh had said Jaxar was her protector as well as her friend. She must have come to see his interests as her own. Maybe he could use that alliance to convince her. He moderated his tone. "Then don't you endanger Jaxar even more by staying?"

"You're not listening. If I disappear and Jaxar cannot account for my absence, Cinath will consider that a treasonous act."

"All the more reason to leave now, by whatever means we can! If the Ar-King is determined to suspect his own brother, he will," Zevaron said. "The only difference is that you will be safely out of it."

"There is no safety anywhere in this world. There are forces at work here, and not just ordinary human politics."

What did she mean? Then he remembered the sea king and the temple at Rorameth. Prophecies and cultish rites meant nothing compared to the cold reality: Meklavar was conquered, his father and brother slain, his mother a prisoner, and he himself an exile, all at the hand of Ar-Cinath-Gelon.

"Explanations can wait," Tsorreh said, sighing. "I should not burden you with a long debate, not when you are weary and newly come to this place."

"I will not rest until we are both away from the land of our conquerors."

She stood, suddenly looking very much the Queen of Meklavar. "Come with me to the laboratory that has been my home, my workplace and refuge."

Tsorreh set about making up a pallet for Zevaron in the far corner, beside the place where she slept like an insignificant servant. Together they sat. She took up one of his hands, running her fingers over the scars.

"Zevaron, you have been a long time away from our people and traditions, but you must remember the stories in the *te-Ketav*, the tale of King Khored."

Memory stirred. Zevaron was once again a child, lying in his bed with his mother's favorite cat curled at his feet, she beside him, a book open on her lap, her voice rising and falling with the rhythm of the ancient verses. With the room almost dark, except for the circle of light cast by the oil lamp, he had closed his eyes, the better to see the marvelous pictures forming in his mind: A great king, bearded, mighty, garbed for battle, stood before his army. Gemstones blazed with iridescent light.

"*And Khored forged a magical Shield,*" Tsorreh had read, "*six perfect* alvara *crystals surrounded Khored's own gem, the* te-alvar, *the soul of the Shield.*"

In his mind, the boy Zevaron had watched the Shield blaze forth all the colors there ever were and even more that had never been imagined. Fire and Ice thundered across the battlefield, white and blazing like a vast, mis-shapen frost-giant. Through his mother's words, he watched as rivers turned into steam and mountains into sand, green fields hardened into ash, and the Sea of Desolation flooded over the battlefield.

"*And it came to pass,*" she read, "*that Khored and his brothers defeated Fire and Ice and exiled its fragmented rem-nants to the far regions of the world, to the mountains of the north, and then beyond the veil between the worlds.*"

Now, seated in this strange room in Aidon, Tsorreh fell silent. Zevaron sensed that there was more she would say, something of great importance that she could not yet bring herself to utter.

"When we have thrown off the Gelonian occupation," he said in a soothing tone, "we will sing those songs once again. I promise you."

"They are not fables, Zevaron. They are *history*, a history that continues to unfold to this day."

When Zevaron snorted in disbelief, Tsorreh gave no sign that she noticed. "What is not recorded is that over the gen-erations, the *alvara* have become scattered. Not all of them, and not all at once. Oh, each descendent of Khored and his brothers was faithful to his task, but the world changed too much. They no longer understood why it was important to keep the Shield intact. For a long time, enough of the guard-ians remained in Meklavar to maintain Khored's magic."

"Much good it did us, when the Gelon came," Zevaron made no effort to keep the bitterness from his voice.

Tsorreh looked sad and thoughtful. "When Meklavar

itself fell, the *te-alvar* went into exile. All that stood between Fire and Ice and the living world were the northern mountains, its prison. The last defense was a physical barrier, do you see?"

She leaned forward, her mood shifting. Her eyes gleamed with more than the reflected light of the lantern, and the touch of her fingers felt hot. A fever burned in her.

"Each land has its own incarnation of evil," she said, her voice low and urgent. "Azkhantian *enarees* preserve the legend of Olash-giyn-Olash, the Shadow of Shadows. The Scorpion god Qr haunts this land of Gelon, growing stronger with each passing day. But Fire and Ice, whose secret name is known only to Khored and his heirs, is the origin of them all. As the power of the Shield failed, so has it grown in strength. Even now, it marshals its resources, searching for a way back into the world."

Zevaron stared at her. She must have gone insane, these four years as a prisoner of her most bitter enemies. Or else she had fallen into an elaborate superstition, or perhaps she had been like that all along, being the granddaughter of the high priest of Meklavar. She had always spent too much time studying the ancient holy texts. Her prayers had not protected her from Gelon. No matter what she said, she was a slave here.

"Now the white star has fallen to earth far to the north, if Jaxar's observations are correct," Tsorreh went on, as if she had not noticed his reaction. "Don't you see? In the *north*. In the mountains where Khored imprisoned the ancient enemy. Before that, Qr had little influence here. The sect was no more than a handful of priests who went around frightening ignorant people." She paused, her focus turning inward. "Now the Scorpion temples are everywhere, and the priests whisper their poison into the ears of the Ar-King himself. And he heeds them."

Zevaron shook his head. What did it matter if the Gelon worshiped a crawling thing? He felt as if he had stumbled into a world where nothing made sense, where grown people believed children's stories.

Yet, in a way, it *did* make sense. His mother had been through a trial of horror and fear, with her husband dead and her city set on fire, fleeing for her life, now alone here, cut off from even another to speak her own language. What woman would not turn to the comfort of childhood beliefs?

He took her hand, the fingers slender and strong between his. "It is late, not a good time to debate explanations."

"You're right," she said. "It's too much to understand all at once, and here you are, a stranger in Aidon. Tomorrow or the next day, you and Danar must explore the city. You will see for yourself what is happening. Everything will come clear in its own time."

Weariness crept over him. He would need his strength for the morning. It would not be easy to convince Tsorreh to flee. Once away from Aidon, he hoped she would see sense. One way or the other, with Jaxar's permission or without it, even if they were fugitives with nothing but their own resources and each other to depend upon, they would find their way home.

He settled on the pallet Tsorreh had made up for him. The laboratory was no stranger than any of the other places he had slept: a bedroll along the road, a hammock onboard the *Wave Dancer*. In fact, it was more comfortable than most. He had no difficulty falling asleep, confident that he would wake at the slightest sound of alarm, as he had learned to do in his years with Chalil.

Chapter Thirty

SOMEONE was in the laboratory, moving softly. Secretively.

Zevaron tensed, his hand reaching for the sword he had placed so carefully beside his pallet. Silently he grasped the scabbard while the fingers of the other hand closed around the hilt, ready to slip the blade free. He slitted his eyes partway open and noticed the rays of the morning sun through the tower at the end of the room. From this angle, the work table obscured a clear vision of the figure moving toward them.

Wait, wait until he gets closer. Zevaron forced himself to maintain a state of relaxed readiness.

"Tsorreh?" came Danar's voice, hushed.

"What is it?" Tsorreh asked, a breath of air, an unseen gesture. "Zevaron's still asleep."

"No, we need just you. Don't worry, Lycian's already gone to the temple."

Zevaron lay motionless except for the slow movement of his chest. Cloth rustled as Tsorreh rose, slipped her feet into her boots, and padded softly across the floor. He waited until the footsteps had died away. Then, taking his still-sheathed weapon, he crept from the room and down the stairs.

Muted voices led him to the garden atrium. Morning sun slanted into the open square, but dew still dotted the leaves of the flowering plants. Hidden in the shadows of the arched doorway, he inhaled the spicy perfume of flowers, perhaps those waxy white blossoms, in the freshness of the morning.

Jaxar waited at a little table, which was laid with a basket of breads and a pitcher. A simple white robe, gathered in ample folds at each shoulder, stretched across his rounded shoulders. A little ways off, two burly men in shorter tunics, short swords hanging from their belts, stood watch. Their faces were grim.

Jaxar's back was to Zevaron, but his words were clear enough.

"...confirms the two men who assaulted my son last night were indeed members of Cinath's Elite Guards."

"Alive and captive, he would guarantee your obedience." Tsorreh did not speak as prisoner to jailor or servant to master, but as one equal to another, and she was clearly worried. "What if Cinath no longer cares about family loyalty? What if he decides to eliminate every rival claimant to his throne?"

"He cannot act openly against me, not yet," Jaxar said. "He must first discredit me for that to happen. I am still too well-respected and am known to have no political aspirations. No, my dear, I fear we must keep on as we have, working quietly, and give him no cause for retaliation."

Zevaron thought, *What folly!* They were all mad if they thought that looking innocent and unthreatening would buy them even the smallest measure of safety. It had not protected him on the wharf at Gatacinne, nor had it prevented the Gelonian army from storming the walls of Meklavar. The scattered exiles of his people had done nothing to deserve persecution.

It was only a matter of time before the demands of kinship and custom no longer restrained Cinath. Then it would be too late to take action.

"If my uncle is determined—" Danar began, but broke off as Tsorreh rose.

Her gaze locked upon her son. She must have sensed his presence, for he had made no sound. Jaxar turned, a painfully awkward movement. The two guards started toward Zevaron before Jaxar gestured them back to their posts.

"Have not fear," Tsorreh said. "My son will not betray us."

Danar scowled. "I'm not so sure. He did threaten us earlier."

"Zevaron, you need not hide in the shadows," Jaxar said. "Come, join us. You have done us all a great service, both in saving my son's life and in bringing to light this most recent plot. Again, I offer you my deepest gratitude. Now that you know the situation, for by your expression you understood what you overheard, you must surely realize why I cannot give you what you ask. Tsorreh herself is in agreement."

But I am not.

They were interrupted by shouting and pounding from the direction of the front door, punctuated by cries of alarm from the house steward.

"Open up in the name of the Ar-King! Out of our way!"

Zevaron whipped his sword free, strode into the middle of the atrium, and shoved Tsorreh behind him.

"What are you doing?" Danar cried. "You fool, put that away!"

An instant later, a handful of armed Gelon burst into the garden. They wore sashes of blue and purple across their chest armor and carried drawn swords. Zevaron counted seven, including a tall, lean man in an officer's helmet. Jaxar's two bodyguards had started forward, hands on their own weapons, but now they hesitated and bowed to the officer.

"Well, Mortan," Jaxar said without raising his voice, "you have a rather unorthodox method of inviting yourself to breakfast."

The officer approached Jaxar. "This is no jest, Lord Jaxar." He pointed at Zevaron. "Tell your man to put down his sword."

Zevaron maintained his defensive stance. The Gelon

quickly took up their positions around the atrium, barring escape.

"Under the circumstances," Jaxar said, "I disagree on the wisdom of compliance. Not without an explanation."

"Don't abuse my patience by pretending ignorance. You know full well that I have come to arrest you." The officer brandished a scroll tied with blue and purple ribbons. "Cinath himself signed the orders. For both you and the Meklavaran witch."

In a glance, Zevaron assessed the situation in terms of combat. He could take three of them, maybe four, before their numbers overwhelmed him. He could not count on the bodyguards, who clearly deferred to the Gelonian officer. Jaxar would be of no use, but if Danar had the wit and will to fight, it just might be possible—

"Indeed?" The mildness of Jaxar's voice did not lessen, but now Zevaron heard the steel beneath the honey. Jaxar held out one swollen hand for the scroll.

The officer placed it on the edge of the table, then stepped back. Zevaron wondered what he had to fear from an obviously ill man.

Witch, Mortan had called Tsorreh. Rumors of Meklavaran sorcery sprang to Zevaron's mind.

Jaxar picked up the scroll, slipped off the ribbons, and read it. No shift of expression showed on his bland features, only a slight tensing of his brows. "I fear you have been taken for a fool, my friend," Jaxar said. "A jape has been committed by a rival, designed to embarrass you and set back your career. These charges cannot possibly be serious. They claim I have plotted with 'the Meklavaran witch' to murder Prince Thessar, overthrow my brother, and free Meklavar."

"Everyone knows my father never meddles in politics," Danar interjected. He peered over his father's shoulder at the scroll. "Are you sure that's really the Ar-King's signature?"

"My son makes a good point." Jaxar looked more closely. "It could well be a forgery. Leave it here with me. I will take it to my brother—discreetly, of course—and begin an investigation."

For an instant, Mortan looked uncertain. Then his features hardened. "Lord Jaxar, there may be some question about your own complicity. I am not in a position to say. But there is no question of *hers*." He pointed past Zevaron to Tsorreh. "*She* has no loyalty to Gelon, and she has every reason to wish the Ar-King harm. It is said that Prince Thessar met his death by black Meklavaran magic, and who better to wreak such vile treachery than the exiled Queen herself?"

Mortan gestured to his men. "Seize her!"

Zevaron lunged at the nearest soldier, using the distracting, circular sword technique of the Denariyan pirates. The Gelon reacted to the feint. The next moment, he went down, clutching a deep cut across one thigh. Two others took his place.

Zevaron was no longer thinking, planning. The steel became a fluid extension of his own arm. His body moved, perfectly placed to seize each opening. Another Gelon spun away, hand bleeding. His sword clattered across the tiled floor.

"Hold!" someone shouted, a word like dust on the wind.

"Stop! Zevaron, stop this now!"

At the sound of his mother's frantic voice, Zevaron faltered. The next instant, he felt the tip of a sword in the hollow at the base of his neck. He opened his hand and let his own weapon fall. Rough hands grabbed him and spun him around. At the edge of his vision, he glimpsed Tsorreh in the grip of a Gelon, one arm twisted behind her back and a knife blade at her throat.

"No more!" Jaxar cried, his voice rough with emotion. "I will come with you, but let there be no further shedding of blood on my account!"

"What about this one?" said the soldier who held Zevaron.

"The penalty for interference with the Ar-King's business—and that includes threatening his agents—is death." Mortan turned away, as if he did not care what his men did.

I'll kill you! pounded through Zevaron's skull. *I'll kill you all!*

"No!" Danar cried. "He is not to blame! As my body-guard, he was only doing what I hired him to do. It is the law—the Ar-King's own law, from the time of Sestos of Un-dimmed Glory, may-his-name-be-revered-forever—that a servant cannot be held responsible for following the lawful commands of his master."

For a long moment, no one spoke. Jaxar's wheezing breath sounded worse than ever. One of the wounded sol-diers groaned as his fellow helped him to his feet.

Finally Mortan said, "This matter can be taken up later. No one was killed, after all, and a fighting man's scars carry no shame. Come, we must conduct these two prisoners to the palace. The sooner they are in custody, the sooner they will be tried, and this whole miserable business will be fin-ished."

Mortan agreed grudgingly to let the two household bodyguards accompany Jaxar, to physically assist him and make sure his needs were seen to, but without their weap-ons. When they were gone, the atrium fell silent. Zevaron stood as the Gelon had left him, a trickle of blood running down his chest.

Danar lowered himself into one of the chairs. Zevaron met Danar's gaze and saw in those gray-green eyes an ex-pression of the same anguish that he himself felt. His hands ached for a sword, but the Gelon had taken his.

"Quickly, let us arm ourselves and go after them!" Zeva-ron said.

"I don't think—" Danar broke off at the sound of light footsteps and a woman's voice in the entry hall. "May all the gods of Gelon save us! My stepmother's home."

Chapter Thirty-one

LYCIAN swept through the front door, demanding to know what all the uproar was about. When Danar told her, she shrieked, fainted, and had to be carried to her bed. Servants wailed, echoing the sentiments of their mistress, and rushed about.

With Zevaron close behind, Danar stormed up to the laboratory. Apparently, this was the only place in the house where privacy was to be found. Danar muttered beneath his breath as he cleared away a space on the central work table, brought out lists of names and rolls of paper, and began writing.

Zevaron could not follow the details of Danar's plan, not even when Danar explained he was sending letters of appeal to his father's closest allies.

What was the point of *writing*? Zevaron shot back. Tsorreh and Jaxar were in the hands of the enemy! To have found her after all these years, and then to have her taken away . . . Anything might happen while they stood idly by. They had to follow—

"And do what?" Danar demanded, scrambling up from the desk to block Zevaron's path. He grabbed Zevaron by the shoulders. "Get yourself arrested as well? What good can that accomplish? You idiot, the only reason you're still

at liberty is because I managed to convince them you're my
bodyguard. So act like one! Guard me—right here!"

Zevaron wanted to jump out of his bones, to hit some-
thing, to *act*. Grudgingly, he admitted Danar was right.
Alone, he had no hope. He could not force his way into
Cinath's stronghold.

"Give me something to do," Zevaron begged. "Carry
messages, carry water, stack stones, mend ropes—I don't
care."

Danar released him. "I must advise Father's friends
about what's happened. Our best hope is to make this arrest
known among the noble houses. Their outrage will be our
strongest weapon and our best chance of making my uncle
see reason. You can't help me write to them, I'm afraid."

One corner of Danar's mouth quirked upward. "The
most useful thing you can do for the moment is to keep my
stepmother away from me. She'll come out of her faint any
moment now and throw the entire household into hysterics.
Jonath and Haslar went with Father, so I'll need the other
servants free to deliver the letters."

Zevaron grimaced. Lycian was the last person he wanted
to deal with, even if Danar thought he, Zevaron, could handle her. "You're sure there isn't a latrine that needs scrubbing out instead?"

"You wanted something to do, didn't you?" Danar
turned back to the desk, the half-smile fading. "Once these
are finished, we can plan our next step. With the most influ-
ential men in Aidon watching, Uncle Cinath wouldn't
dare—won't dare—he—there will be a trial. We must be
prepared."

Zevaron did not know if a trial would be a good thing or
not. He certainly didn't place any hope in Gelonian justice.
Captured pirates were executed summarily. In Denariya,
the injured party or his kin, if he were slain, brought charges
and, more often than not, were granted leave to exact vengeance, according to a complicated traditional code.

". . . so we'll need to know exactly what evidence will be
brought," Danar was saying.

"How can there be evidence of something that never happened?" Zevaron asked. "That doesn't even exist?"

"I don't know! I've never had to deal with anything like this before! Father always— he always . . ." Danar's voice faltered. He blinked hard. With visible effort, he calmed himself. "That's why we need help. Advice on what to do, how to make my uncle see reason. So please, let me get to it. We will take action, I swear to you. We *will*."

Unexpectedly moved, Zevaron bowed and left the laboratory. What would he do in Danar's place? He was even less equipped to deal with the tangle of Gelonian jurisprudence than Danar. Nothing Chalil had taught him would be of any use. He could not slash or sail or bargain with this enemy.

I have to do something! I cannot lose her again!

When Zevaron arrived at Lycian's chamber, she was sitting on a brocaded divan, one maidservant fanning her face with an elaborate concoction of ostrich plumes and silk ribbons, another bathing her feet and hands with lavender-scented water. The white dog lay curled at her feet.

Zevaron explained that Danar had instructed him to protect her. Lycian pursed her lips. Her eyes narrowed as if she were noticing him for the first time and did not like what she saw. Or maybe liked it too well, which thought appalled him.

"You may tell my son that *I* am in no danger from the loyal servants of the glorious Ar-King, may-his-strength-never-falter, and certainly not from an uncivilized barbarian sorceress out of nowhere. I have powerful protection against all such malevolent influences, do you hear me?"

Not knowing what else to say, Zevaron murmured, "I understand."

"The properly respectful address for Lord Jaxar's wife is *gracious lady*."

"Gracious lady."

She sniffed, raised her chin, and turned away. "Nevertheless, I cannot leave matters to chance. My enemies are cunning and resourceful. I must seek counsel immediately."

Throwing off her filmy shawl, Lycian got to her feet. She displayed surprising energy for a woman who, only a short time ago, had been carried prostrate to her bed. In response to her orders, the maidservants brought a basin of petal-strewn water, scented oils, and cosmetics. Lycian dismissed Zevaron from the room, but he remained outside the door, prepared to accompany her when she departed.

Zevaron had seen the work of Denariyan courtesans, the skill with which they painted and perfumed themselves. On several occasions, he had even had the funds to avail himself of their favors. So he was not surprised when Lycian emerged, immaculately groomed and clad in a different gown. She carried the dog, which seemed to have recovered its peevish temper. It had been combed, the hair over its eyes tied back with a pink ribbon. When it saw Zevaron, it yipped and squirmed to be put down.

Lycian clutched the creature even more tightly. "If Danar has ordered you to protect me, then I suppose you must," she said, clearly meaning, *That way, I can also keep an eye on you.*

Zevaron was not happy about leaving the compound. News of Tsorreh might come at any moment. On the other hand, he had agreed to prevent Lycian from interfering with Danar's work, and she certainly could not do that out in the streets.

A servant brought up a pretty little onager mare, white with only a hint of a dorsal stripe, harnessed in red leather with silver bells on bridle and saddle pad. Lycian handed the dog to the servant. Then she settled herself on the onager's back, took up the reins, and proceeded through the gate. She did not speak to Zevaron or acknowledge his presence. With heels and short riding whip, she kept her mount to a brisk pace, leaving Zevaron to trot after her.

Zevaron took careful note of their route through the city. Fortunately, his time at various ports in Denariya had trained him in identifying landmarks, the sense and pattern of any city. As they passed between two hills, Zevaron expected they were headed for Cinath's palace. Surely the building before him, set like a jewel of silver-white columns at the intersection of broad avenues, could be nothing less. Surrounding it were smaller, less ornate, yet obviously important buildings. Statues glinting with gold leaf adorned some of them. Colored banners, streamers, and flower garlands created a riot of color. People, most of them on foot, moved through the streets. The city patrol stood aside, bowing to Lycian.

She turned away from the direct route to the palace and followed a major avenue. They came to a halt in a courtyard outside a structure like a grander, newer version of the Qr temple in Roramenth. The man running forward to take the reins of the onager could have been a twin of the Roramenth priest. The cloth tied around the man's smooth-shaven head bore the now familiar scorpion image.

Lycian slipped to the paving stones, adjusted her gown, and proceeded up the wide steps to the entrance. The doors swung open, revealing a dimly lit chamber.

Zevaron hesitated, caught between reluctance to go inside, his duty as Lycian's bodyguard, and curiosity about her mission here. Tsorreh said that the priests of Qr had the ear and confidence of the Ar-King. Had Lycian come to ask them to intercede for her husband? Just how much influence did they have over Cinath?

Lycian disappeared into the shadowed interior, and the doors closed behind her. Zevaron, fighting a wave of repugnance, reached for the latch. The door opened fractionally and a priest stood there, not the young one who had led the onager away, but another, older man with fiery dark eyes.

"Can I help you, my son?"

"I serve the Lady Lycian. She—"

"She is in no danger here, under our protection. Indeed, there is no place in Aidon, or in all the wide world, where she would be safer than in Qr's holy temple."

Chalil had often said that only a fool would argue with a man on the threshold of his own castle, so Zevaron bowed politely and withdrew. He found the place where the riding animals of those nobles attending the service were kept. Lycian's onager was one of a half-dozen, all of excellent quality and richly harnessed. A boy brought them handfuls of grain and stroked their long ears, singing tunelessly to them. Zevaron hunkered down beside the watering buckets and waited.

In a surprisingly short time, Lycian emerged. Her face was flushed, her breath as rapid as if she had been running, and her eyes gleamed. Zevaron decided she had gotten whatever she had come for, a favorable omen or assurances her prayers would not go unanswered, or whatever the priests thought she wanted to hear.

Perhaps, a poisonous thought wound through his mind, she had told *them* what *they* wanted to hear.

Back at the compound, Zevaron saw Lycian safely back to her own chambers. He found Danar in the atrium, talking to two somber-looking older men. From the understated richness of their clothing and the way they carried themselves, they seemed men of importance. That they had come so quickly and in person indicated how serious they considered the situation.

Silently Zevaron took up a position just inside the inner doorway. He met Danar's gaze with the merest flicker of acknowledgment.

"Who's that?" one of the nobles said, glancing at Zevaron.

"My new bodyguard," Danar said. "Denariyan, you know. Fierce in combat, but doesn't understand a word of Gelone."

Zevaron tried to look stolid and uncomprehending.

"Cinath means to move quickly, while public sympathy for the death of Prince Thessar remains strong," one of the men said.

"The question remains whether the Ar-King, may-he-someday-attain-wisdom, will adjudicate the charges himself, or turn Lord Jaxar and the Meklavaran woman over to the priests of Qr," the other said.

Qr. Where Lycian had gone this very morning.

"Surely, *they* have no jurisdiction over my father and his guest," Danar protested.

"We must not underestimate their influence. After all, was it not at their instigation that Cinath issued the order to arrest any Meklavaran without legitimate business within the city? Understandably, they also claim sole authority to prosecute any cases of sorcery."

"I beg you, do whatever you can to make sure that does not happen," Danar said.

"Would Cinath listen to you, as his close kin?" the second man asked.

Danar looked stricken. Zevaron thought, *He has passed his life in the shadow of his father. He has no voice of his own. Or perhaps he has not yet found his voice.*

"It might be better if you stayed out of sight, to avoid reminding Cinath of the loss of his own son," the first man said. "Some consider Prince Chion unfit to rule, and there is sufficient historical precedent for excluding him from the succession. The Lion Throne has not always passed to the next son, but sometimes to a more competent nephew. Especially the first-born male heir of the older brother," referring to Jaxar's seniority and the accident of his birth that barred him from the throne.

Danar's mouth tightened. "Neither my father nor I have any aspirations—"

"Do you think the Ar-King believes that?" the older man demanded.

"Enough of such talk!" the other said, clearly nervous. "We must not meet again. If Cinath suspects a plot, he will bring us all down."

And that, Zevaron thought, ends any hope that they will help Jaxar or Tsorreh. He caught the faint shift in posture of the two nobles, the hint of withdrawal. *No, they will let Jaxar hang, or burn, or however they execute people here, before they risk their own skins.*

For Tsorreh, they would do nothing.

He waited until they were gone before approaching Danar. Danar looked wrung out, torn in a dozen different directions.

"They will do what they can." Danar struggled for a hopeful tone.

"As long as they themselves are not placed in jeopardy," Zevaron said. "Danar, what about Tsorreh? What will happen to my mother?"

"I know that, so far, we have concentrated on my father's fate," Danar said, raking back sweat-damp hair from his forehead. "Since she is legally in my father's custody, he himself must act as her advocate, and for that, he must be free." He lowered himself to the bench where, only hours ago, he had sat at breakfast. "Do not fear, he will not forsake her."

"I am not worried about his good intentions," Zevaron said, "only his ability to carry them out. If Cinath has turned against his own blood-kin, who then will stand up for my mother?"

"I will." Danar turned to look him full in the face. Zevaron saw a dozen shifting emotions behind those sea-gray eyes: terror, resolution, denial, courage. Which were real, and which the reflections of his own desperate hopes?

The next few days passed in a whirlwind of comings and goings. Zevaron continued to accompany Lycian on her twice-daily visits to the Qr temple. In between, he kept up the pretense of being Danar's bodyguard. Danar went throughout Aidon's rich hill districts, where Zevaron would occasionally be admitted to a meeting with one important man or another. Usually he waited in the entrance chambers. Danar explained that it would be considered a serious insult to require a bodyguard inside the private compound of a noble.

Danar emerged from these meetings looking increasingly more somber. Zevaron did not understand Danar's explanations of what had transpired. The Gelonian legal system, a complex and often contradictory blend of tradition, formal laws, and royal decrees, seemed capricious and arbitrary. There had been Kings as well as Ar-Kings in Gelon's past, and apparently the latter had the power to take any action they pleased.

"So the fate of my father and your mother becomes one of jurisdiction," Danar explained as they sat together in the rooftop observatory. Evening was drawing nigh and the compound lay around them, cooling in the darkness. From one of the manicured fruit trees, a bird sang, then fell silent.

"You mean whether it is a judge who hears the case or Cinath himself," Zevaron said. "A savage arrangement."

"What, did you not have Kings in Meklavar?" Danar replied sharply.

"Of course, as you very well know. But our holy texts tell us that no one man should have the power of life and death over others in more ways than one. If a King is to command in battle, he cannot also judge criminal cases."

"That's very odd," Danar said.

Overhead, the stars glimmered in a milky swath. His mother had sat here, watching the fiery star grow brighter and then disappear into the northern horizon. Jaxar had entrusted her with his instruments, and together they had studied the heavens.

"No, not odd," Zevaron said, regretting having provoked a quarrel with his one ally. After all, if Tsorreh and Jaxar could become trusted colleagues, or even friends, he and Danar should strive to do the same. For the moment, their interests worked toward the same goal. "It's just different."

After four or five days, Zevaron's desperation grew even more urgent. Danar had told him there were no facilities in the royal palace for holding prisoners for any length of time, and it was unusual for a trial to be so long delayed. Danar's efforts seemed to be having a small effect. Jaxar's friends had presented daily inquiries to Cinath regarding his health and welfare, and a few had made speeches in the public spaces calling for a speedy disposition of the case and disclosure of the facts.

"If there is proof of sorcery in Gelon, whether it be from Meklavar or Azkhantia or Southern Firelands, we have a right to know it!" one of the speechmakers had thundered, shaking his fist at the palace. The crowd had responded with such an uproar that the Ar-King's Elite Guard came out to restore order.

Lycian and Zevaron were forced to detour around the area on their way back from yet another visit to the temple. It was late in the day, and the sun dipped toward the western hills. Lycian broke her usual silence to grumble about the inconvenience for the entire rest of the journey. By the time they arrived, twilight had almost faded.

Danar was not at home, although it was unusual for him to prolong his meetings into the evening. The steward, looking worried, said that Danar had been summoned to the royal palace.

"I must go after him, then," Zevaron said.

"You will do no such thing," Lycian said. "All will be well, I am certain of it. I have prayed to Qr, and I have been granted guidance. Do not interfere with the ways of the gods."

She strode from the entrance hall to the colonnade that led to the household chambers, then paused. "Do not stand there like a witless savage, even if you are one. Make yourself useful in the kitchen if you cannot find anything else to do. I specifically forbid you to leave this compound and stir up trouble where none exists."

"Come on, boy," the steward said kindly. His voice betrayed his worry. "There's naught to do but keep ourselves busy until the young lord returns."

If he returns, Zevaron thought.

Zevaron was sitting in the kitchen, helping the cook chop onions and garlic, when he heard voices from the front gate. He could not make out words, except for Lycian's birdlike shrieking, but the clamor had the wrong rhythm for a fight. Excitement, certainly . . .

He put the knife down on the work table in a pile of chopped onions and bolted for the entrance hall.

Jaxar stood there, flanked by Danar, who was grinning broadly, and Lycian, the steward, the two bodyguards, and most of the household staff. The cook had followed Zevaron and now let out a cry of celebration. Everyone was talking at once, hugging each other.

"Free—you're free," Zevaron said, half-stunned. His words were lost in the general rejoicing.

Jaxar met his eyes, and his expression turned somber. He motioned for quiet. "Zevaron—"

"Where is she? *Where is my mother?*"

Silence answered him. His body turned cold right down to his bones, except for an explosion of incandescent fury behind his heart. "Cinath still has her! You walked out of there and left her!"

"It's not like that—" Danar began.

Jaxar cut him off with a gesture. "For the time being, that is true," he said to Zevaron. "I have been exonerated of all charges. My brother now believes that Tsorreh placed me under an evil spell. She is currently being held in one of the cells beneath the Old Temple of Justice, while Cinath deliberates the manner of her execution."

Zevaron felt as if he had been pierced with a blade of ice. His chest muscles locked. He could not breathe.

"Do not lose heart, for this is only the middle of the story," Jaxar went on in a kindly, encouraging tone. "It is not yet the end. We will—we *must*—work on her behalf, and do everything we can."

The sincerity in the older man's voice only fueled Zevaron's anger. These people were Gelon, the enemy. They took care of their own and only their own. Why had he expected otherwise? They cared nothing for anyone or anything else.

A sense of fairness, however, gave him pause. Tsorreh had been brought here as a prisoner, but that was not Jaxar's fault, nor was the madness of the Ar-King.

"My husband, you must rest," Lycian pleaded. "You have been through a terrible ordeal, but it is over now."

Zevaron's vision cleared, so that he looked on Jaxar with different eyes. The older man was clearly worse, his eyes ringed by cadaverous shadows, his puffy cheeks ashen, and his breathing labored. Yet Jaxar refused his wife's supporting arm and kept his attention on Zevaron, waiting for a response.

"Go with her, Father, please," Danar pleaded. "I'll try to make him see reason."

Zevaron dipped his head, ashamed. He had been ready to heap judgment upon a man who had tried to befriend his mother under very difficult circumstances. He searched for words, but none came.

"My boy," Jaxar touched Zevaron's arm, his fingers soft and cold. "I cannot promise—" He broke into a spasm of coughing.

Lycian gave orders to the servants to bring Jaxar to his bed chamber. This time he did not resist.

Danar remained, glaring at Zevaron. "Come up to the laboratory, where we can talk."

When they were safely out of hearing, Danar turned on Zevaron. "How dare you make things any harder for my father, after everything he has done for Tsorreh? Don't you think he is as worried about her as you are? Can't you see what it cost him, those few days as a prisoner? He could have *died*, you insolent lout, and he still might!"

Zevaron fully expected Danar to strike him, so hot and passionate were Danar's words. "I am sorry," Zevaron said slowly. "I hope he will recover."

"You'd better pray to whatever gods you believe in, because if he does not get better, Tsorreh has no hope."

In the space between one beat of his heart and the next, Zevaron saw everything in a different light. "She has *you*."

Danar took a step backward, his face going pale. Zevaron thought he would insist he had no power to help. Then Danar's expression softened.

"You are right. I do not know what I can do, but I have

been finding out. I do not have my father's influence, but I am not entirely helpless. Whether you believe it or not, I love Tsorreh. Perhaps not the way you do, as a mother. These four years—I think I would have gone mad, living in the same house as my stepmother. Tsorreh has been my elder sister, my teacher, my friend."

"I did not know," Zevaron said, mortified. Yet why should it come as a surprise that Tsorreh had made friends even in the stronghold of her enemies? He had seen her only as the mother he had sworn to protect.

"She said," Danar's voice choked and he looked away, drawing a breath before he could continue, "she said the first time we met that I reminded her of you."

And you have been a faithful ally to her. She has not been alone because of you. And Jaxar.

"Let us work together for her sake," Danar said softly. "We are not your enemies, my father and I."

"Tell me, then, what I must do." *Even if it means waiting in silence.*

"Rest, be ready. Tomorrow, if he is able, my father will arrange for us to see her. Then you can give her your strength and courage. The rest—it will not be easy, but we will keep trying."

After Danar departed, Zevaron sat alone in the laboratory, trying to reconcile his jumbled, discordant impressions. For so long, things had been simple. He had known who was on his side and who was not. The fact remained that his mother was in the hands of Meklavar's most ruthless adversary, that once again her life was in jeopardy. There was nothing he could do, alone, to save her.

He went to Tsorreh's sleeping pallet and picked up the folded cloth she had used as a pillow. He buried his face in it, inhaling the lingering scents. And tried not to weep.

Chapter Thirty-two

DURING the night, Zevaron wrestled with the almost overpowering desire to rescue Tsorreh himself. In the end, he accepted that while it might be possible for him to reach her by stealth, there was no chance for the two of them to escape that way. He'd have to rely on Jaxar for that.

The next morning, however, Jaxar was too ill to leave his chamber. His steward dosed him with various herbal infusions and insisted on a regimen of rest. Jaxar's interpretation of rest must have been very liberal, for by the early afternoon, he had arranged for Danar to see Tsorreh, accompanied by Zevaron as his bodyguard. Lycian went about her own affairs, taking several of her own maidservants as her escort.

Danar emerged from his chamber dressed in a cloak over a tunic of linen so fine, it shimmered in the light. The cloak was trimmed in purple and blue, a reminder of his royal lineage.

"You'll do very well as you are." Danar indicated Zevaron's Denariyan clothing.

"I won't attract too much notice?" Zevaron asked.

"That's just what you *will* do. You will be so garish and offensive to the eye that no one will see the Meklavaran beneath the Denariyan disguise." When Zevaron gave his best piratical scowl, Danar laughed. "Everyone knows Denariyans are too barbaric to understand Gelone."

Danar was right. Zevaron was just another strange, colorful servant in a city filled with the exotic. A Meklavaran attempting to contact Tsorreh would only furnish further proof of a conspiracy. That would be all Cinath needed to execute her without further delay.

They walked, following the route Zevaron had taken with Lycian. Danar strode through the more crowded intersections with practiced ease, clearly accustomed to going everywhere in the city on his own feet. Zevaron tried to look fierce, scowling at everyone the way the bodyguard of a son of a noble family should. Whereas he had not particularly cared what happened to Lycian, now he was acutely aware of the dangers Danar invited by walking, unarmed and undisguised, through such crowds. Everyone clearly knew who he was, or whose son he was. Zevaron remembered what Danar had said about the value of making the arrests public.

People are watching. People are remembering.

"That's the new Temple of Justice," Danar said, pointing. "It was built in my grandfather's time." He indicated a broad white stone building decorated with friezes depicting historical events, or so Zevaron assumed. Even ignorant of the niceties of Gelonian art, he recognized the artist's skill.

"Inside, it's even more impressive," Danar said. "The central atrium is three stories tall, most of it taken up by a gilded statue of Ir-Pilant, under whose auspices all legal proceedings take place. My old tutor used to take me through these buildings and lecture me on their architecture. I'll show you another time, if we have a chance."

"We're not going there now?"

Danar shook his head. "There are no dungeons there, so they use the cells beneath the Old Temple. My grandfather believed that if Ir-Pilant—his own personal god, by the way—were pleased with the temple, there would be such perfect justice, there would be no need for prisons."

The stone of the Old Temple might originally have been

a deep orange, but over time had weathered and darkened in streaks. The walls looked to Zevaron as if the skies themselves had bled over them. The entrance was lightly guarded, but as they passed into the dim, slightly dank interior, they were closely watched. Zevaron tried to look stern and stupid as Danar went through a series of brief meetings with one official or another. He could not follow the convoluted legal justification for the visit and was grateful it did not seem to daunt Danar.

In the wake of a senior official, they passed along a windowless corridor, gated at both ends. Zevaron's task was to hold the torch that was their sole light. He grimaced as the barred iron door clanged shut behind them. As they descended the rough cut stone stairs, the temperature fell. The air turned clammy.

"My tutor said these passages were originally mining tunnels," Danar said to the official. "They provided the stone for the foundation of Aidon."

"Yes, indeed," the official replied, "for I once saw an old map that showed the system extending to the edge of the city in the time of our fathers' fathers. Only a small area, here beneath the temple, is presently used."

They came to a landing and another barred gate. From there, the stairs descended into a well of blackness and stagnant air. Zevaron did not want to think what it was like to be locked away in the bowels of the earth, away from sun and air, with the dense oppressive silence and the soul-gnawing fear of being forgotten, penned in the dark for eternity. Danar had said these warrens were not meant for long-term incarceration, but who would know? How many enemies of the Ar-King had simply disappeared into these depths?

The official unlocked the door, and it swung open with a creak. Beyond lay a hallway, wide enough to accommodate a small table and two chairs. In the light of a torch set into a wall sconce, a single guard sat playing with a set of carved bones amid the remains of a meal, a heavy pottery mug and plate with several dry, curled bread crusts. The other wall bore two doors, age darkened wood pierced by an open grate at eye level. Zevaron felt an unexpected ripple of relief, that Tsorreh had at least a little light and the sounds of another human being.

The guard scooped the bones into a pouch and bowed to the official. They exchanged a few words, then the guard unlocked one of the wooden doors and stepped aside for Danar to enter the cell. A faint whispering sound, cloth over stone or straw, came from within.

"Your servant must remain outside," the official said, and by his tone he clearly felt that Zevaron should not have been admitted to the temple in the first place.

Danar paused on the threshold, turning back with a frankly imperious air. "You don't seriously suggest, my dear sir, that I approach this accursed sorceress without protection? What if she should cast a spell, and he were not here to take it upon his own body? The information I must obtain from her is crucial to my father's investigation, but not at the risk of such an attack. I shall depart immediately to inform him of your failure to provide suitable security for this interview."

"No, no," the official said. "Please, it is not a problem. Your bodyguard may enter. I understand completely."

"Then you also understand that whatever is said here must remain confidential."

"You have my oath upon it!"

"And *his*?" Danar said, staring pointedly at the guard.

The official sputtered protestations for a moment, then quickly decided that since Danar had such confidence in his own bodyguard, the most prudent course would be to leave Danar and Zevaron alone with the prisoner.

"That will be sufficient," Danar said, but he watched until the outer door clicked shut behind the official.

"Danar?" Tsorreh stood in the doorway of her cell, a slender shape in the wavering light. The Arandel token glinted in her hair. "Danar—and oh, Zevaron!"

Zevaron caught her, lifting her off the ground for an instant. He felt sick that she had endured even an hour in this hideous place. He heard the sob in her breath, but once she was back on her feet and able to talk, her voice was steady.

"Danar," she began, "I have not words enough to thank you for bringing Zevaron to me. Your soul shines with your goodness."

Danar looked embarrassed. "Father says he will not rest until he obtains your release."

"He must not make himself ill again on my account. Who would nurse him back to health?" She touched Danar's cheek with one hand. "Let us not deceive one another with hope. Cinath must have someone to blame for Thessar's death. With Jaxar exonerated—and not beyond suspicion, do not believe that for a moment—the entire blame must therefore fall upon me."

"Mother, no!" Zevaron broke in, appalled. "Do not say that, not when those who love you are ready to fight!"

"There is still much we can do," Danar protested.

"Do not give in to despair," Zevaron said. "I almost did, after Gatacinne. But you are still alive, and I have found you. We have survived too much to give up now."

"Perhaps you are right," Tsorreh said, with the hint of a smile. "Let us not waste this precious time in argument. Danar, I must speak privately with my son."

Danar left them and closed the cell door almost to the point of latching. A moment later, Zevaron heard Danar speaking with the guard, and the muffled sounds of the outer door opening and closing. What Danar said to the guard, Zevaron could not guess, nor did he spare the time to wonder.

"Quickly now!" Tsorreh cried, her breath as fast as if she had just run across the city. She lowered herself to a patch of filthy straw and held out one hand to him. "We may have only a few moments."

"Mother, are you ill?"

She took his face between her hands, peering into his eyes. "I feared I would never see you again."

"But I am here," he said, covering her hands with his

own. She was trembling. "I am here, and soon we will get you out of here."

Tsorreh shook her head. "I cannot take the risk. This may be the last time. I must take the chance that is given to me."

As if exhausted, she leaned back against the wall, holding on to Zevaron, grasping his hand as tightly as a drowning man thrown a rope. She placed the other hand on her chest, then slipped it between the folds of her gown. The torchlight shifted, so that for an instant, Zevaron saw a gleam like gold shining through her skin.

"Ah!" A cry burst from her lips. Her face contorted.

"What is it?" She *was* ill, he was sure of it. His mind filled with the thousand things that could have happened since her arrest. She could have been beaten, tortured, contracted a terrible disease—

Her fingers clenched around his. He made no attempt to pull away. Instead, he tried to hold her, praying the spasm would pass and she would be able to tell him in what manner she was hurt. He did not know what he could do, but he had a sailor's knowledge of tending cuts and bruises, broken bones, and once a gangrenous leg that had to be cut off.

She was speaking now, words so low and urgent, he could not make them out, only their rhythm, as familiar as the beating of his heart. Verses from the *te-Ketav*, perhaps prayers, supplications, ancient phrases of hope and comfort.

No, not just comfort . . . *purpose*.

"My son, forgive me." Her whispered words shot through his heart. "I never meant to lay this burden on you in this way, I never meant—it is our only hope, believe me, please—*forgive me*."

Her grasp on him tightened, harder now than steel or the inexorable grip of the sea. She clung to him, pulling him closer.

"It's all right," he stammered. "I'm here, I'm here!"

"The stone must not be lost!"

Then she slapped something against his chest. His breastbone flexed and his body shuddered as if he had been struck by a piece of rigging torn loose in a storm. Air burst from his lungs. The muscles of his chest clamped down, adamantine, unyielding. His vision blurred around the edges. In panic, he struggled against her hold. He fought to force breath through his constricted throat.

Darkness lapped at him. Something sang in his ears, high and sweet and terrible, deadlier by far than the sea.

An oval shape, a woman's face, blotted the fading light. "I am so sorry. Remember, Gelon is not the enemy. Qr is only the shadow of the greater. The stone will teach you . . . Forgive me . . ."

Pain seared him, dying away into darkness.

Chapter Thirty-three

"ZEV? I'm sorry to interrupt—Zev?"

Zevaron blinked, and the moment of strangeness passed. Once more, he knew who he was and where he was. Rousing, he tasted the dank air and felt the hardness of the stones beneath his knees, the slime under his fingers.

"I'm all right, Danar. Just a moment."

He could not remember how he had gotten here, half-kneeling in front of Tsorreh. Her hands lay across her outstretched legs, limp, palms upward. From the way she was sprawled and the angle of her head, he feared she had fainted. Before he could reach out to her, she stirred. Her eyes opened and a smile of inexpressible sweetness passed over her face.

"Go," she said in a voice that was thick and slow. "Take my blessings and the hope of our people with you."

He gathered her in his arms. Her body felt all bones, as fragile as a bird's. "I will come back," he whispered against her ear. "By all that is holy, I swear it. I will save you."

"You have already saved what is most dear to me, my Zevaron."

Danar stood at the door, arguing with the official, insisting loudly that Tsorreh be given food, water, and a clean cell. The man lifted his hands and protested that he had no authority to do such things.

"Then you will do it on *my* authority, do you understand? Or I will take every moment of her suffering out of your worthless hide!"

"No, no! You must leave! I have already exceeded my orders! This is all the time granted to you! Away, away with you now! Guard, lock the cell."

Zevaron clambered to his feet. His body felt unexpectedly heavy, as if he had labored hard all day. Behind his breastbone, in the center of his chest, he felt a crushing pain, as if his heart were weeping. He steadied himself against the door frame.

Danar touched his arm. "Let's go, my friend, that we may soon return, and this time with your mother's freedom."

The rest of the day passed in a blur. Zevaron had no memory of returning to Jaxar's compound, only a vague impression of color, of light, of tall white buildings and people sweeping past him. He might have eaten, but what and when he had no memory. Lycian's voice rang distantly through the garden atrium. Someone spoke to him, steward or servant or perhaps even Jaxar himself.

The air turned cold. Behind his closed eyelids, tatters of images, vivid and incomprehensible, fluttered like dead leaves. Here and there, he recognized the shape of a woman on horseback against an ocean of silver-green grass, banners in the wind, an army of lifted swords, mountains of ice, caverns vast and lightless, far deeper than those through which he and Tsorreh had fled. Invisible currents swirled them all away.

He awoke, slowly coming back to himself. He lay on his sleeping pallet in Jaxar's laboratory. A faint tang of metal and chemicals hung in the air. His knee joints popped as he got to his feet. One end of the table had been cleared of equipment and now bore a bowl and pitcher of water and a plate of cold boiled onions, flatbread, olives, and a small piece of salty white cheese. The smell of the food roused a ravenous hunger within him. He ate it all, washed his face and hands, and went downstairs.

Jaxar was sitting in the garden, shaded by one of the willowy trees, his legs propped on a bench heaped with pillows. He glanced up at Zevaron's approach and set aside his pile of letters.

"My boy, you are looking considerably better than when Danar brought you back here after visiting Tsorreh two days ago. You have eaten, I trust? Is there anything else you require?"

"Only to know—*two days?* Surely, I cannot . . . No, I see." That would explain why, although he had just eaten enough for two normal breakfasts, his body still craved food.

Jaxar dismissed the servant at his elbow and indicated the seat beside him. "Do not think harshly of yourself. Even the mightiest man must rest. Our bodies are flesh, after all, not iron. I know something of how they can fail even the most determined spirit."

Zevaron sat, struck by the older man's kindness. In that moment, he saw Jaxar not as a fat old cripple, but a person with a keen mind trapped in a mound of decaying flesh.

"I cannot rest, not truly, until she is free and safe." *And we are well away from this place.*

"How will it help her if you are too exhausted to even get out of bed?"

Zevaron opened his mouth to protest further, then closed it. Had he fainted in Tsorreh's cell? He must have lost consciousness; one moment they had been talking and, within the blinking of an eye, he'd found himself on his hands and knees. In his years with Chalil, he had known two men subject to falling fits. Their limbs would flail about, hurling their bodies to the deck, and when they came to themselves, they had no knowledge of what had happened. Chalil said that for one of them, the fits began after a head injury, but the other had suffered in this way all his life.

It must have been the air, Zevaron thought, the close dank air of the cell, added to the intensity of his feelings at seeing his mother again. He shuddered inwardly at the thought of her remaining in that terrible place for even one more hour.

"What news of my mother?" he asked.

Jaxar's heavy, drooping features turned somber. He told Zevaron there had been no response to his entreaties, nor had Danar been able to visit Tsorreh again. Zevaron heard a new harmonic in the old man's words. He sensed that without sources of information, without connections and relationships, Jaxar was disarmed. Helpless. Blind. Frightened. Anything he said would only sap Jaxar's one remaining weapon, his confidence. The Gelon were creatures of settled lands, of cities and laws. Of traditional family alliances and networks of influence. It was time to make his own plans.

He needed help, that much was sure. Once he had eaten and drunk and bathed, Zevaron's strength returned. When he manufactured a pretext to leave the compound alone, Jaxar made no objection.

In the river-harbor district, it did not take long to determine which of the men drinking at open-air stalls, the layabouts and casual laborers, had ties to Denariya or the sea wolves of the Mearas. A gesture here, a phrase there, established him as one of them. Here he could find men, men without qualms about breaking any number of Gelonian laws. Perhaps men who were eager to do so.

Finding a way into the prison would not be easy, but leaving it would be even harder. He needed men who were resourceful and cunning, ruthless in a fight. And he needed a boat to take them downriver, with a pilot accustomed to slipping past the Ar-King's tax officers. Such men would not come cheap, even those who had no reason to love Gelon. Zevaron identified three sound men, all of them pirates, he would swear, plus two more he was less certain of.

On his way back to Jaxar's compound, Zevaron planned his next step. He would need money for the men and for passage downriver, and then for a fast ship to Durinthe. In his pack beside the pallet in the laboratory, he still had the better part of his fee from the merchant, Ranath. He could negotiate more from Jaxar as his reward. If only Jaxar had let them go when Zevaron had first pleaded for Tsorreh's freedom! Then they would already be free of this place.

There was no point wasting his energy in useless anger at Jaxar when there was work to be done. Zevaron searched his memory for every detail of the old justice temple and the warren beneath it. The guards and gates were designed not to keep people *out* but to keep them *in*. Locked gates had posed little problem to Chalil, and these were simple devices. Zevaron was certain that they could be disabled to allow easy exit. But even at night, he doubted that Tsorreh could simply walk out of the temple. Perhaps there was another way.

The official who had taken him and Danar down to Tsorreh's cell had mentioned a map showing the system of old mining tunnels. How much could he ask of Danar without revealing his plan? Which was the greater, Danar's love for Tsorreh or his loyalty as a Gelon?

Perhaps he could find someone, one of the wharf rats he had bought ale for, who had once been imprisoned under the temple. He could bring a disguise for Tsorreh and create a distraction to get her past the guards, perhaps at night when the shadows would be their allies.

Zevaron returned to the compound at dusk, filled with ideas. It would take a day or two to arrange everything. Even if he refused to help, Zevaron did not think Danar would betray him. It would be better, however, to keep Jaxar himself ignorant and therefore, unimplicated.

He knew from the moment the compound gate opened that something was wrong. The outside bell was answered not by the usual steward, but by one of the kitchen maids. The slanting light could not hide her puffy, reddened eyes. When he asked her what was the matter, she sniffed and shook her head. A wordless shiver, cold like the ringing of steel on stone, passed through him. Jaxar had looked so ill that

morning. If he had gotten worse, had collapsed or, Most
Holy One forbid, had died—

No, he must not think of it, lest, according to Denariyan
superstition, he give power to that evil thought. Despite his
anger, Zevaron did not wish the old man harm. He had
known Jaxar only a short time, but enough to recognize his
worth, and Jaxar had stood as a father to Tsorreh, protecting her as much as he could.

And Danar—how would he bear his father's death?

Zevaron hurried to the house. The entrance hall was
dark and empty. As he crossed the atrium, he heard voices
from the family's private quarters. The steward hurried
along the colonnade with a pile of towels and a pitcher of
something pungent and steaming. He glanced at Zevaron
and missed a step.

"Thank the gods, you're back!"

"What's going on?" Zevaron said. "Is it Lord Jaxar?"

Lycian's voice sliced through the perfumed twilight.
"Danar, stop this unseemly display!"

Something crashed, pottery smashing against stone.
Someone sobbed.

"Get inside," the steward said, but not unkindly. "It can't
get any worse, your being here. And *he* needs you."

Zevaron followed the steward to the private chamber
adjacent to Jaxar's bedroom. A row of oil lamps set along
the wall ledge filled the space with overlapping spheres of
light. Jaxar himself sat in his chair, propped on pillows, his
face the same color as the sun-bleached linen.

*Alive? Then what had put the household into such an up-
roar?*

Danar slumped on one of the benches along the far wall,
his body hunched over, his face buried on his folded arms.
His back shuddered, great ripples of soundless weeping. Lycian stood over him. Her face was contorted, and she'd
raised her hands in a dramatic gesture. She saw Zevaron
and gave a yelp of surprise.

"Now the son has come slinking back to us," she said,

making no effort to conceal her contempt, "doubtless to wring your purse for as much money as he can. Is there no end to these people imposing on your good will, Jaxar?"

"Lycian, you will be still!" Jaxar rumbled.

"Lord Jaxar, what has happened?" Zevaron asked, his mouth suddenly dry.

As Zevaron spoke, Danar looked up. The light of the oil lamps fell full upon his face. Zevaron's gaze locked on Danar's tear-bright eyes.

No.

Before he could draw another breath, before his heart had sent another pulsation through his body, he knew.

No.

The room went dim and then crimson-tinged. Lycian's shrill voice faded. Jaxar shouted something at her, and she swept from the room. The steward set down the pitcher, dipped one of the towels in the infusion, and held it out to Jaxar, but the old man waved it away.

Zevaron opened his mouth to speak, but no words came. The pain behind his breastbone throbbed, fever-sick and hot and frozen.

He wanted to scream, to lash out, to grab the nearest sword and hack the living world to pieces. He wanted to curl into the smallest ball, so tight there was no room for tears.

It could not be true! He had just seen her, alive. How could Cinath have acted so quickly? What about everything Jaxar had said, all his reassurances, his connections and schemes?

Empty promises, all of them. Froth on the tide.

"Zevaron, I am sorry," Jaxar said. "I have no words—"

Zevaron found his voice. "There must be a mistake!"

"I wish there were!" Jaxar told him. "When I could not get an answer any other way, I went myself to the palace."

"*He* killed her?" Zevaron said.

Jaxar shook his head, sending quivers through drooping folds of flesh. "No, I would know if he had ordered her execution. He did not, although he surely intended to."

"Then we have only his word on it!" Zevaron said wildly. Surely Jaxar had been deceived. How easy it was to lie about such things!

The room had fallen silent except for Jaxar's labored breathing and the pounding of Zevaron's heart.

"My brother cannot lie to my face," Jaxar wheezed. "He never could. Even when we were children, I always knew whether he was telling the truth."

"You may believe him. But *I* do not!" Zevaron's voice burst from him, harsh as breaking steel, as the call of the great carrion-birds over a battlefield.

"My boy, I know how painful this must be for you, to lose her so soon after finding her again. If there were any way, anything—for her sake, you will henceforth be as a second son to me. I—"

"She is not dead! She cannot be! I will not believe it, not until I have seen her body with my own eyes!"

Before Jaxar could speak again, Zevaron turned and strode out of the room. He could not bear the weight of grief in the eyes of Jaxar and his son, or their pity, and he did not know what to feel for these people.

Chapter Thirty-four

FOR four long years, Zevaron had believed his mother dead, and he had been mistaken. How unquestioningly had he accepted the words of that Gelonian slave-master. Why should this time be different? Why should he trust what a Gelon—any Gelon—said?

Liars, all of them!

Jaxar might have treated Tsorreh kindly when it was convenient, but he was an invalid who could easily be fooled. He would never stand up to his brother. Cinath would ruthlessly exploit the bonds of blood and loyalty for his own purposes, and would not hesitate to kill anyone who stood in his way.

What if Tsorreh's death were a ruse, a trap? Set for Jaxar, for Danar, for Zevaron himself? Would he be walking into Cinath's prison, throwing his own life away?

What if Jaxar were wrong? What if she were still alive? How could he abandon her in the stronghold of the enemy? How could he leave her to rot in Cinath's black pit?

Was there anyone he could believe? He had to find out, he had to *know!*

He could not think clearly. His senses reeled, and something had gone awry in his vision. One instant, he saw the walled hill compounds of Aidon's aristocracy, the stones and treetops, the flowered garlands. The next moment, a vast shadowy figure, jointed and many-legged, stretched across the city. Brightness faded as the form grew in solidity.

Zevaron reached the bottom of the hill and came out to a moderate-sized thoroughfare. The crowd swallowed him up, a flock of fantastical, brightly colored creatures. He saw the crimson striped sashes of Denariyans, lumbering Xians with the sun glinting on their hairless, tattooed heads, the moon-pale cloaks of the Sand Lands, Gelonian women in fluttering, jewel-colored draperies, onagers and oxen, and even a brown-and-white striped pony. Spices, cedarwood and clove and elixir of roses, wafted on the breeze. The richness and gaiety repelled him.

While Zevaron watched, a troupe of performers made their way through the throng, tumblers and dancers accompanied by pipes and drum. They wore masks. *Like everyone else in this vile land.*

A desperate plan took shape in his mind, a way to gain access to Tsorreh without revealing himself. If these performers could present themselves as what they were not, then so could he. Carefully he composed his features, wiped the sweat from his face, arranged his clothing, and straightened his posture.

He was Jaxar's agent, he repeated silently; he spoke not for himself, but for his master, and as such, he had every right to view the body of the great lord's assistant.

No, he needed a better reason, something more tangible. When he and Danar had visited Tsorreh, she'd worn the Arandel token in her hair. He did not think he would have difficulty convincing the temple officials that Jaxar wanted it.

By the time Zevaron arrived at the Old Temple, he had rehearsed his role so many times, the words sprang readily to his lips. He made his request when a guard, a different one than before, stopped him at the entrance.

"Entrance is forbidden to the public."

Zevaron ached to pummel the man's face into a bloody pulp. Instead, he managed to look vaguely annoyed.

"I am on my master's business, not my own," Zevaron

said in his most ponderous Denariyan accent. "Admit me instantly or suffer his displeasure."

Now it was the guard's turn to look impatient. His gaze flickered over Zevaron's clothing. "I've got orders to keep out the rabble, and I intend to follow them."

Zevaron shifted his expression to one of boredom. He shrugged, as if to say, *It's not my head that will roll.* "Your name?"

"My what?"

"Your *name*." Zevaron emitted an aggrieved sigh. "So that I can report the man who prevented me from carrying out my master's wishes."

"I—er, who did you say your master is?"

"Lord Jaxar."

"Lord Jaxar, the brother to his Glorious Majesty may-his-might-prevail-everlasting?"

"Yes, and I assure you, he has only a limited patience with uncooperative idiots. He will not take it graciously if I am delayed in my mission."

"What does Lord Jaxar want?" The guard now looked more curious than belligerent.

"If my master wished to disclose that information to you, he would not need to send me, would he? The time grows short. Are you going to keep me out here all day?"

For a moment, Zevaron thought the guard might step back and let him in, but the man bade him remain outside while he consulted his superior.

What would a real emissary of an aristocrat like Jaxar do? Wait for the proper permission? Or would he barge inside, as if he had the right to go wherever he wanted? It would do no good to sneak into the temple, where his very presence might result in his arrest. He must brazen it out.

The guard returned a few moments later with one of the officials who had greeted Danar on their previous visit.

"Yes, I know this man," the official said. "On a previous occasion, he accompanied Lord Jaxar's son. A bodyguard, I thought. You," to Zevaron, "what are you doing here?"

"It is true that upon occasion I have been charged with

the protection of Lord Danar," Zevaron replied stiffly. "But Lord Jaxar places his trust in me in other ways. I come now on *his* business."

"Very well. Follow me." Gesturing dismissively to the guard, the official led Zevaron inside.

The interior of the temple was much as Zevaron remembered it and dank with shadows. Torchlight glimmered on the barred gate leading to the windowless corridor.

The official halted. "How may this humble one serve the great lord?"

"My task concerns the woman who was kept prisoner here a short time ago, the one from Lord Jaxar's own household."

"Yes, the Meklavaran witch. A pity she died before her full confession could be obtained. She might have named other conspirators. Do not fear, the priests of Qr will root them out."

Zevaron's heart stuttered. The muscles of his belly clenched. "That is not my concern. My master had given the woman a token, a thing of small value, in the days before her . . . treachery was discovered. He would not have her—" *What did the Gelon do with their dead? Bury them? Burn them? Dump them into the river to be eaten by fishes?* "— have her retain the token in death, since in life she forfeited all claim to his favor."

The official nodded, lips widening in a knowing smile. Why lose the value of even a small trinket? Zevaron wondered if the man had intended to strip the corpse of clothing, anything he could sell.

Although it sickened him, Zevaron forced himself to smile in return. He felt for the coins folded into his belt, selected a large one by feel, and slipped it into the official's hand. "My master would not wish your cooperation to go uncompensated."

The coin disappeared into the man's sleeve. "It is an honor to serve the noble and exalted Lord Jaxar. Please come this way."

The official led Zevaron not to the stairway leading below, but to the far end of the temple itself. If Tsorreh were still alive, Zevaron thought, it would be far easier to get her out of here without having to fight his way back up from the underground, along the narrow stairs.

Uncertainty niggled at him. Would the official be so ready to give a stranger access to her body if he were not certain she was dead? If Cinath had lied, would he not have moved her to an even more secure place, perhaps in the palace itself? And why would Cinath do that, rather than just kill her? Questions buzzed through his mind like swarming wasps. Like the rattling of a scorpion's pincers.

Enough! At this rate, he would go mad with doubt.

The official paused outside a closed door, latched but not locked. He opened it and stood back for Zevaron to enter. The room appeared to be used for storage, with a single high window, no more than a slit for air and oblique light. Shelves lined the walls, laden with boxes and canvas-wrapped parcels. Baskets and wooden crates covered most of the narrow floor. Dust hung on the air, mingled with the odors of stale incense and mildew.

A crude pallet had been fashioned from broken crates and on it lay a long, slender form. Stained cloth covered the body except for a single hand, draped with awkward grace along the floor.

The air turned thick and still. Zevaron went down on one knee beside the makeshift bier. He held his breath, searching for any hint of movement through the cloth, the slightest rise of chest or puff of breath. Behind him, the official cleared his throat. Zevaron could think of no reason he might be allowed to remain alone with the body. He must continue to play his role, performing his brief, perfunctory task.

Beneath Zevaron's fingers, the fabric was stiff with grime. He folded it back. For a moment, he thought he looked upon a carving. This could not be her. Surely, they must have supplied a wax image in her place.

She was smaller than he remembered. Her frailness pierced his heart.

The same gown he had last seen her wear was neatly tucked around her sides. Her body showed no sign of mutilation, no bruises, no cuts or wheals. Her head tilted toward him, cheeks and lips colorless, eyelids delicately shadowed beneath smooth dark brows. She looked unexpectedly peaceful, as if she had been released from all pain, all terror and grief. Whatever light had once shone just below her skin was now extinguished.

No.

He had thought he was prepared. He had not anticipated this clay-pale skin or the utter stillness of her flesh.

Zevaron leaned closer, thinking to make a show of searching for the token. When he brushed her face, the cool flesh yielded slightly. He touched her neck as he moved her hair aside. No pulse flickered beneath his fingers.

He found the Arandel token on a cord woven through one of her braids. He could not untangle it, so he cut the cord. The once-bright silver looked dull, quenched. He held it for a moment before her nostrils, pretending to examine it.

"Is that it, then?" the official asked.

Zevaron's throat tightened. Fever whispered through his veins. The room wavered and turned chill. When he held it up, the Arandel token caught the light for an instant, without any hint of breath. He forced out the words, although they seemed to be spoken by someone far away. "Yes, this is what I was sent to retrieve." *There is nothing more for me here.* "What will . . ." he stumbled. "How will the body be disposed?"

"In the usual way." The official narrowed his eyes. "Does the Lord Jaxar now concern himself with such repugnant matters?"

"No, it was an idle question. Nothing more."

Dead, she is dead.

Dead. The thought pounded through him with each footstep, following the official along the corridor and into the brightness of the day. Outside, the street seemed unreal, a painted mockery. His feet carried him along. He had no idea where he was going.

She is dead.

Their brief time together in Jaxar's house had been a gift, sudden and unexpected, unhoped-for. And never to come again.

Zevaron slammed the laboratory door behind him. There, in the far corner, Tsorreh had made a little home for herself. He lowered himself to her sleeping pallet, trying to feel the impression of her body, to remember the scent of her hair. The room was almost dark, except for a wash of fading twilight through the tower observatory. Fumbling, he lit her oil lamp, battered brass in the shape of a fanciful horse's head, perhaps of Azkhantian make. He would take it with him, leave nothing of hers behind.

At the head of the pallet, beside her pillow, was a small carved box. Inside he found a few hair ornaments and a leather thong strung through a glazed bead, small treasures he knew nothing about. Exploring further, his fingers came upon a battered book, its cream-colored leather bindings showing unmistakable water damage. He opened it, shifting the lamp so that its light fell on the pages.

> *Exiled from Thy sight,*
> *My soul is a realm forsaken,*
> *Filled with lamentations,*
> *Strange portents and darkness.*

The *Shirah Kohav* had been Tsorreh's favorite poetry. Where had she come by this copy?

As he handled the little box and watched the pattern of flame and shadow from the oil lamp, a part of Zevaron's fury eased. As long as he felt himself surrounded by the people who had shattered his homeland, enslaved his mother, and sent him into exile, then all he could think of was bringing ruin to Gelon. Here in this quiet place, in the company of strange instruments and the books that Tsorreh had loved, was the undeniable evidence that she had found comfort here. Something opened up inside him, like an island in a landscape of sorrow.

"My soul is a realm forsaken . . ."

He clutched his chest, kneading muscle and skin to ease the aching within. In the back of his mind, he heard Tsorreh's whisper, speaking of love, trying to tell him something, begging his forgiveness.

"I will come back," he had sworn. *"I will save you."*

And she had answered, *"You have already saved what is most dear to me, my Zevaron."*

Her life was worth a thousand Ar-Kings. Ten thousand.

Gone, she is gone.

Gone as Maharrad his father was gone, and Shorrenon his brother, and Meklavar itself.

Cinath had done this thing. She was dead, and Cinath, may-he-rot-forever, had killed her. Even if he had not slit her throat with his own hand, he put her in that hole. He set the city against her and all her people. He gave the orders to march on Meklavar.

Cinath will pay.

Here, words failed him. It did not matter what happened afterward, if only he could reach Cinath and close his hands around the Ar-King's wretched neck. Or slit his belly open and laugh as his guts spilled across the floor. Or cut off his ears and nose, then his testicles, savoring each scream, each whimper, each plea for mercy.

Gelon would pay. Gelon would burn. By all the gods of Gelon and Denariya, by the ancient powers of his people, by whatever monstrosity the wild men of the Fever Lands worshipped, he would bring down this accursed city, and every city in this thrice-damned land, and every single person in it.

New novels of DARKOVER®
by Marion Zimmer Bradley & Deborah J. Ross

"[*The Alton Gift*] is a must for fans of the series, and reads as if Deborah has been channeling Marion's spirit."
—*Center City Weekly Press*

"Ross has fleshed out Bradley's encyclopedic vision of the Darkovian Dark Ages..."
—*Publishers Weekly* for *The Fall of Neskaya*

To Order Call: 1-800-788-6262
www.dawbooks.com

DARKOVER®

Marion Zimmer Bradley's Classic Series

Now Collected in New Omnibus Editions!

To Order Call: 1-800-788-6262
www.dawbooks.com

DAW 6